Of Two Minds: Location Shoot, It's a Miracle, and Other Strange Stories

Bradley H. Sinor
&
Susan P. Sinor

Print Version ISBN 978-1-945941-10-8
Of Two Minds: Location Shoot, It's a Miracle, and Other Strange Stories
First Edition Copyright © Bradley H. Sinor and Sue Sinor, 2017

Individual stories that have been previously published:

"Raven's Back In Town" by Bradley H. Sinor (first appeared in *The Four Bubbas of the Apocalypse: Flatulence, Halitosis, Incest and...Ned*, Yard Dog Press, 2003)

"The Rhinestone Maidens" by Susan P. Sinor (first appeared in *International House of Bubbas*, Yard Dog Press, 2005)

"Are We There Yet?" by Bradley H. and Susan P. Sinor (first appeared in *Houston: We've Got Bubbas*, Yard Dog Press, 2007)

"We're Back" by Bradley H. Sinor (first appeared in *A Bubba in Time Saves None*, Yard Dog Press, 2010)

"The Rhinestone Maidens Not-So-Excellent Adventure" by Susan P. Sinor (first appeared in *A Bubba in Time Saves None*, Yard Dog Press, 2010)

"Who Rode the Winds" by Bradley H. and Susan P. Sinor (first appeared in *I Should Have Stayed in OZ*, Yard Dog Press, 2011)

"Mack" by Susan P. Sinor (first appeared in *Flush Fiction, Volume I: Stories to be Read in One Sitting*, Yard Dog Press, 2006)

"Crockaroo" by Susan P. Sinor (first appeared in *Flush Fiction, Volume II: Twenty Years of Letting It Go!*, Yard Dog Press, 2016)

"Christmas Shopping" by Susan P. Sinor (first appeared in *Playing With Secrets*, Yard Dog Press, 2004)

"What Comes Around" by Susan P. Sinor (first appeared in *Playing With Secrets*, Yard Dog Press, 2004)

"Location Shoot" by Bradley H. Sinor (first appeared in *Playing With Secrets*, Yard Dog Press, 2004)

"Mama Says" by Susan P. Sinor (first appeared in *Small Bites*, Coscom Entertainment, 2004)

"Bob" by Susan P. Sinor (first appeared in *Small Bites*, Coscom Entertainment, 2004)

"Gag" by Bradley H. Sinor (first appeared in *Small Bites*, Coscom Entertainment, 2004)

"First Date" by Bradley H. Sinor (first appeared in *Small Bites*, Coscom Entertainment, 2004)

"Burglary" by Bradley H. Sinor (first appeared in *Small Bites*, Coscom Entertainment, 2004)

"A Proper Farewell" by Bradley H. Sinor (first appeared in *Space Cadets*, SCIFI, 2006)

"Skimming Stones" by Bradley H. Sinor (first appeared in *Men Writing Science Fiction as Women*, DAW Books, 2003)

"Money's Worth" by Bradley H. Sinor (first appeared in *Places to Be, People to Kill*, DAW Books, 2007)

"Sibling Rivalry" by Bradley H. Sinor (first appeared in *Here be Dragons: Tales of DragonCon*, Bill Fawcett and Associates, Inc., 2008)

"Who Stand and Wait" by Bradley H. and Susan P. Sinor (first appeared in *Full-Throttle Space Tales #3: Space Grunts*, Flying Pen Press 2009)

Each of the following seven stories is by Susan P. Sinor and has never before been published:
"The Memory of Desire"
"To Sleep, Perchance To Dream"
"Bad Day"
"Doors"
"Fairy Story"
"It's a Miracle"
"Petal Attraction"

http://www.yarddogpress.com

Edited by Selina Rosen
Copy Editor & Technical Editor Lynn Rosen
Cover art by Melanie Fletcher

First Print Edition September, 2017
Printed in the United States of America
0 9 8 7 6 5 4 3 2 1

Dedication

We dedicate this book to one another because without us both the collection wouldn't have happened.

Table of Contents

A Brief Introduction

Most of the stories in this collection have appeared in other anthologies. Some of those original anthologies are still readily available, some are harder to find, and still others are fairly rare and/or only available as either electronic editions or as previously-cherished copies.

Under the title of each story we will print the name and publisher of the anthology in which the story first appeared. If you are reading an Electronic copy of this collection, there will be a link to the Eversion of that anthology if we can find such a link.

No, this is not as silly as it sounds. Several of those anthologies have been published by Yard Dog Press, but even if we are not the prior publisher, we like to promote good books wherever we find them.

Enjoy!

Five stories from the *Bubbas of the Apocalypse* universe

This very brief background is furnished for those of you who have not yet had the—pleasure—of becoming acquainted with this universe. (And why not?)

Each of the following five stories first appeared in one of the five themed anthologies that have been published to date.

BACKGROUND: In the year 2025 the worst happened. A deadly virus known only as Yuppie 25 escaped from a secret government lab (it is believed that it was tracked out on a piece of toilet paper stuck to the bottom of a scientist's shoe). The airborne virus spread quickly throughout the fifty states and thanks to unusually low air fares that year within weeks the entire world was infected. Scientists worked day and night to try to find a cure, but most of them were already infected and succumbed to the Yuppie madness before they could find an antidote.

Long story short—within in a few months most of the

population of the earth was dead. Only those who had spent many years eating vast amounts of generic barbeque sauce on grilled meat survived unscathed. In some business professionals, however, Yuppie 25 mutated and they live on as crazed, deranged Yuppies. While all of these Yuppie zombies, sometimes called Yumbies, consume human flesh, mutations differ from one local to another.

Bubbas are now our last best hope for humanity.

GOD HELP US ALL!!!

Raven's Back in Town

Bradley H. Sinor
*The Four Bubbas of the Apocalypse: Flatulence, Halitosis,
Incest, and... Ned*
Yard Dog Press

"So what do you think of my new hat, Ed?" asked Charlie
Clark as he sat down at the Lucky Lady Bar & Grill's lunch
counter.

Ed Roberts set down his beer after taking one last swallow,
reached over into a bowl of pickled eggs and snagged one. He
popped it into his mouth, purple juice running out the sides
of his lips, as he chewed.

"First off, Charlie," he said. "That is one piss poor hunting
cap. It's thinner than shit and wouldn't do diddly towards
keeping your head and ears warm. Secondly, in case you
haven't noticed, you've got the thing on sideways. The flaps
are supposed to go over your ears not hang down in your
eyes."

No one was paying that much attention to Ed and Charlie;
the noonday crowd was pretty much used to their arguments,
and usually ignored them.

"If this isn't a good huntin' hat," said Charlie. "Why else
would it be called a deerstalker? It's one of them English hats,
the kind that ole Sherlock Holmes wore in all his detective
movies when he went huntin' criminals."

"Detective movies? If that hat is supposed to be so damn
special, Mr. Detective, sir, then why don't you solve the mystery
of what's been happening to those gals who've been dying
around here so weird like," said Ed.

"They was just movies!" said Charlie.

"They ain't showing around here, are they?" asked Ed.

"Naw, I ain't seen any since we used to go over to visit my
Aunt Lynn in Coffin's Corner, Arkansas. On weekends we'd
go out to the Canyon Wall Drive-In Movie and Holy Tabernacle.
Watch movies all night and be there for Sunday morning
services," said Charlie.

The mention of the Canyon Wall Drive-in Theatre was
enough to cause Raven Harkness, sitting at the far end of the

counter, to pay closer attention to Charlie and Ed's conversation.

It had been four months since Raven had left Coffin's Corner behind, along with her reputation as "that woman". The people of Coffin's Corner had known her as a hooker, plying her trade with the locals and passing truckers. Which suited Raven just fine, since she was really an undercover field agent for United Pharmaceuticals, working with her partner, Penn Mulroney, to find some clue to the plague immunity that some people had.

Unfortunately, most of the data they had gathered was destroyed during a zombie outbreak at the self-same Canyon Wall Drive-in. The two of them had left town quickly after that. After filing her report Raven had told Penn and her bosses that she was taking a few weeks off to visit her hometown, Lawton, Oklahoma, the scene of her 'misspent youth'.

"It's been more than a few years since we went to Coffin's Corner for a visit, not since Aunt Lynn died," said Charlie.

Hearing that was a relief. Raven had taken pains to change her appearance: red hair three shades darker, different glasses, and a complete change of wardrobe. But you never knew who you might run into.

"Raven? What the hell are you doing back in this town?" Raven smiled as she looked around to see an old friend. Madison Cromwell was the same age as Raven, but because of her diminutive size, (she stood barely five feet tall) she had always been mistaken for her younger sister. Wearing dark glasses and a sleeveless jean jacket, her short dark hair pulled back under a baseball cap, Madison looked hardly any different than when Raven had left town five years before.

"I'm here to raise hell, just like I always have!"

"Then let's get out of here and find some trouble to get into, girlfriend," said Madison.

Madison reached into the cooler that sat on the backseat of Raven's Barracuda and pulled out a can of beer. She popped the top and took a swallow, spewing the contents out of her mouth a couple of seconds later.

"Damn it," yelled Raven. "If I've told you once, I've told you a hundred times. Don't spill food in the car! Or I'll make you clean it up!" She'd been fanatical about the appearance of her car since the first day she had slid behind the wheel.

"Ye gods, what is this stuff?" demanded Madison. She held the beer can up and squinted at it. "Hobb Nail Brewery? Whoever made it should be taken out and beaten within an inch of their lives with a pair of their own hob nails."

"Hey, you take what you can get sometimes," said Raven. "It wasn't as if I could wait to get back here and get the good stuff."

Back when the plague hit there had only been a thousand or so people left in Lawton; too stubborn to leave, Raven's father had said. One of the local industries that had been a priority to keep going had been the beer bottling plant; in fact, it had become one of the major exports for the town. As Raven's father had said "It was amazing how people heard about it and moved to Lawton. This town doubled its population in just a couple of years. You just got to have your priorities, and beer is definitely one of them."

Raven steered the car onto the street and headed toward Cache Road, one of the central streets in Lawton, literally running from one end of the town to the other. On more than one occasion the Barracuda, with Raven and Madison in it, had spent the night cruising up and down the avenue.

"So what the hell are you doing back here, Raven?" asked Madison after riding several blocks in silence.

"I don't know, just got an odd feather up my ass, an urge to see the old stomping grounds. Maybe it was just an urge to see my best friend; it has been a few years. What's a matter, not glad to see me?" said Raven.

"Of course I am. I been tempted to write to you and get you to meet me down in Dallas. We could do some serious partying and then stay over for services at the Tabernacle of the Sportatorium."

Madison had long ago become a convert to the religious wrestling circuit. Raven had been to a few matches herself. Even blood-covered, some of those wrestlers were good preachers.

"Mad, you never were good at hiding things. Something's going on, so talk. What's the deal?" said Raven.

Madison sighed. "All right, then. I take it you remember Peggy, Mary Anne and Jodeana?"

Raven remembered them all right. They had been friends, not as close as she and Madison, but still friends. At times they had been the best of friends and at times they had been the worst of enemies; typical teenagers, in other words.

"Of course. And?" asked Raven.

"They're dead. All three in the past six weeks." Madison told her.

"Was it a zombie attack? Or did they come down with the plague and just go over themselves?" Raven hoped that if it were the latter, none of their families had been the ones to put the girls down. That was the sort of thing that could ruin a relative's whole day

Raven used both her knees to hold the barracuda's steering sheel steady, as she twisted around to grab a beer from the cooler.

"Nope, it was hit and run, all three of them, late at night and no witnesses. Peggy was killed near the Baptist church, Mary Anne on the access road near the water slide and Jodeana out there near Big Bob's Lumber," she said.

"This is that thing that Charlie and Ed were talking about?"

"Yeah, there's a whole lot of talk floating around about it. Fact is nobody knows a whole lot."

"I think I know somebody who would," said Raven.

Raven wasn't sure that she even wanted to go and talk to her grandma, Wanda Davis. Ever since she had been a little girl there had been something about the older woman that made Raven uncomfortable. Problem was, Raven didn't feel like she had a lot of choice in the matter. If anyone in Lawton knew what was going on with the three girls dying, it would be her grandmother. It wasn't that Grandma Davis was a gossip (that was a word you never used in her presence) information just seemed to make it to her doorstep naturally.

Wanda Davis lived in the abandoned air traffic control tower on the south side of Lawton, two miles from the dirt track speedway. Raven's grandmother had once explained that she liked the tower for the privacy it gave her, not to mention the clear field of fire on any strangers.

Standing at one of a dozen rose bushes spread around the tower was a man, a pair of pruning shears in one hand, carefully trimming several branches. He was big; hitting 300 pounds, if not more, and looked like there was hardly a muscle anywhere in his frame. If he noticed Raven, the man gave no reaction, just kept right on working.

"Excuse me, is Mrs. Davis at home?" she asked him.

The man looked up, and then pointed toward the building. It was only when she was well past him that he spoke. "Nice to see you, Miss Raven. I'm Ned."

Raven wondered how he knew her. To the best of her knowledge she had never laid eyes on the man before. More than likely, her grandmother had shown some pictures of her to him, though that didn't really seem like the sort of thing that Grandma Davis would have done.

The door was open just a crack. It only took a touch to make it swing inwards, without a sound.

"Well, don't just stand there like an idiot, girl. Get yourself inside!"

Wanda Davis was in her seventies, at least that had always been the conventional family wisdom. When asked what her birth year was, all you would get out of the woman was an icy stare that definitely suggested it would *not* be a good idea to ask a second time.

Raven spotted her grandmother sitting behind a large wooden table that was covered with a number of paint palettes, display stands and open guidebooks. In one hand she held a brush, in the other a china plate. She moved the brush across its surface.

"Don't get in my light," she snapped, holding the plate up. "So tell me what you think of it?"

"Well," Raven said, deliberately stretching her words out as she studied it. The picture showed a man and a woman in camo, armed of course, standing over the body of a man in a suit with his briefcase open and papers flying around "It's interesting."

"I told you when you were a little girl it isn't nice to fib to your grandmother. This is a piece of shit and I've just wasted the last day and a half on it."

With that she sent the plate flying across the room. It clipped the edge of the couch, bounced and slammed against the wall, shattering into several dozen pieces.

The pewter-colored cat lying on the couch opened one eye, yawned and went back to sleep.

"Now, what'n hell do you want here? And don't tell me it's a family call. You know what I said about fibbing to me," said the older woman, pushing herself away from the table, reaching for the coffee cup that sat on top of a pile of old newspapers.

Raven dropped onto the arm of an overstuffed chair and

stared at her grandmother. "Look, the only reason I'm back was a bit of morbid curiosity to see if this town had changed. Hell, fifteen minutes after I sat down at the Lucky Lady I could tell it hadn't. But then I started hearing some weird shit, that three girls I grew up with all were killed in hit and runs in less than six weeks," said Raven. "That's just a bit too much of a coincidence, even for me to believe."

Grandma Davis picked up her cup and took a sip. She seemed to be mulling over things.

"That is a wee bit odd, I'll admit," nodded her grandmother. "So I'd be looking both ways, anytime I crossed the street while you're back here, if I were you, Raven. But I'm about to make it odder. I know about those three girls being killed. I also know that their bodies are missing."

""I beg your pardon."

"No need, I was quite clear. All three of those girls' bodies were stolen out of their graves within four days of their funerals," she said.

"Why?" asked Raven.

"Pardon me, Miss Harkness." Raven looked over to see the big gardener standing near the window. How he had moved so quietly was a mystery. "There are some things that it might be better if'n we just left 'em alone."

"Look my friend, there are questions that need to be answered," she said turning toward the window.

"Raven," said her grandmother. "I expect you to look at me when you're talking!"

"I was just talking to him," said Raven and gestured toward the window, only there was no one there.

"What are you talking about?" asked the older woman.

Raven was about to say something about Ned, but thought better of it. "So why haven't people gotten up in arms about this whole thing, even if it does sound like something out of a bad drive-in movie."

"There's a lot that can be learned from bad drive in movies, girl. The sheriff might not be the brightest bulb in the package but he's right. With only two deputies, he's got to keep this thing quiet."

"I guess I should tell you that it isn't three girls you know who are dead, it's four. A truck hit Kelly Golden a few days ago. The family kept it quiet, didn't even have a real funeral.

They buried her three days ago. I'm not even sure if the sheriff knows about it, yet."

Another face, another set of memories ran through Raven's mind. She hadn't been that close to Kelly, not like the others. But they had been friends.

"So you think that if someone is going to dig her up, maybe it'll happen tonight?"

Wanda Davis picked up a ceramic mug and began to dab at it with a thick bristle brush. Raven knew when she had been dismissed, and the futility of trying to get her grandmother to talk when she didn't want to.

You owe me big for being out here tonight, real big." Madison told Raven.

"What, did you maybe have a really hot date?" Sitting in a cemetery for three hours was definitely not the way that Raven had planned to spend a Saturday night. Instead of heading for the dance that was going on over at the bingo hall, she and Madison were parked behind the maintenance shed at the Sweet Heaven Cemetery watching the grave of an old friend.

"So, are you going to tell me about this big date that you're missing?" asked Raven.

"I suppose so," giggled Madison, "since you asked so nice and polite. His name is Eric Dawson. He is seriously fine, to the point that I could very easily come in my pants just thinking about him. He works over at the bottling plant, drives a Mustang that he's reconditioned. I met him at the dirt track races three Saturday nights ago. He's smart, intelligent, and I made sure he's falling for *moi*."

"So, have you given him the acid test?" asked Raven,

"What do you mean?"

"Have you screwed his brains out, yet? I'd make sure you were way out in the country. As I recall from more than one or two of our double dates, you do tend to get vocal," said Raven.

Before either could say anything more, a van turned into the cemetery. It took several wrong turns on the unlit roads but eventually came to a halt near the new grave that bore the name Kelly Golden. The vehicle was in fairly good shape but there was a discolored area on the side, as if marking a place where a sign had been removed.

"Bingo," said Raven. She watched two figures climb out of the van: one tall and gangly, the other smaller, both dressed in army fatigues. It was too far to make out their faces, but there was something familiar about the bigger one. Raven just couldn't put her finger on what it was.

An annoying scratching sound from the back window of the car got Raven's attention. Twisting around, she saw a figure standing next to the car, slowly moving its fingers up and down on the glass. There was more than enough light to see the pale skin and eye hanging out of its socket to recognize it as a zombie.

Before she could gun the engine to life and roar away from the undead thing, Madison was out of the car, a two-by-four with a half dozen nails protruding from one end in her hand.

"Shit," muttered Raven, grabbing up her pistol and following her friend.

Madison slammed her club into the creature's head twice in quick succession, then hit it in the back of the legs. That was enough to put the thing on the ground. The sound of wood striking bone, driving nails into it, was very satisfying as she pounded at it, blood and bits of broken bone flying everywhere.

Once the thing stopped moving, Madison turned back to Raven.

"You could have helped," she said.

"Far be it from me to interfere in your fun. Any particular reason why you tore into this one so vehemently?" asked Raven.

Madison leaned against the car, dropping the club at her feet. "Yes. That thing used to be Eric. The guy I was telling you about!"

"Whoops," Raven grinned, but the grin vanished when she saw the look on Madison's face. "So were you going to let him? Get in your pants, I mean. There's a mighty good chance that he might have gone over while you two were doing the mattress shuffle."

"That's gross!" said Madison.

"Well, you don't have to worry about it now."

The sound of the van's engine got Raven's attention as she watched it pull away. The grave was open, and she could just make out a coffin lid peeking out of the hole.

"Let's go." She wasn't sure if the bad feeling in the pit of her stomach was from what was happening or because the chili they had for dinner wasn't sitting well.

The van headed north, onto the old Ft. Sill military reservation, disappearing into the rat's maze of roads that criss-crossed the area. Nearly two hours later there was still no sign of the missing vehicle. Much as she hated to, Raven had reached the point where she was ready to give it up as a lost cause.

Founded at the tail end of the days of the Wild West, Ft. Sill had been intended to help keep settlers safe and Indians under control. After the plague, the army had attempted to hold out at the base for a few years, but had eventually abandoned the site.

"It may be time to fall back to Plan B," muttered Raven.

"What, pray tell, is Plan B?" asked Madison.

"I'll let you know after I think of one."

They were passing a small cinder block church in the center of the base. It occurred to her suddenly that just beyond the church was the large bowling alley, another favorite hangout for teenagers who were trying to see who could scare the others the most.

"There," she whispered to Madison. Parked in the area just behind the bowling alley was the van. "Feel in the mood for some bowling tonight?"

Raven slid her colt 45 into her belt, and then touched her boots to assure herself that the two knives hidden there were ready and waiting. Madison had her own gun, a nine-millimeter with silver grips. She also picked up the same club she had used earlier, the wood and nails now many shades darker because of the bloodstains.

"If you got any blood on the upholstery, you are going to be the one to clean it off, with a toothbrush," said Raven.

"Yes, mommy," Madison laughed. "So, are we going to stand out here all night flapping our jaws or are we going to go see what's going on in there?"

After the two women had gone through the back door, a lone figure came ambling around the side of the church building and looked over at the bowling alley. Ned was wishing that the sign was on; he'd always liked the way the neon pins would fall over and then be picked up, to fall over again across the front of the building.

Of Two Minds

There was no light inside, beyond what leaked in through broken windows on either side of the entrance. If it hadn't been for the flashlights they had brought along, the depths of the place would have been pitch black.

Raven caught a glimpse of her own reflection in the cracked mirror that hung behind the shoe rental area. Here and there in the small cubicles, between rat's nests and trash, she noticed a few unmatched pairs of bowling shoes.

At the far end of the alley, pushed up against the east wall, was a raised stage with a complete drum set in the center and three microphones at equal intervals around it. Shining her flashlight on the drums, one thing struck Raven right away. There was a fine layer of dust on almost everything else in the bowling alley, but the drums and microphones looked shiny new, like they had just come from the music store.

"Is there maybe a concert around here that no one told me about?" asked Raven.

"I suppose you could say that," said a voice from behind one of the alleys. The words were punctuated by the very distinct sound of a machine gun being cocked.

"Dexter? Is that you?" asked Madison.

That name and that voice brought back a memory to Raven: a gangly scarecrow-like figure with an unruly thatch of red hair that looked like it had never been within ten miles of a comb.

"I'm touched that you remember me, Madison. Though a bit surprised, since you, just like the rest, barely acknowledged I was alive, unless you needed me to do something," said the man, as he ducked low and came in below the machinery in one of the lanes. It was the same fatigue-dressed figure Raven had seen earlier.

"Drop you weapons, please," he said gesturing with the barrel of the machine gun.

"Dexter? Dexter McPherson?" asked Raven.

"The same. Now, the guns."

"Are you that good a shot?" asked Raven. "It seems like there are two of us and we have the advantage of numbers and weapons."

"If he's not, I am." From the shoe rental area came the other figure from the graveyard. Only now Raven could see that he was considerably younger, the fatigues hanging loose from him. He was no more than twelve or thirteen at the most; the shotgun cradled in his arms seemed almost bigger than he was.

Behind him came a third man, three times the boy's size at least. It took Raven a moment to realize that it was her grandmother's gardener, Ned.

The two came up behind the two women and began to pull their guns from them, but missed Raven's knives. Ned threw Madison's club against the far wall, hard enough for its points to sink into the plaster.

Once they were disarmed, the boy produced a cord and tied both women's hands behind their backs. Raven found herself forced to sit on one of the curved plastic benches at the end of one of the lanes. Dexter said something to the boy and Ned, and then sat down next to Raven, as the other two disappeared into the darkness.

"Now," said Dexter. "I suppose you are wondering why I called you all here."

"Oh come on, Dexter, get to the point," said Raven. She had already managed to work one hand free of the knots. The kid had been more interested in copping a feel than in making sure the knots were tight.

"Oh, all right," laughed the man. "The truth is, I am putting together the greatest rock and roll band that the world has ever seen. This is our rehearsal hall."

"That's ambitious, Dexter," said Madison. "We all knew you had talent."

The gangly boy had a genius for machines of any sort. He had been the one a lot of people called on to fix machines of every size from a mixer to a bulldozer. The only trouble was, he had always wanted to go further, working with computers and things like that. Those sorts of ideas scared a lot of the people.

"So what's a band have to do with your digging up bodies? Trying to make a band from parts?" Raven asked him.

"Close. I tried to recruit Peggy, Mary Anne & Jodeana, to share my vision with them, but they all laughed in my face, the same way you all did when we were growing up. So I had to get them into the group another way," he said. "Just watch," Dexter pulled a small walkie-talkie from his pocket and spoke a few words that Raven couldn't hear.

The door that Ned and the boy had left through opened.

Even in the dark, Raven could see several people coming through. They moved up onto the stage, each movement seeming mechanical and exaggerated. The boy was the one guiding them into place behind two of the microphone stands and the drums. Over his back he carried guitars that he fitted into the hands of the two figures behind the mikes.

"It's show time, folks!" laughed Dexter. He held his hand up, the walkie-talkie held like a magic wand, and made a gesture with it. Spotlights came on, focused on the stage.

Raven stared in disbelief.

Behind the two mikes were Peggy and Mary Anne, and just peeking over the drum set was Jodeana. At first she thought they might be plague zombies, but no plague victims she had seen had ever looked like that. Their eyes were rolled back in their heads and their skin was fish belly white; every movement was stiff and jerky.

"Play it, girls," yelled Dexter, a smile on his face.

Peggy and Mary Anne began to drag their fingers across the strings of their guitars, but in no coherent way that even resembled music. Behind them, the only sound that emerged from the drum set resembled the sound of a motor that had thrown a rod.

"You sick bastard, what have you done to them?" demanded Raven.

"Oh, just made some improvements. When they turned me down I knew there was no way they would be willing to be my ticket to fame and fortune. So I had to "draft" them. Some arranged accidents, ones that didn't damage their bodies too bad, along with a special preservative I developed and my computer, make them move. Now I have myself a band. I'm thinking of marketing that preservative; it does a great job with fruit and pickles, as well."

Raven stared, incredulous, at the animated corpses of the three women. Her eyes kept returning to the silver necklace Mary Anne wore.

"I had thought about trying to develop a variant of the plague, but this way works much, much better. I can make them into the ultimate rock band. We don't even have to have a bus; the girls can just sit in the closet of my camper. The only thing they need now is practice, and then we can go on the road. Every zombie in the world will be lining up to hear them," said Dexter.

"Dexter, I may have thought you were weird before, but now I know you are one sick fuck," said Raven. "The only thing you should be doing on the road is being run over by a semi. I know a truck driver who would be more than happy to oblige."

"Now," continued Dexter, ignoring Raven, "I've got Kelly downstairs. She needs some work before I can get her ready for the stage. Then I can start on you two; you'll add just the right sound as backup singers."

"Not on your life, little boy." Raven spat in his face, pulling her hands free from the last of the knots and brought her knee up to slam into his crotch. Dexter bent almost double in pain, the air rushing out of his chest in a wave of bad breath and Mentos.

On the stage there was a sudden crashing. One of the spotlights had come loose from the ceiling and fallen, sparks flying everywhere, setting the cheap carpet on fire. The other lights in the alley sputtered and faded out. The "girls" continued to make noise with their instruments, oblivious to everything.

Raven grabbed Dexter's machine gun, ran toward the stage and sprayed the whole place with bullets, concentrating on the girls. Their flesh flew apart, an odd bluish-green liquid spurting out from their wounds. The kid came running out of the door behind the stage, shotgun in hand. Raven gave him his own blast with the machine gun.

She looked around for Ned, but the big man was gone.

Dexter was struggling to his feet. Raven launched a kick at the side of his head and that was enough to put him back on the floor. She pulled Madison, who still hadn't worked her way free from the ropes, to her feet and the two of them sprinted for the door. Already the fire was spreading, acrid smoke filling the place.

"I think it's time to blow this party!" Raven shouted, as she grabbed the other girl's arm and headed them toward the door.

"Yeah, this place blows," her friend answered. "Let's find something exciting to do."

The lights had gone out quickly, so they had to feel their way along the wall toward the door. As they passed the concession stand, Raven looked up into the big mirror. She could barely make out Ned, standing and just looking around like a fascinated child, a yellow circus balloon in one hand and cotton candy cone in the other.

When she glanced back into the alley, no one was there.

"I was tempted to just not untie you and drop you off at your place like that," laughed Raven.

"I'm sure that my neighbors would have loved to see me walking around like that," Madison said.

Raven picked up the coffee cup that sat in front of her. "Hey, I think it would have done wonders for your reputation," she said.

"Gee, thanks. That's just the kind of reputation that I need around this town," she said, rubbing her wrists. "I still have to explain the rope burns."

"What are friends for, if we can't help each other out? Now, pass me the barbeque sauce," Raven told her.

It was nearly noon, but The Lucky Lady was still serving breakfast. Scrambled eggs, grits and black coffee seemed the order of the day. For the past few minutes, besides Alex, who was cooking and working the register, Madison and Raven had had the place to themselves. That suited the two women just fine; there were some things that no one else needed to hear.

By the time they had gotten to the car the whole bowling ally had been totally engulfed in flames. That the fire had spread so quickly was weird, but right then the only thing Raven wanted to do was put as much distance between herself and the place as she could.

In the hours since, she had heard a half-dozen different explanations for the fire; everything from kids starting it to some kind of zombie orgy. Charlie and Ed had suggested that maybe some little green men had come down and set the fire, since they couldn't find a cornfield to leave designs in.

"So how did your grandmother react when you told her about Ned being dead?' asked Madison.

"Now, that is getting really strange, though after last night I'm not sure what that word really means. I went over to see Grandma this morning, but when I mentioned Ned, she asked who was I talking about. She claimed that not only did she not have a gardener, but the only person she had ever known named Ned had died more than twenty years ago. Not to mention the fact that she would be damned if anybody but her was going to touch her roses bushes," said Raven as she poured some sauce over her eggs, not that it helped the taste.

Madison furrowed her brow. "Next thing you're going to tell me is that we hallucinated him," muttered Raven's friend.

Alex appeared with a fresh pot of coffee in his hand and refilled both women's cups. "By the way, Miss Harkness, ma'am. When I opened up this morning I found a big manila envelope stuck in the door. It had your name on it."

"My name?"

"Yeah, it's up here by the register. I forgot about it until just now."

Raven's name was indeed right in the center of the envelope, written in crude block letters with an orange crayon. She tore open the envelope and poured the contents on the counter.

It was a necklace, her necklace, the very same one she had last seen hanging around Mary Anne's neck last night, just moments before she had blown her face off.

The necklace wasn't the only thing. Lying next to it was a length of string tied around the stem of what remained of a yellow circus balloon.

The Rhinestone Maidens

Sue Sinor
International House of Bubbas
Yard Dog Press

"We done got us a letter, Reenie!" Loretta yelled from outside the house to her twin sister.

"We did? Well, what's it say?" Lorene called back, as she continued to stir the pan of scrambled eggs that sat on the low fire, and threw in some sliced hot dogs and chopped onions. Not the fanciest dinner in the world but given their budget - two professional singers just starting out in the business who were not pulling in that much money - not too bad at all.

"Hallelujah, we got in, we got in, we got in!" Loretta whooped as she ran into the kitchen.

"Got in what, Loretta? Will you make some sense for once in your life."

Loretta grinned like a Cheshire cat and held out the letter for her sister. "Got in the USO tour, you dummy. What else were we tryin' to get into? We leave next week."

Lorene rolled her eyes up in her head; this was just like her sister. "Next *week*? This is Friday, for Elvis' sake! And we've got us gigs tonight and tomorrow, in case you've forgotten. We don't have time to get ready!" She reached up and pulled a couple of plates out of the cabinet. "Besides, you're the one who wanted to get on that tour. You just want to see Lester again. How do you even know that we'll play where he is?"

If it were possible for Loretta's grin to get bigger, it did. "Because, Miss Wet Blanket, it says on this itinerary that we'll be playing at the base in Germany where he's stationed. I'm goin' to write him right now and tell him when we'll be there."

Lester was Loretta's high school sweetheart who had joined the army right after they had all graduated from junior college.

"And I'll tell him we want him to play with us again, just like when we was startin' out. It'll be *fun!* Plus it will get us some good exposure, which never hurts. Not to mention that we'll get to see where Great Granny and Grandad grew up in Germany."

Lorene didn't like the whole thing, it didn't feel right. But Loretta was the driving force behind their singing career, and most of her ideas seemed to have worked out.

The girls had grown up in a small town that sat right exactly on the borders of Arkansas, Oklahoma and Texas. Country music had been a staple in their lives from the cradle, especially the Grand Ol' Opry on the radio, and Hee-Haw on cable. In fact, Loretta had been named for Loretta Lynn. Since she was born first, she got the country-singer name. Lorene was named for their grandma on their mother's side.

They loved the flash and glitter of the costumes and decided they were going to be Country Singers, too. Thus were born "The Rhinestone Maidens", the name coming from an attempt by their high school principal to instill some appreciation for "culture" in his students. He had taken them all to a performance of the opera "Das Rheingold" by Richard Wagner. Loretta and Lorene were mesmerized, not by the music, but by the mermaids swimming around in the river, the Rhine Maidens. They didn't think of water, though; they thought of rhinestones, and longed to wear lots of them. They had started appearing at local fairs, clubs and even going out of state every now and then, not making much money but having a high old time. Lorene hadn't thought much about it when her sister announced that she was sending a tape of one of their shows in as part of an audition for a USO tour. Hell, even when Loretta had dragged her to the in-person auditions, the chances of their being picked felt remote.

Now, there was this damn letter. Lorene enjoyed singing as much as her sister, but traveling to other countries didn't figure prominently in her plans. She'd just started dating a local computer techie. She knew practically nothing about computers, but he was just majorly cute and seemed to be head over heels for her.

"I don't know, Retta. How long will we be gone? I don't want Travis to forget about me and find someone else."

"Come ON, Reenie, you have to go! We're a duet, not a solo act. Travis will be waiting for you. Besides, there'll be a lot of men on the tour. Maybe you'll find someone else and not want to put up with Travis. Besides, you know how much I miss Lester. When he gets out of the army we're goin' to get married and we can be a trio again. Pleeease," Loretta pleaded.

Lorene hated to hear her sister whine; it reminded her of

her own voice. "Geez, Retta. You know I'll go. What would I do by myself? Now eat your dinner and get ready for the show."

"Thanks, Reenie. I knew you would. Now pass the barbeque sauce."

"Five minutes, Reenie!" Loretta called as she came through the dressing room door. They'd been on the tour for a couple of weeks; this was the biggest dressing area they had had and it was barely the size of a closet.

"Five? How do I look? Is my hair OK? How's my makeup?" Lorene frantically ran her hands over every part of her costume, pushing and pulling, tugging and twisting. Loretta stepped up beside her and in the dressing room mirror they looked like two images of the same person. Few people could tell them apart; only their parents and Lester had that ability.

"Goodness, you two are a sight for sore eyes. My, y'all look purty. Are those new costumes? You sure do sparkle," Lester said as he peeked in the door. "Especially you, Loretta."

"Lester!" Loretta whooped as she ran over to him. "Are you ready to play with us tonight?"

"I can't wait to get outta the army and back to playin' with you." Lester wore his army uniform, but he liked his rhinestone cowboy outfit better, and he said so.

Over the monitor came "Now here they are, straight from the heartland of America, The Rhinestone Maidens!" After one last deep breath they raced from the dressing room.

The crowd went wild as the girls ran onstage, followed by Lester with his guitar. The tour band played for all the acts, but it was hidden at the back of the stage behind a curtain for some of the acts, including this one.

They started with a Patsy Cline standard and followed with an early number by Loretta Lynn. Everybody seemed to be getting into the music. Before they had a chance to start the George Jones song, there was a disturbance in the audience. Two soldiers had attacked a third one. In a matter of seconds a dozen more solders had gotten into the act, with the rest of the audience following moments later. The ones who weren't fighting, or running away, had dropped dead where they sat.

Neither girl was really sure what to do, so they kept on singing, finally stopping in the middle of a Kenny Rogers ballad, since it was fairly obvious that no one was listening to them.

"We'll just have to sing louder, Retta," Lorene suggested. "That oughta get their attention. How about some Jerry Lee? Great Balls of Fire?"

Just then Lester ran up from the back of the stage. "What's going on? What's the fight about?"

"Don't know. But we're fixin' to get our audience back," Loretta said.

"Don't bother," yelled a trumpet player named Randy, as he rammed his trumpet into the head of another member of the tour band. "Some of the guys dropped dead, but some of them have turned into ....I don' know what, some kinda zombies. They're munching down on some of the others that didn't drop dead. Let's get the hell out of here, like yesterday."

"Why doesn't anybody shoot 'em?" Lorene asked. "These guys are soldiers; soldiers have guns."

"Not at the concert," Paul, who played clarinet, explained. "The guards are the only ones who are allowed to be armed. And it looks like most of them turned into zombies and are trying to eat anyone who didn't. If we don't get away pretty quick, we'll be zombie food!" He grabbed Lorene and ran toward the tour bus. Lester, Loretta and Randy were already running in that direction.

When they had all barricaded themselves in the tour bus, Lester asked, "But we all seem OK. Why'd that happen to them and not us?"

"I don't really know, but I heard something from one of the guys who'd been checking news on the internet. He said that there were a lot of reports of things like this happening, all over. It sounds like some kind of drive-in movie gone crazy, killing most folks, but turning some people into zombies - who eat human flesh," Paul explained.

"Ew!" the girls shuddered in unison.

"He left his computer here in the bus, so I'll try to find out what's going on by checking the news sources," Paul said as he belly-crawled toward the back. The others hunkered down on the floor, peeking up only occasionally.

"You know how to do that?" Lorene asked.

"Sure, although I've spent a lot more time looking at music stands than computer screens," Paul explained, as he booted up the wireless connection. Outside of the bus zombie-looking figures, some in army uniforms, some in civilian clothes, were running around the parking lot, chasing after normal-looking people and tripping over bodies lying around everywhere.

"Ah, here we go. I've opened the "Stars and Stripes" online. Let's see what I can find. Here's a post from a few days ago. It seems to be describing what's going on back home. Lots of people dead, lots more turned into flesh-eating zombies; seems like it's everywhere. There are some places where nothing seems to be happening. I think one of them's where you folks said you were from."

"Thank Elvis," Loretta said. "I hope our families are okay. I wonder what's caused all this."

"I wish I knew, too. I'll keep checking every once-in-a-while. Maybe we'll find out."

Lorene looked around. "I'm scared, but I'm hungry, too. Is there anything to eat in the bus?"

"You're *hungry*? Reenie, there's dead people all over the place and zombies runnin' around eating anyone that's still alive, and you're hungry?"

"Yes I am. And I'll bet you are, too, if you'd think about it. We haven't eaten in hours. You know we didn't have time to eat before the show."

"Okay, I think there may be a loaf of bread back here, and I've got the bottle of barbeque sauce I brought to give Lester."

"You brought me some barbeque sauce? Oh, that was sweet."

"I've got some sausage in here," Randy piped up. "And there's some beer, too, I think." He crawled toward the back where the cooler was.

"Uh, guys, I think the beer's gone, and that sausage won't last long," Paul said regretfully. "But I know where to get more. There's this restaurant in town that some cousins of mine own. I keep in touch with them, and last night when we got in town I went over there to see them. I'd like to check up on them, too. I'll drive; I know how to get there."

No one was moving when he looked out the window. Dead bodies were scattered around, some of them partially eaten, but no zombies were in evidence. Paul climbed into the driver's seat and tried to figure out how to start the bus.

"I'll drive; you just tell me where to go," Lester insisted. "I used to drive a bus back home. I don't think this one is much different."

"You drove a school bus," Loretta reminded him. "I don't think this is a school bus."

"No, but it's not that different. Y'all sit down 'cause I'm startin' the engine. Which way do we go, Paul?" Lester did something and the motor came to life. "Looks like we got enough fuel to get somewhere, anyway."

A half hour later the bus pulled up to the curb in front of Paul's cousin's restaurant, two kilometers from the base. Lester punched the horn several times.

"What'd you do that for? We don't want the zombies to know we're here." Loretta thumped Lester on the head as she yelled at him.

"I expect they heard us comin'. Besides, we're pretty well locked in here. I don't think they can get to us." Lester honked again.

Paul noticed a twitch of the curtain at the window of the restaurant. He leaned close to the windshield and waved, yelling, "Heinrich, it's me, your cousin Paul! You still alive?"

The curtain opened and a face peered out, then the front door opened a crack and the barrel of a gun protruded. Paul quickly unlocked the bus's door and got out, holding his hands high.

"Don't shoot. It's me, Paul, and I brought a few friends. We're not zombies! Can we come in, please?"

A head appeared above the gun barrel, then a voice called out, "Hurry."

Just as they were starting to get off the bus, they heard a shot.

"Duck, he's shooting at us," Loretta yelled.

Paul ran back. "No, he shot a zombie. Come on." He grabbed Lorene and led her to the door as the rest followed.

The last of them scrambled through the door just as it was slammed shut behind them. A moment later slow, unmethodical pounding started on the door. It looked like the zombies had arrived.

"So, Paul, why don't you introduce your friends?" said the man Paul had identified as his cousin. Two women, one older, one younger. appeared from the back of the restaurant, both with rifles in their hands.

"Thanks for letting us in, Heinrich," Paul said as he put his arm around Lorene. "This is Lorene, and that's her twin sister, Loretta. They're "The Rhinestone Maidens" in the USO show at the army base. The guy in the uniform is Lester, Loretta's boyfriend. And the other guy is Randy. He's a trumpet player in the band."

Then Paul turned to the refugees. "This is my cousin, Heinrich. He owns this place. That's his wife, Inger, and that's their daughter, Bridget. Hey, where are your employees? I know there were more people working here last night."

"There were; some are dead, dropped in their tracks, a few turned into these flesh eating things; we had to kill them. The others made a run for their homes. I fear they may not have made it."

Just then the pounding, which had died down, resumed even louder.

"The first order of business is to defend ourselves. Paul, take this rifle. I've more behind the bar and in my office, enough for you three men and myself." He turned to get the other weapons.

Heinrich passed out all the weapons and ammunition he had, including knives from the kitchen. "Everyone hide. We'll pick off all we can when they come through the door. Get the ones that get past us with the knives, but don't take chances. We don't want to lose anyone."

Lorene and Loretta, holding butcher knives, hid behind the bar. "Boy, Heinrich can really speak good English," Loretta commented.

"Paul said he grew up in Mississippi, with some of Paul's family, and went to college there before he moved back here to Germany. So I guess that's why." Lorene peered over the top of the bar.

Right then the door burst open and a zombie lurched in. Heinrich, who had turned a table over and was crouched behind it, shot the zombie, but more poured through the open doorway. Paul and Randy were behind another table, each with a handgun. Paul shot at a zombie that was heading toward them, but missed. Randy shot, also, but only grazed it in the side. They both tried again, but the zombies were coming too fast and furious for them to make a dent.

Heinrich and Lester were doing a pretty good job of picking them off, but more kept coming, and Paul and Randy kept missing.

Finally, Loretta said, "We can do better that that." She and Lorene dashed to the table shielding Paul and Randy. "Give us those guns. I bet y'all couldn't hit the broad side of a barn with a cat."

"Hey," Randy replied. "We're musicians, not, uh, whatever you call people who shoot guns."

They handed the guns over in exchange for the knives, and the girls started popping up and squeezing off shots like prairie dogs popping up from their holes. They were good shots. In fact, between them and Heinrich and Lester, very few zombies got through to attack the knife-bearers.

The number of zombies coming through the door slowed to a trickle, then stopped. The door had been broken in and they couldn't bar it anymore, so they decided to abandon the restaurant.

"We live upstairs," Heinrich said, "but I don't think it would be safe there. However, I do have a cellar where I store food and supplies. We can carry whatever we'll need to last us a few days into the cellar and barricade ourselves down there." He looked at Loretta and Lorene. "Would you two guard the door for us? You seem to be pretty good shots."

"Thanks. We learned to shoot from our Granddaddy. I bet we could still hit a tin can on a fence post at fifty paces." Loretta was justifiably proud of her and Lorene's marksmanship.

The rest of the group started carrying boxes of food, drink and other necessities into the cellar. It turned out to be snug and comfortable. There were several rooms, a mini-kitchen, a full bathroom and a couple of fold-out couches and recliners.

Heinrich explained, "We've used this as a guest room at times, when we've had company that we didn't have room for upstairs."

They went back up to get the girls, who had shot a few stragglers while they were waiting.

"We left some stuff in the bus that we should get, and the rest of our stuff is back at the base," Loretta said. "I think we should try to go get it. If Lester comes with us, and everybody else stays here and watches for us, we can get it and be back real quick."

"Don't you think it's a little too dangerous to go back out?" Paul asked.

Loretta answered. "Look, we love our costumes, but we don't want to live in them. And I don't think your cousins have anything that'll fit us. Inger and Bridget are just too small. We'll take two of the guns and a knife. We'll be in the bus; we'll be fine."

With that she took off out the door and Lorene and Lester followed.

They saw a little action on the way to the base, but most non-zombie live people had holed up in safe places. They saw a number of zombies lurching around, a few of them lunching on the very recently dead. A couple were about to attack a woman who was trying to unlock a door. Loretta slid open the bus window and calmly shot the attackers.

"*Danke!*" the woman cried as she got the door open and dashed in, slamming it behind her.

When they pulled up to the base's community center, where the show had been held, all they saw were bodies lying around. They quickly ran into the building, locking the door, and crept toward the dressing rooms. They packed their things and checked the other rooms for any more live people. They didn't find any, so they grabbed their belongings, along with as many weapons as possible, and raced for the bus.

"I want to stop at my barracks before we go back. There are some things I want to get. I promise I'll hurry," Lester said as they settled in their seats.

"We'll help. I don't want us to get separated," Loretta told him.

They stopped at the barracks door, still seeing no zombies or survivors, but seeing plenty of dead bodies, many with guns nearby.

Lorene said, "I'll go pick up some of those guns. You never know when we'll need more. Why don't you see if you can find more ammo inside, too."

"That'll be in another building, but that's a good idea. We can stop there, too. This won't take me long, so you'd better hurry. I don't want to be outside any longer than necessary." Lester ran into the building while Loretta stood at the door, covering both of them.

Lorene was able to pick up half a dozen rifles, and as much ammo as the bodies had on them. She got back to the bus just as Lester reappeared, dragging his footlocker.

They stopped at the armory before they left the base and gathered up additional arms and ammo. By then they were a rolling arsenal.

"We're baaack," Loretta called when they arrived at the restaurant. "Come help us with this stuff."

Paul peeked out, holding his shotgun. "I've got some bad news. Some zombies got in and got Randy. He's dead. We shot the zombies, but it wasn't in time to save him."

"Oh, no!" Lorene cried. "He seemed like a real nice guy."

"No time for sentiment. We need to get your stuff in and all of us down in the cellar before more come."

Heinrich appeared at the door. "I took his body out back. There are a lot of bodies around. We can't bury everyone. What did you bring us?"

"Lots of stuff, including more guns and ammo. Lorene and I'll stand guard if you all will take everything inside. Don't leave anything in the bus that isn't built in. We might need it. And take care of that bottle of barbeque sauce. That's the only one we have."

They soon had everything stripped from the bus and put away in the cellar. While the twins and Lester had been pillaging the base, Inger and Bridget had gone up to their living quarters and carried down as many supplies as they could. They might have to stay down there a week or longer.

When the twins had changed into more comfortable clothes and everyone had cleaned up, they sat down to take stock of the situation and get to know everyone else better.

Inger spoke up for the first time. "Are you girls really "The Rhinestone Maidens"? I think that's what Paul called you."

"Yep, that's us," Lorene answered. "But you couldn't have heard of us. We're just a small town country act."

"Oh, yes, we've heard of you. Some of my relatives live in Austria. They heard you play when your tour stopped there. They knew you were coming here next and said we should try to see your show. Often civilians can buy tickets, if there's enough room. but we couldn't get any. I guess that was for the best, or we would be zombie food by now. But we never got to hear you."

"Tell you what," Loretta piped up. "Let Lorene and me fix y'all some dinner and we'll put on a show right here. Lester's got his guitar with him and that's just how we started out, just the three of us. Now, you've got some of that bratwurst sausage, don't you? How about some barbequed brat?"

"You would share your barbeque sauce with us?" Heinrich said. "Could you teach me how to make it? I learned to love barbeque when I lived in Mississippi, and I've tried to make it for my family, but it never was as good as I had in America.

But I keep trying."

"Of course we will. Now let's get something to eat. I'm hungry, and we have a show to do."

After dinner Lester got his guitar. "Ready girls? Okay. Now here they are, The Rhinestone Maidens!"

They started just as they had earlier that day, with Patsy Cline, followed by Loretta Lynn and George Jones.

Paul was out of the room during the last song, and when he got back he told the group, "I heard footsteps upstairs while I was in the bathroom. Do you think we should check it out?"

"I'll take the rifle and look. If it's a survivor who has nowhere else to go, we should offer sanctuary," Heinrich said.

He climbed the stairs, with Lester right behind him, and cracked open the door. They saw a young man in an army uniform poking at a zombie lying on the floor, apparently dead.

Heinrich pointed the gun at him and he raised his hands above his head. "Don't shoot me, please. I'm not a zombie," he said in English.

"It's OK, Heinrich. I know him. Ted, are you OK? How did you get here?"

"Lester, I'm so glad to see you. This zombie was chasing me, so I ran in here. I hid in the kitchen and looked for a knife or something, then I heard the singing. I was trying to figure out where it was coming from when the zombie found me. It started to grab me, and then it just dropped dead. I didn't touch it."

Heinrich went back to the door and called down the stairs, "Girls, keep singing. Sing loud. Boys, hide behind the table and keep the rifle ready." Then he went to the front door, looked out and waved his arms.

Shortly he ran back into the room, followed by two zombies. They staggered toward him, and he led them past the cellar stairs. When they heard the music, they stopped, looked at each other, and dropped to the floor, stone dead.

"Everyone, come on up," Heinrich shouted. "I have a plan."

When they were all there, he pointed to the dead zombies. "When they heard your singing, they just dropped dead."

Loretta looked at the zombies and then looked at her sister.

"Everybody's always a critic," she said.

Are We There Yet?

Bradley H. & Susan P. Sinor
Houston: We've Got Bubbas!
Yard Dog Press

"Houston, we have a problem," Madison Cromwell said as the engine of their battered old pickup truck sputtered several times, then gave a shudder and sent a putrid-smelling puff of smoke out the tail pipe.

"Houston, are you listening to me?" she said. Her cousin, Houston Mayhew, continued to stare at the comic book he had been reading, rereading, actually, for the fourth or fifth time in the last hour.

"Yeah, Mad."

Without looking up, Houston reached down beside his seat and pulled out a pump action shotgun. He fired one-handed out the passenger window, barely even turning his head; taking out a trio of shambling yumbies that had appeared in the entrance of what had once been a fast food restaurant. Stray shotgun pellets impacted the faded clown face painted on the side of the building, marking it with bits of rotting grayish flesh.

Madison had seen him do it before and never understood how the recoil kept from breaking his arm.

She had her gun out, a Smith and Wesson .32, before the echo from the blast had faded. Madison wasn't as good a shot as Houston, but she could hold her own. If the guns failed, she had her Louisville Slugger baseball bat and definitely knew how to use it.

"I was hoping we wouldn't run into any yumbies. Not in my town." Ever since Houston had found out that there was a town in Texas that had his name, he had proclaimed it as "his town."

When Madison had announced her intention go to Houston, Texas, on a religious pilgrimage, her cousin had informed her that he was going with her; this was his chance to see "his town," and nothing or no one was going to talk him out of it.

Madison knew from experience not to even try. She just told him to pack extra ammunition and a good supply of beer.

He had also brought along a couple of dozen of Sherri Dean's homemade Moon pies and some of his momma's barbeque ribs.

"Ain't we there yet?"

Madison sighed. "No, we're not there yet, but we're gettin' close."

Houston may have been a really good shot, but he had the attention span of a sheet of paper. He was fine around home, friends and family, but any time he was in an unfamiliar place he acted like a five-year-old child.

Madison was just as anxious as Houston to get there, since *there* was the home of the only all-American sport and biggest religion to survive the 2025 plague – Professional Rasslin'.

After seeing some of the traveling revivals, Madison had decided that she wanted to go to the Tabernacle itself, the Sportatorium. She had even considered "taking the tights" herself and going into the squared circle as a wrestler or a referee or, at the very least, a ring girl carrying the sign around announcing the next match and the new hymn.

Originally the Sportatorium had been located in Dallas, just west of Nightingale on the inter-dispersal loop. Unfortunately, the Yumbies had gotten really bad in the Dallas area over the last couple of years and attendance had been way down. So the matchmakers of the Sportatorium had sought a better location and moved their operation to Houston.

Getting to Houston hadn't been easy, but really had been no worse than Madison had expected. Madison had a real good memory for directions so when Houston misplaced the maps it hadn't been that much of a problem.

Taking a deep breath, with a number of swear words in mind if it didn't work, Madison turned the ignition key. She smiled as the engine kicked to life; it still wasn't running well, but at least they were moving again.

"Are we there yet?"

Madison sighed again. "No, not yet! But it won't be too much longer. You just keep a lookout in case more yumbies show up. I've got enough to do drivin' this piece a junk."

"Okay. I'll watch." Houston started bouncing up and down in his seat. If this truck had had a bench seat like pick-ups used to, Madison would have bounced out the window.

She whapped him on the back of his head. "Stop it! You do

that again and I'll make you walk."

Madison may have been five feet nothing to his six feet two, but she'd gotten her bluff in on him when they were three years old, and it'd stuck.

"We're almost there!" Houston repeated this mantra in a singsong voice, which, had it gone on much longer, would have driven Madison batty.

Fortunately, they *were* almost there, though she wasn't sure where there was going to be. No one seemed to know exactly where the Sportatorium was located. According to the locals, matches happened in different places around town, with word being spread a day or two before. Someone suggested that they look out at the old NASA Space Center southeast of town.

"Well, it's almost dark," she told Houston, as they cruised up and down streets in what had once been a residential area. "We need to keep an eye out for some place we can hole up for the night."

"Mad, I hear somethin'. Sounds like music comin' from over there." He pointed to the right and slightly ahead of the truck. Madison heard music, too, and at the same time noticed a large metal sign that said National Aeronautics and Space Administration, Gate Three.

Just then two motorcycles came roaring past on either side of the truck. One of them popped a wheelie, riding on one wheel for at least fifty feet. It was a pretty safe bet that whoever was on those bikes, they weren't yumbies.

A quarter mile further, between two hangers, Madison spotted a half dozen semi's parked in a neat row; one of them had the logo of United Pharmaceuticals on its side, others bore paintings of everything from a stagecoach robbery to flying saucers. Scattered between them were a couple of dozen cars, several with rocket engines strapped to them, and pickup trucks, with a smattering of motorcycles mixed in among them.

The strong smell of roast pork hung in the air, reminding Madison that it had been several hours since the two of them had eaten. Stretched between the two buildings was a big banner with the words WELCOME TO THE DOUBLE DEUCE, HOUSTON'S BIGGEST OUTDOOR BAR AND GRILL.

Madison pulled over and got out. She guessed that there had to be at least a hundred people, some dancing to the band that had set up on a stage, others hanging around the bar and the good sized fire pit, where several very large pigs were slowly turning over a bed of red hot coals. To one side, a huge buffet table had been set up on sawhorses, where the remains of another pig were resting next to an industrial size bowl of barbeque sauce.

Madison was still a bit wary. True, there were no yumbies to be seen, but her momma hadn't raised any foolish children, and some normal humans could be as bad a problem as the yumbies.

She had intended to tell Houston to stay back at the truck while she looked around, but he was headed for the buffet table before Madison had slammed the door. The last time she had noticed her cousin he had two large plates of food in his hands and was talking away to a blond-haired man wearing an eye patch.

"Can I be getting you something to drink?" said the dark-haired man behind the bar. In spite of the scar that ran up the left side of his face, he was kind of cute, in a rakish sort of way; for a fat guy.

Madison dropped a couple of coins, enough to cover her drink and Houston's trip to the buffet, on the table. They quickly disappeared to be replaced by a short brown bottle. She'd had better from the brewery back home in Lawton, but this was tolerable.

"So, what's the occasion?" she asked, gesturing at the revelers.

"No occasion, just an ordinary night at the Double Deuce," said the bartender. "Name's Nick Jonas. Welcome to the best bar in all of Houston. I'm the owner, bartender and chief bottle washer, as well."

Madison spotted a few figures moving around on the rooftops that overlooked the "bar." Since no one seemed upset about them, she guessed they were some necessary guards or bouncers or both.

"So what happens when it rains?"

"We just make sure that the important things are kept dry, like the roasting pit," laughed Nick. "Actually, come winter we'll move the club inside one of the hangers, during the summer they tend to get a bit warm. So what brings you to the Double Deuce?"

Madison took a swallow of her beer. "My cousin and I just got into town today. I am here seeking the Sportatorium, where I will find my destiny in the squared circle," she said, slamming her hand down on the bar three times in quick succession.

Nick stared at her for a moment, and then the thin line of a smile broke his face. He reached across the bar, took her wrist and raised her arm straight up.

"Sister, you have found your road."

"You're a religious man?"

The bartender laughed. "Before I hurt my shoulder taking down a referee who had gone yumbie in the middle of a tag team match, I was the number three contender for the light heavyweight championship belt," he said proudly.

Madison looked askance. If he'd been what he said he was, it had been awhile.

"Well, it was a few years back," he said defensively, noticing her stare. "So, you want to join the flock. Got any experience?"

"Not in the ring. But I'd do just about anything, pass out programs, usher, or be a ring girl. How hard could that be? But someday, I am sure I could be the main event."

"Well, darlin', you've come to the right place. Since I retired from the ring, I've become a scout. I've sent a number of talented performers on to the Sportatorium, where they have made a name for themselves in the pulpit of the squared circle. I could give you names – but I won't. I'm not a name-dropper. So, what do you say? Will you sign with me? I can make you a star."

Okay, the smart thing would probably be to say no and go on looking for the Sportatorium on her own. But Madison realized that this might also be one of those one-in-a-million chance meetings that could change her life. Before she could say anything gunfire started echoing from all around her. She grabbed her bat and came around, expecting to see yumbies. Instead, there were a group of men wearing biker gang colors, featuring a shot of a bare butt made of iron, backing away from each other.

"Don't worry," laughed Nick. "There's hardly a night goes by where some of my rooftop bouncers don't have to interfere."

"That's a relief," she said, dubiously.

Nick set a fruit jar on the bar in front of her. He pulled out a metal flask and poured an inch of clear liquid into it.

"Let's celebrate our new relationship," he said.

"I suppose it couldn't hurt." Madison sniffed it and then

took a tiny swallow; she had learned a long time ago how to make it look like she was drinking more than she really was and that seemed like a good idea right now.

"It's going to be a few minutes till I can get someone to cover for me here. Why don't you grab yourself something to eat off the buffet table. One of the women who cooks for me makes enchiladas so hot you'll be dehydrated by the time you finish 'em.

"Then we'll find your cousin, head over to the Sportatorium and get you signed up for the training school."

That sounded like a plan to Madison, though she never made it to the food. The last thing she remembered before passing out was Nick staring at her with that smile of his.

The last time that Madison had woke up with a hangover had been six months earlier, when her best friend from high school had come back to town for a visit. That had been fun; this wasn't.

It took a minute or so for the room to stop spinning and her eyes to focus. In what felt like, to Madison, a superhuman effort of will, she pulled herself up into a sitting position on what she realized was a bed.

The room was no bigger than the attic bedroom she had back home. That was where the resemblance stopped. These walls were metal, though they did have several black velvet paintings hanging on them. These didn't show decent things, however, like Elvis or dogs playing poker, but men and women doing things that, at least in one case, looked either anatomically impossible or like a twister game on some heavy drugs.

"Well, nice to see you're awake."

"That's just a filthy rumor that someone is spreading."

Madison focused on the person sitting near the door. She looked to be about Madison's age, with short brown hair, wearing a nearly non-existent halter and the smallest and tightest pair of shorts that Madison had ever seen.

"Don't worry about your head," the girl smiled. "It's just a side effect of that drink dear Nicky gave you."

"He promised he would help me find my cousin and then he was going to take me to the Sportatorium training camp," said Madison, although speaking seemed to make her head hurt worse.

"You too, huh," the brunette sighed. "Trust me, they won't let him anywhere near the Sportatorium. They do call this place The Training Camp, though."

That revelation just made Madison's head hurt more.

"Just where are we? This looks like a cat house."

"You got that right off," the other girl said. "We're in one of the rooms on McMahon Station, the world's first orbiting brothel."

"Orbiting? You mean like up in space?"

"Exactly," she said. "Oh, by the way, you can call me Sunset."

Madison turned to the right. The movement was enough to send her rolling over. Ever since she woke up, Madison had heard a low throbbing, the sound and pitch gradually cycling through enough to where she realized it was not just in her head.

Just then the throbbing sound stopped and she found herself floating an inch over the bed.

"Got to be careful there, honey," said Sunset with a chuckle. "Gravity in this part of the station is less than half what you're used to and it sometimes goes out entirely. Of course, it can be handy, though, when some of our "gentlemen callers" get a wee bit inventive."

Space? She was up in space. This was just too weird. It had to be a joke. "How did we get up here, a flying saucer or what?"

"Or what. I'm not real sure how; all I know is we went into this glass room back there in Houston. I felt all tingly and then we were here. They call it a matter transporter. I don't understand how it works and I don't want to," she said.

"When you're feeling a bit better I'll take you over to the main view port. When you see out, there's going to be no doubt where you are. I have to admit, Ole Nick there picked a heck of a good place to set up shop. There ain't no rent up here and I sort of doubt we're going to be getting a visit from the local sheriff any time soon."

"It's just a little hard to wrap my head around. You say this is a brothel and that you work here?"

"Same as you're going to," Sunset nodded.

"Me?"

"Hey, you're even dressed for it. So I'm guessing they plan for you to go to work pretty quickly."

For the first time since she woke up, Madison looked down at herself. Instead of the work shirt and cutoff jeans that were her normal attire, she wore a see through pink top and a pair of panties that felt like the next thing from nothing around her lower regions.

"If that lying bastard tries to touch me, or let anyone else touch me that I don't want to, I'll not leave enough of him for a yumbie to even bother with!"

Pain like she had never felt before hit Madison, running from her leg up through every inch of her body. As quickly as it had begun the pain was gone, the memory of it left her trembling.

"There, there, darlin', I'm sure that we can motivate you in your new line of work," laughed Nick, standing in the door to the compartment, a shit-eating grin on his face.

It took Madison several minutes before she could really focus on him. The desire to go after him was overwhelmingly paramount, though she held it back. There were times to attack and there were times to wait. This was the latter.

"Honey, have a look here." Sunset held up her left leg to show a wide band around her left ankle. Madison looked at her own leg, where there was an identical band.

"Pain by stimulation of your nervous system," chuckled Nick, holding up a small box that pulsed with a sickly green color. He barely touched his finger to one of the dial and Madison felt a shock like touching an electric outlet run through her body. "As I understand it, the signal makes your nervous system think you're hurting, but doesn't do any physical damage; after all, I need to keep my stock in good condition. But don't think for a minute that me and "the boys" won't get physical if need be."

Behind Nick a bald man appeared, a pair of bandoliers criss-crossing his chest. "Excuse me, boss; we got that party come in and I need the key to the ammo closet and the liquor vault."

"Be right there, Sam. You ladies just rest yourselves. I got a feeling its going to be a long and profitable evening."

The lineup.

That was what Sunset had called it when she and Madison took their places with eight other girls in the reception area of the station. Three huge monitors gave a view of the earth and the sky that proved everything Sunset had said was accurate.

The first customer of the evening was a little ferret-faced man who leered at each girl. His breath was repellent enough to frighten skunks as he leaned close to each girl, picking his 'date' for the night. Standing there with practically nothing on, Madison felt humiliated, like this was a meat market and she was prime rib. Nevertheless, the customer chose a taller, more voluptuous girl named Velvet.

Madison was relieved, but she knew her time would come unless she found a way to escape, and quickly. There were two problems, as she saw it - the ankle bracelet, and how to get the hell out of this place.

Trusting Sunset for information was dicey at best, though the brunette seemed friendly enough. She didn't think it a good idea to ask any of the other girls about the bracelets, which they all wore; there was too much of a chance they would go blabbing to Nick or one of his men.

The arrival of a new customer was announced by a loud buzzer. Unless they were entertaining, the girls had two minutes to get to the main room, so she had been told.

Nine men were standing there.

One, who wore a hooded sweatshirt and sunglasses that obscured his face, pointed toward Sunset almost immediately. She smiled, extended her hand and the two walked down a short hallway. Madison felt a slight twist in her stomach when she heard the sound of a compartment door closing.

One by one the other men picked girls, and went off with them, until only one, a pock faced man in a much repaired letterman's jacket, remained. He stopped and stared down at Madison; he was at least eight inches taller than her.

"I'll just take this little lady here." A small sack went flying out of his hand. Nick caught it. "There's enough money to cover any extra charges, in case there are any "repairs" to the merchandise might be required later."

That was not the sort of thing that Madison wanted to hear.

The man in the letterman's jacket closed his hand on her shoulder and the two of them headed down the hallway. Madison suspected that this was not the first time he had been a visitor to McMahon Station.

There was very little in the room they entered: a bed, a table and a couple of chairs, all of them securely clamped to the metal floor. There were manacles and chains hanging from the wall.

When the door sealed shut Madison knew she had only a few moments, so she threw a punch at the man. That was when the constant humming of the gravity generator, a sound that in only a few hours she had grown used to, stopped. Her momentum sent Madison flying off the floor. She would have collided with the man, but he ducked to one side and managed to grab her around the waist.

The two of them went rolling through the air for several seconds. Madison couldn't see what was happening; the see-through night gown she was wearing rolled itself up around her head, tangling around her face and hands.

The lights dimmed and then came back up, along with the gravity, and the two of them plummeted like a hackysack to land half on and half off the bed, her on top of him.

"Somebody needs to have a long talk with you about foreplay," she muttered.

"Are you all right, Miss Cromwell?" he asked.

"How do you know my name?" She had only been required to give her first name during the lineup.

The man didn't answer; instead he struggled to his feet, going over to the door. It had remained sealed and no one seemed interested in what was going on inside.

"If we're lucky, if they heard anything, they'll think things are just getting "interesting" in here," he said.

Madison just stared at him, not sure what to say.

The man reached under the collar of his shirt, slowly ripping the skin away from his face. Only it wasn't blood and muscle that remained as the man's face peeled away, but a black and red mask that covered his entire head.

"Good evening," he said.

Madison stared at him for a full minute before speaking. "I know you! You're The Shade! I saw you last year in a three way handicap match in Lawton!"

"Oh yeah," he chuckled. "Me, the Crazy Lady and Hans von Hans. Ol' Hansie nearly took my leg off with that figure four hold of his."

"You preached a hell of sermon afterward, though," she said. "What is going on?"

"Looks like I'm here to rescue you, among other things," he said, pulling a pocket watch out from his jacket and checking the time.

"We may have a little problem there," Madison pointed at the ankle bracelet. "Not to mention the fact that we're in orbit."

"Trust me, we know all about that and have, shall we say, made arrangements to deal with it, plus a few other things," said The Shade, as he opened the door. Madison had barely taken a few steps into the hallway when the lights dimmed again; she grabbed for a handhold on the wall, expecting the gravity to disappear, but it didn't.

"One of my tag team partners is a little squirrelly, but a whiz at tech stuff," whispered Shade.

Madison spotted the big bald guy who had been talking to Nick earlier. He had found a flashlight and was moving intently across the central area of the station. Other figures were moving unsteadily in the dark.

One man came charging in, one hand holding up his pants, while he tried to load a pump action shotgun with the other. Before he got very far he tripped on his pants legs and crashed into a couch that Velvet and another girl that Madison hadn't met were clinging together behind.

"Let's get ready to rumble," yelled Shade.

At those words the gravity generator cut out. The masked wrestler launched himself into the area, flying at the bald man. Out of the darkness three others also launched into the area, each of them wearing the same kind of mask as Shade, and each of them tackling one of Nick's men.

The fight didn't last more than a minute, though at times it looked more like a comic dance than a down and dirty street brawl. Shade had the bald-headed man in a sleeper hold; the others were making swift ends to their opponents with everything from iron claws to bear hugs.

Gravity came back on as quickly as it had vanished, sending everyone down to the deck.

Madison heard a string of cussing that would have made a sailor blush coming from a small storage room. Inside she found Nick frantically dumping out drawer after drawer. Everything from silverware to rubber bands and copies of something called National Geographic were piling up on the floor.

"You," he screamed seeing Madison. The green glowing box had barely come out of his pocket when a loud splat echoed through the room, blood and brain matter flying everywhere at once.

She looked past Nick and saw one of the wrestlers standing there, a Louisville Slugger in his hands. Slowly he reached up and pulled off his mask to reveal a very familiar face.

"Yo, Mad," said Houston, with a big grin.

It wasn't until she actually had some clothes on again that Madison realized how cold she had been. Once the lights were back up and the gravity restored, one of The Shade's men brought her a pair of coveralls and slippers.

She felt marvelous.

The Shade, Houston and she stood in the main operations center of the station. "Don't take this wrong, but what the hell are you folks doing here?"

The Shade laughed. "I told you we were rescuing you," he said. As he spoke he reached behind his head and began unlacing his mask. When it came off, Madison found herself looking at the same blond-haired man she had seen talking with Houston back at the Double Deuce. His left eye was milky and obviously sightless; an eye patch completed his transformation.

"My name's Andy, by the way," he said.

"If I look confused, I am," said Madison,

Houston laughed and put his arm around Madison. "It's really simple, Mad. You were looking for the Sportatorium, I found it for you," he said.

"We owe you a great debt, Miss Cromwell," said Andy. "Nick used to be part of the Sportatorium, but we kicked him out for ripping off the parishioners. Then about six months back we heard rumors that he was claiming to be recruiting for us.

"We've had people watching him and the Double Deuce for more than a month. One of them, Sunset, disappeared two weeks ago. If I'm not mistaken, you met her earlier. When you and Houston here turned up, and Nick seemed so interested in you, it gave us our chance to track his operation down. I admit that I didn't think we would end up here," laughed Andy, gesturing at the main view screen.

"All I wanted to do was find my way to my destiny in the squared circle," she said, shaking her head, this was all a little too much to take in.

"You may have done more than that," Andy said reaching

out, taking her arm raising it up in the air. "We've been looking for the ultimate home for the Sportatorium; what better place to reach for the championship belt than the stars."

Houston had wandered over to one of the terminals and was staring at moving lines. "Hey, Mad, are we there yet?" he looked up and said.

"Yeah, Houston. We're there."

We're Back!

Bradley H. Sinor
A Bubba in Time Saves None
Yard Dog Press

The first thing that Madison Cromwell spotted as she drove around the curve was Mount Scott. True, the mountain itself was just a dark outline against the cloud-filled night sky, but she still got a silly grin on her face.

It had been six months since she had last seen her hometown of Lawton, Oklahoma, and the nearby Wichita Mountains in her truck's rear view mirror. Right now, home sounded pretty good to Madison.

She and her cousin, Houston, had gone looking for the holy temple, the Sportatorium, home of the one true religion, Professional Wrestling. And they had found it! Madison reached over and patted her dark brown gym bag; inside were two sets of brand new tights, emblazoned with red and blue lightning bolts, not to mention her own sweats and a half dozen pairs of dirty socks.

After months of training, Madison would soon start her new life as the wrestler Lighting Lass, a speaker for the Lord, and hopefully, a contender for the women's championship belt. Her debut in the squared circle was set for a tent revival and weekend Wrestling Extravaganza over at Texhoma.

However, in a couple of days, it would be her parent's twenty-fifth wedding anniversary, and Madison had really wanted to be there. The chance to go home and show off what she had already achieved didn't hurt her ego in the slightest. It had been raining off and on for most of the day, more on than off, so Madison had dropped her speed from 85 to 75 m.p.h—all in the interest of safety. Her old truck did have a tendency to fishtail on a wet road.

The Rhinestone Maidens CD in her stereo had just clicked over to their cover of "Ring of Fire" when Madison caught sight of a Volkswagen laying on its side, blocking part of the road ahead of her. She jammed her brakes down hard, the tires screeching loudly as she managed to bring the truck to a halt twenty yards or so from the overturned car.

There was steam coming out of the VW's radiator and various types of fluids pooling on the ground around the car. Whoever was driving had probably taken the curve too fast and lost control, rolling over several times and colliding with the rocks that had been set up like a guard rail. Otherwise, the car would have shot off into the field and the chances that Madison would have spotted it were next to nothing.

There wasn't an inch of metal that didn't look like it had been broken and bent. Even the racing number on the side was cracked and wrinkly looking, definitely something that her not-so-bright cousin Houston would have called "a real ouchie."

She had left Houston with the trainers at the Sporatorium; they seemed to think that he had a possible future in tag team wrestling or running the concession stand and passing the tithing plate.

It would have been so much easier to just head on down the road. She could highball it as fast as she wanted, since there wasn't any kind of traffic, as few people as there were anyway. Lawton wasn't more than a couple of miles ahead, so she could grab a couple of people and come back with help. But Madison knew she had to check the wreck, in case anyone was in there that might need help.

Her mama had always been adamant about the parable of the Good Samaritan and insisted that if someone needed help and you could do anything, you had better do it. None-the-less, she made sure her pistol was loaded and she had a good grip on her Louisville Slugger baseball bat. She took a quick look about for yumbies; those damn things had a habit of just seeming to appear and there was enough rain to mask the smell of decaying flesh. Helping someone in a time of need was one thing; there was no need to end up as a late night snack for yumbies.

Madison had just approached the wreck when the bottom dropped out from her stomach—a wave of nausea ran over her from the top of her head down to her toenails. The feeling passed in just a second or two, but for that moment, all she wanted to do was go as limp as a dishrag. It took her a minute or so to regain her equilibrium and get her eyes to focus on the car.

Then she heard moaning coming from inside the car, so

somebody was alive. Madison got down on all fours and pushed her face up against the driver's side window. She heard another moan. This time there was something familiar about that voice.

"Raven, is that you?"

"Mad, get me the hell out of here before I start puking."

"Wouldn't be the first time," Madison laughed, remembering more than one party she and Raven Harkness had gone to where puking had been the end of the evening. "You know, if you just wanted to hang around, you should have called. I might have brought beer."

"Just get me the hell out of here," said Raven.

She wasn't sure how her best friend from high school had ended up here, but that didn't matter. There was no way that the door could be opened; all that remained of the handle was a broken piece of metal. Madison moved around to the front of the car and applied her bat to the windshield; it only took a couple of hard swats to start the glass to breaking loose.

"Can you use a hand there, little lady?"

Madison looked over her shoulder. A tall man dressed in jeans and a down hunting vest stood there. A covered jeep had pulled into place beside her truck. She cursed herself for not hearing its arrival. That was the sort of thing that could make you yumbie lunch meat.

"Yes, sir," she answered, shifting just a little so her pistol could be more easily reached, just in case it was needed. "My friend had herself a little accident and needs a hand getting out."

The man looked at the car for a moment and whistled. "Looks to me like this poor car has been through a demolition derby. Let's see what's what. By the way, you can call me Jingo."

Madison couldn't put her finger on it, but there was something about Jingo that looked awfully familiar. A little voice in the back of her mind kept saying, "You know this guy." It wasn't as if she knew everyone in Lawton the way her mama did.

Between the two of them, it just took a couple of minutes to get Raven free.

"Lord, I have felt better," Raven said.

"You're going to be all right," Jingo said. "I think we need to get you both inside and have someone who knows a little more first aid than me look at you." Jingo produced a couple of slightly oil-stained army blankets and wrapped them around both girls' shoulders.

"We'll take my Jeep. I can send some boys out at first light to get this car and your truck," he continued.

Not two miles from the accident, Madison caught sight of a lighted building near the roadway. She didn't recall anything like that out this direction, but it had been six months and things do change.

"A hospital?" she asked.

"Nope, that's the Indian Bingo Hall!" yelled Jingo

What? The Indian Bingo Hall on the north side of Lawton had burned down when Madison had been four years old, twenty years ago. Nobody knew exactly what caused the fire. Some people still insisted it was because the caller and some of the players had "gone yumbie". The resulting fire fight had ended when the building was engulfed in flames.

Jingo slid his jeep to a halt almost exactly at the front door of the building.

"Marcus Cromwell, what kind of stray sheep have you found, now," said a woman who came up to the jeep on the driver's side and kissed Jingo.

"Lilly, I couldn't just leave them," he said with a sigh in his tone.

As Madison climbed out of the jeep, she got her first good look at Jingo. It was a very familiar face, this was Marcus "Jingo" Cromwell, her paternal grandfather, looking more like the family photos from before she was born than the grizzled gray-haired figure she remembered; even the familiar scar on his left cheek was gone.

"Grandpa?" she whispered "What the hell is going on?"

"Take yourself another sip of this."

For once in her life, Madison did exactly what she was told and didn't regret it. The liquid was warm and felt good going down. It was actually a thick soup of some sort; she could taste vegetables and maybe a hint of cinnamon.

"It's very good," she said, wrapping her fingers tightly around the mug. It wasn't until she had started to get warm that she realized how cold it had been in the rain.

Madison and Raven were sitting in the Bingo Hall kitchen, there had been a stream of women, many of them that Madison thought looked vaguely familiar, coming to check on them, so neither had had a private moment since they arrived.

This whole thing was weird, and seemed to get weirder. Madison had a few vague memories of being in the bingo hall, more feelings of things that seemed familiar than really remembering something.

"We need to get you some dry clothes. I surely don't want you catching your death of cold," said the woman who had given her the soup ."That idiot Jingo should have given you his vest to wear. Men! If it isn't cars, stills or hunting, then it doesn't exist, except if there's beer involved."

"Well, he was there when we needed him," said Raven, who was sitting on a stool just to the right of the stove.

"He does have his uses," she laughed. "Oh, where are my manners anyway? I never introduced myself. My name is Stephanie Spingesi."

Most of the Spingesi family had moved away several years before Madison had lit out to the find the Sportatorium. She had a vague memory of the matriarch of the clan being named Stephanie

"It's a pleasure. Thank you so much for the soup. My name is Madison Crom…Cromton."

"Just call me Raven," her red-haired companion said.

"Well, you girls get some rest. You two are welcome to spend the night at my place. It's not big, but it beats the heck out of camping in the rain," said Stephanie.

After the older woman left, Madison stepped over to the door and looked around, once she was sure they were alone she came over and embraced Raven.

"Girlfriend, what the hell is going on?" Raven said.

"And they said I was the slow one in school," said Madison. "I don't know how, but we've ended up in our own past. From a couple of things they've said, and people I've seen, I'm guessing twenty, twenty five years."

Raven nodded. "Normally, I'd ask you to share whatever you've been drinking or smoking, but I remember *this* place burning down. And I haven't got a better explanation"

"What are you doing back, anyway? The last I heard, you and baldy were headed for Scotland or some damn place like that," asked Madison.

"We did go, it took a while to find a ride back. Penn had to report in to the trucking company and then he's going to meet me here. I wanted to introduce him to my grandma since she's all the family I got left."

"Meeting your family? Sounds serious."

Before Raven could say anything else, there was a huge crashing sound coming from the main part of the hall. Madison grabbed her bat and was out the door in a moment, with Raven behind her.

She was expecting to hear shooting and see a bunch of yumbies overrunning the place, even though if this was a quarter century in the past it was a period where there hadn't been that many yumbies turning up around Lawton for a couple of years. Only, instead of yumbies, they found a half dozen people surrounding someone who was lying on the floor in front of a cherry picker that had been extended up to the ceiling, where several neon bulbs were sputtering. How they had gotten the cherry picker inside was a mystery.

"What happened?" Raven asked.

Stephanie Spingesi came over, shaking her head. "I've told them a thousand times; that gate on the cherry picker needs to be fixed. Jason Cromwell was trying to change one of the lights so the bingo caller could see to finish the game. The gate gave way and he came straight down."

"Is he all right?" asked Madison.

"Oh, of course he is," said Stephanie. "It would take a lot more than a swan dive off a cherry picker to hurt Jason. Though I think he may have broken his leg."

Even banged up and with his leg in a splint, Jason Cromwell was hot.

For the fifth time in the last half hour, Madison had to remind herself that Jason Cromwell was *her father* and she didn't need to be thinking such things. Though it was hard to think of that dark-haired, well-muscled figure with the six pack abs as Daddy.

Daddy hot? Go figure.

"This hurts like hell," Jason yelled. Someone passed him a bottle filled with clear liquid and he took several long swallows from it.

"Jason, the break is clean and it should heal up in about eight weeks," said the man that Madison thought might be Dr. Wicker, though she couldn't see him clearly. "I'll get you some crutches tomorrow."

"But I'm still going to be able to drive in the dirt track race on Saturday, won't I Doc?"

Madison could hear the anxiety in her father's voice. She had always believed that her daddy could do just about anything. Okay, there was that time he tried to ride the Brahma bull onto the raft out at the lake, but everyone makes mistakes.

So as she walked away from the main part of the bingo hall, she was sure that whatever the reason that was so important, her daddy would be in that big race. That was when she happened to see the big cross-stitched calendar hanging on the Bingo Hall wall.

Saturday would be April thirteen; then it was just a month until her parents got married. Then it dawned on her

If there was one thing that Madison knew right then, Jason Cromwell not only had to be in the big dirt track race on Saturday, but he had to win it.

"I guess you could say that I am 'The Prize'," giggled Ginny McDevitt.

Madison hadn't been crazy about the idea of looking up her mama. Thing was, she ended up with not a whole lot of choice about it; turned out that grandma McDevitt and Stephanie Spingesi were the best of friends, so the next day, when Grandma came to meet the newcomers, Ginny got dragged along.

It wasn't long before the older women had suggested that the "girls" go out and get some sun. In other words, the two older women wanted to gossip, but didn't want to admit it to the younger ones.

Ginny led them to a small tidal pool along Cache Creek, and stuck her hand down into the water, almost to the elbow. She yanked hard and her arm shot out of the water with a mason jar. Setting it on the shore, she reached back and continued feeling around for a moment, then pulled a second jar out.

"You girls thirsty?" she smiled. The jars had contained a cold clear liquid that burned as it rolled down Madison's throat.

"Finest kind," giggled Raven.

All three girls stretched out on the grass next to the creek, Madison was dangling her feet in the water and giving some serious consideration to dropping her halter top and shorts and just diving in. the water.

"I've been chasing Jason Cromwell for the past year," said Ginny "He *is* a smart guy, sweet as you would ever want, a hard worker, and smart on a lot of things, but not so sharp when it comes to girls."

"I've known a few guys like that." Raven punctuated her comment with a hiccup.

"Well, I've done everything but lay down in the middle of Main Street with my legs apart and yell "take me." Sure, we've made out, but he says he cares too much about me to go all the way, so I told him that I would marry him if he won the big dirt track race next Saturday night. Hell, I'll marry him even if he doesn't; I'll do him either way," she laughed.

"Yeah, but you can only chase a guy until he is ready to catch you under *his* rules, even if they are really *your* rules, but you can't let him know about it," said Madison.

"Oh that is so, so true," laughed Ginny, as she excused herself to go and visit a secluded place behind the trees.

Once they were alone, Madison turned to Raven and motioned for her friend to pull closer. She couldn't take any chance of Ginny, she refused to think of her as mama, overhearing.

"I got a major problem," said Madison.

"You mean something more than being stuck a quarter of a century in the past?" asked Raven.

"Yeppers, I know that race. Daddy won it; a month later the two of them were married and eight months after that I showed up. They celebrated his winning in the bushes behind the grandstand, fucking their brains out, so let's just say I was not a preemie," she said.

The problem was, Madison had never heard anything about her daddy winning that big race with a broken leg. She also knew that he would have a hell of a time shifting with that leg of his in a splint, so there was a question in Madison's mind if he would win or not.

No win, no celebration...no daughter named Madison.

"You sure this is going to work?" asked Madison.

Raven zipped up the heavy leather jacket and buttoned it at her neck. She tied her long red hair up in a bun, wrapped her lower face in a scarf and pulled a big black crash helmet down over her head.

Madison stared at her for a few minutes. The clothes were

the same as Jason would be wearing; those had been real easy to find. The helmet had been a little harder, but Raven had found one. Sure, Jason was a half dozen inches taller than Raven, but given the clothes and the crutch that he had been hobbling around on, this might just work. Of course, since neither of them could think of a better alternative, it had to work.

"So you're sure that you can win the race?" asked Madison. "I mean you did just roll your car."

"Don't be stupid, just do your part and leave the rest to me." Raven smiled.

Raven had always been one of the best drivers in the whole of Southwest Oklahoma, pulling off some tricks with a car that afterwards, even Raven wasn't sure how she had done it.

The two of them were holed up in a storage shed just outside of the track area. Their conversation was interrupted by a knock on the door. Jason Cromwell was standing there, his clothing mirroring Raven's outfit. Madison motioned her friend to get back into the shadows before she opened the door.

"Well, hello there, Jason," she said a moment later. "I was hoping that you would get my note."

"I surely did," he said, limping into the shed. The doctor had given him two crutches, but Jason insisted that one was all that was necessary. "I would have been here sooner, but I had to help them get the BBQ pit fire going, and Ned never did learn the right way to tap a beer keg. Of course, I also had to check out my car. That puppy is going to kick some serious ass when I get behind the wheel."

"I know you'll go out there and make them all eat your dust," Madison said, letting her words flow into what she liked to think of as her seductive voice.

"Well, thank you, Miss Madison," said Jason, eyeing the girl carefully.

"I just wanted to wish you good luck." Madison let herself flow up against Jason, wrapping her arms around him. He didn't pull back; on some level she wanted to scream at him and ask what he was doing.

"Now, you know I've been seeing Ginny McDevitt," he said slowly.

"I do and I'm sure she's already wished you good luck, but

it can't hurt to have someone else wish you good luck, can it?"

"I suppose not," he said, leaning closer to Madison. Their lips were only inches apart when Raven's hand came around Jason's head and jammed a folded up piece of cloth soaked in chloroform under his nose.

The whole thing couldn't have taken longer than fifteen seconds before the crippled racer sagged in Madison's arms. She gently let him down, not wanting to injure his already broken leg.

"What took you so long?" she demanded.

"I just wanted to see if maybe you would kiss your father," said Raven. Even though her face was hidden by the scarf and helmet, Madison knew her friend was grinning like a Cheshire Cat. "He probably wanted to tongue you as well."

"You have a filthy, sick mind."

"I try my best."

It was the smell that sent Madison grabbing for her Louisville Slugger. That decaying flesh odor, with just a touch of old spice still lingering, was a dead, pardon the expression, giveaway that yumbies were around. She got up next to the door and stood stone still.

There was a bump, when something hit the outside wall of the shed, followed by a low moan. That was enough to tell Madison where the yumbie was. She drew a short breath, held it, threw the door open and jumped out in time to see the critter turning toward her; he was a youngish fellow, the remains of a suit hanging on his frame. Rather than critique his clothing, Madison brought her bat hard into the side of the yumbies face; bones cracked and a blackish substance squirted everywhere. She followed up with two more blows, smashing the head and spine and sending the yumbie hard into the side of the shed.

"That's some right fine swinging, Miss Madison," said Jingo Cromwell. Her grandfather had been in the process of jamming another clip into his rifle when she had appeared; he had some mud stains on his clothing, but other than that, the only sign that he was hurt was a bloody line across his cheek, in the same place the scar that she had known all her life would be.

"What happened?" she asked, knowing how dumb a question it was, but that was the only thing she could think of asking.

"Just a couple a' three yumbies made it past the perimeter guards. They stumbled onto the track just as the race was ending. Two of 'em got took out by cars. This one got away; guess he wanted to watch you take batting practice," said Jingo as he pulled out the makings and rolled himself a cigarette. He offered one to Madison who shook her head. Smoking was one of the things that her trainers at the Sporatorium had been adamant was no longer part of her life.

"Just doing what I need to do," she said. "By the way, who won the race?"

Jingo got a big grin on his face. "My son Jason did, like there was any doubt."

"Tell me again why he's asleep?" Ginny asked. She was wearing a tight blouse, with two buttons strategically open, along with a leather mini-skirt and flip flops decorated with rhinestones.

Jason was lying on an army blanket spread out on the ground in a little grove of trees not far from the racetrack grandstand. Raven and Madison had managed to get him there, not without some difficulty though, since maneuvering a six foot tall, 180 pound dead weight in the dark was not easy.

"He just tripped chasing after that freaky, zombie-looking fellow and hit his head," said Madison. "I figure he ought to wake up in a little while."

"And I'll bet you a nickel," chimed in Raven, who was leaning up against a nearby tree, "that there is nothing he would like better than waking up and finding you in his arms. You might even be able to get him up sooner."

Ginny grinned, looked over at Jason, and unbuttoned two additional buttons on her blouse. "You bet your ass, I will."

Jingo Cromwell closed the hood on Madison's truck and turned around to look at her. He had a crooked grin on his face. "I know there was nothing wrong with it, but I looked over your truck anyway, never hurts to do some preventative work as well. I got to say that your truck is in good shape. Whoever worked on it seems to have forgotten more than I've ever known about engines."

"Thankee," said Madison.

Raven walked over to her car and patted the Volkswagen's side door, rubbing her hand on the faded number eight decal. "I've got a feeling that my ride is dead."

Jingo reached into the cooler that he had taken out of his truck and pulled out a brown bottle, twisted the cap and took a drink. "I've seen worse, a lot worse. I've gotten a lot worse running and running well enough to leave a lot of rubber on the street. It will take some doing, but I think we can get you rolling."

Madison had her hand on the roof of Ravens' car when the bottom dropped out from her stomach again, a wave of nausea ran over her, from the top of her head down to her toenails. The feeling passed in just a moment, but for that moment all she wanted to do was go as limp as a dishrag.

Then she realized that she was back out on the highway, it was dark, raining and the Volkswagen was lying on its side.

"We're back," she muttered, feeling the rain hitting her face.

"Mad! I think I know that. Let's get the hell out of here, before I start puking," said Raven, her face flushed white as she collapsed down onto the asphalt.

"Wouldn't be the first time!" laughed Madison.

"What are you girls doing out here? You're going to catch your death of cold," said Jingo Cromwell as he came walking up to his granddaughter, his battered old jeep parked a few yards behind him. Madison stared at him for a minute and then threw herself into Jingo's arms; this was the Jingo Cromwell she had known all her life, the grizzled grey hair, the cocky attitude, the worn out down hunting vest that he refused to throw away. She ran her finger up and down the faded scar on his cheek.

"Is something wrong?" asked Jingo.

"No, I'm just glad to see you, grandpa" Madison said, a few tears mixing with the rain.

"Look, it's been raining for three days. Can we get you two into the jeep? We still got to get to your folk's anniversary party. If we're late, your grandmother will shoot us," laughed Jingo.

"Well, we're back and everything looks normal," said Madison. The two women sat in the furthest back booth at the Lucky Lady Bar and Grill. After the big anniversary celebration for her parents the day before, Madison still had a slight hangover.

"Looks that way," said Raven, between mouthfuls of pancake covered in molasses and brown sugar. "You know, it was strange seeing your parents and everyone else so young. I sorta wish my folks hadn't been out of town back then."

Madison picked up a piece of toast and covered it in butter and homemade pear honey. "Yeah, that whole thing was weird, but you know how sometimes you find out things about your parents that you really would have preferred not to know? That happened to me."

Raven cocked her head at her friend. "What do you mean?"

"Well, you remember when we lingered outside the glade, after Ginny...err Mama, went in there?"

"Yep."

"I would never, in a million years, have figured my mama for a screamer."

The Rhinestone Maidens Not-So-Excellent Adventure

Sue Sinor
A Bubba in Time Saves None
Yard Dog Press

The lights dimmed and brightened. Loretta and Lorene bowed, then Lester, guitar hanging from his shoulder, joined them, clasping hands. During the bow, Loretta felt something, a sensation like she had never felt before, passing over her and through her. Out of the corner of her eye she could see that Lorene and Lester seemed to have felt the same thing.

At the front of the stage were small pots with what looked like candles replacing the jury-rigged stage lights that were supposed to be there. In the audience, people were getting out of their seats and walking away, which was exactly what she expected to see. But there did seem to be a lot more people than had been at their concert in the first place.

"This ain't right," said Loretta as they rose.

"What are you talkin' about?" asked Lorene, looking where Loretta was pointing. "Those things're on fire!"

"Lorene!" said Lester. "Lookie here." He and Loretta had turned around and were inspecting the stage. "This ain't our stage no more."

"*Their*" stage had been a raised open-air platform with steps at the back and light trees at the front as spotlights. "*This*" stage was larger and inside a building, with a vast dark curtain across it. It also had an orchestra pit in front of the stage, from which they could hear voices and the familiar sounds of musicians dealing with their instruments. At either side of the stage was a staircase curving into the large, emptying audience area.

"Dang!" Loretta cried. "This *ain't* our stage. What in the name of George Jones happened here?"

Just then the lights at the front of the stage dimmed and went out. The darkness loomed around them as they huddled together, wondering what to do next as the huge curtain began to move, pulling apart slowly as stage hands began to circulate around the stage.

"Howdy!" Loretta called, approaching the busy people. "Kin you folks kindly tell me where we're at?"

A man carrying a lantern stopped what he was doing, looked at her and said something in German that Loretta didn't quite catch. In the time since the yumbie outbreak had stranded them in Germany, the three of them had tried to learn at least a little German, though a lot of the people they were around spoke English. They had got fairly good at understanding it, though.

"Pardon me," she said slowly and loudly. "Do you speak English?"

"Englisch?" he said with a pronounced accent. "Nein! Nein!"

The man muttered something that Loretta didn't understand and made a shooing motion with his hands. He herded them down a stairway, past the rows of elegant seating, through a large and opulent lobby and then outside. The grand front door slammed shut behind them.

"I guess that meant 'Go away'," Lorene said.

The front of the theater was decorated in soaring arches and gargoyles, much like some of the buildings they'd been living near since the yumbie plague broke out. Gas streetlamps and horse-drawn carriages, though, were definitely not what they had expected to see when they had been thrown out of the building.

"Dang," Loretta said. "We're really not in Kansas anymore."

"An' we don't even have our little dog, Toto, neither," continued Lorene.

Lester put his arms around the girls. "Don't worry; I'll take care o' y'all. Maybe we kin find somebody who kin talk English. Maybe somebody kin tell us what happened."

In the next hour, although they asked politely in their bad German for help, all they got were disapproving stares and, sometimes, laughter.

"Dadgummit! Ain't there nobody in this town we kin talk to?" Lester was frustrated.

"Now sweetie, don't be mad," Loretta chided her husband, even though she was trying not to panic, herself. She didn't want to fuel his mood. "We'll find somebody. Right now I'm cold and hungry." She pointed to a nearby restaurant. "Let's go in there. Maybe we can get something to eat. At least we can get warm. I love these costumes, but they ain't meant for cold weather."

As they neared the restaurant, they heard laughter and music. They opened the door and stood just inside, looking around at the crowd. It was a boisterous group of men and women, talking, laughing and drinking beer.

"Our kind a' people," Lester grinned.

A passing waiter noticed them, looked at them questioningly, and asked, in German, of course, "May I help you?"

Lester stepped forward and tried to say, also in German, "Yes, please. We are cold and hungry, but have no money to pay. Is there some work we can do to earn our meal?"

The waiter looked them over, his eyes lingering on Lorene, then said, "Wait here. I will find the owner."

"Mebbe we could wait over there." Lorene pointed at a blazing fireplace at the center of the room. "I'm still cold."

"Well," Lester answered. "He said to wait here. I guess we could move a little closer to the fire."

They started to sidle toward the warmth, just as the owner walked up, eyeing them curiously. Still in German, the owner spoke, "I am Peter Heinz, the owner of this restaurant. I hear you are looking for work. Where have you come from?"

"We're *from* the United States, but we've been living in Munich for awhile." Lester tried to make it clear.

"The clothing of the young ladies is indecent. If you want to be admitted to my restaurant, you must wear acceptable clothing."

"But this is all we have!" Loretta cried.

"Then you must leave. We require proper dress to patronize this establishment, and to work here, also," Herr Heinz said as he herded them toward the door.

"Now what're we gonna do?" Lorene whined as they stood on the sidewalk staring at the door that had been slammed behind them.

Loretta put her arm around her sister. "Lester'll take care of us. Don't you worry. What're we gonna do now, Lester?" she demanded, without looking at her husband.

Lester pursed his lips for a moment and looked up and down the street before motioning for his wife and sister-in-law to follow him. It was only a matter of five minutes' walk before they were standing in front of the theater where their journey seemed to have started.

"Look, Loretta." Lorene said as she stared at the big sign

that they had not noticed before. "It says "Das Rhinegold." Wasn't that the name of that op'ra we all went to in high school? 'Member? The one the principal took the whole school to see in Texarkana. Looks like somebody's puttin' it on again."

"Yeah, that's the one we got our name from. Come on; I think the stage door's this way. Maybe we can get in that way and get warm." Loretta started walking down the side of the building.

Lester led them down the alley to the stage door and began to pound on it. After a minute or two with no response, he noticed a ground level window.

"I'll see if I can get this open. At least we'll be warm," he said.

Lester tugged at the window, but nothing happened. There was a heavy black cobblestone lying on the ground that looked like it might solve their problem, but he never got the chance to try it because a loud whistle echoed through the alley and a small thin man in a uniform stepped into the light.

"Stop! Thief! Stop!"

The three of them headed toward the back of the building, but almost immediately found themselves against a dead end where the theatre butted up against another building.

"We're trapped," Loretta cried, cringing behind Lester.

"What are you doing here?" demanded the policeman, pointing to them.

"We were only trying to find a warm place to stay," Lester replied, in the best German he could manage.

"I don't believe you," the officer replied, appearing ready to use his nightstick on them if they blinked wrong. He pulled out the whistle and began to blow it again. Two more officers arrived within minutes, neither of them looking like they were interested in hearing any kind of explanations.

"What are you going to do to us?" Lester asked, as the three policemen surrounded them.

"Take you to jail, of course," the first officer told him. "Be quiet and come along peacefully, and you might avoid a beating."

The police station proved to be a massive building with high ceilings. There were a dozen people scattered around the room, some in uniform, some in civilian clothes with handcuffs binding them.

"Sergeant, I found these three strangers trying to break

into the Opera House," the first officer told the uniformed man sitting behind the desk in the entranceway. "They claim they were just trying to find a place to keep warm, but I don't believe them. Look how they're dressed. Maybe they're Gypsies."

The sergeant looked the captives over disapprovingly before he said, "Lock them up. They'll be interrogated later."

The constable shoved Lester into a cell with several other men, then led Loretta and Lorene into another room where they found themselves locked up with a couple of women.

"Hey, honey. You sure are pretty," one of the men in the cell said to Lester, gesturing at him. Lester thought he understood what the man said, but figured he must have misunderstood.

He began to speak slowly, using his best German, and said, "Hello. My name is Lester Pritchard. The two women with me who were taken away are my wife, Loretta, and her sister, Lorene. Thank you for complementing my shirt. It is my costume. What are your names?"

That earned him laughter, and the other men in the cell began taunting him, although he wasn't able to understand it all.

"What did you say to me? I didn't understand you. Please repeat what you said," he kept saying to them. Before long, when the others couldn't get a rise out of him, or a fight, they moved away and began talking among themselves.

In the other cell, Loretta and Lorene had been getting to know their cellmates, who were friendlier and spoke a little English.

"I was arrested for being a prostitute," the woman, who called herself Hannah, said. "It is untrue, but here I am anyway. They said I am dressed indecently. The police are so suspicious."

"I know," replied Loretta. "They called us Gypsies."

"Well, you *are* dressed in an unusual manner. I have seen Gypsies, though, and their dress is much more modest than what you're wearing."

"These are our costumes; we wear them when we're singing," Loretta said, indicating the sleeveless, low-cut mini-dresses they were wearing. "They're covered with rhinestones, see, because we call ourselves 'The Rhinestone Maidens.' We don't wear them all the time, of course! We were just wearing them when what happened, whatever it was, happened."

"The Rhinestone Maidens? That sounds like something out of the new opera, 'Das Rhinegold'. I have read about it in the newspaper. Are you in the cast of it?" Hannah asked.

"Yep, it's from 'Das Rhinegold,' all right. We saw it in Texarkana," Loretta said. "We loved the glittery water those rhine maiden characters were swimming in. It reminded us of rhinestones. That's why we call ourselves "The Rhine*stone* Maidens."

"You must have seen a rehearsal, because the very first performance of it was tonight. I would like to have seen it, but I couldn't afford tickets" Hannah protested. "And where is this Tex-ar-can-na?"

"No, we saw it about five years ago," Lorene insisted. "Texarkana's right on the border between Texas and Arkansas. We lived on the Arkansas side, before we came to Germany on a USO tour to see Lester, that's Loretta's husband. That was when the yumbie 25 virus broke out."

Hannah thought for a moment before replying. "I don't think I understand. You couldn't have seen 'Das Rhinegold' five years ago, because it premiered this evening, September twenty-second, eighteen sixty-nine, right here at the Munich Opera House. And what is Yum-b 25?"

Loretta looked at her new friend, then at her sister, not sure if she had heard Hannah correctly.

"September twenty-second, eighteen sixty-nine? That's not right; it's September twenty-second, all right, but it's twenty twenty-six, not eighteen sixty-nine," Loretta said.

"I can assure you," the other woman, named Bridgette, said, "This is the year eighteen hundred and sixty nine. I know it is. This is my twentieth birthday, and I was born in eighteen hundred and forty nine."

"Well, happy birthday," Lorene squealed. She had always loved birthdays. Anybody's birthday. "It don't look like it turned out too happy, though. What happened?"

Bridgette was about to answer when a large man appeared at the cell door, unlocked it and motioned for the two sisters to follow him.

Eventually they came to a small room where Lester was sitting at a table. The officer indicated that Loretta and Lorene should take the chairs next to him.

A few minutes later another man came in. He had large

mutton chop sideburns and several pins on his collar that Lester suspected indicated his rank.

"You three were caught trying to break into the opera house last night, were you not?" said the new man.

"Well, we were trying to get inside so we could get warm," Loretta told him, trying her best to be as polite as she could. "As you can see, our costumes will not keep us warm."

"Yes, I can see that they are very...revealing. Why are you two girls wearing those, did you call them *costumes*?" the officer replied.

After her explanation, the officer just stared at her for a minute, then pulled out several pieces of paper from a folder. "I understand that the two of you are singers and that this man," he pointed to Lester, "plays accompaniment for you. He said that you call yourselves 'The Rhinestone Maidens' after the characters in Herr Wagner's opera that opened tonight. How did you know of these characters so quickly?"

Loretta repeated the story of their viewing of the opera. "That's where we got the name. We were already planning to be singers." Loretta leaned closer to the officer. "We just want to go home, but the girls in our cell said that this is eighteen sixty-nine. A few hours ago it was two thousand twenty-six. How did we get here, uh, now, uh, whatever?" She started to cry quietly.

"Do you really expect me to believe that you are from the future? I am not a stupid man, and not easily taken in." The officer looked at the three sitting at the table. "If you will not tell me the truth, I will have to send the three of you to the mental institution outside Munich for as long as it takes for you to confess to your crimes." He stepped to the door and motioned for the sergeant to take them away.

Lester's, Loretta's and Lorene's hands were chained together in front of them after the two girls had used what Lester referred to as "hurt puppy " eyes and talked the guard into binding them so they would be more comfortable as they rode. The paddy wagon wasn't comfortable, even with their hands in front of them.

"Don't worry, sweetheart," Lester told Loretta. "We'll get away somehow. I know we will."

The sergeant, who was sitting on the bench opposite them, said something they didn't understand. From the tone, Lester suspected that meant be quiet, but the officer didn't seem to know English.

Loretta leaned close to Lester and whispered, "What should we do? Do you think we could conk him over the head and jump out?"

"That'd be kinda hard with our hands chained together," he answered. "Maybe when we get there we could just run for it."

"We could sing something," Lorene suggested. "Mebbe that'd make us feel better."

"A lullaby. Mebbe it'd put him to sleep." Loretta gestured toward the guard, who already smelled of liquor and looked like he was ready to drop off.

"Hush little baby, don't say a word..." It didn't take long before the guard's head had drooped down to his chest and snores filled the wagon.

"Keep singing," Lester whispered. "Just get softer 'til you stop."

They sat for a few more minutes before Lester very gently opened the door at the back of the wagon, which was, fortunately, unlocked. Since the three of them were chained together, each had to jump down and walk behind the wagon until they were all outside and Loretta could close the door so the driver wouldn't know he had lost his passengers.

They made a break for the tree line, then tried to get their bearings. Lester finally said, "I don't know what we're lookin' for. We've never been here before." He motioned for Loretta and Lorene to follow him as they headed away from the road.

The three fugitives walked until they were deep into the woods. Before long, they came to a rocky clearing. Lester found a small, sharp-edged rock and pounded on the chains until they broke. Loretta did the same for him, and soon they were all able to hold their arms apart.

"Well, looks like the cuffs ain't gonna break." Lester said after attempting to remove Loretta's. "I knew I should of paid more attention when my cousin tried to teach me how to pick locks. We better get on... Mebbe we can find somebody with a hacksaw to get these cuffs off for us."

They resumed walking, trying to parallel the road they had been traveling on, wanting to get back to the city, though they didn't really know why.

By that time the girls' high-heeled, rhinestone-spangled

shoes were dirty, and their feet were killing them.

"I'm cold, an' I gotta take my shoes off before my feet come off with 'em," Loretta said, stopping next to a large log.

"Mine, too," Lorene agreed. "But we can't walk through here barefooted. It'd ruin our pantyhose. And our feet."

Lester thought for a minute. "Tell you what. You take your shoes off. Then take your pantyhose off and tie the feet around your shoes. Hang them around your necks and nothin' will get ruined."

"But our feet!" his wife and sister-in-law chorused..

"I'll give y'all my shoes. You can wear one each. I'll keep my socks. That way we'll all have something to wear."

"Well, I'll still be cold," Loretta complained.

"Sorry, but I can't do anything 'bout that. I'm cold, too." Lester waited for their answer.

The girls thought that the shoe idea might work, at least for a while, so they followed Lester's directions.

"Now you watch where you put your feet, Lester," Loretta told him. "Don't want you steppin' on a thorn or somethin'. You got to get us outta this perdicament."

"How big is this dang forest, anyway?" Lorene complained, as she walked with her arm around her sister to keep from falling. "We've been walkin' for hours."

"It shore seems that way," Loretta agreed. "I'm wore out. Ain't you, Lester?"

"I'm doin' okay," Lester claimed. "But we can stop for a rest if you girls need to." He pointed to something ahead of them. "Wait a minute, do you see that?"

A thin plume of smoke rose just above the trees, coming from a small cabin, about the size of their daddy's hunting 'lodge', as he called it, though this was not in near as good a shape. The door hung loose and there were burn marks on the walls.

Lester motioned for the girls to stay back, noticing that Loretta had picked up a rock and held it ready. He tentatively knocked on the door jamb.

"Hello? Anyone here?" Lester said in English, and again in German

No one answered.

"Look 'round back. Mebbe there's a barn,"Lester said.

There was, but it was empty.

There was also an outhouse, which, by that time, everyone

needed.

"Let's look inside. Mebbe they're asleep or somethin," Lorene suggested, although it was early afternoon at the latest. They tiptoed through the door into a two-room cabin. The fireplace was at one end with several chairs and a table near it. A man lay on the floor, with a big chunk of his head missing.

"Yumbies!" yelped Lorene.

"But we didn't see any," said Loretta.

"If it ain't yumbies, what did that?" said Lorene, pointing to the man's head.

"She's got a point, honey," said Lester to his wife.

"Then where are they? An' how'd they get here?" Loretta pointed out. "Oh my dear sweet Elvis! They followed us from the future. They got here the same way we did, however that was."

"Then we got to find 'em and kill em'," said Lorene.

Lester looked at the bread and cheese that was lying on the table. "We might as well eat this. We're starving, and this poor guy won't need it."

At the other end of the cabin was the second room. "We better check in there first, in case the yumbies are hidin'," Loretta told him.

"I guess," Lester admitted. He looked through the door into what was used as a bedroom and found the man's wife in the same condition as her husband.

"Oh, that poor woman," said Loretta, looking around Lester. "I guess she won't need those clothes hangin' on the wall. Looks like they'll fit us, Lorene."

"I found a bag," said Lorene, holding up a medium-sized carpetbag. "We kin put our costumes in it so we won't lose them. And here's some men's clothing that oughtta fit you, Lester, sort of."

Even if there was a yumbie disaster to avoid, Loretta insisted that they bury the dead couple.

"It's the Christian thing to do," she said. Lorene agreed and they sang two hymns once Lester had covered the bodies with stones.

Then they went back into the house and ate as much as they could find, which wasn't much, but given the circumstances tasted awfully good.

It was the middle of the afternoon before they could get on the road again. Lester saw more bodies only a few miles away from the cabin, all with large bites taken out of their heads.

"I'd say we're on the right trail," said Lester.

They had just stepped back onto the road when they heard a voice.

"I would stop right there, if I were you," the voice spoke from behind them. "I've been looking for you all morning."

It was the sergeant who the three of them had left sound asleep in the paddy wagon. He had a rather formidable-looking gun in his belt, but didn't pull it out.

"That was not a nice thing you did," he said. "Though the singing was lovely. I'll just say we slept in the forest because a wheel broke. Get in!"

Just then they heard a very familiar low moaning sound, followed by a high keening. As it got closer, they could hear the word 'brains' over and over. Soon they could see several shambling figures headed their way.

"There they are! Look!" Lorene pointed at the yumbies.

"Demons!" the sergeant screamed, and started to run, the gun in his belt forgotten.

"Sing!" Lester told the girls. "Sing loud!"

So Loretta and Lorene began to sing as loud as they could. Even Lester chimed in, though his voice was not as good as theirs, as they sang 'Great Balls of Fire' and then 'Your Cheating Heart.'

The yumbies moved toward them, one heading for the wagon, but as the singing continued, they began dropping, spasming violently and then becoming still. By the end of the second song, every one of them lay motionless on the ground.

The driver stared at the scene in front of him, his face as pale as a sheet. He looked at the yumbies, then at Lester, Lorene and Loretta, shaking his head. "How did you do that; kill them by singing?"

"I don't know; it just works. My wife and her sister sing, and the, uh, demons die. We do not know why," Lester told the driver. "There may be more of them."

"More? We must find them," the driver said. "Get in and I will drive you."

In less than an hour, thanks to the officer driving like a moonshiner with revenuers on his tail, they reached the center of town, the girls and Lester killing yumbies along the way. This went on all afternoon, the locals all staring at them and shaking their heads.

Peter Heinz, who owned the restaurant they had been thrown out of, had been in a group watching them work. He brought a plate of schnitzel to them, and a bucket of beer.

"You must be hungry and thirsty after all that singing," he told them, handing over the plate.

Lorene whispered to Loretta, "That's the man at the restaurant who threw us out last night."

Loretta whispered back, "Well, be nice to him. He's bringing us food and I'm starved."

"You came in my restaurant last night, I believe," he said.

"Yes, that was us. Do you like our singing, Herr Heinz?" Lorene said, as she took a bite of the schnitzel and exclaimed, "My goodness, this is good. And we sure are hungry."

Loretta took a bite and echoed her sister. She offered the plate to Lester.

"I apologize for throwing you out of my restaurant, but your clothing was really not suitable for public dining."

"We understand," replied Loretta. "That was why we were so cold. We appreciate the food, though. We are very hungry and the beer is wonderful"

Two more yumbies approached; people screamed and ran like they had before, but not too far. Everyone wanted to watch what would happen when the girls began to sing.

The girls started singing again, with the expected results of yumbies dropping to the ground and rounds of applause from the people watching. By then, the girls had sung their entire repertoire, including some songs they had learned during their time stranded in Germany. They were exhausted, having been awake for more than twenty-four hours, and were hungry again.

"Boy, that was a lot of yumbies," remarked Lester. "Ya think they all came back when we did?" Loretta and Lorene shrugged as they finished off the last of the beer.

"Shore wish we had some more of that schnitzel," Lester said, sitting down on the curb between his wife and sister-in-law.

"That would be right good," agree Loretta. "And a bed would be nice, too. I don't think I've ever been so tired in my whole life."

"That all would be real nice right now, but what are we gonna do next? We still don't have any money or a place to live." Lorene grumbled.

Lester was about to say something when he noticed Peter Heinz coming toward them.

"I hoped you would still be here," he told them. "I have been thinking about how you saved so many people from the, what did you call them, yumbies, today. I would like to offer you a job singing at my restaurant."

Loretta, Lorene and Lester looked at each other. Then, as one, they said, "Thank you. We would love to work for you."

Herr Heinz helped them get settled with new clothes and accommodations. He wanted them to start right away, while what they had done was fresh in people's minds.

"Look, Loretta," Lester said, when they went in to rehearse. "There's the stage. It ain't too big, though, but I guess we'll fit."

"Looks wonderful to me," Loretta told him. "I'm so ready to start singin' again."

Opening night was a success, with much applause and cheers. Within two days, Herr Heinz was turning away customers.

They had barely come off the stage the first night when it was obvious that the waiter they had seen the first night had more than a passing interest in Lorene. They learned that he was their new employer's son, Max, and that he was also single. He sat in on their rehearsals, occasionally joining in on some of the songs.

A few weeks after they had appeared so abruptly in the opera house, Lorene told Max, "We want you to sing with us on the stage tonight."

"Oh, no. I couldn't do that. My voice isn't very good," he protested.

"Of course you can. You have a good voice, and we can rehearse with you for a few days," she told him, punctuating her words with a kiss on the cheek.

"I hope I don't embarrass you," he said.

At the end of their set, Loretta and Lorene took their bow. Lester and Max joined them and, clasping hands, they bowed again. During that bow, Max felt something, a sensation like he had never felt before, passing over him and through him. Out of the corner of his eye he could see that the others seemed to have felt the same thing.

The quartet rose and looked around.

"We're home!" Lester, Loretta and Lorene cried. They had almost forgotten the stage they had disappeared from and just now reappeared on. The audience was in place, but bobbing and turning heads were evident. Many of the people in the chairs were wearing strange clothing, probably from the places and times they had been sent to. An occasional unfamiliar face could be seen, likely having come with people who belonged in this time.

Then Loretta remembered the newest member of the group and looked over toward Max. He was still holding Lorene's hand, but was staring slack-jawed and wide-eyed at his new surroundings.

"What has happened?" he exclaimed.

"We're back home!" Lorene told him. "We're back in our own time, and you came with us."

"Your own time? You mean you were telling the truth?

Who Rode the Winds

Bradley H. Sinor and Susan P. Sinor
I Should Have Stayed In OZ
Yard Dog Press

Nathan Grayson was humming "Rule Britannia" when Dorothy came into the room. He didn't see her, which irritated Dorothy no end. After all, they were not only *not* supposed to be here, Nathan was in the process of committing a crime by opening a wall safe that did not belong to him. Not to mention the fact that he was severely off key. From past experience, that was a good sign; it meant he was close to finishing.

"You realize I could hear you halfway down the hall," she said quietly.

Nathan stopped what he was doing and looked at Dorothy. "Bring the light over here."

Dorothy rolled her eyes; Nathan was only two years younger than she, but sometimes he acted like he was still around fourteen, complete with the cocksure arrogance of someone that age. There were definitely moments, like this one, that she wanted to take a two by four to him.

"You were also supposed to have been done fifteen minutes ago," she said, and picked up a lamp, setting it on the table close to Nathan.

"Relax, my dear Miss Gale, you cannot hurry true artistry, and I, Madam, am an artist."

Nathan plastered his ear to the metal door of the safe and began to work the dial.

Outside the window the lights that illuminated the grounds seemed to have grown brighter. Dorothy suspected it was only her eyes growing more accustomed to the dim light inside the house.

Since Jay Gatsby had come to West Egg, Long Island, he had thrown parties every weekend, with several hundred people circulating among the tents set up on his lawn. Doing something like this in the middle of a crowd wasn't their ordinary type of job. Nathan's and Dorothy's usual forte was empty apartments, office safes, and even the occasional bit of corporate espionage.

However, finding a box, apparently appearing out of nowhere, on her kitchen table had gotten Dorothy's attention. Inside had been information about Gatsby, his parties, invitations dated for the next Saturday, and the location of the safe. How it had gotten there she didn't know, and that scared Dorothy, since, outside of Nathan, there were not more than a half dozen people who knew what she did for a living.

This whole thing seemed like an elaborate practical joke on someone's part. Of course, if it was a joke, it was an awfully expensive one, since there had been five hundred dollars, in non-sequential bills, included with the instructions. The money, which now resided in her safety deposit box, was a good argument for the job being on the up and up.

"What the hell," said Nathan. "I don't have a date Saturday, so we might as well earn the money."

There was a sharp click and Nathan yanked down on the handle of the wall safe. Dorothy didn't have to look at him to know that he had a large grin on his face. Nathan stood up without even looking at the safe and walked over to a small table near the window where he poured two fingers of an amber colored liquid into a cut glass tumbler.

She pulled open the safe door and looked inside. Their instructions had said that they "would know what it was when they saw it."

There was a small pile of papers in the safe, along with several boxes, not to mention bundles of cash. The problem was, there was nothing in front of her that said *"Take me."* Dorothy found a package pushed to the back, pulled it out and began to unwrap it.

"Find something?" asked Nathan.

"Don't know," muttered Dorothy. "It feels like a shoe."

Pulling the last of the paper away, Dorothy could see it was a silver slipper. She stared at it for a moment, then collapsed unconscious on the floor.

"What happened?" Dorothy's voice was raspy and, if she hadn't known what she had said, she wouldn't have understood herself.

"Very original," Nathan said, helping her to sit up. "You fainted."

Dorothy hated those mealy-mouthed girls who would get the vapors, as her grandmother had called it, and pass out at the drop of a hat. Those were the ones who seemed to think they could run the world by just fluttering their eyelashes

That was when she realized the silver slipper was still in her hand. Everything became fuzzy again and she felt herself starting to slump backward.

A blonde-haired man, in a well pressed tuxedo, came bursting out of the shadows and pushed Nathan aside to grab Dorothy by the shoulders.

"There's some brandy by the chair; bring it!" the man told Nathan. His voice had a tone that said he was used to being obeyed. Nathan looked around nervously, then returned with a half-full snifter that he gave the man.

The liquid was warm as it rolled down Dorothy's throat. She looked down at the slipper. It seemed a normal pump, but the surface was silver and reflected even the tiniest bit of light.

"Who are you?" Nathan said from behind the man.

"Actually, I'm the one who should be asking you this question, old sport. Gatsby's the name. Jay Gatsby. And you are?"

Dorothy could see the color drain out of Nathan's face. Finding yourself face to face with the person that you were attempting to rob was not something you plan for.

"Nathan Grayson. I hardly expected to see you here tonight, Mr. Gatsby. Nice party," he said.

"Thanks, I don't usually go to them, myself," Gatsby said. "I was in here when you arrived, so I decided to watch."

"I usually don't work with an audience," muttered Nathan.

Dorothy ignored the two men for a moment, looking down at the silver shoe. It fascinated her; it was beautiful and familiar and yet there was something frightening about it.

"This shoe," she said. "I think that it's what we were sent here for."

"Now, that's interesting, young lady. But let's get you up off the floor," said Gatsby.

Nathan pulled a leather chair over while Gatsby helped Dorothy stand. She was steadier on her feet, though she grabbed onto the edge of the desk for support. She didn't actually need it, but it never hurt to give the impression you were less than you were.

Gatsby went behind his desk, stopping to stare out the window at the crowd of partiers. For a moment there was a

faraway look in his eyes, which disappeared almost immediately
"So you were sent here to steal that shoe. Why?" he asked.
"By the way, we haven't been formally introduced."

Dorothy smiled. She considered for a moment giving a
phony name. The driver's license in her purse identified her
as Eliza Santee, but there was something about this man that
suggested he would recognize a lie when he heard it.

"Gale. Dorothy Gale."

Gatsby stared at her for a minute, then reached into his
pocket and pulled out a ring of keys. Selecting an odd green-
colored one, he used it to unlock a drawer in his desk. He
brought out several photos that he handed to Dorothy.

She looked at them and felt the bottom fall out of her
stomach. Images rolled through her head, faces that she had
long ago pushed back in the recess of her mind as dreams,
nightmares and things that couldn't be.

Nathan stepped up to the desk and looked at the photos
spread out in front of his friend. The first photo was rather
blurry, just a figure with some kind of bird hovering above it.
He had to look at it for several seconds before realizing that
the bird looked like it had arms and what might have been a
tail. He picked up the other two pictures and saw the same
thing, but with two more of the creatures in them, baring
their teeth like they had been captured in mid snarl.

"What the hell are these things?"

"Flying monkeys, the most vicious, nasty creatures you
can imagine. In a herd they can make piranha look like
goldfish," said Dorothy. "But they're not real, just the
nightmares of a poor sick little girl who lost her family and her
mind in a tornado."

"Actually, Miss Gale, those creatures are all too real," said
Gatsby. "And those nightmares of yours, well they were real,
too."

Dorothy felt herself on the verge of tears, but pushed
those feelings back, refusing to show them to Gatsby, Nathan
or herself. This whole evening had turned into some totally
bent version of reality. Part of her wished she had burned
that damn package the moment she found it on her kitchen
table, but another part of her, the little girl who watched her
world disintegrate in the whirling chaos of the twister, was
grasping for something that said the dreams had been real.

"Oz? It was real?"

"Oz," echoed Nathan. "Wasn't there some sort of book or something called that?"

"Yes. A best-seller, as a matter of fact, as-well-as a Broadway musical not to mention a couple of movies. All of that thanks to a nosy reporter named Baum getting his hands on part of Miss Gale's case file. He got a lot of the story right, but a lot wrong, as well. Those sequels were total balderdash."

"Wait a minute," Dorothy said. "You're trying to tell me that it was real; Oz, the tin woodsman, the scarecrow, the wicked witch. That, it wasn't a nightmare after Auntie Em and Uncle Henry were killed when the tornado hit the house," she said. "No. No, the doctors told me over and over again it was just a dream."

"But dreams sometimes do come true," Gatsby said gently. "We needed you to believe that it was a dream. That was the only way to protect the place. That's what a lot of us have done for a very long time. We weren't certain that you, at that age, could keep secret the idea that the place was real."

"I became involved because one of the men in the company I commanded during the war was dying and felt like he had to tell someone," said Gatsby.

"Then what are we doing here? Why do you have the shoe?" said Dorothy. She still wasn't sure if she believed him, but pushing ahead and asking questions would keep her from dwelling on it and those long cold years where the doctors kept telling her it had all been a dream.

"I've been holding the shoe for its proper owner. It looks like that's you. Otherwise, it wouldn't have glowed when you touched it," he said. "As for who sent you here, I suspect that your answer lies in Omaha, Nebraska," said Gatsby.

"Nebraska," said Nathan. "Hasn't that place dulled away by now?"

"Dorothy, you need to go there to see Oscar Zoroaster Phadrig Isaac Norman Henkel Emmanuel Ambrose Diggs," said Gatsby.

"Who?" said Dorothy.

"My dear Miss Dorothy Gale, you're off to see the Wizard, the Wizard of Oz."

"Didn't I play this scene before?" Dorothy Gale asked herself.

"What scene?" asked Nathan, as he paced back and forth on the sidewalk. Omaha, Nebraska was not the smallest town in the world; there were several that Dorothy remembered from Kansas where the entire town would fit on the street outside the train station.

"Going off to see the Wizard, except that wasn't a yellow brick road we just spent far too many hours on," she said.

"So are you remembering that stuff that Gatsby was talking about?" asked Nathan.

"I never forgot it; really. Those doctors drugged me up enough that I believed that it was really just one long nightmare," she said. "It's just hard now accepting the fact the whole thing was actually real. Do you see a telephone booth anywhere?"

They walked a half block away from the train station before spotting a phone booth. The phone directory was small, made of pulp paper, and the pages were stained and torn from too much handling and being out in the weather.

She paged through the book to the Ds and ran her finger down the listings. "Hm, nobody named Diggs. Do you think he could have moved?"

"I doubt it," Nathan said. "Gatsby wouldn't have sent us here if he had. Look in the commercial listings, maybe under entertainment. He's supposed to be a wizard."

Dorothy paged to that section, surprised to see how big it was for a town this size. For a moment it seemed like this was another dead end. Then she saw it: Oz the Great – Stage Magician – reasonable rates. Call 359.

"Well, call 359," Nathan told her, reaching into his pocket. "Here's a nickel."

Dorothy hesitated. "Do you think he can really help us...me?"

"Call him; then we'll know." Nathan reached into the booth and put the nickel in the slot. "Call."

Dorothy gave the number to the operator; when no one answered, she admitted to herself that she felt relieved. At least for a while she wouldn't have to look into the face of the unknown.

"I don't know about you," said Nathan. "I noticed a diner down the street. What do you say to a couple of blue plate specials?"

"I think that would be an excellent idea for all three of us. I could use a bit of sustenance myself."

Dorothy and Nathan turned to find themselves facing a

rather portly man with a large nose, wearing a top hat, with a green watch chain coming out of his vest pocket. He looked a lot like a vaudeville comedian named Fields that she had seen perform a few weeks before.

"Were you speaking to us?" said Nathan.

"Indeed I was, young man," said the newcomer. "Miss Gale, I believe?"

Dorothy and Nathan looked at each other, then at the stranger. "Who might be asking?" Dorothy said to him, though she had a feeling that this was not the first time she had laid eyes on the man.

"I am Professor Oscar Zoroaster Phadrig Isaac Norman Henkel Emmannuel Ambrose Diggs; *Oz* Diggs." He said with a flourish.

"I remember you," said Dorothy "You're the Wizard!"

"The very same," the man said. With that, Dorothy slapped him, the sound a crack that could be heard above the west wind that had picked up in the last few minutes.

"How could you let them treat me like that? Make me think that I was crazy," she said, her voice halfway between anger and tears.

"I'm sorry, Dorothy. It was for your own good. Better a few years of thinking that you dreamed it all than decades in a lunatic asylum," he said gently.

"It was also to protect Oz itself, the fewer people who know, the better."

"Professor," said Nathan. "Why don't we get something to eat and talk there."

"Young man, you are exactly right."

"We'll have three blue plate specials," Professor Diggs said to the waitress. "Put it on my tab."

They had taken a booth at the far end of the diner, several tables away from the establishment's few other patrons. Dorothy continued to stare at the man who called himself Oz. Memories that she had locked away came flooding back, events, impressions, sights, smells.

"How was your journey from West Egg?" said the professor

"How do you know where we came from?" asked Nathan.

"Oh, I know many things: where you came from, where you're going."

"*We* don't know where we're going; how can you know

that?" asked Dorothy.

Just then their meal arrived. They ate for a few minutes before Diggs spoke. "Perhaps I should start from the beginning, Miss Gale. May I call you Dorothy? First let me apologize for the things that my colleagues and I put you through when you returned from Oz. It was necessary to protect that wonderful place."

"Indeed, there are not many of us who know of its reality; Gatsby, myself and a few others, but those of us who do try to protect it. You can imagine what people would do if they knew a 'magic' land existed."

"How well do you know Gatsby?"

"Oh, I've known him for years, since he lived in this part of the country. A really nice young man, although I can't say I approve of his business interests, but we all have our crosses to bear," said the wizard.

"And no one has found proof, after all these years?" said Dorothy.

"Not many. The books and the movies and that play only helped make everyone think it was nothing more than a fantasy story. We did have a problem with a young archeology student named Jones a year or two ago, but we diverted his attention into other areas," said Diggs between bites. "What few artifacts find their way here are kept hidden."

"Like that silver slipper," said Nathan.

"Indeed, it was the power of the silver slippers that returned Dorothy to this world. Dorothy, my dear, touching that shoe brought back all the reality of your time in Oz. I understand how painful that has been, but it was necessary," said Diggs.

"Necessary?" Dorothy asked. She had always been hesitant when someone told her something was necessary. There were too many memories connected to that word, memories leading back to her time in the "doctor's care."

"We need your help in protecting Oz from a very great danger," said Diggs; his friendly face had gone hard. Under the right circumstances, it was an expression that might have sent chills up someone's spine.

"And that would be?" asked Nathan.

"Both the best thing and the worst thing to ever happen to the land of Oz. I am referring to L. Frank Baum."

Nathan pursed his lips for a moment, as if struggling to remember something. 'Wait a minute," he finally said. "I think

I remember something about this Baum fellow dying a few years ago."

Professor Diggs paused to take a sip of his coffee.

"Indeed he did. In fact, Baum was a good man who stumbled on the whole Oz matter by pure accident. He amassed quite a collection of Oz memorabilia, including a few things that actually came from Oz."

"Am I right in guessing he has the other silver slipper, since we only have one of them?" said Dorothy

"Exactly. It was their magic that returned you from Oz. They can take someone back. In the wrong hands that would be a disaster," said the old stage magician.

"True, but his son, Frank Joslyn Baum, has gone into business with a Captain Hugh Fitzgerald, who has taken over the memorabilia collection and knows that Oz exists," said the professor.

"And you need someone to steal that silver slipper," Nathan said.

Dorothy smiled and looked over at Nathan. He had always been sharp and adaptable, willing to work with any situation. That had been one of the things that had attracted her to him.

"So I had to find out if you were as good as your reputation suggested before I pulled you into our little project. That's why I sent you the information on Gatsby's safe. I needed to know if you were good enough. It was a test and you passed with flying colors," he said.

"So how do we find this silver slipper that the good Captain has?" asked Nathan

"One slipper will always know where the other is," said Diggs.

"Does this mean we have to go back to West Egg and get Gatsby's slipper?"

The wizard smiled and shook his head. He gestured at Dorothy's purse sitting on the seat next to her. Without a word she opened the bag, pulling out her compact, wallet and key ring. When she looked back in her purse, the silver slipper was there.

"Nicely done, sir," she said, pulling out the slipper with two fingers. The feel of the material in her hands left them tingling. She remembered the feel of them on her feet, the way the sensation had spread up through her when she had clicked the heels together and thought of being 'home'.

"It was there all along, just a spell that made no one notice it until I took it off. It's not something I can do very often anymore. I'm not as young as I used to be. But it is very handy. I have to save my strength for bigger things." he said.

"All right, Oh Great and Mighty Oz. Give me one good reason that Nathan and I should do this little job that you're asking us to do."

Professor Oscar Zoroaster Phadrig Isaac Norman Henkel Emmanuel Ambrose Diggs picked up his coffee cup and took a sip. For a moment he had a vague distant, almost sad, look in his eyes.

"I'm not asking you to do it for me, for Gatsby or for any of the others that you haven't met. I'm asking you to do it for that little girl, scared out of her wits, who rode the winds into a land of dreams and wonder."

They were all three silent for a time, then Dorothy picked up the slipper and put it back in her bag. "When's the next train?" she asked the Wizard.

"There I think I can help you out a little bit," said the wizard as he pulled an envelope from inside his jacket and passed it over to his younger companions. "That will fill you in on Captain Hugh Fitzgerald. Now, I need you to just go through that door over on the left."

The door that Diggs referred to had the word Storage stenciled on it. Dorothy looked at him oddly and saw the same twinkle in his eyes that she remembered from the first time in the throne room in The Emerald City.

"Go on, my dear," he said gently.

I thought you said this guy was a stage magician, a fake," said Nathan.

The door that the wizard had directed them through had led down a short corridor and out onto the street, only it wasn't a street in Omaha.

They were standing near the Busy Bee Dry Goods store; just down the street she could see a grove of several dozen trees covered with what looked like oranges. Looking back toward the door the two of them had come through, Dorothy saw nothing but a wooden wall covered with advertising posters.

"I guess I was wrong," Dorothy replied. "Do you have that

envelope he gave us?"

Nathan paused for a minute, patting his pockets, and Dorothy didn't like the look she saw on his face, he did have a tendency to lose things.

"Bingo," he proclaimed pulling the papers from his inside coat packet, along with several other scraps of paper and a leather case that she knew was his picklock set.

"Okay, let's see what the professor has in mind," she said unfolding two typewritten sheets. "It looks like we're in Hollywood, California. I wonder if we'll run into Charlie Chaplin?"

"Coming out of Busy Bee Dry Goods? Hardly," said Nathan.

Nathan disappeared into that same store. Two minutes later he was back out on the street smiling "This Fitzgerald fellow's address is number 22 Orange Drive. Although, apparently, Captain Fitzgerald won't be home tonight; he's attending a party at Pickfair."

"Pickfair? As in…." said Dorothy.

"Mary Pickford and Douglas Fairbanks place. If we had time, I wouldn't mind crashing that little shindig."

It took them nearly an hour to find the house. By that time the sun was sinking into the west. Even though she couldn't actually see the ocean from where they were, Dorothy stopped for a moment to look in that direction. Growing up in Kansas, the ocean would have seemed as far away as Oz, and now here she was, only a few miles from it.

On the far side of the property they slipped over the fence and made it up to the house without encountering anyone. Nathan saw a basement window and had it open and was through it in only a matter of minutes.

"Your turn," Nathan called out to her, reaching up to grab her as she wiggled through the narrow space.

"We're in; now what?"

Dorothy remembered the words of the Great and Powerful Oz, "one slipper will always know where the other is."

"I suppose we could ask the slipper," she said.

The fact that she hadn't thought about the silver slipper since their last moment in Omaha bothered Dorothy, but not much. Magic just seemed to have stepped back into her life like it had never left.

Her hand tingled as she held the slipper. Walking up the staircase, the sensation increased as they moved into the main part of the house.

"So where are we going?" asked Nathan.

"We're following the yellow brick road." Dorothy gestured at the floor where a long winding yellow strip had been painted. The slipper was also leading them along the same path. She felt an odd sensation of déjà vu following it right up to a large door painted with the royal crest of OZ.

"Dis must be the place," Nathan said.

The door wasn't locked, though the hinges groaned loudly as they opened it. If there was anyone else in the house, that surely would have alerted them that something was going on.

"Don't turn any lights on," she muttered.

The room was filled to overflowing with OZ memorabilia: props, books, advertising posters. Dorothy paused in front of the hat that had belonged to the Wicked Witch of the West in one of the movies and felt like she could still hear that evil woman's cackling laugh; the memory was frightening, yet oddly reassuring.

From the other side there was a sudden flapping noise followed by a crash as Nathan fell. Dorothy turned and saw her partner on the floor, his hands flailing at something.

Running to his side, she saw there was an animal of some kind on Nathan's chest, pawing at his face. Thinking it was a cat, she grabbed for the scruff of creature's neck and jerked backwards. Only, this was no cat; it took a few seconds for her to realize she was holding a small monkey with wings! Her stomach twisted in fear, and she fought down an urge to scream and run away. Then just as quickly, she slammed her fist into the creature's stomach; it slumped and went limp.

"What the hell is that?" said Nathan as he struggled to his feet.

Before Dorothy could say the words "flying monkey" she heard the sound of footsteps in the hallway outside the room. She grabbed a heavy green cabinet and began pushing it up against the door.

From outside the door came a voice. "I tell you I heard something in there! It sounded like all hell was breaking loose."

Something pounded hard against the door, but the barrier held, although Dorothy had her doubts for how long.

"Get Dorkins; we'll break the door down and then send someone for the police," said a second voice.

"Nathan, we need to get out of here now," she said, looking

around.

The problem was, there were no windows. Every inch of the walls were covered by display cases, bookshelves or framed posters. As best Dorothy could guess, this room was in the center of the house, so that left only one exit, the main door.

"Maybe there's a secret panel or a tunnel of some sort?" said Nathan.

Just then Dorothy spotted the silver slipper lying on the ground where she had dropped it going to Nathan's rescue. Instinctively, she grabbed it up. As soon as her hand touched the slipper, it tingled like it never had before.

In the middle of the broken remnants of the display case that Nathan had fallen into, Dorothy caught a glimpse of something silver. Frantically, she began to push shattered pieces of wood and glass aside. Its content was a single shoe, a silver slipper. Dorothy grabbed it up, a warm feeling running through her as held them.

The pounding on the door began again and, without thinking about it, Dorothy pulled her shoes off and replaced them with the silver slippers.

"I'm open for suggestions on how to get out of here," said Nathan as the pounding on the door increased.

Dorothy reached over and took his hand. "Just believe," she said, then touched the heels of her slippers together. "The last time I did this I ended up back in Kansas."

Exactly what happened next was unclear to Dorothy. Everything seemed to whirl around her, and, for one terrifying moment, she was back in the tornado that long ago day in Kansas. Then she and Nathan came crashing to the ground, rolling over and over until they stopped. Dorothy opened her eyes and looked around. She and Nathan were lying in a field of the most beautiful flowers she had ever seen. Around the field were stately trees bearing rich fruit. She felt her breath come in gasps for a moment. She knew this place; it was Munchkinland in Oz.

"That hurt." Nathan groaned as he looked around. "You said the last time you used those shoes you ended up in Kansas. Well, I don't think I'm wrong when I say, we're not in Kansas."

Mack

S. P. Sinor
Flush Fiction, Volume I: Stories to be Read in One Sitting
Yard Dog Press

So there I was, hangin' out with my buds, my peeps, the guys, at the usual place. The food's not bad and there's a terrific view. Seems like we're there all the time, watchin' the world go by. Lots of Big People out there, walkin' by, payin' us no never mind. Except occasionally one'll stop and peer through the window at us, like he's tryin' to pick out a pet, or decide what's for dinner. Those guys give me the creeps, all big eyes and big teeth.

Anyway, the guys and I was just hangin', when one of those Others swoops in and grabs me. I'm outta there so fast it makes my own head spin. I fight, but it's like I'm swimmin' upstream. So I kinda lose track of what's goin' on until I find myself dumped into another place, not too unlike the place I was just unceremoniously yanked out of. The new place wasn't as big, the clientele was somewhat smaller and the decor left a lot to be desired, but what the hey, I'm up for new experiences.

"Yo," I said to the group. "I'm Mack. I'm new here. What's hangin'?"

"Hi, Mack," they said in a lackluster chorus.

"I'm Joe," one of 'em said. "We figured we'd be getting a new guy after Fred went belly up. I'd say welcome, but, well, none of us really want to be here."

"Yeah, it does seem a little smaller than the last place I was in. So, whadda ya do for fun around here?" I was ready for a little action.

"Nothin' much," said Joe. "Like you said, not much room. We hang around and talk. Where're you from, anyway, Mack?"

"The big city," I said. "I had lots o' friends there. It's a much bigger place. We got good grub and didn't get hassled much." I was pretty proud of my former lodgings, and I didn't mind spreading the word.

"Well, don't count on good grub around here," Joe replied. "Sometimes we're lucky to get any grub at all, and other times there's more than we can eat. Nothing's consistent."

I decided to keep my big mouth shut until I could come to my own conclusions. I'd snoop around a bit to see what I could see.

Joe went on. "Tell us what it's like where you came from." It's not like they'd ever see it for themselves, so what the hell.

"Well, you see, it's big, and there's lots of people. And talk about things to do, well, no one's ever bored where I come from." I went on like that for awhile. They were eating it up; I had them hook, line and sinker. I didn't mention the Others; I'd save them for ghost story time.

"Wow," Joe said. "I'd sure like to go there. It sounds a lot more exciting than hanging around here with nothing to do all day." I never thought anything would come of that statement, considering the type of demoralized, downtrodden guys I was with now.

And, since I was here, I decided to get to know the rest of the gang, such as it was.

Time went by, and my current situation was becoming unbearable. I'd thought higher status in a smaller area would be to my advantage, but it wasn't worth it. The walls started closing in around me and I felt myself drifting aimlessly; floating along in a sea of despair. I needed an anchor, a purpose in life. I needed something to do. I thought about what Joe had said a while back, about seeing where I'd come from. Just thinking about it made me homesick. I tried to think of a way to escape, and take the other guys with me, but everything I thought of seemed too dangerous. Besides, I wasn't sure that everyone would want to go.

"Hey, guys," I said to the rest. "I was thinkin'. How do you all feel about staging a jail break?" It had gotten to the point that I'd do almost anything to break outta this prison. "Whadda ya' say? Who's with me?" That caused a ripple of excitement amongst the group.

"What do you have in mind? Joe replied.

So we got in a huddle to discuss the logistics of escape. One suggestion was that we scale the walls.

"I don't know," said Joe. "I'm not sure we can survive the atmosphere out there.

The environment looks really alien."

"Oh, it's not that bad. The Big City is pretty much the

same. Ya' just gotta be careful. However," I went on, "we shouldn't jump at the first suggestion. Any other ideas?"

Talk went around like a whirlpool, but nothing much came of it.

Finally, Joe said, "The only one of us who ever got out of here was Fred, and he bit the big one."

Which gave me an idea.

"Say, what did They do to make sure Fred had really kicked the bucket?"

"Well," Joe answered. "Not really anything we could see. They just grabbed him up and we never saw him again."

I thought a minute. It might just work. "Listen to this. Hows about we try it the way Fred did, only we're not really dead. We're just playin' like we are, until the Big People take us outta this place; then we make a break for it." I wasn't sure if the guys would go for it, or even if it was a good idea. It was just the only one I could think of.

They mulled it over for a while, then Joe said, "I guess we might as well try. We've certainly got nothing better to do."

So we gave it a shot and played dead. When the Big People saw us just layin' there, one of 'em grabbed us all up and ran. We thought we'd be tossed away and could sneak off, but we ended up in another place that had a big white bowl in it. We were just about to blow our cover 'cause we couldn't breathe the air out here after all, when we were tossed into that bowl and we could breathe again. Next thing, we heard a loud noise and a slide opened up under us and away we went. My plan had worked! We were free! Next stop, the Big City.

Crocaroo

Sue Sinor
Flush Fiction, Volume II: Twenty Years of Letting It Go!
Yard Dog Press

Have you ever seen a crocaroo? Yes, a crocaroo. At least, that's what I call what I saw last summer. What, you say, IS a crocaroo? Let me tell you a story.

My Uncle Beezer and I were hunting in southern Louisiana last summer. We were somewhere to the east of Grand Bayou, hunting for whatever was edible and legal.

"Jimmy," Uncle Beezer said, "Look over yonder. What does that look like to you?"

I looked. "Looks like a jackrabbit to me. A big one. What does it look like to you?"

"Well, for a minute it looked a little like a kangaroo, but with a strange looking head." He stared for another moment. "Yeah, I guess you're right. We don't really have 'roos around here."

We walked on, looking for deer or squirrels or whatever we'd have for supper. Possums would be okay, too, but we didn't see any of those, either.

"Jimmy," my uncle said suddenly, "Do you believe in Sasquatches?"

Now, I knew my uncle had some strange ideas. He believed in monsters and astrology and ghosts, things like that, so it didn't surprise me that he asked me that question.

"I've never seen one, so I can't say yes, but I've never seen a lot of things that I know exists, either. Why do you ask?"

He looked around for a moment without saying anything, then, "Jimmy, I've been thinking about going up to Washington state for a while to look for one."

We walked on. "How would you get there? You don't drive."

"Oh, I can drive. I just prefer to have other people take me where I need to go. Like you."

"You've got to be kidding!" I stopped in my tracks and faced him. "I've been taking you places for years, thinking you couldn't drive, and now you tell me that. Don't you dare ask me for a ride again."

"But I don't have a car," he whined.

"And whose fault is that? I saved up to get the junker I drive. It was all I could afford with my crappy job."

"Yeah, it is a junker, all right. But have I ever complained? Of course not. It's your car."

"Well, now you can buy your own car to take you where you want to go. I quit!"

I stomped off, leaving him to think about what I said. That's when I heard him yell.

"Jimmy! Watch out!"

I turned and saw the scariest thing I've ever seen not five feet from me. It had the body of what looked like a kangaroo, but its head was shaped like a crocodile's head, with rows of razor-sharp teeth. I stood frozen, trying to make sense of it. Fortunately, Beezer thought faster than I did and ran toward me swinging his rifle.

He whopped that thing upside the head, which only made it look at him.

"Run!" I yelled to him. I raised my rifle and looked through the site. I couldn't get a clear shot, so I started running, too.

Beezer started running in a zigzag pattern to confuse the critter, and when he found a suitable tree, he climbed it as far as he could get.

But the damned thing could jump. It tried to catch him by jumping up the tree, but I got close enough to get a bead on it and fired. I don't think I hit it, but I scared it. It started hopping away toward the bayou and we hightailed it back to my car. We decided that take-out would do for supper, and the next time we went hunting, we'd go to Arkansas.

"You know," I mused. "If I'd killed that thing, we coulda had crockpot roo for dinner."

Christmas Shopping
Susan P. Sinor
Playing With Secrets
Yard Dog Press

Larry peered at his watch by the light of a nearby lamppost.
8:00 P.M.

"Time to go shopping," he said.

He was normally very prompt about doing things, but Christmas shopping was something that he always waited until exactly 8:00 P.M. on Christmas Eve to do. After all, it was a tradition, and traditions were important things, especially where he had grown up.

Start at 8, finish by midnight. Four hours was pushing it, but he had never had any problems before, and there was no reason to expect any this year.

Midnight: the Witching Hour; or rather, Clausing Time. Larry grinned at his own joke. Since childhood he had been proud of his sense of humor. He loved puns and other outrageous jokes. The people he'd grown up around had certainly been cheerful, but they would never have appreciated Larry's sense of humor.

He checked his bag one more time: lock picks, rope, latex gloves, plastic bags to use a shoe covers, black ski mask and an assortment of odd items that he thought might come in handy. You never know what you might need.

Under a black flight jacket he wore a matching jumpsuit. He had worn it to work, but then it had been appropriately decorated for the season. The pins and other things were now safely stored in a plastic bag under his car seat.

Most of the other male hairdressers at Madame X's salon dressed outrageously, trying to outdo each other, but Larry was fairly conservative. That's how he got so many of the older, richer clients. They might like to look at the more outlandish dressers, but they wanted their hair done by someone who was expert in the classic styles. And someone who could carry on a conversation, meaning listen attentively.

He didn't have a family anymore. He'd left home a few years before and had never looked back. Marilyn and Chuck

Ryan and their twins, Tracy and Stacy, were Larry's best friends. In fact, if he was being brutally honest, they were really his only friends. Larry had met them when he'd first come to town, alone and broke. They had all but adopted him and he owed them a lot. They were his family now.

He wanted to give them nicer Christmas gifts than he could afford.

Larry checked his shopping list.

The first stop would be at Mrs. Richardson's, for that sterling gravy boat. She had bought it for her newly-married granddaughter, but the pattern also matched what Marilyn had. Then to the Smiths. What Mrs. Smith didn't confide to him, Mr. Smith did. The computer games they had bought for their grandchildren would thrill the twins. After the Smiths, he would pick up a silk shirt for Chuck at the Arnold's. It should be just the right shade of blue, providing Mrs. Arnold had bought the shirt Larry had so thoughtfully suggested.

He didn't have anyone special in his life at the moment, although he did have his eye on someone who worked at the small art gallery next to Madame X's. His name was Mark. Larry had stopped in the gallery a few times, mainly to see Mark. They hadn't gotten to the getting-together-after-work stage, yet; certainly not to the Christmas gift stage, so three gifts would be all he needed.

The Richardsons, Smiths and Arnolds were all going to be at the Hobart Johnson's Christmas Eve party. Besides New Years, this was the one night of the year that they all stayed up, and out, until after midnight.

Even though Pam Johnson had invited him, somehow Larry didn't think he would make it.

"Larry, why don't you drop by and join the party? You already know most of the guests, and you're such an amusing young man. We'd love to have you."

Amusing. That word really grated on his nerves. What he wouldn't stoop to for his career. All three ladies had been eager to discuss with him what they would wear to the party. They seemed to value his advice, and especially, his attitude. Larry had learned when he was very young what an asset the correct attitude could be.

When he couldn't even fake the "correct" attitude his family demanded, he had decided to leave his home, and had never regretted it. Here, he had been able to maintain an attitude that had gotten him to the position of senior hairdresser at Madame X's. With just a bit of luck, it would eventually get him his own salon.

Maybe he should go to the party, just for a few minutes. The Johnson's house was so big, like the guest list, that he could be there for ten minutes, say he'd been there all evening, and no one would know the difference; an alibi of sorts, just in case.

He could also pick up something there, for himself, since he had no way of knowing what it would be. The other gifts should be no problem. His clients always bragged about how elaborately the stores wrapped their packages, just the sort of information that one filed away for future reference.

Larry parked his dark green Volvo a few doors down from the Richardson's house. The car was old, but it was a classic and he took good care of it. One must keep up appearances. It was just the kind of car no one would pay any attention to in an upper class neighborhood like this.

The winter wind whipped his hair as he put the ski mask and other 'protections' on. It had been a dry winter so far, and tonight was clear and dark, just perfect for Christmas shopping.

He slid along the walls of the house until he came to the back door. Carefully, he worked the door lock until it snapped open. That gave Larry thirty seconds to reach the alarm box and punch in the deactivation code. He did it with ten seconds to spare. When the system was being installed last spring, Mrs. Richardson had let slip what the code was, which, knowing her memory, would never be changed.

He paused for a moment in the living room door. Even without lights he could see the Christmas tree, decorated in silver and red. The gravy boat was in a green foil box with a gold ribbon and bow, marked **To Maria, From Grandmother**.

He hid it inside his jacket and retraced his steps, closing the door carefully behind him, not forgetting to turn the alarm back on or to remove his ski mask.

One down, he thought.

The Smiths didn't live very far from the Richardson's. Everything in this part of town was old: houses, trees, people, and money. Most of his clients lived in this neighborhood, knew the same people, shopped at the same stores, got their hair done at the same salon, by the same person.

Larry wasn't too concerned about being found out. He never shopped at the same homes two years in a row and never took more than one gift at a time. No sense taking chances. Larry researched each *store* very carefully: security, pets and the possibility of someone still being home on Christmas Eve.

The Smiths lived on a block with an alley. The backyards had high stone walls and alley-entrance garages. Larry already knew of a spot on the wall where he could boost himself over.

As he hit the ground, he heard the yap, yap, yap of a small dog.

"Oh, no!" He could see the dog jumping and barking furiously about ten feet away. "Where did that thing come from?"

He thought of just going back over the wall, but that would mean giving up the games for the kids. He knelt on one knee and softly called the dog.

"Here pup, pup, pup. Come on, I won't hurt you. Come on."

To his surprise, the dog ran over and began to lick his hand.

"Well, hi, fella. What are you doing here?" There was enough light from the yard lamp to read the dog's tags. Muffy, Owned by Robbie and Nicole Smith.

"Oho, so that's it. Just visiting, are you? I suppose that you can't stay in the house with the cats, because you might terrorize them. Let me tell you a secret, Muffy. Those cats could have you for lunch. Better you do stay outside. How about I try to find you a snack while I'm inside. Would you like that?"

The Smiths didn't have an alarm system, thinking that the wall around the yard was all the security they needed. Maybe he should discuss that with them—next year.

He had no trouble jimmying the back door, careful to not leave any marks. Their tree wasn't lit, either, but light coming in from the window bathed it in a glow, and he could see that it was decorated beautifully. The Smiths had always had excellent taste.

He carefully looked through the packages under the tree until he found the right one: To Robbie and Nicole. Then he saw another one like it. Two! He hadn't thought of that. He couldn't take both, but which one?

"I guess I'll just play eenie, meenie to decide. I hope I pick the right one."

He set both gifts on the floor and waved his hands over them until they settled on one. Placing the other one where he had found it, Larry hid his choice inside his jacket and made his way to the kitchen.

"Mustn't forget Muffy," he said, looking in the pantry and the fridge. Nothing. What were they doing, putting the little furball on a diet? Then he noticed some leftover steak wrapped in plastic. "I'll bet Muffy will love this."

Bribe in hand, Larry stepped out into the backyard, just as the dog came yipping around the corner of the house.

"Okay, okay. Here you go." Larry tossed his present for Muffy under the bushes where any remnants wouldn't be noticed.

Now *he* was getting hungry.

"Maybe I should take a break and visit the Johnson's party."

Larry checked his watch by the dome light of his car, it was only 9:30. He was doing well enough that he could allow himself an hour at the party and still make the last house on his shopping list.

It wasn't far to the Johnson's. He parked in an inconspicuous place and started putting back on everything he'd taken off: a scarf—red and green, of course; a pin here, an earring there, and several rings.

He combed his hair and locked the car behind him; *can't be too careful around here at night, especially with so many expensive cars.* Besides, he'd heard about a gang of thieves who ripped off Christmas presents from cars.

The front door would not be a good idea; after all he "had been here for some time". There were party noises coming from the rear of the house as he turned the corner into the backyard.

A dark figure stumbled out of the bushes and ran right into him. "Who's 'at?" the figure, a man, slurred, clutching at Larry's arm. "Why, it's Mr. Larry! Hey, how long you been here? Great party, huh?"

Larry was amazed at the change in Mr. Smith since he'd come by the shop that morning for a last-minute holiday trim. The dapper retired stockbroker's shirt was hanging loose from his belt, there was a stain of what looked like mustard on his pant leg, and the man's breath smelled strong enough to strip a varnished table.

"Why, Mr. Smith, you let me in the front door about an hour ago. Don't you remember? Oh, well, I suppose you might have been a bit distracted. I saw who you were talking to. Don't worry, I won't breathe a word. Now, I thought I'd help myself to a bit more of that wonderful shrimp dish. I just can't help myself."

Larry was glad that Mrs. Johnson had discussed the menu with him. Knowing about the shrimp might help avert a potential problem, if not disaster. Although, in his current condition, Mr. Smith would be lucky to remember what country he was in, let alone what happened an hour earlier.

"You go right on ahead. I'm just goin' to get a little fresh air." Mr. Smith giggled as he staggered around the corner of the house.

Larry smiled to himself as he walked through the back yard. He saw an almost empty glass on the deck railing and picked it up to serve as a prop. Putting on a big smile, he slipped in through the back door.

Larry had been in the house before and knew that there was a small bathroom near the back door. He went inside, sprinkled a little of the bourbon from the glass on his face like aftershave, emptied and washed the glass, and put about half an inch of water in it. Then he flushed the toilet and went back out. He drained the glass, making sure to be a little unsteady on his feet as he made his way toward the dining room, nodding to people he didn't know and exchanging pleasantries with those he did. Larry felt sure that he had left the impression that he had been there for a while until he ran into Mrs. Johnson.

"Why, Larry, I didn't know you were here. When did you arrive?" She didn't seem nearly tipsy enough to fool for long. Best not to spin too elaborate a tale, he thought.

"Mrs. Johnson," he exclaimed, putting an arm around her shoulders. "I didn't see you when I got here, and then I got into a fascinating conversation with one of the other guests. You know, I don't remember what he said his name was, but he seemed to want to talk about his golf game, and before I knew it, it was an hour later.

"I'd had a couple of drinks and just had to get some fresh

air. I sat on your delightful deck until I got cold and hungry and decided to come back in and indulge myself at your wonderful buffet. I do hope there's some of that shrimp dish left, but I'm sure that you would never let anything run out. You are such a marvelous hostess."

He was babbling, he knew, but it fit in with the festivities and he certainly didn't want her to be suspicious.

"Why, Larry, thank you!" Maybe he had fooled her, after all. "Please, go eat. You shouldn't be drinking on an empty stomach. I'll see you later; I must check something in the kitchen."

She waved him toward the dining room.

The table was covered with nearly two dozen dishes, all of them looking expensive and very fattening. Larry had always been small and slight, so he didn't worry about calories as he loaded down a plate. After having the bartender fix him a real drink, he looked around for a somewhat secluded spot to eat.

He found one behind a sofa in the den, nearly tripping over someone who was already there.

"I'm s-s-sorry," the man whispered. "I'll move over. I'm trying to hide from my wife for a little while. She doesn't want me to have any fun. Said I couldn't have any more to drink, because I might embarrass her. She's a real tyrant, but she also has money, so what can I do? She'll probable find me pretty soon, but 'til she does I can do this." He took a sip of a very substantial drink he had hidden between the sofa and the end table. "Are you hiding from your wife, too? I won't tell on you if you don't tell on me. Say, do you play golf?

"I could play golf all day, and sometimes I do. Myrna doesn't play, says it's a stupid game, but she doesn't make me quit. She's always busy with her club meetings and things and she says it keeps me out of her hair. I'm pretty good, too, if I do say so myself. I've got a real low handicap, and the pro at the country club says with a little work, maybe I could turn pro myself..."

Larry couldn't get a word in but he really didn't have anything to say anyway. Golf interested him about as much as watching grass grow. He settled back to eat and let the man talk. The poor guy was obviously starved for some attention. He didn't sound drunk, but either he was, or his elevator didn't go quite to the top.

After a while, Larry glanced at his watch.

11:00! How did that happen?

He had one more place to go before he was finished, and he didn't have much time, not even to find himself a present from the Johnson's. After making a quick excuse to his new "friend", he went into the little bathroom again, washed his hands and flushed, and casually walked out onto the deck. There didn't seem to be anyone outside right then, but just to be on the safe side, Larry clung to the shadows as he worked his way out to where he had left his car.

Fortunately, the Arnolds didn't live that far.

In less than ten minutes he was cruising their street. Apparently, one of their neighbors was having a party, too, and the block was lined with late-model cars. Finally he saw a small space just around the corner.

There wasn't any kind of fence or wall surrounding their property, but they did have a thick growth of hedge. They didn't have an alarm system, either. The neighborhood itself was protection, they assumed. "And who am I to argue with them," Larry mused.as he slipped through a space next to the alley-access garage. Sometimes he found his lack of size to be an asset.

Thankfully, there would be no Muffys, here. Mrs. Arnold abhorred dogs and was allergic to cats.

He gently worked at the door with his lock pick, eventually hearing the click that told him it was open. Pushing the door ajar, he stood in the threshold. It took a few minutes to get his bearings. While Larry had heard about the house, he'd never been inside.

The kitchen was to the right, with a utility room to the left. Straight ahead was a short hallway, ending in a closed door. He tiptoed to the door and listened for a minute. He could hear nothing except the ticking of what he assumed was a large grandfather clock.

He turned the knob and eased the door open as silently as possible. Still no sound. He took a cautious step, peering through the dim light down another hallway. There was the living room, to the left. The entryway was a large squared-off opening with double doors. The grandfather clock stood to one side. It said 11:30. No problem.

Even from there, Larry could see the majestic tree, gorgeously decorated, at least seven feet tall, standing in the bay window at the front of the room. He would have liked to see it lit, but that would have been too risky. He stood entranced for a moment; it had been years since anything associated with Christmas had filled him with such awe.

The only part of Christmas that had ever really excited him had been the Christmas tree. Selecting the perfect one, setting it up, and especially decorating it, had thoroughly fascinated him. He missed that now, since he could fit only a very small tree in his apartment. Nevertheless, he decorated it as beautifully as he could.

"Come on. You've got work to do, and you're running out of time."

He pulled off the ski mask and began searching carefully through the pile of gifts for the one wrapped in multi-colored foil and tied with a red satin bow.

"Here we go."

He picked the package up, and saw a second package, wrapped in identical foil and bow. Then he saw another, and then another.

"Four! Two at the Smiths was bad enough, but four! And the tags don't help; they're all for Mr. Arnold. Couldn't that old biddy have been more original?"

It was obvious he would either have to unwrap each one, take them all, or just grab one and take his chances.

"I certainly can't take all of them, and if I just grab one, it will be pajamas or underwear or a bowling shirt."

Taking a deep breath, Larry sat down on the floor and began to carefully unwrap the first package. Being foil, the paper didn't tear when he pulled off the tape. That was fortunate.

"Houndstooth pajamas. How tacky."

The second package yielded a golf shirt.

Just as Larry began to peel the tape from the third package, he heard a very strange sound.

Hurriedly replacing the boxes where he found them, he looked around for a place to hide.

He was afraid that it was the Arnolds returning home. It was just midnight, he heard from the large mantle clock, a replica of an antique wind-up clock, or probably it was the actual antique itself. Whichever, they shouldn't be leaving the party yet, much less be home already. He knew there would be a midnight toast to Christmas, and they wouldn't leave before that.

Just as he started to crawl behind a corner chair, he heard a chuckle that was horribly familiar.

Larry turned slowly toward the fireplace, which until just now, had been empty even of gas logs. Most of the area was obscured by a crouching, rotund figure dressed in red and white, and holding a bulging sack over one shoulder.

The new arrival put down the bag, straightened and turned toward the chair that Larry was peeking around.

"You!" the figure and Larry cried, simultaneously.

They stood, staring at each other for what seemed like hours before either of them spoke.

"Nick."

"Well, well," the newcomer said. "Fancy meeting you here. I'd wondered if I'd ever cross paths with you again, Laric."

"Now, don't tell me that you live here. You'd never be able to afford a place like this, and besides, except for Christmas trees, your taste was never quite this traditional," Nick gestured at the holly wreath, the manger scene and the candles on the mantle. "So tell me, what are you doing here at midnight skulking around someone else's Christmas tree?"

Larry just stood with his mouth hanging open, then swallowed. "Uh, nothing. I'm not doing anything. I'm just visiting here. That's right, I'm spending Christmas with my friends, the Arnolds, and I couldn't sleep, so I thought I'd sit here in the living room and look at the tree for a while..., and call me Larry!"

"Laric, you know you can't lie to me. You never could. Now tell me the truth."

"Hey, wait a minute. What are you doing here, Nick? These people don't have any small children. Why are you bringing presents to this house?" Larry decided that belligerence should be the next course of action.

Nick picked up his pack and moved toward the tree. "No, they don't. But they do have grandchildren who will be here early Christmas morning. Remember, I know everything when it comes to this sort of thing.

"Now, don't you think it's about time you came back home? I'll even give you a ride. I could use some help; I'm not getting any younger. Oh, by the way, we'll put back those presents you took earlier this evening while we're in the neighborhood."

Larry felt a chill run down his back. "I don't know what you're talking about. And no, I'm not going 'home'. I am home.

I always hated it at the North Pole. That's why I ran away." He slumped into the chair he had hidden behind. "I never fit in. My lifestyle...wasn't exactly encouraged there. I'm not going back with you. I've got a good life here. For the first time I'm happy. You'd better get finished and go. I imagine that Arnolds will be coming home pretty soon, and you don't want to get caught."

"No fear of that, or don't you remember?" replied Nick. "Have you forgotten that on Christmas Eve at midnight, time all over the world stops until I've finished all my rounds? I have, literally, all the time in the world. And I don't mean to leave without you. Now, you can come with me willingly or not, your choice."

Nick settled into another chair, looking like he could wait forever. From one pocket of his jacket he produced a blackened briar pipe. He inspected the bowl, produced a small bag of tobacco, refilled it and put it between his teeth. A long thin line of white smoke emerged.

"I could just leave, you know. You can't hold me here." Larry looked toward the door.

"Go ahead, make a break for it," Nick urged. "You'll see."

Suddenly, Larry ran for the door, half expecting something like a force-field to be protecting it. He jumped just as he reached it, as if to break through, and landed on the floor of the living room. He stopped rolling at the base of the Christmas tree.

"What?" he cried, and tried again. Picking himself up, this time from in front of Nick's feet, he finally realized what Nick had been trying to tell him. The only reality at that very point in—time—was that very room. The only way he could get out of it was when Nick left.

"Oh, I see. I'm stuck, huh? Well, go on; leave your presents for all the good little girls and boys and go on to the next house. I told you, I'm staying."

"No, you weren't listening. I said I'm not leaving without you. You're not supposed to be here in the real world, Laric. You're an elf, not a human. You don't fit in."

"Yes, I do. I do fit in," Larry insisted. "Much more than I ever could at the workshop. That bunch can be very intolerant of alternate lifestyles. I'd be miserable for the rest of my life.

"Besides, I hated putting those toys together. It was boring. I hated smiling all the time. OK, OK, I have to smile a lot now, but now I don't mind. I'm doing something I enjoy. And I'm planning to open my own shop soon.

"At least I'm not tied down to the same thing day in, day out. Talk about a dead-end job. Even a ditch-digger can aspire to better things, here. At the North Pole it's either elf, reindeer or you. I'm obviously not a reindeer and I can't see you retiring soon. Please don't make me go back! I'll do anything you want if you'll let me stay here."

Nick hesitated, his eyes locked on Larry's. "I'll consider it, but there are conditions. First, you return what you've taken tonight. Oh, I know what you've been doing. I've known about it from the beginning, but I could never catch you before now. Second, you'll stop these, what do you call them, shopping expeditions. Third, you'll pay back every one of the people you've stolen from. How you do it is your business, but they must each be paid back the value of what you've taken by Christmas next year."

"Nick, give me a break. I don't make that kind of money!"

"Then take a second job. Take it or leave it, Laric. Like I said before, it's your choice." Nick pushed himself to his feet and began to place additional presents around the tree. "Now hurry up. I'm not even half through and I've got a hot bath waiting for me at home."

"All right, I said I'd do anything. I'd better hurry if I'm going to return the other things. After all, it's midnight, isn't it."

"It is. I'll tell you what. We'll pick up the other two packages from your car and I'll deliver them for you. You can go on home and think about how to repay the rest of the people you stole from. Oh, by the way, I'll be back next year to check on you"

Larry, what a nice way to thank your clients for their patronage," Mrs. Richardson commented as she handed Larry a red and green foil coupon with the words "Complimentary Visit...Merry Christmas" printed on it.

Larry had tried to calculate the values of all the 'gifts' he had acquired from his clients over the past several years. Then he figured how many free salon visits it would take for each client to be compensated for what had been stolen. It turned out to be quite a tidy sum. If Larry hadn't had enough customers he had never "shopped" from, he wouldn't have been able to pay his station fees to the salon owner, or to cover his own living expenses.

"It's the least I can do to show my appreciation to my very favorite clients. Now, not everyone got my Christmas coupons, so let's be discreet, shall we?"

"Of course, Larry. I certainly wouldn't want to embarrass anyone. You have a wonderful holiday, and I'll see you on New Year's Eve." Mrs. Richardson waved her fingers as she left the salon.

He had exchanged nearly those exact words with several other clients this week. Now it was Christmas Eve, and he was relieved. That last appointment with Mrs. Richardson had completed his obligation to repay all his debts.

"Just let Nick come. I'm ready for him," Larry thought defiantly as he cleaned his station before leaving. He was spending Christmas Eve with his friends the Ryans. Last Christmas he hadn't been able to give them anything, due to his unfortunate meeting with Nick. He'd apologized to his friends, but they had been entirely unconcerned.

"Larry, your friendship is the best gift you could possibly give us. Now don't be silly and come eat."

However, this year he wouldn't show up empty-handed. He'd shopped early and frugally for them, and had done better than he'd thought he would. He'd found lovely sweaters for Marilyn and Chuck at a close-out store, and had found CDs for Tracy and Stacy there, too.

And, this year he was spending the night with them, and going to sleep before midnight. He didn't want to repeat his encounter with Nick, despite his recent thoughts.

"Merry Christmas, everybody!" Larry cried as they all crowded around the Christmas tree. "I hope you like your presents."

Marilyn and Chuck loved their sweaters, and the twins liked the CDs, which was a relief to Larry. They'd been used to getting much more expensive gifts, and, regardless of their reaction to last year's lack of gifts, he'd been apprehensive that they wouldn't like what he had bought for them.

"Larry, there are a couple of envelopes on the tree with your name on them," Marilyn said, picking the envelopes off a branch.

"Oh, yeah. A couple of my clients gave them to me

yesterday, so I brought them with me to open today." Larry had brought only one envelope with him, but he had an idea where the other one came from.

He opened the unfamiliar one first. It was just a piece of paper with the words "Well done" printed on it. Even though it had no signature, he knew who it was from. He had accomplished the task set by Nick one year earlier. That was a weight off his shoulders.

Then he opened the other envelope. He knew it was from Mr. and Mrs. Smith. Mr. Smith had dropped it by the salon yesterday, but had said not to open it until Christmas Day. Larry pulled out a lovely card. Inside the card was a handwritten note saying "We have a business proposition for you. We know you want to open your own salon, and if we can come to an agreement, we might be willing to finance it for you. Come see us after New Year's."

WHAT COMES AROUND
Susan P. Sinor
Playing With Secrets
Yard Dog Press

It had turned into a bitch of a day.

My supervisor had just informed me, along with the rest of her work group, that weekends would be mandatory for a while; something about reorganizing files due to a new acquisition by the company. It wasn't just that I'd have to work weekends, as-well-as the extra hour a day I'd been putting in for the last month, but I had plans to go out of town for the weekend to visit an old college friend that I would now have to cancel.

And she was so damn smug about it. Oh well, that's Charlene, Queen of Darkness, smugness personified. There are times I'm certain that she has but one mission in life: to prevent me from having one. A life, that is. Who has time? Charlene doesn't care that I'm 32 years old and not only single, but not even involved with anyone? Who has time?

I didn't make it home until 7:30 that evening. I hadn't left the office 'til 6:00. I'd had to call my friend and cancel our plans, and then I had to go by the grocery store. Not that I'm doing much cooking these days, but I still need things. I picked up a burger on the way home – I'm doing a lot of that, lately – and ate while I watched TV. Some things I won't give up, and *Buffy, The Vampire Slayer* is one of them. Fortunately I bought a good VCR a couple of years ago and I use it often. In fact, I have a whole library of shows I've taped to watch later, but haven't – yet. I'm hoping I'll break my arm some time and will have to stay home a few days. Or maybe get something contagious. I'll catch up on my shows then.

Anyway, after I ate and cleaned up the postage stamp-sized kitchen in my three-room closet of an apartment, I got out a box of old childhood stuff I'd brought home from my Mom's. It was either that or have it all sold in a garage sale. Mom wants to sell her house and move who knows where. She recently retired and wants to go crazy. At least that's how I see it. She has a nice income from what Dad left her, plus her own Social Security. I think she should stay at home, play bridge with her friends and grow old gracefully. She refuses to grow old; she says she hasn't got time.

But this isn't my Mom's story; it's about what happened to me.

I was sitting there, cross-legged on my couch when I found myself looking at some of the best parts of my past, old Barbie dolls. There had been four of them, plus a Ken doll. Hey, what's Barbie without her principal squeeze? I absolutely loved those dolls, so much so that, as I took them out of the box I could see that they were kind of ratty looking by now. My oldest Barbie's arms had come off. I found them at the bottom of the box, along with the hair from another and one leg from a third. Our dog had snacked on the other leg, but I couldn't bear to throw the doll away. The fourth was the newest and hadn't fallen apart yet. Ken, on the other hand, had lost his head. Isn't that just like a man? I had to hunt around to find it, inside the remnants of one of Barbie's prom gowns.

That was when the doorbell rang. I wasn't expecting anyone and really was in no mood for company, especially since I'd be going to bed soon. I couldn't ignore it, though, any more than I can leave a ringing phone unanswered.

It was Karen, my down-the-hall neighbor and best friend.

"Wat'cha doin'?" she asked, walking in and plopping into the only comfortable chair I had, which I'd just vacated to let her in. I'd met Karen the day I moved into my apartment ten years earlier, and we'd hit it off immediately. We were each an only child who had desperately wanted a sister growing up. Since our respective parents hadn't supplied us with any siblings, we'd had to find our own.

"Just looking through some old stuff." I sat down on the futon that doubled as a guest bed, or would if I ever had a guest.

Karen rummaged around in the box. "Wow, you've got some great junk here! Is this left over from high school? I've got a box like this at my folks' house. Oh, look, here's Ken's head; where's his body?"

"I had just found that when you came," I replied, holding out a naked quasi-male torso. "Give me that. It's the closest I'll get to a man probably for the rest of my life." It had been a long dry spell for me since my last boyfriend.

"Poor baby! What's the matter, having a bad time at work?

Well, I can fix that. Let's go shopping tomorrow. I need some new clothes."

"That's just it; I can't go anywhere tomorrow except back to work, courtesy of Charlene. We're on mandatory weekends now, indefinitely. I think that means only Saturdays, but I'm not really sure. She couldn't have meant Sundays, too, could she? I guess I'll find out tomorrow." I fell over on the futon, narrowly missing the armrest with my head.

"What a bitch! I wish there was something we could do about it."

"How about more hours in the day, or maybe doing without sleep? Or, I read a story once about a guy going into some kind of fast mode when he wanted to. He could move faster than everybody else and speed through his work while everyone else was on coffee break. Then he could drop back into normal time and take the rest of the day off. Of course, his dead body was found in his apartment a year later. They said he died of natural causes, which wasn't unusual for a man of 90. He was only 35 at the beginning of the story, so I guess that's out."

"Figures," chuckled Karen.

I leaned over and picked up the newest Barbie. "She has more of a life than I do." I looked at her more closely. "Hey, you know what? This doll looks a little like Her Highness Charlene, Queen of the Dark. You met her a couple of times, didn't you? She's not as thin as the doll and her hair's different, but the face looks kind of similar. Here, if we pull the hair back in a bun and pad the body a little..."

I twisted the hair behind the head and looked at it. There was a definite resemblance.

"Do you have any gauze? We'll need some tape, too, if we're going to pad her up right." Karen headed toward the bathroom, an evil grin on her face. "Where are her clothes? Never mind, Jill's got lots of Barbie clothes. She'll never notice if I borrow some."

"I'll be right back." She handed me the gauze and tape she'd found and opened the front door. "It's the kids' weekend at Stupid's...I mean their Dad's. I was hoping we could go out, but this might be even more fun than fishing at Stanley's Chock Full O'Men."

It was not a sad day when Karen had finally dumped her ex-husband, Steve. He'd been domineering and demeaning, when he wasn't ignoring her and the kids completely. But once she divorced him, his mission became to be named "Father of the Year", apparently. In fact, she came fairly close to not getting custody. The judge had been smart enough to realize that Steve's allegations were grossly exaggerated. Karen got full custody and he got limited visitation rights.

I sat there looking at the padded-up doll with the slicked back hair and thought about all the times Charlene had loaded me up with unnecessary work, had taken credit for work that I had done and had belittled me in front of our superiors. I got madder and madder. I felt like throwing the stupid doll down and stomping on it. So I did, almost. My foot was about to come down on its little plastic head when Karen burst back into the room.

"I got some great clothes...hey! What are you doing? Give me that doll! If you break the head it won't look like Charlene anymore and it won't be any good. OK, we'll dress it in this suit. We can safety-pin the clothes on since they don't fit anymore." Karen can work and chatter at the same time. She calls it multitasking. "Now, doesn't she look good? Just like the bitch, herself. Tell you what, get some straight pins and stick 'em in her. That ought to make you feel better."

Karen had an evil gleam in her eyes. I learned a long time ago, when she looks like that you may as well go along with her, because nothing will dissuade her from what is now her supreme goal in life. So I got straight pins from the never-used sewing kit stored under my bed and began to poke them into the newly constructed model of my boss. At first just one or two, but then I got into the swing of things. By the time I finished, my old Barbie bore an amazing resemblance to a pincushion. It occurred to me that I did feel a lot better now.

The two of us had a good laugh about it and I shoved Karen out the door, reminding her that tomorrow was a workday for me, and promising to get together for brunch on Sunday. Unless, of course, I had to work.

After she was gone I took another look at the doll. I swear, the little thing looked like it was in pain.

I wasn't surprised that Charlene wasn't in the office the next day. After all, she had volunteered me and the rest of her peons for Saturday duty, not herself.

Several of the others in my group were already there,

slaving away. It was beyond me, and anyone else, why we had to get all this done so fast. If it was that important, why couldn't we get some temp help 'til it was finished? It wasn't that complicated. Of course, temps would have to be paid, and since we all were on salary, overtime was essentially slave labor. Nobody told us to come in Sunday, so we all voted to stay home and catch up on life.

Sunday morning I called Karen about the brunch I'd promised her.

"Great! And have I got something to show you. I'll be right there."

A few minutes later the door burst open. It was a good thing I'd unlocked it or it might have come off the hinges.

"Nancy, look what I've got. I found some of Jill's old dolls and decided to experiment."

Karen emptied a paper sack onto my dining table. "Here's one that I've made up to look like *my* boss, Marge. I thought I'd try something on it. What do you think?"

"I think we're being ridiculous, that's what I think. Oh, did I tell you that Charlene didn't show up yesterday? Figures."

Karen looked at me strangely. "Hmmm. Do you know why she wasn't there? Was she sick?"

"Don't know and don't care. If *she'd* been there yesterday, *I* might have to be there today. Let's go eat."

The next day Charlene wasn't at work again. She hadn't called in, either, so her boss called her. Seems that she'd been suddenly taken ill Friday night with sharp pains all over her body. She'd taken strong drugs and hadn't even woken up until he called to check on her. She said she felt better and would be in by noon.

When she walked in it was obvious she didn't feel well. Her hair was drab and her eyes were flat. Her skin was pale and she walked slowly, as if it hurt just to move. The few times she spoke it was in monosyllables, like every word hurt.

I told Karen about Charlene that night, and she said, "Serves her right"

I didn't feel right agreeing with her, but I'd bitched about Charlene for so long I couldn't disagree, either.

"Let's try something again. On her; I mean on the doll. To see if it was the pins. You know, to see if sticking the pins in the doll was what made her sick. We could put it in the freezer this time. Maybe she'll come down with pneumonia." Karen was getting that gleam again.

"No! Absolutely not. That's ridiculous; it's stupid. It's – superstitious, that's what it is. We're rational people here, we don't believe in magic. It was just a coincidence. Putting that doll in the freezer won't do anything but maybe damage the doll."

"If you'd cared about those dolls you wouldn't have thrown them in this box and left them at your Mom's all these years. OK, I'll put it in *my* freezer, and I'll put my doll there, too. If Charlene and Marge both come down with pneumonia, then we'll know."

Karen grabbed my Charlene doll and dashed out of my apartment to keep me from protesting again. Actually, I didn't really want to protest. I secretly wanted her to do what she proposed (just to see what would happen), but one of us had to sound rational, after all.

I wasn't really surprised when Charlene appeared to be much better on Tuesday. She was still somewhat subdued, but getting back to normal. When she discovered that we had taken Sunday off, she was furious. She declared, "When I say weekends, I mean BOTH days. You can come in at noon on Sunday, but you'll need to stay until 6:00. Until further notice. Nancy, I'll bet you're to blame for this." We all groaned, but she just glared and went back to her office.

I reported what had happened at work to Karen that night. She said that Marge had been her own evil self, too, so obviously the experiment hadn't worked.

"I'll take them out of my freezer and give your doll back to you," she sighed.

"NO! Leave them in there! I don't care what happens, now. The Queen of Darkness has made me so mad I'm ready to build igloos for them, or at least for mine. I don't want to look for another job, but this is becoming almost unbearable." I ran out of steam then and settled for looking miserable.

Karen smiled and said, "OK. I'll leave them until tomorrow night, but I have to buy food, most of which will be frozen since I don't have time to cook and live at the same time. When I get home, the Eskimos have to leave the North Pole."

I agreed and went home to my cold, narrow bed (which was Queen-sized with an electric blanket).

On Wednesday Charlene was at work, but was sniffling and sneezing. It did my heart good to see that. Of course, I couldn't believe it was due to her doll being in Karen's freezer, but something in me wanted to continue "the experiment." That evening I told Karen that I'd take mine and put it in my freezer.

"Put mine in there, too. Marge seemed to be just fine today. I was hoping that she'd at least be sneezing. I feel kind of achy, though. I guess I could blame it on all the bending and lifting I did today. Filing; I hate it! But no one else will do it, so I guess I could consider it job security. Anyway, stick my doll in there with yours and we'll give it another try."

When both dolls were ensconced in my freezer, behind the ice cube trays and on top of a box of frozen waffles, I fell into bed, exhausted. This schedule was really beginning to get to me.

Thursday Charlene was at work again. She still looked like she felt bad. I had an attack of conscience and was just about to suggest she go to the doctor, when she announced, "Everyone will have to stay late tonight. At least until 8:00. We're behind because nobody came in on Sunday. We'll cut lunch breaks to thirty minutes, too. We've got to catch up, people." Then she glared at me yet again.

My conscience was overpowered by my anger once more. A few strategically placed pins, in addition to life in the freezer, might keep her home the next day. Even if it didn't work, the idea made me feel a lot better.

It must have worked, because Charlene was absent on Friday.

I talked to Karen that night. Her kids, Jill and Scott, were home that weekend, so we sat in her kitchen, drinking coffee (decaf) until midnight. I knew I'd better not take a chance by staying home on Saturday. It would be just my luck that Charlene would be better and decide to be there. Also, her other victims might not take my absence very well. Especially since they had no idea what was going on.

Karen looked at me a minute and then said, "Marge was in today, but she wore a sweater. Nancy, it was at least 75 degrees in the office, maybe warmer. The rest of us had our little desk fans going and Marge was wearing a *sweater!* She kept shivering and sneezing, and this afternoon she called her doctor. She almost cried when they told her she couldn't get in until Monday."

"So, what do you want to do? I could go a few more days before ending this 'experiment'. But if you think we should quit...?" I was running hot and cold on the issue and didn't want to commit. It was sort of scaring me.

"NO! Let's keep going, at least until Monday. I'll see how Marge is and you can find out if Charlene's back. Let's get together Monday night and compare notes. We'll decide then."

I went home and went to bed, not knowing whether to dread or look forward to the next day at work.

Charlene wasn't there on Saturday. And she wasn't there on Sunday, either, although the rest of us were. We all worked feverishly, trying to complete the project that none of us felt was that urgent, but that we wanted finished and done with.

We dragged in on Monday morning to find the message that Charlene had had a heart attack. It had happened Saturday morning at home, and no one had found her until later that morning. The heart attack had been mild. She'd thought it was just stress combined with a little indigestion, so she had just gone to bed. Later her sister, Joanne, who's a nurse, had showed up for a visit and rushed her to the hospital. According to her doctor, she was lucky her sister had found her when she did, although he could find no apparent reason for the attack. No high blood pressure, no artery blockage, no high cholesterol, no anything.

But I knew what had caused it. It was that big silver pin I'd stuck in the doll's chest. I'd poked it in pretty good, but it had fallen out right away when I dropped the doll and I hadn't bothered to stick it back. I'd put Karen's doll in the freezer, but that was all the room I had because I'd been shopping, so I'd put mine in the vegetable bin. That may be what saved Charlene from having pneumonia, too. I left early, pleading a splitting headache, and went home to get the doll out of the fridge and wrap it up in a heating pad (low setting). Boy, was I having my own attack – of conscience.

I called Karen at work.

"We've got to stop. Charlene had a heart attack." Then I told her what I'd done. "I took your doll out of the freezer and wrapped it up with mine in a heating pad. And I'm going to visit Charlene in the hospital. Talk to you tonight."

I really felt awful about what I'd done, at the same time not really believing that I'd had anything to do with what happened. I didn't believe in magic and I wasn't superstitious. However, I wasn't going to take any chances. As much as I didn't like Charlene, I didn't want her hurt, sick or dead. I just wanted her to find another job, maybe in Outer Mongolia, and to go torment someone else. Which gave me an idea. What if I took the doll and sent it somewhere? I had a good friend, Tony, who lived in Kansas City. What if I sent it to him with a request to hold onto it for me? He was the sort of guy who wouldn't ask questions, even about odd behavior like this.

That's what I suggested to Karen that night. I'd gone to the hospital, but Charlene hadn't been in her room. Her sister was there and said something about another round of tests. I asked her sister to tell Charlene I'd been by. Her sister seemed really nice, nothing like Charlene. But then, Charlene might seem nice to someone who didn't work for her.

Anyway, Karen wasn't sure about sending the dolls off. I'd offered to ship off hers with mine. I said my friend wouldn't know, or care, what we were doing. He'd just put them in a closet until I asked for them back.

But Karen wanted to keep hers. "I'm not through with mine. Marge is still being a bitch and I know she'd never leave town. I'm just not ready to stop tormenting her."

"Karen, you don't *really* think all this is anything but a coincidence. Do you? Come on, I admit it's a really strange, even eerie, coincidence, but still only a coincidence. What are you going to do to the doll?"

"Oh, I don't know. But I'll tell you if it works. Hey, if you don't believe it's more than just a coincidence, why get rid of the doll?"

"Just to get rid of temptation; just in case."

She hurried out with her doll, and I swear I could see the wheels turning in her head.

I wrapped my doll and mailed it to Tony with a note the next day. I told him that it was a birthday gift for Karen's daughter, and I just didn't have any place to hide it here because I was doing a lot of babysitting for her and I knew she'd find it. Just a small lie. In fact, it was all true, except for the birthday gift and the babysitting parts. Besides, I'd complained to him more than enough about the size, or lack thereof, of my living space that he'd understand.

I felt much better then, as though I'd reversed everything

that it was just slightly possible that I was responsible for. I was a little concerned about Karen, though. She seemed to be getting a little fanatical. I worried that she'd go off the deep end about Marge and do something dangerous. I wasn't sure what, but I knew she could find something.

Tuesday Charlene called in to say she was much better. Her doctor had held her overnight because he was baffled by her condition. She had gone from what he considered a heart attack (with no apparent cause) to seemingly perfect health in less than a day.

When she had no further symptoms by Tuesday morning he had to release her or she'd have checked herself out. He had made her promise, despite her protests, to stay home and relax the rest of the day.

Wednesday she showed up looking much better than the last time I'd seen her. She was acting different, too. Other times when she'd been out sick, she'd come back in a lousy mood, complaining about all the work that hadn't gotten done while she was out. This time she was nice, which was actually scary.

She actually complimented us for finishing all the extra work faster than she had expected.

"I can't believe how quickly you all got the extra filing done. I thought it would be the end of the month before it was completed. I'm sorry I pushed you so hard, but I really thought it would take that long. I know that all of you have lives away from this office, and I guess I was somewhat jealous. I don't really have anything besides my work."

I felt like raising my hand and saying that I didn't, either, but I couldn't, after her surprising admission. This speech from our nemesis was really confusing. Now we didn't know what to expect. On the way back to our desks we discussed, in hushed tones, the situation.

My next-cube neighbor, Sherry, said, "I don't know what's worse, the evil we know, or the good that might or might not cloak the evil that we know. Does that make sense?"

"Perfectly, and I totally agree," responded my other side cube neighbor, Gary.

Things at work went more smoothly after that, even though we were all waiting for the other shoe to drop. We got to know Charlene a little better, and she turned out to be a fairly nice person after all.

At home, though, thing were getting stranger. It had been a couple of months and Karen had become obsessed with trying to get back at her boss, Marge, for all real or imagined offenses.

I couldn't believe the things she did to that doll. She put it back in her freezer. She had to eat a half-gallon of ice cream to make room, but she was willing to make the sacrifice (OK, I helped). Before it went back into the cooler, she stuck pins in it. She screwed screws into it, turned its head around backward, and even broke one leg and cut off one hand.

Nothing worked. Finally she asked me to try something.

"Nancy, help me. What you did worked, but I can't make anything affect Marge. You must have some power that I don't have. Please! I'm desperate! Take the doll and do something, I don't care what."

"Karen, I didn't make anything happen; it was just a coincidence. I sent my doll away, remember? And Charlene's still here. Which is fine, because she's become a nicer person to work for, now, and I don't want her to leave."

"Pleeease!" Karen looked half crazy, and I was worried about her.

"OK, I'll take it. But don't expect anything to happen. Charlene's problems were just a fluke. I didn't have anything to do with them. And don't ask me any questions. Just tell me if anything happens, which won't."

"Thank you, thank you, thank you! I owe you for this."

"You're damn right you owe me. I'll let you know what it is and when it's due."

I had no idea what to do with the poor doll. If what Karen had done to it hadn't affected Marge, then nothing I could do to it would. I knew if I kept it in my apartment Karen would eventually find it, so I decided to take it with me to work and store it in my desk while I tried to think of something.

A week or so later Charlene asked us all to come into her office. She had an announcement she wanted us all to hear together.

"Everybody, I have wonderful news. I'm getting married. It's the strangest thing. A couple of months ago, after I recovered from that strange episode, I went to Missouri to visit a cousin. We went to Kansas City to see the Hallmark museum and to shop, and I met this wonderful man. He's a friend of my cousin's, so she introduced me to him.

Well, we hit it right off and have been emailing ever since. We even met halfway a couple of times for the weekend. We get along really well, and we're not getting any younger, so we decided to throw caution to the winds and get married. It's going to be just a small family wedding in Kansas City. His parents can't travel and it's important they be able to attend, so... Anyway, I'll be moving there to be with him. This company has an office there, and I've been told I can transfer, so I don't even have to quit. Isn't all this great?"

Everyone was speechless. On the one hand, we were happy for her, but on the other hand we were not happy for us. Everything was going so well now we hated to lose her. If anyone had said, three months ago, we'd feel that way, I would have told them they were dreaming.

We all congratulated her and went back to work.

At home I called my friend in Kansas City to ask for the doll back. If there was any chance of keeping Charlene here, I'd take it. She could bring her fiancé here with her.

"Tony, hi. It's Nancy. I've called to ask for my package back. But first, how are you? What's new?"

"Nancy, you won't believe it, but I'm getting married. It's so strange. Her cousin is a friend of mine. I ran into them when she was visiting Vickie and they came to the Hallmark museum. I got a job there three months ago. Anyway, it was like I already knew her. She just seemed so familiar. Oh, about your package. I'm so sorry, but my dog, Archie, got ahold of it and chewed it to bits. I could barely tell that it had been a Barbie doll. Tell me which one it was and I'll replace it. I feel terrible about it."

Not as terrible as I felt. Now I'd never get Charlene to stay.

"Oh that's OK. Jill decided she doesn't want to play with dolls anymore, so I'll have to get her something else, anyway. So, the confirmed bachelor's getting hitched, finally. Tell me about her."

"She's just wonderful. Her name's Charlene. She happens to work where you do; I just remembered that. She came to visit her cousin Vickie shortly after she'd been sick. In fact, she'd been in the hospital because of a heart attack. Anyway, we're getting married in a couple of weeks, and it will happen here because my parents can't travel. You knew that, didn't you? And she'll transfer to the KC office. That's about all, I guess. Please tell me what I can do to replace the doll Archie chewed up."

I'd have liked to tell him he had to move here, but I couldn't explain the whole awful mess to him. He wouldn't understand. And I knew he'd never leave KC.

"Just be happy. That's all I want. And congratulations; I'll send a gift."

Well, just call me Cupid. Maybe we'd get a good replacement for Charlene. They're not all bad; they can't be.

A week later Charlene made another announcement. "They've hired someone to take over for me. Her name's Marge and she's from outside the company. She says she felt drawn to our company, that she really needed to work here. Her credentials are fine, and I'm sure you'll all make her feel welcome. Tomorrow's my last day. I've got wedding planning and moving to do. I'll miss you, but we all move on sometime."

I'd already told Karen all about losing Charlene, but I hadn't known who would be replacing her and hadn't told Karen the rest of the story. That evening Karen dropped by so excited I could barely stand it.

"It worked! Whatever you did worked. Marge has quit. She got another job. Tomorrow's her last day. It's just like her to wait until today to tell us. She wouldn't tell us where she's going, but who cares. It's somewhere else. What did you do, anyway?"

"I said no questions, remember? Maybe someday I'll tell you, but not today."

"OK. Doesn't matter, anyway, as long as she's somewhere else. Talk to you later."

Sure enough, on Monday Marge walked through the door into Charlene's office and took control. *And it was all my fault.*

That afternoon I got the Marge doll out of the back of my desk drawer, took it home, and shipped it to a rural post office in Alaska, general delivery, with no return address.

One lives in hope.

Location Shoot

Bradley H. Sinor
Playing With Secrets
Yard Dog Press

"So, when are you going to get a 'real' job?"

For some damn reason Maggie had her mother's perennial question flashing through her mind when she stepped in the gopher hole.

All right, so they didn't have gophers on this world. But, it was very definitely a hole; it was very definitely there; it was also very definitely just enough to knock her off balance and send her falling forward, straight into Bambi. Of course, Bambi wasn't that easy to miss, being six-four, dressed in chain mail and leather, and weighing in at around 250 pounds, not to mention the fact that he was standing less than two feet in front of her.

Bambi realized what was happening and managed to twist enough to put his sword to one side, away from Maggie. So when she hit him, it was leather armor and flesh that impacted. Still that was enough to send them both crashing to the ground in a tangle of metal, legs, brush and briars.

"Cut!" yelled the second unit director.

Maggie lay still for a moment, half on top of Bambi, her face buried against his chain mail covered armpit, feeling like a rank amateur. The big mans labored breathing bouncing her head, like it was a child's toy.

When she finally got up on her knees, she saw several people moving toward them.

"We're okay," she said, waving them off.

The words coming out of Bambi's helmet weren't in any language that Maggie knew. The translation spell that allowed the movie company and the natives to understand each other only worked with the local tongue, plus a couple of regional dialects. The big man's words weren't in any of those, but from his tone Maggie had a pretty good idea of exactly what he was saying.

"You are okay, aren't you, Bambi?" she asked.

"Yeah, yeah, I'm fine. Nothing seems to be particularly

damaged, dignity bruised but it will heal," he said, switching to English. "But, I'll tell you this, for certain, if that son-of-a-bitch calls for a retake, I'm going to cut his balls off!"

*"**But Mama! I have a job** and I'm good at it! I'm in show business! You know.....**The Movies!**"*

"Yeah, sure, show business! All you ever do is leap off buildings, jump through windows, get into fights, and crash cars. Is this any way for a well-bred young lady to earn a living? How do I tell the neighbors what you do?"

"Our neighbors know all about what I do!"

"Half the time when you come to see me you've got some new set of bruises or a broken this or that! If I didn't know what you did, I'd think you were into something really kinky. You aren't are you? No wait, I don't want to know."

"Don't worry, mom, nothing kinky."

*"And besides, even if you are in show business, how is anybody going to know that it's you up there on the screen?! They all think its **Miss Silicon Tit Implant!**"*

"That's what being a stunt double is, mom. If people recognized me, then that sort of negates the whole thing. I do have my name in the credits."

"Yeah, but it's always buried so deep in those credits that nobody but the projectionist and I ever see it!"

"At least you know where to look."

"Of course I look, I'm your mother!"

Maggie reached out to help Bambi to his feet. Her hand felt like a toy compared to his huge mitt. At five foot three Maggie tended to be towered over by a lot of the stunt men and women, both locals and company people, but she liked to think she made up for height in other ways.

Of course, Bambi wasn't his real name. Maggie was the one who had dubbed him that, since the House badge on his shield featured a stag that had reminded her of a grown up version of the Disney animated character. Besides, calling him Bambi was easier than his real name, M'Gerna N'cal Hastolka.

The nickname didn't bother him, in fact one night the entire stunt team had staged a special showing of the Disney video just for Bambi's benefit. He had been rolling in the aisles with laughter. So from then on he had been Bambi the Barbarian.

Of course, he had taken pains to explain to everyone that his people were most definitely not barbarians. They were, after all, completely civilized; though if someone really wanted to know about barbarians Bambi assured them he could name a few tribes and races that would fit the bill.

Once on his feet, Bambi moved a bit stiffly, favoring his right leg. This wasn't the first time that Maggie had noticed him walking like that.

"The pike wound still bothering you?" she asked.

"It's nothing," said Bambi.

Maggie didn't believe him. She suspected that it was more likely that Bambi was developing arthritis in that leg. As best Maggie could calculate, the years in this world were somewhat longer than those on earth; Bambi would be in his early forties. He had been a mercenary since he was fourteen; a long time in a profession that was not known for the longevity of its practitioners.

A few years ago Bambi had organized his own mercenary company, The Nightwinds, who were currently in winter quarters fifty miles from the filming location. Bambi had heard rumors about the movie company and decided to come see for himself. It didn't take Maggie long to recruit him for weapons training and stunt work.

"Hey, will you two move! You're right in the middle of my shot," said an assistant director. "I've got to get it now, before we lose the light!"

Bambi gave the man a look of utter disdain.

"Do you think that just maybe this means we're through for the day?" asked Maggie.

"I suspect so. Also, if I remember correctly, it's my turn to buy the first round of ale," said Bambi.

"It's not ale, its beer," she laughed. "But whatever you want to call it, I like the way that you think, sir."

At the time she had gone to the Paragon Pictures production offices, Maggie had only the vaguest idea of what the movie was to be about. She didn't even know what the name of it was. The producer, a little worm named Rudolph Meriweather Carmichael IV, hadn't even been willing to send her a copy of the script, even when she'd offered to sign a standard non-disclosure agreement.

When she walked into Carmichael's office she understood

the reason for the secrecy; didn't necessarily agree with it, but understood it nonetheless. Standing by the window was Ean Findley, the living personification of eccentric director.

As a director, depending on whom you talked to in La La Land, Findley was either a genius or a total raving lunatic, possibly both. His penchant for secrecy on projects was legend. One thing Maggie knew for certain, movies Findley directed, whether they were trash or classics, made money, a lot of money.

"Let me explain to you, Maggie. My movie is going to be something special, unique in the annals of filmmaking. This is going to be a tale of high adventure, of an age undreamed of before history, a story that mixes allegory and fantasy, without losing touch with modern sensibilities," Findley had told her. "For it, I need the services of the best stuntwoman in the business."

"Well, she's busy, so you'll have to settle for me."

"Yes, yes, I like her, Rudolph. She has just the right sense of humor, not to mention the sort of credentials that we will need," Findley said. "Maggie Ferguson is the person that I want in charge of all our stunt work."

"You're the genius, Ean, I won't argue that. It's just my job to juggle the bottom line, and keep the cash flowing," said Rudolph. "Okay, Ferguson, here's the deal. We can give you a crew of fifteen stunt people to work with, nothing more; the budget won't allow for it. Can you be ready to leave for the location in three days? We have a tight, a very tight, transportation schedule and no leeway in it."

Three days? They had to be kidding. Normally Maggie insisted on at least a month to design and prepare all the stunts. She didn't like the feeling this caused in the pit of her stomach.

However, she was free. Her son, Jack, was spending the summer with her Ex at his place in Maine. Plus her bank account was a lot leaner than she liked it, which alone was good motivation to take the job. Yet, she still had the strange feeling it might be better to just get up and walk out of here.

"Three days? That's cutting it a bit tighter than I like, but I don't foresee any problems."

"Good, I'll messenger you over a script tonight." said Rudolph. "Meet us for lunch at the Polo Lounge tomorrow; we'll start discussing the details of just what this movie is going to need along with the budget that you'll have to work with."

"Ah! There you are, Maggie!" Ean Findley came striding across the field toward her at a pace that was just short of running. The director had a tendency, even when he was standing still, to give the impression that he was about ready to run a marathon.

"Hello, Ean. Bambi and I were just heading over to the tavern tent for a drink. Would you care to join us?" asked Maggie.

"No, no, no time. Far too much to do," he said. "Have you looked at the schedule for shooting tomorrow? Remember you're doubling Caitlin in the fight on the tavern roof, and in the fire wall leap."

"I've already inspected the fire wall set up, twice today. I'll do it again tomorrow before we do the shot. With a bit of luck we can get everything in one shot. I don't fancy having to jump into and through that fire wall more than once," she said.

The stunt was really very simple, in theory at least. Maggie would take over for Caitlin as she fought two mercenary soldiers up onto the tavern roof. A fire that was supposed to have started downstairs in the great room would begin to eat its way through the roof.

"One take, yes, that would be wonderful," said Ean. "If I position the cameras right, then that might just be all we would need. But we will do more, if necessary."

"One better be all that is necessary," muttered Maggie.

"I have faith in you Maggie," smiled Ean. "That's why we picked you for this picture. Just one thing, remember this woman that you're playing is more than just a sword swing adventurer. She's the soul of her nation, of her people, fighting the oppression that has held not only her, but her people in bondage for centuries. Think of her as a Jungian prototype image brought to life amidst the shifting chaos that is reality."

"Of course, Ean." Maggie had quickly figured out that sometimes the best route with the eccentric director was to just agree with him.

"Alright, I'll leave it in your capable hands." With that he turned and headed off toward one of the production trailers, muttering under his breath as he went.

Once he was out of ear shot Bambi looked at Maggie and asked, "Did you understand any of that?"

"Not really, but that was just Ean being Ean."

The tavern was actually a huge army surplus tent, erected next to a barn that the company had leased as a scene shop. Looking around at the mixture of movie people and locals, both human and non, it didn't seem any different to Maggie than any other studio commissaries that she had been in over the years.

Maggie grabbed a Diet Pepsi for herself and a can of Coors-Lite for Bambi. It hadn't taken long for the big mercenary to develop a distinct taste for Colorado Kool-Aid.

He snapped the pull-tab off his can and held up the small piece of metal. "This little thing is truly amazing. So simple, so obvious and efficient, yet no one in my world has ever conceived of any such a thing," he said.

"There're a lot of things that I imagine people around here have seen in the last few weeks that no one has ever seen before," said Maggie. She remembered watching a local woman trying to figure out how to use clothespins to hang her wash the first week they had arrived. "There's a fortune waiting for someone who is able to duplicate even a few of these things, when we leave."

"There is indeed," mused Bambi.

Maggie had learned very quickly after meeting him that the mercenary had a sharp eye for business and not just military matters. If there was going to be money made because of their visit, she suspected it would be Bambi who made it.

"Yet it still makes me wonder how a world that could produce such wonders as these can also produce such a...a, what is the word that I heard you using to describe him? Oh yes, a jerk, like Rudolph Merewether Carmichael." Bambi stretched out the producers name for emphasis.

"The Fourth," Maggie reminded him. "We mustn't forget that part of his name. Proper names are very important, to self-important twits like him."

Bambi nodded, smiling. "Oh, yes Rudolph Merewether Carmichael the Fourth," he said. "Dear, dear Rudy." The producer hated the shortening of his name, and was quite vehement about the point. So naturally, everyone took every opportunity to use it.

"I can understand when Ean does something strange; it's usually for the sake of his art, " said Maggie. "Rudy, on the other hand, just manages to irritate people by trying to act like he knows things that there is no way he can know."

"Did you know that yesterday he tried to tell me the proper way to use a short spear?"

"Whoops," giggled Maggie. "I do hope you offered to demonstrate the working end of the spear, on him."

"Naturally," laughed Bambi.

A three a.m. call was not all that unusual for Maggie. She had done more than her share of them, and a lot of other improbable things in the dozen years since she came to Hollywood. At least there weren't any costumes or makeup calls to deal with. Plus, and most importantly, there was plenty of coffee.

Once at the studio they had directed her to a gray van, part of a long convoy of trucks, R.V.'s, and buses that were supposed to head off for wherever the first location was supposed to be; Ian and Rudy had been very vague about details like that.

Things got even stranger when the signal came to start the cars. Instead of heading off, they were directed to form up in a big circle in the studio parking lot.

"Are we, maybe, expecting an attack by Indians or something? Or is this some scene that Ean wants in the movie?" Maggie asked the driver of the van she was riding in.

"Lady, I don't have the slightest idea. It's not even something that I need to know. I just do what they tell me, drive here, and drive there. As long as the check clears it beats long haul trucking all to hell. When I got here tonight they just told everyone to do this and make sure no one gets out," he said. Maggie made a pillow of her windbreaker and tried to sleep, but failed.

So they waited, for nearly an hour.

No one else in the van, or the other vehicles, seemed to know anything beyond that. Later a few restless people got out and began to prowl around the parking lot. One of a dozen security guards, using a bullhorn, directed them back to their vehicles.

Under the light of the full moon, a limo followed by a black '64 Thunderbird pulled in and drove to the center of the circle. Maggie watched as Ean and Rudolph got out of the limo, followed by two other people that she recognized immediately;

Caitlin de Vres and her husband, Joseph Alexander Ellison.

"Oh great, prima donna city," Maggie said, under her breath.

In the space of less than ten years the two of them had become the reigning couple in Hollywood. It seemed like no picture either or both of them appeared in finished anywhere but number one at the box office. Joseph was reported to be one of the nicest people in the business. Caitlin, on the other hand, was an egotistical bitch who seemed to take great joy in abusing the people she worked with. She couldn't conceive of anyone more talented than herself.

But it wasn't the two actors that held Maggie's attention.

A fat man wearing a full-length robe and carrying a carpetbag embroidered with astrological symbols got out of the Thunderbird. He stood for a long time just staring at the various vehicles. Then, without speaking to anyone else the man rummaged in his bag and took several instruments out. He carefully paced off distances and placed the items at various points around the caravan.

That whole procedure went on for about ten minutes. Once the man in the robe seemed satisfied, he produced a large brush along with what looked like a paint can and began to draw a number of symbols on the ground. Maggie leaned out the window and stared at the one he inscribed near her van. It seemed to be some kind of notched triangle.

Finally the fat man pulled a propeller beanie from inside the carpetbag, placed it on his head and began to chant. Whatever it was he was saying, the whole thing sounded like gibberish to Maggie.

Maybe she should have taken that job in real estate that mom had kept harping about, but even there you get your own set of whackos . This guy seemsed harmless enough, she hoped.

Then it happened.

Later she wasn't sure how to describe it, but that was the moment that, for Maggie, the world was awash in colors and spinning shapes, everything around her, the people, the cars, the air itself, glowed, twisted and changed. Blackness wrapped itself around Maggie.

When she woke up the first thing she noticed was the pounding inside her head. Maggie had had the occasional hangover, most of them well deserved, but what she felt right then made any of its predecessors feel like nothing. Eventually she decided there was nothing else to do but open her eyes.

It was still night, but the sky had an odd coloring and two moons hung there. That they were no longer sitting in a parking lot at Paragon studios in Burbank, California was pretty obvious. Now the entire convoy, every R.V, truck, van, car and bus was parked in a huge field with only some farm house-looking buildings anywhere to be seen.

Near the limos Ean was in deep conversation with a man dressed in chain mail and a cape. Caitlin and Joseph were leaning against the limo. Of the Thunderbird and the man in the propeller beanie, there was no sign.

"I suppose it beats the freeway, at rush hour," she said.

With her fiery red hair and supermodel figure, Caitlin de Vres resembled some of the Irish heroines of legend. At least that was what was in all of her press releases; every word of which, Maggie was certain, Caitlin believed.

When she came into the tavern tent she was wearing the chain mail bikini, knee high boots and sword that comprised her character's principal costume. There were some others, mostly made of gauze, bits of metal and leather, none of which covered more of Caitlin than the one she currently wore.

Maggie had always suspected that Caitlin had a large streak of exhibitionism in her and just generally enjoyed shocking people by prancing around in next to nothing. Two Playboy layouts, not to mention the covers, had certainly helped cement that idea. Maggie had also seen the gown that Caitlin had worn to the Oscars last year. Maggie owned swimsuits that had more material than that dress.

As Caitlin's stunt double, Maggie had identical costumes to Caitlin's hanging in her tent. She was none too fond of the one Caitlin had on just now. In spite of the lining inside the bra and panties portion, the metal rings had a tendency to push through and pinch, usually at the most inopportune times and in the most inappropriate places.

"Maggie, darling, I should have expected to find you around Bambi," said Caitlin, her voice was just dripping with friendliness. "You really should give the rest of us a chance at him."

"I'm surprised that you're even here today, Caitlin. I figured that since you and Joseph had the day off you would be taking it easy," she said.

Caitlin laughed and got a dreamy smile on her face. "Oh, we had planned on a nice little private picnic today, at that wonderful waterfall about fifteen miles or so from here. The local mayor told me about it. Joseph and I went out there briefly last week. It was fantastic."

"Oh, I know that place," said Bambi. "Very private, perfect for ..."

"That's exactly the sort of thing we had in mind, dear boy. Wine, cheese and some assorted things were all packed. As a matter of a fact we were supposed to have the next couple of days off. We'd planned a little camping expedition, just us beneath the stars for seventy-two wonderful hours.

"But then our adored director took it in his pointy little head that there were some scenes with Joseph that had to be shot now; ones that weren't even on the schedule for a week! I was fit to be tied and Joseph certainly wasn't happy. I had to physically restrain him from going after Ean with a horsewhip.

"Knowing our dear director, he'll call for forty or fifty retakes of each one of the new shots. Which means, if I'm lucky, I may see my darling Joseph around midnight. Then Rudolph, that little worm, decided that *I* should have some more publicity shots taken. So I had to put this outfit on and go shake my tush in front of some pointy eared photographer who looked like a reject from a Star Trek convention," said Caitlin.

"I'm sure Joseph will make it up to you, and with great enthusiasm," said Bambi.

"Oh, you better believe he will, dear boy," she said with mock fierceness. If there was one thing that overrode everything else about Caitlin, it was her love and devotion for Joseph. "But since Joseph won't be back till late, and I didn't feel like just sitting around reading a book, I'm having a few of the other girls over to my trailer. We can kill a couple of bottles of wine, gossip and just have a great time. Why don't you join us, Maggie?"

"I wonder if they're all as thrilled at that prospect as I am," thought Maggie. "I'll try,'" she said. "I've got several props being built that we need for tomorrow's shot. I want to make sure they will be ready. It's the tavern shot and the fire wall leap."

"Oh, yes. I have to admit that scares me. But that's our

Maggie; always there to make sure everything works right. I know it will work and you'll make me look fantastic. So, I'll expect you about eightish!"

"Of course," Maggie sighed, sagging back in her chair, accepting the fact that she couldn't get out of it.

Caitlin hadn't gone more than five feet from the table before Maggie reached over, took Bambi's beer and finished it in two swallows.

Bambi, wisely, said nothing.

The few R.V.'s that were being used for living quarters had been parceled out among Joseph and Caitlin, Ean and Rudolph. As chief stuntwoman, Maggie was entitled to a private tent, but she had opted to share space with two of her friends, Jenny Carshaw, a sound mixer and Sherry Hartley, a costume designer. The three of them had worked on a number of other projects together, enjoyed each other's company, and were quite tolerant of the others' crazy schedules.

Thankfully, this afternoon both Sherry and Jenny were out and if Maggie remembered the schedule correctly would be until well after sundown. That suited Maggie just fine; right now she wasn't in the mood for company, no matter how congenial and understanding.

Dropping a CD of Mozart's fourth concerto into her Walkman, Maggie fitted the headphones over her ears, turned the volume up until music was all she could hear, slipped out of her jeans and boots and just stretched out on her cot. The music washed over her, letting her push everything else away.

A century or so later the music was suddenly drowned out by the most horrendous sound. Maggie thought for a moment that there might be something wrong with the player, but when she punched the off button the sound continued, this time coming from outside her tent.

It was a scream. She dropped the Walkman and sprinted through the tent doorway to see what was going on.

The camp was in chaos. There were people running in several directions at once, screams coming from all over the camp and the sound of crashing wood and metal everywhere.

"What the hell," said Maggie, though there was no one standing anywhere close to answer her.

That was when she saw the dragon. Maybe twenty feet long and eight or nine feet high, it seemed to fill the sky.

Greenish silver scales glistened in the afternoon sun as its roar echoed everywhere.

One of her stunt people ran past Maggie and yelled, "Come on! The damn beast knocked one of the camera towers down. Jim Hanson is trapped underneath."

The camera tower was actually an old windmill that Ean had converted to the company's use. From there the camera was able to cover several different sets that had been erected.

As they got closer, it was obvious that the windmill's days as a camera tower were ended since all that remained was kindling of various sizes.

It turned out that Hanson wasn't trapped under that pile of wreckage. If he had been, he would have been deader than vaudeville, someone observed. He had been able to leap free and seemed to have come away with only a badly sprained ankle.

"You'd still better have the Doc check you out," Maggie told him, as she examined his ankle. "I think you're going to be okay, Jim. You know if you could do that kind of fall on a regular basis, I could use an extra hand on some of the stunts."

"No thanks, Maggie. I'm crazy sometimes, but you guys make me seem stone cold sane," he said.

"That's part of the reason you love us so much."

"Hey, it's leaving!"

The dragon twisted in the air and sailed off toward the south.

"Thank God that's over," said Hanson. Around them people were staring at the sky and at the havoc the beast was leaving in its wake.

Maggie wasn't so sure it was over. She couldn't be a hundred per-cent certain at this distance, but she thought she had seen somebody gripped in the dragon's claws. From here it sure looked like that somebody was none other than their lead actor, Joseph Alexander Ellison, his ownself.

*"**Maggie! I need to see** you,* right away!" Rudolph's voice always seemed to hit the highest notes when he was either angry or scared. There was a pool going around among the crew to see who could get him to hit that high note the most number of times before the production wrapped.

"Yes, Rudy," she said.

"You've got to stop her!" His face flushed red with every

word.

"Stop who? Did one of your ex-wives manage to follow us over here?"

"No! Caitlin, of course, who do you think I'm talking about!" said Rudolph. "Look around you. Look at the place! This is a major disaster of epic proportions. The camp is in ruins. Half the equipment has been trashed! Our leading man has been carried off by some flying lizard. Now my leading lady has just announced that she is going to go off to play Xena, Warrior Princess and rescue him. This picture is ruined!"

"Rudy, you're the one who is always saying that you're in charge. I think this falls under your job description, not mine. So why don't you go and tell Caitlin that you will go rescue Joseph? That way she can stay here and finish the picture."

"Like she would really listen to me? When I tried to tell her she couldn't go she turned her back on me and started muttering something about ripping my lungs out through my ears," said Rudolph.

Now that sounded like something that Caitlin would say. Of course, Maggie might have suggested amputating a somewhat different portion of Rudy's anatomy, and through a different aperture.

"You've got to convince her to stay. Ean is sulking in his RV, but he says he thinks that we can still salvage the picture. It can be a final tribute to Joseph. His last, greatest work! This will be the movie they will remember him by!"

"You make it sound like he's dead," said Bambi, who had come walking up just a moment before. The mercenary's left arm was in a sling. He leaned on a make shift crutch, favoring his bad leg. Maggie cast a quizzical look at him.

"Tripped over one of the script girls during the attack. But getting back to the dragon, I would say it's very likely that Joseph is alive and healthy, for the time being at least. The stories I've heard about dragons is that they like to collect their food, keep it alive, at least for a while, play with it and then eat it raw," Bambi said.

"Thank you for sharing that wonderful bit of culinary information with us," said the producer.

"Seems Caitlin is determined to go and try to rescue Joseph," Maggie told Bambi.

"You two will have to move fast. Dragons can fly a long way very quickly," said Bambi.

"Two?" said Maggie.

"I'd go with her, myself, but not with this arm," said Bambi. "Look, you can handle yourself and are able to think on your feet. Those are skills that Caitlin may not have in abundance."

"Yes, yes. If you can't talk her out of it, go with her, bring her back here alive," said Rudolph.

Maggie had worked in Hollywood long enough to know when an advantage presented itself.

"All right, Rudy, it's a deal. But only on my terms."

"Terms? What terms? We don't have time to be bickering about terms! You have to go with Caitlin!"

"I told you I would do it. But, I'm only going to do it on my terms. You see, my fee for this little escapade is going to be that you have to produce my script," she said.

"A script! A script! Why is it that everyone in Hollywood has a script!?" shouted Rudolph.

"Maybe it's something in the water," said Bambi.

"All right, all right. You've got me over a barrel. When we get back I'll look over your script."

"No, you'll do more than just look it over. I want you to agree, right here and now, to green light my project for production. We can discuss the budget later. It's either that or you borrow one of Bambi's chain mail shirts and go with Caitlin yourself," she said.

"He agrees," said Bambi, laying his hand on the producer's shoulder. "Don't you Rudy?"

"Yeah, yeah I agree," he sighed, what little color was left in his face drained away.

"I knew you would see it my way," said Maggie.

"Now where the hell is it?" Caitlin was pawing through the things in a closet at one end of the RV. Maggie had knocked, but when her third attempt went unanswered, she just walked in.

After a minute or two Caitlin took a black leather whip from inside the closet, pausing to shake a couple of loose socks out of its coils. Maggie considered for a moment asking why she and Joseph had a bullwhip in their closet, but then thought better of it. That sort of discretion was something she had learned soon after arriving in Hollywood.

"You really think you're going to need that?"

"You never know," Caitlin said. "I suppose that sniveling

little worm Rudy sent you here to try and talk me out of going. Don't even bother wasting your breath."

"Fine, I won't. But I wasn't intending on stopping you. I just wanted to let you know that I would be going with you."

Caitlin looked at her for a moment. This was definitely not the Caitlin de Vres that Maggie, and the rest of Hollywood knew. The 'star' egotist was gone, replaced by a different woman, a very determined woman, looking out from the familiar green eyes.

"Like hell you will! I know what's really going on. You just want me to forget the whole thing so that Ean can get his damn picture finished. Well, you can go back and tell him that I don't give a flying fig about finishing the picture. I don't care if they blackball me back in La La Land. I'm going after Joseph," said Caitlin.

To emphasize her words, Caitlin flipped her wrist out and cracked the whip across the trailer's length, expertly tearing into the pillow just to Maggie's right.

"Not bad, you've got good control with it," said Maggie. "Look, Caitlin, for one thing it wasn't Ean, it was Rudy who sent me. You can yell and scream all you want, but it's not going to do you any good. I'm going along, that's a fact so live with it. The longer we stand here arguing about it, the further away that dragon is going to carry Joseph. So, whether you like it or not, I'm going with you and there isn't a damn thing that you can do about it," she said.

"I want to leave immediately."

"No problem. By the way, you are going to change clothes, aren't you?" Caitlin was still wearing the chain-mail bikini. The actress didn't say anything, just gestured over to the couch where breeches, boots, a work shirt and an assortment of weapons lay. Maggie made a mental note to see just how good she might be with them.

"Glad we could have this little talk."

"I was afraid of this," said Caitlin as she stared through the binoculars.

In the last five days the two women had ridden hard, stopping only to sleep for the briefest of periods, as they headed for a mountain range that Maggie estimated was sixty or seventy miles from the company's campsite. All along, Caitlin seemed to know exactly where they were going. That part bothered Maggie. But she decided it would be better to wait for the other woman to explain things

"Afraid of what?" asked Maggie.

"That." Caitlin passed the stuntwoman her binoculars and pointed toward a place above the tree line, maybe a hundred yards away. There sat Joseph, apparently unharmed, seemingly all by himself, only the chains around his wrists keeping him from getting up and walking way. As pretty a picture as any rescuer could want to find. It virtually screamed trap.

"You may be right. When it looks too good to be true, it probably is. So this is obviously an ambush," said Maggie.

"Oh it's an ambush. There is no doubt about that, and Joseph is the bait. Look to the left and about twenty yards up into the rocks."

It took Maggie a moment to find the place that Caitlin had indicated. The dragon was not hiding, but had wound itself among a number of rocks and boulders.

"Looks like he's waiting for someone."

"I know this lizard, that's exactly what he's doing." said Caitlin.

"You know him?"

"Yes, I do. His name is Halymer. He's waiting for me," said Caitlin.

"You?"

"Good morning, Joseph!"

Maggie had waited to speak until she was close to Joseph. His face showed the shock of seeing her. He twisted around to look up toward the rocks. The dragon sat silently, watching them both.

"Hello, Maggie. I must say I didn't expect to see you here. I hope you know what you're doing and maybe brought some help," he said.

"No, just little old me. You don't think Ean would turn loose of enough people to make a decent-size posse, do you?"

"Caitlin didn't come with you?"

"Nope. No way would Ean or that spineless shit Rudy let her go. You know the show must go on and all that. Rudy said that they were going to make this picture *your final movie*, a tribute to you," she said.

"Oh, how nice of them. I suppose they even have the

acceptance speech written for my posthumous Golden Globe award."

"Not to mention your posthumous Oscar as well."

The dragon rose up on its hind legs and roared.

Maggie looked up at him and shook her head. "Would you knock it off! We're trying to have a conversation, if you don't mind," she said. "Has he been this noisy and obnoxious since he brought you here?"

"'fraid so," said Joseph.

The dragon roared a second time.

"Look, I know you can talk. So stop acting like a wanna be Rudolph Merewether Carmichael the Fourth. One of him is enough!"

"Where is she!" The dragon's words were gravely and loud, echoing off the rocks around them.

"You remembered how to talk. That's better. Now maybe we can talk like two civilized creatures. Let's start with names. Mine is Mary Margaret Ferguson," said Maggie.

"I am Halymer! I am your death, if you don't tell me where she is! Is she a coward to ignore my challenge!"

"Oh come on," said Maggie. "Here we had such a nice relationship started and you go off on this macho bullcrap. What's next, you and Joseph going off to beat drums together?"

That was when Caitlin appeared on the rocks above the dragon. She waited only a moment and then launched herself from her perch, crashing down onto the dragon's neck.

Halymer began to twist from side to side, trying to throw her off. However, she seemed to have gotten a good grip, straddling his neck. A few seconds later the bullwhip flashed over the beast's face. It struck several times, cutting into the leathery flesh.

"Stop it now! Stop acting like a spoiled brat!"

The sound of Caitlin's voice enraged the dragon even further. He began to buck, attempting to throw her off. His tail struck the boulders around him hard enough to shower the area in a rain of pebbles.

"I said to stop it!" shouted Caitlin. "Stop it now or I'll have to tell Mom and Dad not only about this, but about that stunt you pulled on Aunt G'may!"

"You wouldn't dare!" The dragon stopped in its tracks, shoulders arched, the only thing moving was the tip of his tail slowly twitching.

"Think so? You just try me."

"I'm going to assume that you have one hell of a lot of questions," said Caitlin.

"You could say that," said Maggie. "It looks like you were right when you said I wouldn't need my sword."

"Well, I couldn't let you go trying to play St. George and kill him. After all, as much of a pain in the tail as he is, he is still my little brother," said Caitlin.

Maggie, Caitlin and Joseph were seated near the edge of a stream. As soon as the confrontation with Halymer was over, others, both dragons and humans, appeared from the rocks. The younger dragon had snorted and then flown off to sulk on the side of a hill in the distance.

Food was brought out; plates of vegetables, a meat dish and mugs of warm beer. Several dozen other people were scattered around the landscape, some eating, others were talking, a few walking back and forth attending to various chores. Nearly a dozen dragons of sizes varying from ten or so feet to nearly thirty were dispersed over the side of the hill, some watching what was going on, others just sitting in the sun.

One thing that Maggie did notice was that several of the people walking near them resembled each other and more than a few had striking resemblance to Caitlin. This definitely had the signs of being a family picnic

"Okay, let's cut to the point. Caitlin, what the hell are you?

"I suppose you could call me a were-human. Dragons are able to take human form for a period of time. It's just another form of camouflage," said Caitlin. "I was born a dragon; my birth name is S'lina. About a dozen years ago, because of a head injury I sustained then, I was locked into human form. Not even our most powerful magi could find a way to let me take dragon shape again. Needless to say I was not happy."

"That's where I entered the picture," Joseph said. "Before you ask, I'm completely human. Plus, I come from the world that you and I both call home. The wizard who sent us here is my brother-in-law; a third rate magician and a fourth rate klutz. What my sister sees in him I will never know. About ten years ago one of his spells went wrong and he accidentally kicked us in this world. It took him quite a while to figure out how to get us back. But by that time I had met Caitlin, we fell in love, and she came back with me," said Joseph.

"It turned out that I had a flair for acting. With Joseph's help I manufactured an identity and the career along with it. The egotistical bitch goddess routine was just to keep people from suspecting that I was different.

"And it worked. Then about six months ago, just right after we had signed to costar in this picture, we got an invitation from my parents to attend a massive family reunion and celebration of their golden wedding flight anniversary," said Caitlin. She picked up a knife and cut into a melon and passed a piece to her husband.

"Problem was, we were committed to this picture. The contract was iron clad. Luckily, I was able to convince Ean that if he filmed in a true fantasy world, a world that magic worked in, it would add just that special touch to the picture. He fell for it hook, line and sinker," said Joseph. "By this time my brother-in-law had perfected the transportation spell, along with a number of other ones. I made sure he got the contract."

"I'm sure you made Ean think it was his idea."

"He never suspected a thing. According to the original shooting schedule we were supposed to have four days without any scenes at all. The plan was that we were going to go off on a camping trip. My cousin S'gan would pick us up and fly us to and from the reunion. Then that idiot Ean got some 'wonderful new concepts for the film' and started changing the schedule and out of the blue my little brother shows up," said Caitlin.

"Yeah, why did he do it?"

"Who can know for sure? Adolescent rebellion? A need to show off in front of his friends by beating up on his big sister? He's really a good kid at heart. The family couldn't interfere in an official challenge between siblings. It was up to me to show him who's the boss," said Caitlin.

"Would he have hurt Joseph?" asked Maggie.

On that she could see Caitlin hesitate. "I'm not sure. He's a kid, kind of the equivalent of a wanna-be human juvenile delinquent. You know how unpredictable they can be. Let's just be glad it didn't come to it."

"So what are we going to do about this? We certainly don't want Ean to know the truth about Caitlin," said Maggie.

"That will bear some thinking about," Caitlin nodded. "But

I think I have something in mind."

"We're running out of time, Ean," said Rudolph Merewether Carmichael.

Rudolph had found the eccentric director in the editing tent at the far end of their camp, his face only inches above the screen of a movieola. Every minute or so he would pull another frame through the viewer.

"According to the schedule, we've only got two more scenes before the Caitlin and Joseph stuff has to be filmed. After that, everybody is going to be sitting around on their duffs twiddling their collective thumbs," said Rudolph.

Shouting from outside the tent interrupted anything that Ean was about to say.

One of the assistant film editors stepped into the tent. "It's the dragon, coming back!" the man said.

"Are we being attacked again?" asked Rudolph.

"No! Maggie, Caitlin and Joseph are all three riding it."

Ean pushed his coffee cup toward Rudolph. "Be a good fellow and get me a refill, please."

"She was trying to what?"

"I think I said it clearly enough the first time, Rudy. S'gan was trying to audition, just like any other actress. Maybe it wasn't your ordinary cattle call, but you have to admit she did make an impression," Maggie said.

Rudolph stared at the dragon; luckily no one had noticed the slight difference in coloring between S'gan and Halymer. Maggie was fairly sure she heard the producer say something about S'gan looking hungry and wanting to know why she kept staring at him.

"You think it would be a good idea to hire her?" asked the producer.

"As a matter of fact, it would. She protected Joseph, got us back here in a couple of hours, where we would have taken a week if we had walked, and seems to have a good bit of acting talent as well," said Maggie.

"She's an actress? But...but...how can we negotiate a contract with something that doesn't even talk? Even if we could, she couldn't sign it, no hands," said Rudolph.

"Just wait." Maggie turned toward S'gan and nodded. The

dragon roared loudly. The sound was enough to send shivers through everyone on the set. Then S'gan stretched her wings wide, raised up on her hind legs and then vanished.

In the dragon's place was a woman.

Now that's making an entrance, Maggie said to herself.

This newcomer was tall and striking. Her face was sharp angles and lines. Hair the color of rust hung down below her waist. There was no doubt that this was the same being, even though the forms were utterly different, every movement, every nuance was the same.

"Rudy, m'boy, this is Ms. S'gan."

"What just happened?"

"Oh, did I forget to mention that dragons are perfectly capable of shape-shifting into human form?" asked Maggie.

Ean was standing off to one side of the small group. When he saw S'gan he stood just staring at her. Maggie knew the expression on the director's face.

"Yes, you will work perfectly. I already see ways to integrate you into the remaining scenes," he said. "In fact, your very presence changes my whole concept of the true subtext in this story. This is going to make my movie a mega-hit. Please come along with me and we can talk about it."

"Hold it right there," said Maggie. "We had an agreement and I fulfilled my end."

"Maggie, baby," said Rudy. "You're exhausted. You need to rest. Take some time off. Let's put that project on the backburner until this production is done. Once we're back in our world, call my office and we'll take a meeting over your script."

"Look, you SOB! You gave me your word!" she said. Maggie's hand settled onto her sword pommel, fingers slowly tightening around it. Several of the people around her noticed and began to move away. Bambi shifted to one side, not to join in but to keep anyone from interfering.

"I'm afraid it will just have to wait. Then we will see if we can come to an agreement on your project," said Rudolph, putting on his full executive mode. He began to stroke his chin; as if he were trying to consider what ways he could completely turn this situation to his advantage.

"I don't think it will wait, Mr....Rudy was it? I believe that you did give your word to Maggie that you would, what is the phrase, 'green light' her project for production. Among my people keeping one's word is a matter of life and death.

"I feel that if you don't keep your word to her, then I'm not sure I can trust you to keep any agreement that we make." S'gan's voice was soft and sexy, while her expression had that same hungry look that had made the producer nervous.

"Rudolph! I must have her, if I am to be expected to finish this film and to make it the masterpiece that it was always meant to be," said Ean.

"She's just trying to save you from yourself," said Caitlin. "After all, you are a man of your word. Everyone in Hollywood knows that."

"Yeah, but who's going to save me from her? She looks hungry," said Rudolph.

"Trust me, Rudy, I'll save you," said Maggie.

"Besides," said S'gan. "It is doubly to my advantage for you to keep your promise to Maggie. I will know that your word is good on any agreement we make. Plus I will also be getting 15% of what Maggie receives."

The color ran out of the producer's face at S'gan's words. "Fifteen percent? That sounds an awful lot like you're....you're....her ...."

"Agent," said Maggie. "Besides being an actress, and we're going to train her as a stunt woman, S'gan will be working as an agent. I'm her first client."

"Hmmm......An agent who looks like a supermodel, acts, has brains and isn't afraid to breath fire when necessary," said Joseph. "I think she will fit right into Tinsel Town with no problem at all."

"I'm not sure if Hollywood is ready for this," said Caitlin.

"Then it better get ready," Maggie and S'gan said in unison. Bambi was standing to one side, struggling to keep from laughing.

"Maggie, you're good, very good. Are you sure you won't stay here and join The Nightwinds?"

"What, and give up show business!"

Mama Says

Sue Sinor
Small Bites
Coscom Entertainment

"Now children, when you play in the yard, be sure to watch out for dangerous animals. Always stay together and don't go far from the house." Mama always said the same thing every time we went out to play. I didn't believe her; I'd never seen a dangerous animal around here. My brother, Sam, said he thought he'd seen one, once, but he ran in so fast it must not have seen him and went away.

"And if you do see one, run in the house and tell me and I'll scare it away."

"Yes, Mama, we will," we all chorused as we ran out into the yard to play hide and seek.

Sam and my sister, Sasha, went off to hide while I hid my eyes and counted. I could only count to ten, so I counted real slow to give them enough time to hide. Then I turned around and called, "Ready or not, here I come!" That's what you say to let them know you're coming to look for them, so they'd better be ready. I knew where they'd probably be; they always hide behind the big rock next to the front door. Most of the time, I just go over to it and tag whichever one I can get to first. But today I decided to take my time finding them. That meant they'd have to be quiet longer, and they always have a hard time being quiet.

I started looking by going to a big tree around the side of the house. I called their names and looked up into the branches, though they'd never be able to climb the tree. Then I went to a big rock around the other side of the house, but I knew they weren't there, either.

There are a lot of big trees and rocks around our home. That's because we live in the woods. It's usually pretty peaceful here in the woods, but Mama says that sometimes big, dangerous animals come around and try to kill us. I don't know why they'd want to kill us; we don't try to hurt them. But anyway, that's why Mama always tells us to be careful when we go outside.

I'd gone behind that rock and was about to head over to where they were when I saw the animal. And I saw that it saw Sam and Sasha. It was standing up on its hind legs, and was holding a long stick in a front paw. I was afraid it was going to run up and hit them, so I hollered, "Stop!" and ran over to it. That brought Mama out and she yelled at it, too. That must have scared the animal, 'cause it took off running on its hind legs.

"That was a brave thing you did, Sally," said Mama. If you hadn't yelled at it, it might have shot at Sam and Sasha. See, I told you humans are dangerous animals. Now don't you forget it."

Bob

Sue Sinor
Small Bites
Coscom Entertainment

Zombies have an advantage over vampires. Even if one is killed, they're pretty easy to make. They can be out in the sun and they take orders really well, which is why I had them guarding my bedroom. More accurately, it's the crypt that houses my coffin.

Zombies are quiet and they stay out of sight unless someone attacks my home. Then they have permission to go after the attackers' brains. This means they're pretty well-fed, since I'm attacked almost every night.

After all, I'm famous! Haven't you heard of me? In case you're wondering, my name is Francine, Cajun Voodoo Queen. I'm the only vampire known to be in existence. *Of course* everyone wants to get famous by killing me.

There is one zombie that's been with me for a long time, relatively speaking. Bob. I picked him up about five minutes after he was killed; run over in a dark alley by a speeding car which was being pursued by the police after a bank robbery. Bob had the bad luck to be in the wrong place at the wrong time, got hit, and was thrown against the brick wall of the building next to the alley.

I was watching from a fire escape, scouting for dinner, and saw it all. The bank robbers, of course, didn't stop, and the police weren't going to let the bad guys get away just to see to some guy who was surely dead anyway. (That's cops for you.)

They did call an ambulance, though, but Bob was already on his way back to my crypt by the time it got there.

I learned long ago how to make zombies. The best ones were fresh, and this was the freshest I ever saw.

I rifled his wallet and found, besides his driver's license, a membership card to a local gym. He looked like he went there every day. Big muscles are something I appreciate very much.

I got vamped when I let my guard down once in the 19th century, but I don't mind too much. After all, I'm 148 years old and don't look a day over 22. And I can still make zombies with the best of them.

There's a possibility that Bob might not have been completely dead when I zombied him, 'cause all his *really* important parts still work. That's why I take such good care of him. He guards my coffin while the others patrol outside.

And sometimes he guards it from the *inside*.

Gag

Brad Sinor
Small Bites
Coscom Entertainment

Shifting hurt, but Halin had long ago learned how to push the pain into a distant corner of his mind, letting the changes come as quickly as possible.

Ten feet below, on the far side of the room, he could see Paige on the floor, covered in wreckage from the wall. The fire was all around her, traveling up walls and curtains in waves of orange and red and blue.

The fire was close, closer than he liked. Halin ripped off his plaid work shirt, revealing the full pelt of fur that covered his chest and arms. He could have taken full wolf form, but he would need his hands to get her free, so it was a humanoid "wolfman" who flung himself downwards, between two flame engulfed posts, toward the floor where he landed in a crouch near the girl.

Once she was free, he clutched the unmoving girl tightly to his chest and looked for a way out through the flames that roared around them.

"You smell like roasted dog!" she screamed, and began to twist out of his grip.

Halin fought to hold her for a moment, then let her fall to the floor.

"Cut!"

Figures scrambled out of the darkness, maneuvering around cameras, fire extinguishers in hand. The flames were a thing of the past in minutes.

Halin looked up to see Ean Findley, one of the most eccentric directors in all of Hollywood, come walking toward him, shouting, "What the hell just happened?"

Paige stood up and turned toward Ean. "You didn't tell me that "he" would be smelling like a moldy roasted rug!"

The director said something to Halin, but the lycanthrope did not hear him. After snarling at him and making a grab at the director's leg, he reached within himself, allowing the human part of himself to reassert itself.

A quick glance at the shiny metal side of one of the light reflectors assured Halin that he again he looked like any other 12 year old.

"Don't worry, we will reshoot," the director said. "I have a new concept for this scene. It will be magnificent."

"I don't think so!" The new voice was one that sent a shiver down Halin's spine. It belonged to someone who scared *him*, whether in human or wolf form. Mrs. Davis, his teacher; a thin woman in thick glasses stood, arms crossed, staring at him and the director.

"Halin, as well as Paige, has worked his allotted four hours for the day. It's time for them to go to school," she said to the director, then turned toward Halin and Paige. "If either of you so much as growl at me, you will so loaded down with homework you won't finish it until the next century!"

As they walked away, Halin heard Ean muttering, "I should know better than to work with animals and kids, but nobody warned me about teachers."

First Date

Bradley H Sinor
Small Bites
Coscom Entertainment

Just after noon I was cut off by a couple of zombies. I suspected that they had once been yuppie businessmen because they still held tightly onto briefcases. I was trying to avoid one of them and would up taking a header over the edge of a cliff.

I was out for maybe a few seconds. When I came around I hurt, landing in a briar patch will do that. Only there wasn't much time for me to recuperate, because as soon as I scrambled to my feet I spotted three more zombies.

Only they weren't after me, in fact those rotting brains of theirs didn't even seem to register my presence. These critters seemed far more interested in something a little further down the way than me.

Common sense said I should get of there and do it quickly. Only thing is, more times than not, I've never been known for doing the smart thing. So I decided to see what it was that caught their attention.

Turned out they had a girl, who looked to be in her early twenties, backed into a crevice and had blocked any chance of escape. The girl was doing a pretty fair job of keeping them at bay, with a broken branch that ended in a ragged point.

Normally any reasonably alert person can avoid most zombies; they are not the fastest things in the world and certainly not the smartest. Most casualties seem to occur when they gather in packs or people run out of ammunition.

Now there were only three of them and I had more than enough bullets. My .357 had stayed in my shoulder holster when I fell. The only reason I hadn't used it on the other zombies was they had come on me too suddenly and kept me off balance.

I waited until I was less than ten feet from them before firing off three rounds in quick succession, right into their heads

The girl looked at me for a moment. "What took you so

long? You had a clear shot way before that!"

"You're welcome. You have any plans this evening?"

"This going to be our first date?"

"More like a second, I'd call *this* our first date." I laughed at my own joke, pointing at the zombie remains, but the sound died in my throat when I saw my "date" heft her stick and throw it at me. I ducked to one side, turning as I did to see the improvised spear burying itself directly between the eyes of one of the briefcase-carrying zombies I had encountered earlier.

"Pick me up at seven," she said.

Burglary

Bradley H. Sinor
Small Bites
Coscom Entertainment

Patrolman Eric Baxter was not happy. Standard operating procedure specifically said that any officer who came on a possible burglary in progress was to wait for backup. No ifs, ands or buts about it; you waited for backup.

It had been more than half an hour since he reported the broken rear window of the Enchilada Express to the dispatcher, and still no backup. The big delay was because an oil tanker had turned on its side out on Route 20, causing a 12-car crash, backing traffic up for a couple of miles. That had priority over the possible burglary of a fast food place.

Baxter was fairly sure this was the work of local teenagers. Several names came to mind as possible nominees for the Guilty Party Award. He'd had to run off a number of them hanging around in an Enchilada Express parking lot over the last few weeks. His gut told him that there was a better than even chance that some of those teens were still inside.

As his watch hit midnight Baxter muttered "To hell with this" as he picked up his flashlight from the seat next to him. He made a mental note to have a talk with the fast food joint's owner about the flimsy locks on the doors, and about the advantages of an alarm system.

At first there didn't seem to be anything inside. It was just possible Baxter concluded that the little brats had satisfied themselves with busting in the door, grabbing some food and getting out of there.

That was when he heard something off to the right. Whipping his gun up, Baxter pointed his flashlight toward the prep table.

"Police, freeze!" he yelled at the top of his voice.

Instead of a teenager, he saw in the center of the table the small trembling form of a Chihuahua.

"Talk about your major crime figure." He re-holstered his gun with a smile. "Who locked you in here, little one?"

Baxter reached over very slowly toward the table. He knew

the little dog was scared and didn't want to frighten it any more than necessary.

That was when the tiny dog bit two of Baxter's fingers.

Pain shot up through him like an electric shock, especially because the Chihuahua's teeth were holding tightly onto him. It was a struggle to free himself, and when he did, backing a step or two away from the animal in the process, blood was flowing freely.

"Shit," Baxter muttered, cradling his injured hand against his chest.

That was when, all around him, other small forms appeared. Chihuahuas of varying sizes and colors were on the floor, every table and appliance, and even a pair on the light fixture above him. In the next instant they attacked, hitting him from every direction, their claws and teeth ripping though cloth and flesh, forcing him to the ground.

It flashed through Baxter's mind, before he lost awareness that his was like some bad, low budget, drive-in theatre movie: *Attack of the Feral Chihuahuas.*

A Proper Farewell
Bradley H. Sinor
Space Cadets
SCIFI

"*Isn't a bar the traditional* place to stage a wake?"

Luke Weber didn't look up. It wasn't necessary. He hadn't even had to hear the voice to know it was Steve Hauula. There wasn't that much noise in Academy Park, especially at 2 a.m., so hearing, and recognizing Hauula's familiar gait had been easy.

Hauula was a senior at the Space Academy, a year ahead of Luke. Graduation would see him leaving, heading out where Luke and every other cadet at the Academy wanted to go – *the stars*.

Of course, that would be nothing new for Hauula; the older cadet had grown up on Elliso III. He was the first colonist that Luke had ever met. The ones who came to Earth didn't always move in the same circles that Luke's family did. Then again, neither did most of the other cadets at the Academy.

Luke wasn't really sure if the two of them could be called friends; he just knew that they weren't enemies. Sometimes that was the best that you could ask for.

"Who said anything about this being a wake?"

Without waiting for an invitation, Hauula dropped onto the bench where Luke sat.

Luke was not in the mood for company, hadn't felt the need for companionship for some time...but he also found himself unable to muster the energy to suggest to Hauula that he might find somewhere else to sit. Instead, Luke stared out across the well- manicured park lawn.

Across the way he caught sight of a squirrel working its way down the trunk of a gnarled oak tree. The animal stopped just before venturing onto the grass. For a brief heartbeat the squirrel locked eyes with Luke. Just as quickly as the encounter had begun, it was over. The squirrel broke the stare, firing itself out onto the grass, and covered the distance to another tree in three very long leaps.

Whether the animal might be completely Terran was a

question. The Academy Park had become home not only to local fauna but to a number of off planet critters as well. Of course, officially, no unauthorized animals had ever broken the strict quarantine of the port.

Naturally that meant that reports of rather odd looking animals that had been reported over the years were actually nothing more than "simply figments of over active imaginations", if you believed the official press releases.

The screeching of the metal as it fought the atmosphere echoed through the ship like an unholy chorus of banshees. Luke's hands criss-crossed the control board again and again. Everything he had ever been taught to do in an emergency flashed through his mind. None of it worked.

He looked out the control panel window: the approaching ground was awash in the reentry fire as the small ship moved through, a lighting fast brick with nowhere to go but down.

Hauula extracted a silver metal flask from the inside pocket of his uniform jacket. He unscrewed the lid and took a swallow before offering it to Luke. That the upper classman had already done some serious drinking was obvious from his breath.

It seemed strange to see Hauula like this. He had always struck Luke as a straight laced type, one who would eventually end up as a ship's doctor or a base psychiatrist.

"Of course it's a wake," Hauula told him, his words slurring slightly. "Some of our brother and sister cadets died a year ago this very night. They deserve to be honored. A proper farewell, the Academy way, isn't some fancy memorial service; it's with a wake. So don't deny that this is a wake; I won't hear of you trampling on an Academy tradition, Weber."

Luke nodded, accepted the flask. The taste was sharp and bitter. He was tempted to spit it out.

"What is this stuff? It tastes like flavored paint solvent."

"Antarean Brandy."

"I don't think I slept through my interstellar law class, in spite of it being at six in the god-awful a.m, but isn't this stuff illegal?"

"Yes, yes, Antarean Brandy is illegal. If it's made wrong it can be poisonous as all hell. On the other hand, if it's made right, as this batch is, trust me, it can be ambrosia," said Hauula.

"It could get you expelled."

"Sure could. You going to turn me in?"

"Nope."

"Damned nice of you. Besides, I doubt that Ryan and Gianade would care one bit about the illegality of what we're toasting them with," observed Hauula.

Hauula didn't have to tell Luke what Nate Gianade and Elaine Ryan would think. Luke had known Nate since the first grade. The two of them had met Elaine in high school and had become as close as any teenagers could be.

"I don't think that the two of them would want to be honored by the man who killed them."

"Did you put a blaster to their heads and pull the trigger? Or poison them with some exotic designer drug you created? Look, Weber, I read the commander's report. I know what happened. Did I miss an appendix that said you were responsible?"

Luke kicked at a leaf that had blown up against his foot, sending it off into the air to settle a half dozen inches away. He knew what was in the report. After all, he'd been the officer in charge of Training Flight Delta 712, one of the dozen Babylonian scout ships that the Academy used to train its students.

"It doesn't matter what the report says," replied Luke. "I was in command. I was responsible for bringing them and the ship back in one piece. In case you didn't notice, the only one who lived through that mission was me."

Hauula laughed. The sound reaffirmed the conviction that everything Luke felt was right. Luke fought down an urge to throw a punch at the upperclassman.

"Damn it, Weber! Those Babylonian class ships are accidents waiting to happen. If you check the records, there have been three other crashes in the past five years. One of the crew chiefs told me that every time one of those death traps manages to land without killing someone it has to be due to divine intervention. Of course, it's not like you just walked away from the crash without a scratch; seven and half months in a med facility and then another three in rehab sort of say what kind of shape you were in."

Luke's power chair came to a halt just inside the morgue door. He drew a long hard breath, forcing himself to stare at the two coffins, knowing what was inside of them.

"This is wrong, so wrong," he said, not bothering to fight
the tears rolling down his face.

"The truth of the matter is that I'm considering resigning
from the Academy." There. He had said it. Hearing the words
that had been inside him for so long was almost a relief.

Hauula laughed again. "Oh, please, not that routine; it's
too melodramatic! Are you maybe hooked on those old Errol
Flynn vids or something? You know the one I'm talking about,
where the hero feels he has disgraced his regiment, resigns
his commission and goes off to redeem himself."

"What would you do? Grin and bear it, stiff upper lip and
all that other crap," snapped Luke.

He waited for an answer; he wasn't sure if it would be a
pithy one-liner or something deeply philosophical – but Hauula
said nothing. In the distance he could hear the sound of a low
throbbing; he suspected it was a generator at the zoo
compound. When Luke finally looked up he realized that the
upper classman was slumped back against the wall, sound
asleep.

He reached over, gently pulled the flask from Hauula's
fingers, and took a long swallow. "Here's tomorrow's lead vid
story: *Killer Cadet Found Drunk in Park*," he muttered.

"Oh, give me a fucking break!"

That voice sent a chill through Luke. He knew it, knew it
all too well. It wasn't Hauula. The other cadet was still snoring
away. Turning toward the speaker took every ounce of courage
that Luke Weber could summon, right then all he wanted to
do was run away.

Standing next to a tree was another Space Academy cadet,
dressed in the same uniform that Luke wore. A single red hair
hung, out of place, across the newcomer's forehead.

"Nate?"

"Of course it's me. Who else would show up to kick your
ass when you start feeling sorry for yourself? I mean, it's not
as if I don't have a whole lot of experience. I've been doing it
since first grade," said Nathan Gianade.

The nineteen-year-old, who also was Luke's oldest friend,
had been a last-minute addition to the flight; replacing a
freshman named Stackpole who had fallen and broken his
collarbone in three places.

"Nate," repeated Luke, the feeling in the pit of his stomach going into overdrive, sure now that he had gone over the edge. "I don't know what to say."

"'Hello' might be a good place to start," said Nate, brushing the lock of hair back into place.

"Hello," stammered Luke. "I don't want you to take this the wrong way. It's not that I'm not glad to see you, but aren't you supposed to be dead?"

"As a doornail."

Nate strolled along the walkway stopping a few feet away from Luke.

"You're looking pretty good for a dead guy," said Luke. They told me that there wasn't much left of either of you."

"Most of what was left was pretty much crisped," Nate told him. "As for how I look now, what can I say? Being dead has some advantages in the way you can appear."

"I believe that we are all due a weekend pass when this pleasure jaunt is done," said Nate. "What do you say to using it to do some serious partying?"

Luke smiled as he stepped onto the command deck. The weekend pass was a tradition for a crew after its first solo flight.

"Let's not get ahead of ourselves," said Elaine Ryan from the co-pilot's chair. "While I'm sure you have some serious debauchery in mind, I, for one, would like some time to relax."

"Yeah, right. I've seen that silver bikini of yours," Nate laughed. 'I'm sure debauchery never crosses your semi-virginal mind."

"Okay," said Luke. "If I recall the flight plan correctly, we still need to successfully rendezvous with three satellites, take readings and get ourselves home. Then we can worry about weekend passes."

"Yes, Daddy," Elaine and Nate said simultaneously.

"No," Luke shook his head, staring at his friend. "No, this can't be right. You can't be here."

Luke could remember, all too well, the very long talks he had had with Commander duPene, the Academy's chief psychiatrist. Hauula, who was on her staff, as a teaching assistant, had sat in on some of the interviews. They had talked a lot about survivor's guilt and how it might affect him.

Looking at his best friend, Luke was sure that they had been right; it had pushed him over the edge and into a complete breakdown.

"Nate, I would give anything in the universe to really be talking to you. But I know I'm not, I can't be." His voice was quivering with each word.

"Oh, I'm here, old buddy. Trust me on that one." Nate sniffed at the open silver flask.

"Antarean Brandy? You've been drinking that stuff? You're braver than I would be," he said. "Sleeping Beauty there has to have been your supplier. You're too straight-laced to even know where to get it."

Luke smiled. That remark only helped to cement that this was Nate, be he real or hallucination. People had asked both of them why they picked on each other. The reply from each had been the same. "Because I can, and he's a close enough friend that I know he'll never hold it against me or carry a grudge."

Just then a pair of hands grabbed Luke by his left arm and spun him around. He had a brief glimpse of long brown hair and caught the scent of jasmine before a pair of lips slammed into his and arms wrapped him in a tight hug. A soft form pressed against him, tongue probing into his mouth. An eternity later Luke broke the kiss, pulling his head back.

"Elaine! But you're...."

"I know, dead," laughed Elaine Ryan. At five foot five with dark hair and green eyes, she had an exotic, almost gypsy, look to her.

Luke stumbled over a million words in his head before he finally managed to utter real ones. That they were in any coherent order astonished him. "Why did you kiss me?"

"I figured I wasn't going to get too many more chances, so this seemed as good a time as any. It was something I've wanted to do for a long time."

"You wanted to kiss me?"

"You bet your cute little ass I did," Elaine said.

"If you had only said things like that to me," said Nate with a sigh. "It would have been a dream come true."

"A dream for you, sweet cheeks, a nightmare for me." She told Nate.

Luke was more confused by the minute. Elaine, here, kissing him? A part of him wanted to say it was all part of the hallucination that had started the moment that he had seen Nate. But the feel of her arms around him, the taste of her lips, that seemed too real not to be real.

"I'm sorry," Luke said.

Nate hopped up on the wall, letting his feet dangle over the edge. "Yeah, yeah, I know you always wanted to be a hero, and I think that saving people is one of the requirements, page 47, section A, of the *Heroes Manual*. I'm glad that I slept through that course."

"Nate, you were probably too hung over to have been awake," said Elaine.

This all felt so right, the three of them together, bickering, but it was all wrong. Luke knew it; he knew that Nate and Elaine were dead. He had been at their funerals, watched their caskets lowered into the ground.

Luke turned away from both of them, though his hand brushed against Elaine's. The touch of her was electric, but it was also as solid as that of any human being.

"I've got to be off my rocker," he said.

"My grandmother said that anyone who wanted to leave a perfectly fine planet and go out into space had to be a little nuts," said Nate.

Luke wasn't even sure just when he became aware of the fact that Nate, Elaine and he were standing in the cramped command area of a Babylonian class training vessel. Hauula was with them, scrunched down in the co-pilot's seat, still asleep, still snoring away, unaware of any changes.

The space academy insignia had been stenciled on the wall near the main hatch. Out of habit, Luke's eyes scanned the control panel, checking the readings. He recognized which ship this one was when twin cracks in the console caught his eye. It was the ship that would be designated Training Flight Delta 712. The same one that he and the others had ridden would ride down, to a fiery meeting with the Sahara desert floor.

"When are we?" he asked.

It couldn't be more than a month before the accident. If it had been any sooner than that there would have been a red acid stain on the decking near the command chair, left by one of the Academy techs who had been doing some routine maintenance. That incident had been recorded in the ship's log that Luke had gone over the night before the flight.

"Very good," said Elaine. "See, Nate; I told you he was a quick study."

"Follow me," said Nate. The three of them moved back through the cramped command area, past three seats and into the engine compartment. The Babylonian class was a long range scout fighter known for speed and maneuverability, nothing else.

"See anything?" Elaine pointed toward three gages near the ceiling. Luke scanned them, then checked the readings again. They seemed normal; there were minor aberrations, but no cause for alarm.

"I have a feeling, since you asked; there is something I should see."

From his pocket he produced the multi-purpose tool that was as much a part of the uniform of any cadet as the rank insignia on the collars. He pulled three screws loose from a piece of plating and set them on the floor. The gauges inside and the conduits were a small rainbow of lights and wiring.

A row of silver specks appeared along the coolant tube conduits. Luke could see where two of them were criss-crossed with tiny black marks.

"Micro fractures, so fine that it would take a full Class Seven diagnostic to find them." Elaine told him.

"And they don't do Class Seven diagnostics, except once a year," said Luke.

"If that often," Nate chimed in. Class Sevens required a full system shutdown and an examination of every inch of the ship down to the hull plating. That detailed a survey could take up to three days to complete, so a Seven was normally only required during the yearly inspection, a full ship refit, or life-threatening battle damage.

"So if it isn't found, the micro-fractures can rupture and push you up into a full scale engine breech," said Luke. "You end up with a shitload of power and no way to control it. Which means..."

"*Ker-splat!*" said Nate. "And not a damn thing you can do about it."

"God, I love it when you use those technical terms, Nate," said Elaine. "Luke, what Nate is trying to say, in his own way, is that the three of us were just in the wrong place at the wrong time. Once that breech occurred we were as good as dead. That you came out of it alive is a total anomaly."

"I wish to hell it had been a three-way anomaly," offered Nate.

Luke understood that Elaine was right—but understanding it was one thing; believing it with his gut was a different matter.

"I'm thinking of resigning."

"That is utterly stupid," said Elaine. "I've known you long enough to know you're many things, but stupid isn't one of them, and resigning is stupid."

Luke began to prowl through the ship, twisting and turning around the instrument panels, seats and other projections.

"Believe me, there are reasons for you to stay in the academy," said Nate.

This time Luke was aware of the change, a gradual shift of everything around him. The ship was gone, replaced by broken walls and the sound of firing in the distance. Luke gauged the noise as a combination of energy weapons and old fashioned projectile weapons.

Elaine's hand closed around Luke's, for a moment, then released it.

Nate was standing over the prone form of Hauula. "This guy could sleep through anything."

Half a dozen figures came running into Luke's field of vision. They were dressed in black, all heavily armed, a few of them with large backpacks marked with insignia that Luke did not recognize.

The solders ignored the four ghostly visitors.

"I want a perimeter up, plus a full sensor sweep of the area!" snapped a young woman, her voice intense. "We need it five minutes ago!"

Each of the solders, four men and two women, moved quickly to make the area as secure as it could be in the middle of a battle.

"What's going on?" asked Luke.

"Bit of a civil war, a rather nasty one," said Elaine. "The planet is called Bootstrap, don't you dare ask for the formal designation, you know I never remember those things. It's out in the hind end of the Krishna Sector. That young lady is one of the leaders, or will be; I'm a little unclear of the chronology. Her name is Kate Meadows or Beddoes or something like that."

Luke found his eyes locked with those of the girl. Kate

seemed almost aware of him, or at least of *something* looking at her. From her expression Luke could tell she was under a lot of pressure. She wasn't beautiful, especially covered in grime and camouflage make-up, but there was something about her face and manner that had grabbed hold of Luke and wouldn't let go.

"Hey, big boy, you never gave *me* that kind of look," Elaine said, "I may be dead, but I think I'm going to start getting jealous."

Nate picked up a rock and threw it right in front of Kate. She blinked, shook her head, and motioned for two of her companions to move toward a far wall.

"Look," said Nate, "you ought to know that you could be very important in that lady's life." He paused. "Or maybe you could end up a drunken second engineer on some dilapidated trading colony station."

Around them the firing started again. The soldiers swung their weapons up, waiting for orders. Luke shook his head. This whole thing was too real, yet there was still the certainty that it couldn't be.

"So let me get this straight," he said at last. "You're saying that this girl and I will end up together?"

"And they said *I* had an ego," chuckled Nate. "Maybe you will, maybe you won't. There are a lot of variables down the road. Maybe you'll just be responsible for putting someone else in a position to be important to her. Of course, if it were me, naturally the two of us would end up together."

Luke let himself drop toward a perch on a broken piece of wall. By the time he reached it he was back in the park, with Hauula still snoring on the bench next to him. There was no sign of either Elaine or Nate.

"I'm in worse shape that I thought," he muttered, letting his head drop forward to rest in his hands.

"You've been in worse." The voice came from the same squirrel that he had seen earlier. The animal was standing on its hind legs at the edge of the sidewalk just in front of Luke.

"I don't need this right now," said Luke

The squirrel shrugged, turned to walk away, but before he got more than a few feet Luke managed to say "Wait a minute! I have one question."

"Shoot," said the squirrel.

"Do the pain and the guilt ever go away?"

"Some says it do, some says it don't" answered the squirrel. "Me, I don't claim to know."

The last thing that Luke remembered as he sank into darkness was the scent of jasmine and the sound of Haulla's snoring.

"You look like hell!"

Hauula looked up from his desk. Standing in the door to the broom closet that was laughingly referred to as his office was Chief Academy Psychiatrist, and his boss Commander Erin duPrene. That she had deemed to come to the area where the teaching assistants were housed was out of the ordinary, to say the least.

She set a mug of coffee on the desk in front of Hauula; he grabbed it up and wrapped his fingers around it, savoring the heat and the smell.

"Good morning to you, too," he said. "You try slipping into someone's mind and mucking about, all without them knowing it, and I guarantee you, Commander, you won't come out looking like you were ready for a red carpet Vid premiere."

"This stuff helps," she said, picking up Hauula's flask. The Antarian Brandy had been mixed with several compounds that helped to lower the mind's defenses.

Duprene took her glasses off and rubbed the bridge of her nose. That she didn't really approve of telepaths was well known. That she had also admitted, reluctantly, but publicly, that they had their uses in the medical field, was just as well known. So having her as his academy advisor, not to mention department head, had proved a challenge for Hauula.

"So are you going to sit there all day or you going to give me your report," she said.

"I figured that you wouldn't want to see it until I had written everything up," said Hauula.

"If I did, do you think I would be down here in the basement. This place doesn't smell any better now than it did when I was a teaching assistant. Don't give me details; save that for your report. Which, by the way, is due on my desk by two. Just give me the highlights," she snapped. "Making him see ghosts was, shall we say, a novel choice of therapy. I gave you the case because Weber was close to the edge. I hope this little "charade" didn't send him over."

Hauula considered his reply carefully. "I let him see his

friends. That was what he needed. I don't even know if he will remember the whole thing consciously, but it let him get a chance to admit to himself that he wasn't responsible for the crash and to say a proper farewell to them. He might have a chance now; he had none before."

"That's the best we can hope for, I suppose," DuPrene nodded as she headed for the door. "Finish that report, and then get some rest. You may be on staff as a teaching assistant, but you're still a cadet. I happen to know you have a midterm in Bennett's Fluid Dynamics class coming up and it will be a real bitch."

"Yeah, I was afraid of that," said Hauula said as he took a swallow of coffee and reached for his notes on Weber. "Pity I can't really call up ghosts – like maybe the ghosts of some past students who aced Bennett's exams."

Skimming Stones
Bradley H. Sinor
Men Writing Science Fiction As Women
DAW

Lying flat on my stomach with my face less than a foot from the river was not the way I had planned to spend Friday night. Especially when I knew that waiting at the Shadow Creek bar, there was a martini, possibly several, with my name on it.

Not that I had a whole lot of choice in the matter. I work for the City of Tulsa as an electrical maintenance engineer, so I end up doing a lot of work in places that I would prefer not to even think about, if I didn't have to, all in the name of keeping various facilities around town running.

The hours weren't the greatest, but I was pulling down decent money and didn't have to spend my days in a cubicle. This girl wasn't complaining; I'd gotten enough of that from my ex-husband, Luke; he didn't like my hours, the fact that my pay check was bigger than his or much of anything in our relationship. When he finally took off, three days after our first anniversary, with that dye job blonde, Denise, I couldn't have been happier.

With budget short falls and layoffs my department was short-handed. Truth be told, we'd never had enough people, so making due was a way of life. That was why on a Friday night, I was in coveralls, laying on a stage floating on the Arkansas river, instead of wearing my new leather mini-skirt, boots and suede jacket and bar hopping with my best friend, Jani.

The floating stage is anchored in a small cove. They use it for outdoor theater productions, performances by musicians, and any formal city-type ceremony that the politicians want to conduct under the open Oklahoma sky.

The problem with the place is that it was designed by an idiot. At least once a month my department got a frantic call from the stage manager saying something was wrong and it needed to be fixed, yesterday. Since Tulsa Opera was supposed to do a benefit preview at two on Sunday afternoon, the powers-that-be thought it would be sort of nice if things worked.

I had come out with a four man crew around noon, then at six my boss called and told the others to go home. Less overtime, I suspect. "Look, Nancy," he had said. "You can handle it by yourself, shouldn't take you more than a half an hour or so."

Yeah, right! Three hours later I was closing the last access port and breathing a long sigh of relief when I heard something hitting the side of the stage. I trailed my flashlight along the water to find see what it was. There was something I thought it might be a mannequin, thrown away by frat boys at one of their drunken parties.

Okay, call me a Girl Scout, but I figured there was a chance I was wrong, so I dropped my flashlight and made a grab for whatever it was.

That took me several tries. The problem was, I couldn't get a good enough hold, and he dropped back into the water several times. In the process I heard the sound of coughing, that was proof enough that I wasn't trying to rescue a dummy or a corpse.

Once I did get him up on the stage I pushed his hair out of the way and discovered two important things, 'he' was a 'she, and *she* had my face!

Beyond a knot on the side of her head the size of a goose egg, some bruises and a cut on her cheek, my new-found twin didn't seem to have anything obviously wrong with her. City regulations, not to mention common sense, said I ought to call 911 or get her to the nearest hospital.

It was just that looking at that face, my face, just wierded me out so much, that I just could not see going by regulations right then as being the smartest thing in the world.

"Take it easy. You're okay. I got you out of the water," I told her.

"Where am I?" she said, her voice a cracked whisper.

"Tulsa," I said.

Don't ask me why, but right then I figured the best thing to do was get her away from there. The only place I could think of to take her was my house. I live in a suburb of Tulsa, somewhat isolated, which suited me just fine. I had been astonished when Luke had been willing to sign the place over to me as part of our divorce settlement. I took it, of course, after making sure he hadn't secretly mortgaged the place to the hilt.

Since her legs didn't seem to want to work for more than three or four steps at a time without going out from under her, getting my guest inside was not easy. My cats, Paranoia and Schizo, were on the sofa but decided to take off for other places when they saw us come through the door.

Her clothes had dried some, but were still smelly and wet. I managed to get one boot off of her and was just untying the other when my guest said, "If it's seduction you have in mind, I'm afraid that you're going to be rather disappointed. I'm not feeling up for anything just now."

"Don't worry about that. I've got better ways of picking up dates than fishing them out of the river. Besides, I don't think you're my type."

"If she's not, Nancy, am I?"

Standing in the living room door was Kent Sabiani. At six-one, his lanky frame and gray-streaked goatee gave him a vaguely satanic look, which went over great with some of my more religious neighbors.

He moved so quietly that sometimes you would just look up and there he was. Kent was an Emergency Medical Technician, so I had called him on my cell phone to come give my visitor a quick once over.

"Damn it, make some noise when you come in the door!"

"Hey, I did make noise; it's not my fault that you didn't hear me. So who's your friend?"

"Name's Sian," she said in a whisper.

I saw the look on Kent's face when he got a good look at Sian. He was cool, didn't say a word, just cocked an eyebrow at me and went to work.

I excused myself to the kitchen, where I found a couple of beers in the back of the fridge. Kent was just unwrapping a blood pressure cuff from Sian's arm when I came back. I handed him a beer.

"Thanks. Other than the obvious, bruises, scratches and contusions, Sian seems in pretty good shape," he said. "How far did you fall?

"Don't know, but it hurt like hell," she said.

"Must have felt like hitting concrete."

Sian nodded

"All right, that's enough," Kent said. "I would say a few

hour's sleep are in order. The interrogation can wait."

The next morning I came in the kitchen and found Kent rummaging around in the cabinets, a look of frustration on his face. "So, where did you put the frying pan *this* time?" he asked when he saw me.

"Just for using that tone, I'm not telling you." After all, it was my kitchen and *I knew* where it was. "Besides, why should I help you? You left your socks and shirt hanging on the dresser mirror, again."

"Be that way and you get to cook." He grinned.

That was a good argument. I'm a decent cook, but it's nice to have someone else do the work, and I stand in awe of what Kent can do in a kitchen. "Cabinet! Just to the right of the stove!" I said quickly.

Kent pulled the skillet out, fetched eggs, milk and a variety of other things from the refrigerator. I've never been able to figure out if he has specific recipes or just works with what's there. The results speak for themselves.

"Is there anything I can do to help?"

Sian walked into the kitchen wearing my heavy red bathrobe. A shower and some sleep seemed to have done her a world of good. The bruises were still prominent, but in the light of day looked like they would heal. She moved a bit stiffly, favoring her right leg, but, given the circumstances that was understandable.

"Just grab a stool," I said. "Kent is working his magic."

A moment later he presented us each with a tall glass of orange juice. The odor of blueberry muffins began to fill the kitchen, followed a few minutes later by Kent setting a plate of them in front of Sian and me. He turned his attention back to the stove. I knew omelets would soon follow.

"Okay," I said. "So, feel like answering a few questions?"

"Ask away," Sian said, slicing a muffin and layering butter onto it. "This is very good. She was right when she called it magic."

"Thank you. So, what happened?" Kent said, without turning around.

"You wouldn't believe that I just got a little bit plastered and fell into the river?" I just arched an eyebrow at her and didn't say a thing. "Well, I didn't think so, especially if you've looked in the mirror anytime. The long and the short of it is,

I'm you."

"Really?"

Sian nodded as she took a sip from her glass.

"If you were able to run a DNA test on the two of us you'd see that we are genetically the same person. Only I'm not from this world."

"Unless you were cloned by aliens, or are a part of some sort of secret government conspiracy, that leaves only two possible explanations," said Kent. "Time travel or parallel world?"

Sian looked at him, shocked. "I'm impressed. You keeping him around on a long term basis?" she asked me.

I didn't answer. Instead I reached across the counter and grabbed Sian's left arm, pushing back the sleeve. Midway up the arm was a formation of veins, making the letter H, clearly visible beneath her skin. A jagged scar, about four inches in length, bisected it. I bared my arm to show an identical mark, but reversed. I'd definitely call this a bit more than circumstantial evidence.

"I *am* from a parallel world," she said. "Where history, as you know it, ran differently, because of different choices."

"So how did you end up in our corner of the time-space continuum?" asked Kent.

"To make a long story short, I'm a run-away princess." Kent had to struggle to keep from laughing, this was beginning to sound like something out of those fantasy novels he's so fond of reading.

"Let me see if I have this straight," I said. "You're me, from a parallel world, where you're a princess. But you decided to take it on the lam from your life as one of the royals and came here."

"Not at first. I left just over a year ago. I've probably been in seven or eight different worlds before this one."

Sian made a gesture in the air and a small globe of light appeared just above the palm of her hand. It hovered there for a moment and was gone.

"Kent isn't the only one who can do magic. It looks like magic, but there are sound principles of science behind it," she said. "Problem is that is about all I can do."

"A handy talent. So why *did* you leave home?" Kent asked.

Sian laid the remnants of her muffin down on a napkin.

"They wanted to make me Queen."

"Queen?" I said. "I don't think you have any glass ceiling where you come from."

She cocked an eyebrow at me but went on. "My Daddy had decided it was time for him to have a co-ruler; someone who would do most of the work while he took it easy. I may be the eldest, but my brother is far more suited to the throne. When he wouldn't let me abdicate I faked my death and ran. Problem was he didn't he didn't believe it. He commissioned the Guild of Head Hunters to find me and bring me home. They've come close too many times."

"You figured to hide from them here in Tulsa?" Kent asked.

"Actually, no," she sighed. "I left a trail for the Head Hunters to follow. I had planned to lay a trap for them and then permanently lose them in the desert."

Permanently lose? To me that said kill them and dump the bodies.

"So, why are you in Tulsa?" asked Kent.

"Because of her," Sian pointed at me. "For reasons that I don't understand, whenever I enter a new world, I tend to end up close to myself, if I'm still alive in that world. There have been a few where I was dead or had never been born."

"I bet that was a fun discovery," I said.

Kent picked up a muffin from the tin and began to gingerly peal the paper cup from around it.

"Sian, one thing that you haven't mentioned is just how you're able to go hopping from parallel world to parallel world. So what went wrong?" I asked.

"What makes you think anything went wrong?"

"A thirty foot drop into the river sort of suggests that things didn't work the way you planned them to work," I said.

Sian laughed. "Oh, they definitely didn't work the way I had planned them. Travel between the worlds is a combination of making your mind perceive things differently and then stepping through the gate. Ideally you need a set of rune stones to open that gate. I grabbed some of the best before I left home

"The only trouble is that I lost my rune stones. My father's chief warlock taught me ways of duplicating the rune door with my mind, using a variety of herbs, native flora and pharmaceuticals. The problem is the last two worlds haven't had what I needed and I had to use substitutes. They didn't always work right."

"So you're saying, when you do this you're on drugs," Kent grinned. "Talk about your ultimate bad acid trip. So if you don't know where you are, does this mean that those Head Hunters of yours won't be able to find you?"

Sian stared at the counter for a long time. "I can only hope so."

"Well, I never had a sister, so you're about the closest I'm going to come to one," I said, putting my arm around her shoulder. "You're welcome to stay here for as long a visit as you want."

If she was going to stay around, Sian was going to need "a life", at least on paper. Kent just said to leave it to him. He knew a hacker who could do the job.

"Is this guy good?" I asked.

"Oh, yeah," he grinned. "The guy I have in mind is the one who teaches the CIA forgery department how to do things."

That done, it was time to do something else just as important. I looked at Sian's clothes we'd left in the laundry room. They were not in good shape. She was going to need more than what I had found her in, and more than just borrowed things from my closet. Time to go shopping.

We hit the local mall and found everything Sian would need, not to mention some neat things for myself. Just after noon I decided it was time to introduce Sian to native dishes, i.e.: pizza. Meals in hand, we found a table near the stage at the center of the food court.

There were a bunch of guys there, dressed in combat fatigues, faces painted in camouflage paint all holding weird looking metal guns. The weapons looked like the sort of things my cousins Tim and Randy had played with when we were growing up, not practical looking but the sort of thing that thrills a twelve year old male.

When they began showing off some round balls and inserting them in the guns it dawned on me that these weren't real army types, but paint ball gamers.

I explained the concept to Sian and she just shook her head. "They do this for fun?"

I was about to turn my attention back to a slice of pizza when I looked toward the rest rooms. The air in front of them had begun to shimmer and fold in on itself. Then someone was standing there. He was big, six-four at least, wearing a dark floppy hat and a leather jacket.

"Slowly look over toward the rest rooms," I told Sian. "I think we have a visitor."

"I don't have to," Sian was staring at the shiny metal wall of the Chinese fast food place. She could see a slightly blurry version of this fellow without a problem.

"A Head Hunter? Does he know you're here?" I said softy.

"Remember what I said about being drawn to this area because you were here. Look up on the stage." She pointed at a man standing at the back of the group of camo dressed performers. He was shaggier and maybe didn't weigh as much, but I could see the resemblance.

I was about to suggest that we ease our way out of there, when things began to go a bit haywire. One of the paint ball guys tripped over something, his own feet probably, gun in hand and almost fell. One thing he did do was accidentally squeeze off a shot that went straight out into the audience and hit the Head Hunter square on the chest. I can imagine where he would have hit if there had been time to aim.

The Head Hunter looked down, touched the fresh paint with one finger. "I just had that cleaned!" he said and headed for the stage.

Not being your shy retiring type, Sian grabbed one of the metal chairs that filled the food court. As the Head Hunter passed she brought it down hard across the man's back. That proved effective enough to put him on the floor, surprise is the best weapon. A quick grab under his shirt and she jerked something loose.

"Let's go!" she said.

We made it to the car and I hit the gas. How we got out of there without being stopped, I still don't know.

"Damn, damn, damn," she muttered as I pointed the car toward the street.

"What was that you got from him?" I asked.

"These," she opened the small leather bag and poured out a half dozen flat stones, each one of them carved with an intricate rune.

Sian spread the rune stones out on my dining room table. There were six, none bigger than a quarter. All were slick and cool to the touch.

"This isn't good. If one of them found their way here, that means the others know where he went. So if he doesn't report back, and he can't without these, then they will come looking for him," she said.

"Then why did you take them?" I asked. "I know, I know, it seemed the thing to do at the time. Can we just smash them and hope the others don't show up on our doorstep?" I got my answer with just the look in Sian's eyes.

Smashing those pebbles would be a very last resort.

"How long will it be before the others show up?" asked Kent.

"If I've read these alignments correctly," she nodded. "I should judge sometime late tonight, give or take a couple hours. They are going to try for an area along the river, probably somewhere north of where I arrived, something solid I would expect. They can't walk on water any more than I could."

"Good, then maybe it's time for you to stop running," said Kent.

"I'm not going back!" protested Sian.

"You don't have to, if we work this right." The look on Kent's face suggested that he had something in mind. "It strikes me that there is a fairly simple answer to your problems, in my never-to-be-humble opinion."

"Oh, really?" asked Sian.

"Sure, we're just going to have to kill you."

Standing, at two a.m. on an abandoned bridge a mile north of the floating stage, with a strong northeasterly breeze blowing off the river, I was definitely not what you would describe as a happy camper. More like an irritated, cold and angry camper. I didn't think that Sian or Kent were any more comfortable right then than I was.

When Kent had breezed back in late that afternoon he was carrying half-a-dozen large boxes. "Have a look at these," he said. "I think you'll find them interesting."

Interesting was a good word. I was wearing the contents of several of them; a one piece black leather cat suit, covered in chains and metal studs that was so tight I could barely breathe. Sian had had to help me get into the thing and get everything zipped. Even the ankle length duster didn't do a thing to keep me warm, though it did provide a place to keep a loaded Beretta and a fully charged Taser.

If Sian had read those stones correctly, this was where the Head Hunters were supposed to show up. That was a big if to my way of thinking. Of course we might get lucky, have them miss and end up drowning in the middle of the river. I wasn't counting on that.

Frankly, I was about ready to give up this idea and revert to Plan B, once we came up with Plan B, when something happened to the air about twenty feet off to my left. I motioned for Sian and Kent to stay hidden.

The air seemed to waver for a moment, fold in on itself and then there were two men standing in the center of the bridge. After our first Head Hunter I think I expected some sort of cross between a barbarian and a biker. That wasn't what we got; more like a matching pair of lawyer boys, one was scarecrow-thin with a smile that seemed to take up three fourths of his face, the other was short, bald and looked like one of my cats could take him two falls out of three.

"I think this may be the place we're looking for. It feels right," the tall one said.

"I hope so, it's about time our luck changed," his companion said.

That was my cue. I pushed the duster back and strode forward. "All right, you two scum balls. This time you are completely out of luck. You're mine!" Hey, even if I was cold and scared out of my wits, I think I presented a fairly fierce picture right then.

Seeing me, they just stood staring for several seconds. That was enough time for Kent to come over the side of the bridge, where he had been perched, and clobber one of them with a blackjack. I enjoyed very much using the Taser on the other. Once they were down, I made sure they were still breathing, then we hogged tied them; feet and hands together behind their backs, with nooses around their necks.

"I guess this is places for Act Two," I said as Kent waved capsules of smelling salts under their noses.

They jerked awake and it didn't take them too long to figure out that they were in trouble. The smaller one looked around and started to speak, but thought better of it. The other one just stared at me, his face impassive and waiting.

"Good evening, boys. So, do the two of you have names of any sort?"

"Aye, m'lady," the taller one said, pronouncing each word

carefully. "I'm Carson Sal'se and he's Vernon Myth'rn. If we have offended you, or broken any local laws we do most humbly apologize."

"Well, isn't that just too, too cute. You've made a serious mistake, showing up on my lands, just when I'm in a very, very bad mood!" I said.

I began to pace back and forth. In the distance I could see the lights of the 21st street traffic bridge, flanked by the expressway bridge fifty yards beyond that. I couldn't help but grin at the idea of how the passing drivers might react to this scene. Of course explaining this whole scene to any police officers who showed up might be more than a bit difficult.

"The treasury is a little low right now and the price of two prime slaves like you two would certainly help fatten it up. I understand that there is a shortage of workers in the okra fields to the south. They'll be here shortly, for my little package over there. You fellows wouldn't happen to be with her, now would you?"

It wasn't easy for either of the Head Hunters to see where I had pointed, but they tried. One of Kent's other boxes had contained a filmy affair of white silk and transparent gossamer fabric.

Wrapped around Sian it looked as exotic, in its own way, as what I had on. It made what I had on look warm and comfortable. Kent dragged her forward to stand closer to the rest of us. Sian was blindfolded and her hands bound behind her.

"It's her! I told you we would find her!" said Myth'rn. He tried to get to his feet, but got no more than a couple of inches when the rope around his neck choked him off.

"You dared to violate my territory for that?"

"Yes, m'lady. She is to become a queen in her own right."

I began to laugh. "I doubt that she will be good for anything like that, not now anyway. This wench showed up here three days ago, tried to take me in a fight and lost. Instead of killing her I had her dosed with a drug that I use a good deal in my business. The stuff helps new slaves adjust to life in the bawdy houses I operate. That is if I don't decide just to get rid of her, like I'm thinking of getting rid of you two." I knew one thing; I had to keep them more than a bit uncertain of just what was going on, before they started asking too many questions, like how we happened to be there just where they were going to show up.

The look on the faces of the two Head Hunters was something akin to grief and shock, with a healthy dose of fear thrown in for good measure.

"This wasn't how you had wanted things to work out?" I asked.

"No, m'lady. Our guild accepted the commission to return her to the throne. It's obvious now we have failed," he said. "When we return we will be in disgrace."

"If I allow you to return. Maybe I should just feed you to the fishes. Can either of you swim?"

"Swim? N...no, m'lady."

"You two are such pains. But then so is she, and I'm not in the mood." I pulled out the Taser and jammed it against Sian's neck. The effect was quick and certain, she jerked like a marionette whose strings had been dropped, then crumpled to the ground. She lay there, eyes open and empty, her tongue hanging limply from her mouth.

"We'll just compost what's left of her," I said.

I let my words digest with them for several moments as their eyes darted between me and Sian's still form. Then I reached over and pulled their shirts open, just as Sian had told me to expect, there were two identical leather bags hanging around their necks. I yanked them free.

"I was going to kill you, and dump you over the bridge, but the river's too polluted as is," I said. "I have a better idea."

I gestured for Kent. He grabbed the shoulders of the smaller man and I grabbed his feet. We rolled him on top of the other one, face to face. I shoved one rune stone each between their lips.

"Don't swallow fellows," I laughed. "You've got one chance, scum. I'd advise you to take it."

They understood what I was talking about, leaned forward and touched the stones together. The air shivered, folded in on itself and the two Head Hunters were gone.

"That's one way to make an exit," Kent said.

Sian moaned and began to blink her eyes. Kent scrambled to her side, checking her vitals. "Did it work?" she managed to ask.

"You betcha, sis," I said. "I have a feeling they're going to be required to think very fast to explain what happened. In fact, I'm fairly sure they won't be able to admit a thing about what really happened. As far as your father is concerned you are gone and will not be returning anytime soon."

"That's good; I just wish it didn't have to be this way. I love Daddy, but he can be hard headed," she said. "Oh, but that thing you hit me with, sister mine, hurt like you wouldn't believe. Look, before we go much further, would somebody mind untying me. And I would appreciate a coat of some kind. It's cold out here."

Kent took a knife and cut the ropes around Sian's wrists, helping her stand up in the process. "We need to have a long talk, Kent, about your taste in women's clothes." she said. I didn't have to look over there to know he was putting on his totally innocent "I don't know what you're talking about face just then.

I had to say it had been an interesting weekend. I reached in my pocket and touched the rune stones. It occurred to me that smooth and flat as they were they would be perfect for skimming. I wondered how far I could throw them.

"No, maybe another time," I said to the wind.

"I don't know about you two, but I could do with some hot coffee," said Kent.

"What's coffee?" asked Sian.

Money's Worth

Bradley H. Sinor
Places to Be, People to Kill
DAW

I had my hand on the dagger before I was fully awake. Sleeping with a knife under your pillow isn't the most comfortable thing to do, though you can get used to it. I'd rather be uncomfortable than wake to a sword at my throat.

When I had leased the villa last month the caretaker had apologized profusely about the number of things that needed fixing; after all, the place had been empty for nearly two years.

One of the problems he had mentioned was the hinges on the master bedroom door; they squeaked and needed replacing. He had sworn by any number of local gods that he would have it fixed quickly.

It hadn't been. Right then I didn't have a problem with those squeaky hinges. They had been enough to awaken me.

There were two intruders, small hunkered forms clinging far too closely together as they came across the floor. When they sprang I threw my blanket over them as I rolled over the other side of the bed.

"So what enemies have tried to ambush me?" I demanded, my voice as melodramatic as possible, since I already knew the identities of these intruders. I threw the blanket aside and fought hard to suppress a grin at the scene in front of me, a jumble of legs, arms and tangled hair, mixed in with gasps and giggling. "Is it some demon or perhaps an advance scout for the Kelmigie Horde? Whatever foul creature it is I will crush it under my heel and serve the remnants to the dogs!"

"No!" The bundle of arms and legs separated into two forms and scrambled madly toward the far side of the bed.

Kellian was eight; his sister Jayce was two years younger, but nearly as tall. Their red hair came from my side of the family. Their chaotic nature was a legacy from both their father and myself.

"It's us, Mother!" Kellian yelled.

"Really it is," his sister added.

"I don't know! Those could be very good disguises. You could de dwarfs from the deep mines. I'd best beat you severely, just in case."

Jayce turned to her brother. "I told you this was a bad idea, that Mommy would be mad and punish us."

I wasn't mad; I was actually quite pleased with the two of them. They had been at each other's throats for the last several days, over some incident that they had both forgotten by now. That they had made peace and decided to attack *me* was a good sign.

"Mother, we were just playing! We thought it would be fun to play Kyber assassins!" Kellian proclaimed.

Kyber assassins?! It didn't surprise me that they had heard of the Kyber Guild.

There were half a hundred tall tales about the Guild, told by children and adults to frighten each other, most all of them far, far from the truth.

Nothing in my possession had the Guild name on it; only a seal, hidden away in a compartment in one of my trunks even bore the emblem.

"All right! I believe you aren't dwarves wearing a disguise spell to make me think you are my children. I will let you off, this time, young Kybers." I picked up a piece of fruit from the table next to my bed, and broke it into several smaller sections. "But only if you help me eat this. Do you agree to my terms?"

"Yes!"

Six weeks ago I had announced that I was taking an extended holiday, officially to escape the seasonal heat in the capitol, as were many others who could afford to move to the mountains or the sea for a few months. Unofficially, I just I needed some time away from not just the Kyber Guild but the various businesses I ran as a part of my "everyday" identity.

I had chosen Yallon's Bay because it was several days' travel from the capitol, far enough away for some privacy but close enough not to be completely out of touch.

Of course, this was not the first time I had come to Yallon's Bay; that had been decade and a half before with my beloved Micah.

Here he was remembered as one of the five thousand men lost in the Battle of Summer Falls. I had no intention of disillusioning anyone about that tale; besides, who would want to hear that he had died in an attempt to assassinate General Zyon, one of our officers who had defected to the other side. I preferred to let our "friends" think of Micah as a dead war hero and myself as a rich, respectable widow.

The down side of Yallon's Bay was a number of "social" obligations that I would cheerfully have ignored; however, attending them was part of my public persona.

"Lady Danya, it is most gratifying to see you again," Lord Junius had said as I arrived at his home for what had been billed as a small gathering. Conservatively, I estimated that, excluding servants, there were well over fifty other guests: human, dwarves, and elves, along with a smattering of other races.

"Danya, are you alright?"

I turned to look at Cyma Tamu, her thin face furrowed as if she was uncertain of what she wanted to hear me answer. She was an inquisitive sort, but Cyma did have the good sense to know there were some questions that were best left unasked.

I realized that I had been staring out at the bay, studying the ships. There were three new ones that had arrived on the morning tide. They were small, compared to the large merchant men more common near the capitol. But Yallon's Bay was off the major trade routes and too shallow to take the really large vessels.

"Oh, it's nothing, Cyma," I said. "It was just seeing the bay right now, something about the way the light is falling on it reminded me of the first time that Micah and I came here."

I let a long sigh write a look of nostalgia on my face. Let Cyma take whatever interpretations of it that came to her mind; she was very good at that. Truth be told, Micah and I had first come here seeking a hideout. A mission for the Guild had gone wrong and we needed to be someplace where no one knew us.

That had been a good time. For a moment I let myself miss Micah more than I had in a long time.

"Now, Danya, you must accept the fact that Micah is gone. Remember always, he died a hero of the Empire; that is something that you and the children can be proud of. While I didn't know him, I have the feeling that he wouldn't want you to lose yourself mourning for him forever. You are still young and very beautiful."

I smiled. "Beautiful, hardly; but thank you, Cyma."

"You are definitely beautiful, don't deny it," she laughed. "In case you haven't noticed, someone can't take his eyes off you."

"Indeed?" I asked, searching my memory for any recent arrivals that I was not aware of.

"Oh yes." Cyma gestured toward a tall man, dressed in silken finery, at the far end of the room. Even at this distance I could see the marks of Elvin blood in him - silver streaked hair, long fingers and a narrow face.

"Interesting" I said

"He's been asking about you," Cyma said, a slight purr in her words.

"Does he not have the courage to come and face me himself?"

"Who knows what will happen. This gathering has at least several more hours of life in it. Then there is the rest of the night." The suggestive purr was back in Cyma's voice.

"Indeed." I admit I was a bit intrigued. I looked back to where he was standing but the man was nowhere in sight.

An hour later I found myself back at the balcony, having made a half transit of the room, speaking with a number of my neighbors, letting them see the "me" that I wanted known around the town. It would be a bit longer before I could withdraw and return home without committing a social faux pas.

I caught sight of the stranger only twice, always at a distance. It seemed an odd little dance the two of us were doing.

The sun had begun to disappear over the horizon, letting dusk streak itself across the waters of the bay as the three-quarter moon appeared in the sky. The full moon would come in a day or so.

"Is the wind from the south, Lady Sable?" It was my admirer stepping up beside me. His words were pitched low, intended for me alone.

"Pardon me, m'lord?"

"Is the wind from the south, Lady Sable?"

I was a little taken aback. No one should have known my Guild name, let alone *that* phrase, in Yallon's Bay.

"Ask about the weather and it will change in a blink."

Sign, countersign.

"How do you know me?" I demanded.

"The Widow told me," he said. "After the proper payments, of course. I hope I get my money's worth."

I wanted to turn and walk away. This man knew far too much about me for my liking.

"Very well, but this is not the place to talk. There are too many ears attached to wagging tongues," I said.

It wasn't that I really wanted to hear what he had to say, or, frankly, gave a damn. I just didn't want anyone else hearing it.

Besides, I was not happy at his being here at all. Of course, knowing The Widow, enough money would make her forget my decree. She also knew, of course, that I would say no; that is an option all of us have. I'd been very specific about my wishes; but the Guild would have the money, the introduction fee was non-refundable.

"Fear not, I've laid a minor glamour around us. All anyone will hear will be whispers that no one can quite make out and none will approach, thinking it a near romantic tryst," He reached up and took my hand. He didn't lean forward and kiss it, just did a slight bow.

"You are prepared."

"I try"

"I need you to kill someone, and it must be soon."

No big surprise there. "First, there are some niceties to be observed, m'lord," I told him. "The courtesy of your name would be a good start, though I suspect I could find it out easily from any one of a dozen people around us."

"My name is not necessary. The only name you need is that of she who I want you to kill."

"On the contrary, it is very necessary. You have sought me out, at some great expense if I know The Widow. Obviously you know who and what I am."

"A killer," he said with a certainty in his voice. "As are all the Kyber Guild."

"Understand this," I said. "I know of five ways to kill you where you stand without even breaking a sweat or staining my clothing with blood. Three of them would look like you had just died a natural death. So shall we start again?"

I could see him thinking, wondering just how far to take my challenge to him, wondering perhaps just how far I would go right now.

"Very well. I am Rathbin of the House of De Costa."

I vaguely knew the family name, one of the lesser Elvin houses, too much human blood for the High Houses to give them more than the briefest acknowledgement, too much elf blood to "fit in" as more than a token among the higher born human clans.

"See, that didn't hurt at all," I said.

De Costa scanned the garden just below us. He gestured toward the far end where I could see a woman, dressed in a fur edged cape.

"That is her, your target. Her name is Layra. She is my sister."

On more than one occasion I had heard my children threaten to kill each other, but the next moment they would be laughing and playing together. De Costa was taking sibling rivalry a good ways further along the track than normal.

"I must decline your offer."

De Costa's face went paler than it had been, then ran red with anger. 'What! You can't! She must die by your hand!"

"Not by my hand. Do it yourself if you are that adamant. I decline. I'm on holiday; there is no argument that will persuade me otherwise"

He grabbed me, his face a grim mask of hate, long finger tightening around my arm. "It must be you!"

With my free hand I slapped him hard and then drove my knee into his groin. That was more than enough to get him to let go of me. I stepped away and saw him draw back, my unexpected attack being quite effective.

In spite of the glamour that de Costa had cast, that little exchange caught more than a few people's attention.

Cyma came running up. "Are you all right?"

"Lord de Costa just needs to learn that when I say no, I mean no."

I left Cyma doing what she did so well, draw the wrong conclusion.

Over the next two days I saw de Costa a half dozen times, always silently staring with the same grim face. I didn't give a rat's ass if he wanted his sister dead, I just couldn't figure out why he insisted that I had to be the one to do it.

That was why, two hours after sunset, on the third night since the party, I was sitting, concealed in the branches of a tree just outside of his house.

I had plumbed certain local sources to find out what I could about the man. It turned out not to be much. He had come from the south, but no one knew exactly where, arriving in Yallon's Bay a month before, having purchased the house through an agent earlier in the year. That proved he had money, but I knew that since even a chat with The Widow can cost an arm and a leg, not to mention your firstborn.

What bothered me was that there was even less to discover about his sister than about de Costa, save that she lived only a mile from her brother. There was endless speculation, but no hard facts.

I had taken to my bed early in the afternoon, complaining of a sour stomach, leaving instructions that I was not to be disturbed. If anyone looked into my bedroom they would see a figure enshrouded in heavy blankets.

De Costa had spent most of the evening in the house's library, studying a number of documents and books that looked very old. Just before midnight he finally blew out the last candle and left the room. I remained on my perch for a slow count of a thousand before dropping onto the balcony outside his window.

Once inside I lit a small candle and put it into the metal holder I had brought; the shutters could be opened one at a time to direct the light where I wanted and to keep it to a minimum

I sat down and began to study what he had left behind. The books were old and had the smell of ages on them. One of them left the palm of my hand tingling after I touched it. I could make out only a single word embossed on the cover, *Aubic.*

There were also loose papers, written in a clear concise hand, spread over the desk top; most were business dealings, nothing personal.

"I think you might find something interesting in the lower right hand drawer, Lady Sable." A section of the bookcase on the far side of the room had swung open. De Costa stood there, a much too satisfied look on his face.

Damn it! I would have read the riot act to any first year apprentice who didn't check for hidden doors when they invaded a room.

"Good evening, Lord de Costa. I get the feeling that you

were expecting me. I presume that you've got a spell on the chair to keep me from getting up."

"Actually, no," he said leaning against the bookcase frame. "But before you decide to bolt or to use any number of those skills that I know you possess, I think you really should look at what is in the drawer."

I rose up slightly, just to test his words and could feel no restraints, sorcerous or otherwise. It would only be the matter of a few seconds to get me out of the window.

Opening the drawer, I found a wooden casket. The wood was smooth, almost silky, to the touch. The hinge and latches were almost impossible to find; whoever had made it had been a master craftsman. I doubted that there would be any sort of contact poison. That seemed to be a far cry from what de Costa had in mind.

Inside was a silver blade laying on a red silk piece of cloth. Two glyphs were emblazed on the blade; I recognized one of them as a Dakarian Moon, the other I did not know but even the sight of it sent a shiver down my spine.

"A Moon Dagger?"

Moon Daggers were few and far between; no more than a dozen were even rumored to exist. They were said to have been forged from sky metal by a Dwarven smith nearly a hundred years ago for an order of sorcerers that had been destroyed in the Three Sabers War.

I personally knew where six of them were; safely buried under several tons of rock in the ruins of the Fulgrham temple. If this happened to be one of those, then there was a lot more to de Costa than I thought.

"I searched for more than a decade after I first learned of them," he said. "Then one day I saw it lying on a fishmonger's table. He accepted a rather large payment and never knew what he had."

"Some people have all the luck."

"I want you to use it this very night."

"On you perhaps?"

"I'm sure that would please you to no end. Before you try, I would suggest that you look at what else is inside that casket." He moved over to a bookcase and picked up a small statuette, running one hand across its surface.

I lifted the cloth and found a pair of small hand mirrors. De Costa nodded, indicating that this was what I was looking for.

Hefting one of them I stared deep into it and felt my heart drop out from me.

Instead of my own reflection I saw my daughter. She was asleep. In the other one I saw my son. Both children were seemingly undisturbed. A small dark spot hovered over each, gradually shifting form into that of a dagger, identical to the one lying in front of me.

"Those are echoes of the Moon Dagger. I assure you that neither of those fine young people will come to any harm, they will simply sleep the night away," said de Costa. "Provided you do as I have requested. The spell that I am weaving will require the heart blood of the house of de Costa. You have two hours to plunge that blade into my sister's heart. If you don't, those blades in the mirror will plunge into your children's hearts."

"You slimy bastard." It took all my concentration to control myself. Losing my temper would not save my children. "I should use this on you."

"I wouldn't. I crafted the spell so that should anything happen to me, then the knives do their work," he said casually. "As for my sister, with her defenses, I can't enter her sanctum, nor she mine, without an invitation. Trust me; neither of us is going to be issuing the other one of those. Now, be on your way, the moon is full. I need her blood spilled with the dagger while the moon is full."

He picked up the two mirrors and looked into their surfaces, smiling.

Given the minimal amount of time involved, there was no way to plan a quiet way into the house of de Costa's sister, so I opted for something simple and straightforward—I went in the front door.

It wasn't barred and there was no sign of any guards. Given the siblings' magical interests, that didn't surprise me, any more than the distinct feeling that I was being watched from the moment I crossed the threshold.

If I believed de Costa, then his sister would be asleep in the master bedroom, toward the rear of the house. He seemed to think that I should be able to waltz right in, carve her like a goose and wander away at my leisure. I, on the other hand, had my doubts about that plan.

"Why don't we have a drink and talk about it?"

I had barely stepped into her bedroom when Layra de

Costa spoke. Like her brother, she seemed able to turn up when no one expected her.

It took a moment for me to locate her, sitting in a large throne-like chair just to the right of the bed.

"I'm not going to insult you by assuming that you don't know why I'm here." I said.

"Lady Sable, you're quite direct. I like that." That she knew my Guild name made wonder just how many people had paid The Widow for information about me.

I suppose I expected Layra de Costa to make some sort of magical gesture and conjure up a globe of light or some such thing like that. Instead, I heard the very distinctive sound of flint being struck, followed by sparks and a shard of wood glowing as its tip burst into flame.

She held it out to the wicks of several candles nearby; the light was enough for me to see her face. Layra de Costa wore green, so dark it was almost black. Her silver streaked hair spilled loosely over her shoulders. I could see the resemblance to her brother.

"Half-brother, actually; our father, shall we say, got around a bit and had a taste for human women. In our cases, two different human women," she said.

"Interesting, you can read minds." That would be all I'd need in someone I had come to kill.

"Not actually; it just seemed a logical thing that you might wonder," she said.

Simple and straightforward, I liked that. I reminded myself that no matter how much I might like her; there was the matter of those two ghostly daggers hanging over my children.

"Did he at least provide you with a reason that he wants me dead?" Layra said, pouring two glasses of wine and passing one to me.

I waited until she had taken a sip before lifting my own, not that I drank from it, but there are ways of appearing to.

"Nothing specific, something about tapping the power of your late father, though he did give me some damn good motivation to follow through on his wishes." I held my hand on the pommel of the Moon Dagger, its metal now ice cold to the touch, letting her see the weapon.

"Did you see a very old book, with the word Aubic on the cover?"

I nodded and mentioned the fact that touching it had left

my hand tingling.

"Our father's grimorie; then it is obvious that my dear brother has broken the seal and found the spells that were the source of our late father's power. From what our parent said, it *would* require the blood of our family to do such a casting," she said.

"Wouldn't your father have had to have a Moon Dagger to do it in the first place?"

Layra reached down to the side of her chair and brought out a blade identical to the one I held.

"He had one," she said.

"It figures," I muttered. Then I let fly with the Moon Dagger.

I probably should have been a lot more discreet, given the large bag I was carrying, when I went back to deCosta's villa. I wasn't in the mood for subtlety; I just wanted to make sure my children were not within reach of his slimy fingers one minute more than they had to be.

De Costa was behind his desk when I entered. "Welcome, Lady Sable, welcome," he said. "I trust all went well and as I requested."

"It did, and I have brought you proof of my deed." I laid the bag down on the floor, near the bookcase with the sliding panel. Very carefully I untied the ropes at the top and pulled it open. In the dim light Layra's face was pale as her head rolled lifeless to one side.

"Unnecessary; her blood on the Moon Dagger would have been sufficient. If you felt you had to bring proof I would have been happy with just her head," he said. "Oh, sweet sister, I've never been more pleased to see you." For a moment it was as if the two of them were alone in the room.

De Costa came around the desk and toward the body. I stepped in between him and his goal.

"Hold it right there. You get her, and I frankly don't care what you do with her," I said. "But only when you fulfill your end of the bargain by taking those ghost daggers from my children's throats!"

I watched his jaw tighten as he stared at me, unblinking. I already knew that he wasn't used to people telling him what to do, and didn't like it when it happened, but I didn't care. I was prepared to do some serious damage to him if that was what was necessary to keep the children safe.

"Very well, Lady Sable," he said at last, his voice as casual as if talking about the time of day rather than children's lives. "You did as I asked and my word is my bond."

De Costa went back to the desk and picked up the casket that the Moon dagger had been in. I could see the two mirrors from where I stood and I felt a tug at my heart seeing the vague forms in them that were my son and daughter.

Holding the mirrors in one hand, he smashed them down against the corner of the desk. Shards of glass flew everywhere. For a moment I felt like I could see the forms of the blades over the pieces of glass, then they dissipated.

I wanted that to be the end of it. But what you want and what happens are often two different things.

"As promised, both of your little darlings are safe," he announced.

"One thing," I said.

"Our bargain is completed. Your Guild will have its fee, and you have your children. What more is there to say?"

"There *is* more," I continued, ignoring his attitude. "Why me when there are any numbers of street thugs, mercenaries, even other Kybers you could have hired? Why did you insist on me?"

De Costa laughed: it was a sickening cackle. "The night I acquired the Moon Dagger I had a vision: my sister, dead, the hand that had wielded the blade was yours. You were a key pivot point to achieving my destiny," he said. "Does that satisfy your curiosity?"

I nodded and stepped to one side. I've dealt with any number of magic users over the years. The necromancers like him left me repulsed. Kneeling beside her, the man moved the cloth further away from her head, and then gently ran his fingers along her hair.

"Not that you weren't planning to do this to me, Layra. You shall bring our father's power to his rightful heir, me."

De Costa grabbed the bag and began to rip it down the center, revealing Layra's blood stained blouse right over her heart. I caught myself wondering if the man knew where that was; he certainly didn't seem to have one.

Even with his back to me I could tell when he realized that something was wrong.

"The Dagger, where is it?" he screeched in a voice that was almost feminine. "I will need it to finish this night's work."

"Oh, is this what you want?" I asked innocently, holding the blade up.

"I think not, brother," said Layra. Her eyes were open, a look of pure hatred on her face. Since she couldn't enter the house without an invitation, I gave her one. It wasn't that I didn't trust de Costa fully to keep his side of the bargain, but it pays to have a backup plan.

Layra brought out the other Moon Dagger. Her aim was good; as close as she was to her brother, it would have been hard to miss. The blade drove easily through cloth, flesh and bone and into de Costa's heart.

I could tell when the shock passed and pain swallowed Rathbin de Costa. Blood began to run around the edges of the blade, spewing out after a few moments to strike Layra, the furniture and even me. He trembled and then collapsed backwards.

Layra struggled out of the bag and to her feet. She stared at her brother for a time and then began to chant. I couldn't understand the words; there are more dialects of elfish than there are grains of sand in the desert.

Any possibility that it might be a mourning chant passed quickly. I could feel the magic stirring in the air around me. I realized she was doing exactly what her brother had planned. I had the feeling that this was not a good thing. Apparently, she had known more than she had let on.

Vague images formed in the air above the body, most of them things that I did not want to even put a name to. But when I saw Killian and Jayce there, I knew what I had to do.

I stepped up behind Layra, threw my arm around her neck and brought the Moon Dagger around. This time it did not strike into the chair to one side of her, as it had earlier, but drove directly up under her rib cage and into her heart.

"I could ha...."

That was all she got out before the light faded from her eyes. I let go of her and she fell down into the arms of her brother.

"I guess you got your money's worth." I told the dead sorcerer.

Sibling Rivalry
Bradley H. Sinor
Here Be Dragons: Tales of DragonCon
Bill Fawcett and Associates

As to why they stole the fire extinguisher, I didn't know and I didn't care.

I had taken the redeye flight into Atlanta, and then discovered that my hotel didn't run a shuttle service to the airport. At first, the only choice that presented itself was the long line of car rental counters. Spotting the MARTA (Metro Atlanta Rail Transportation Agency) sign presented a very workable alternative.

Hey, I've always had a weakness for trains.

Earlier today, I had returned from picking up lunch at the Greek place across the street from my office to find that I'd had a visitor. The interesting thing was the door was still locked tight.

One of my exes keeps telling me I should put in an alarm system, but when you're in a building that would have been old in the Depression, it seems a waste of money. Besides, I didn't think that the wiring could handle the additional load.

Even though I was on the 12th floor, I checked the window anyway. It was locked tight, just like the door. Since there wasn't a fire escape, someone would have had to know a few magic tricks to get inside. Stage magic has always been a hobby of mine, bringing in a few dollars when the P.I. business was slow, and getting in through the window would be beyond me.

Whoever my visitor had been they had left a manila envelope sitting in my desk chair. I opened it to find several things of interest: a round-trip airline ticket, a hotel room confirmation number and a membership in something called Dragoncon.

"What in the hell is Dragoncon?" I asked the empty office.

I've been a private investigator for eight years, so finding answers is my bread and butter. In this case it was easy; I just Googled the term and had the information in a matter of a few key strokes.

Dragoncon turned out to be a large-scale sci-fi convention,

with a lot of actors, musicians, writers, artists and that sort of thing. It had been going on for twenty years and got a shitload of people who were apparently willing to come from far and wide to hang out with their fellow sci-fi geeks.

I had actually been thinking about taking a few days off to go fishing. It looked like the trout would have to wait, though, since included with the other paperwork were twenty pictures of Benjamin Franklin, all of them with non-sequential serial numbers.

This whole thing had piqued my curiosity. I've had more than one person tell me that my curiosity would be the death of me; one day they may be right.

I'd been on the train for a half hour, and had had the car to myself for the last few minutes. That was when the gang-bangers showed up, none of them any older than sixteen; dressed in baggy pants, do rags and vinyl vests.

They stood in the door of the car, surveying the whole scene, before dropping onto one of the plastic bench seats that ran along one side. Three of them were pointing out the window and speaking in low voices; the fourth was lost in whatever was on his IPod.

We'd passed two more stops when IPod boy suddenly stood up and marched across the car. I shifted a bit, just in case there was trouble in the offing. He didn't make a move toward me. Instead, he went to the back of the car and began feeling around under one of the plastic benches. It took a moment for him to find and open a compartment that had been built into the thing. He pulled out a fire extinguisher that had been stored there. With a satisfied look on his face, IPod boy carried it back to where his friends were sitting and slid the thing under their bench without a word being said.

Two stops later the gang-bangers were up and heading for the door before the train had come to a complete halt, IPod grabbing the extinguisher and hefting it onto his shoulder.

"There's something you don't see every day," I muttered.

***"I'm sorry, sir,"* said the** girl sitting below the sign that said Pre-Registration O-Z.

"This membership has already been picked up."

Ms. O-Z was dressed in a tee shirt that bore a cartoon-looking figure of a big-eyed girl in a mini dress and pigtails. Her own hair was dyed black, but had blonde roots showing, and she had a spider web tattoo peaking around her neck.

"Really?" I said.

The girl nodded and looked back at the laptop in front of her. I watched as she moved the mouse around and pulled up several screens. I could see my name in a list of other attendees, and the column next to it indicated that the membership had been picked up.

"Is there a problem here?"

The young woman who stepped up beside Ms. O-Z didn't look too much older than her. I did notice that her name badge, which featured a mini painting of a dragon curled around a rose, had the name Carla.

"No problem," I said. "Except your system says that they gave someone else the membership that was in my name."

"Indeed?" Carla stared at the screen over Ms. O-Z's shoulder for a couple of minutes before she finally looked up at me. I had the feeling that Ms. Carla thought this was just a minor glitch, no doubt expecting much larger ones as the day progressed.

"Can I see your ID?" she asked.

"Certainly," I flashed my driver's license, voter registration and library card. I was carefull not to show my PI license or gun permit; there are some things that people don't need to see.

"Okay, here's the deal. They did apparently give away your membership to the wrong person. That's not a problem. I can print and laminate a new badge for you. I'll meet you at the Special Services area with them in fifteen minutes." She gestured toward a desk in the far corner of the hall with a half a dozen people standing around it.

"That sounds like a plan to me," I said.

Carla was as good as her word. Fifteen minutes later I had a badge that was still warm from the laminator and a manila envelope full of papers. I decided to celebrate this small victory with coffee from a vendor's cart just outside of the hotel.

I had just taken a swallow of a large double latté with triple chocolate chips, when *she* came stomping through a crowd of people in Star Trek uniforms, with an expression on her face that looked about Category Four angry and reaching for Category Five. The girl was maybe an inch shorter than me, dressed in a black tee shirt, cargo shorts and hiker boots, her hair tied in a ponytail.

In no more than three seconds she was in front of me and growling something that sounded like "You son of a bitch" before she drove her fist into my chin.

I didn't go down, but only because I managed to grab the edge of the coffee cart. There were a few stars flying around my head and a flash of light that filled up the world for a couple of seconds, but I don't think I lost consciousness. The next thing that I knew, a Good Samaritan had me by the arm, steadying me.

"Easy there, mate," he said with a distinctive Australian accent. "That's not exactly the way to start the day."

Out of the corner of my eye I caught a glimpse of someone pushing my attacker up against the wall, pinning her between the cart and a big concrete planter. It took a minute or two for me to recover. When I did, I looked back toward where the girl should have been, but saw no one; the only thing next to the planter was a crushed up fast food bag.

"So what the hell did you do to her, mate?"

The pain in my jaw had faded into a dull ache. My newly-made friend, "just call me Reg" had suggested that we go find a good stiff drink, strictly for medicinal purposes, to help me deal with the pain.

That sounded like an idea I could live with, but the rumbling in my stomach presented an argument for a different course of action. I hadn't had anything to eat that morning; the free continental breakfast being offered in the lobby of my hotel had been less than appetizing. Since the main hotels where Dragoncon was centered were in downtown Atlanta, there was no shortage of food possibilities.

So Reg led me through a covered skyway bridge to a large food court, which suited me fine. From the size of the place, it seemed intended to serve the needs not only of hotel guests, but a good portion of the daily business population of downtown Atlanta. People in costumes ranging from Spiderman to SpongeBob Squarepants were mixing with tourists and shining examples of business casual dress.

"I wish I knew what I did to her, or at least who she was. Maybe I would feel like I deserved that whopping," I said finally.

"Well, if you've forgotten her, then you must have done some heavy-duty drinking. She was a nice looking Sheila," he said. Reg was an older guy, mid to late fifties was my guess. His pale hair and skin give him a kind of ethereal appearance. It sort of fit with everyone else I had seen at the convention.

I grabbed a piece of pizza from an Italian fast food place, along with a replacement container of coffee. Reg did the same, taking a Dr. Pepper instead of coffee and pointed toward some empty tables at the far end of the food court. Garish signs, announcing Coming Soon, covered over several unoccupied store fronts in that direction.

Before he had a chance to sit down, Reg's cell phone rang. After a few quick words he announced that the call had been from his office. Apparently, there was some kind of crisis that only he could solve. He apologized, suggesting that maybe we should meet for a drink later and then hit a couple of the convention parties tonight.

So I dropped down into the chair and looked back toward the hallway. From the corner of my eye I noticed someone come through a maintenance door just to my left and up to my table. Just when I thought things were not going to be getting any weirder, I looked up into my own face.

"I think we need to talk," I heard myself say.

"So, are you my evil twin Skippy?" I asked.

Alright, I know that remark scored rather high on the flippant and stupid meters. It was honestly the only thing that I could think of to say right then.

My other self grinned. I'd like to think it was because he understood my reaction. Hey, coming face to face with your identical twin brother, especially when you don't have any brothers, is not business as usual.

He took the seat opposite me with his back to the wall, keeping an open path to the doorway he had come through, and laid a canvas messenger bag on the table between us.

"Why don't you call me Bucky; that will keep things from getting even more confused than they already are," he said. Nobody had called me Bucky in more than twenty years. To the best of my knowledge, there was no one alive who even knew that had been my nickname.

Now that I got a closer look at him, I could see that Bucky had a black eye, some cuts, and, I suspected, a nice collection of bruises. Obviously I was in better shape than my "brother." Damn, even with the nickname, terminology was going to be a bitch.

"Okay," said Bucky. "Let's get down to it. The easiest way to explain this is to be upfront with the fact that I am you, and you are me."

"And we are all together," I said. "Right?"

Bucky chuckled at the reference. It was reassuring to know that my "brother" was a fan of the lads from Liverpool like I was.

"The long and the short of it is that somewhere along the line I made one choice and you made a different one," he said. "We don't have time to compare personal histories, just know it happened and has happened thousands of times. There are a lot of us, a lot of everybody when you get down to it."

At the other end of the food court someone dressed as Hellboy had been deep in conversation with a rather anorexic looking girl in a Wonder Woman costume. Apparently, the lady did not like what the big red guy said, since she dumped the contents of her drink over him and stomped away.

At the sound of the ruckus, Bucky's hand pushed inside his jacket, exposing the butt of a pistol. I've never cared that much for guns; the results of using them are far more final than I like. After a moment he relaxed and turned back toward me.

"So how did you end up here?" I asked. "And what am I doing here, anyway?"

"About two years ago I discovered I could slip between possibilities. I've developed a little sideline of handling cases in different timelines. Only problem is, one of them has gone more than a bit wrong," he said.

Just then a racking cough shook Bucky. I had a feeling that, in addition to the bruises, we were dealing with some broken ribs, not to mention a possible punctured lung. Bucky boy there was going to need to get himself to a doctor as soon as possible.

Once the coughing jag was over, he reached inside of the messenger bag and pulled out a long wooden box that he laid on the table between us. The workmanship was highly detailed with inlaid ivory designs in swirls and geometric patterns. Obviously a lot of time and skill had gone into making it.

"What's in it?" I asked

"Not my business. This was supposed to be strictly a courier job. Pick up the package and get it to my client. Unfortunately, someone took umbrage at the idea of my possessing it; otherwise I would have taken this thing back home, pocketed my fee and then headed to Bora Bora for the weekend."

"Would, by chance, one of those people who got in your way be a good looking girl with dark hair and a hell of a right cross?" I asked.

"You met her, did you?" Bucky grinned. "She's a bit of hellion, I'll give her that. I'm surprised you didn't notice the family resemblance."

"A family resemblance?" I didn't like where this was going. "Are you saying she's another version of the two of us, from some other timeline?"

"Nope, though I have run into female versions of us, but she's not one of them. She's our sister, Elaine."

Oh, damn! I felt my stomach twist in a dozen different directions. My older sister Elaine had been killed in a hit and run accident when she was in the sixth grade.

"Let me make an educated guess," I sighed and pointed at the box. "She is one of the crew that tried to stop you from getting that."

"Give the man a gold star for getting it right on the first try. Not only is she part of the crew, she's their boss. I stung them badly, but," he shrugged painfully, "they gave as good as they got. Unfortunately, during our little "family reunion," the compass unit I use to find my way home to "my" exact world got smashed."

"And without that you can't go home again?"

"How very Thomas Wolfe, but, unfortunately, accurate. I could go 'home,' but the odds on it being the exact timeline that I came from are pretty slim. The thing is, *that* is where my client knows to find me. I would like to get paid." Bucky said it all with the same faux Boston accent that used to drive one of my ex-wives bonkers when *I* did it. I was beginning to understand her point of view.

"I'm not exactly a map maker."

"That's alright, because I had a spare unit. Unfortunately, during our little commotion, I had no time to use it. I had to hide it to keep Elaine from getting the thing. It's none of her business who I'm working for, client confidentiality and all that. Problem is, even though I got away from her and her bully boys, I'm in no shape now to try and get the compass unit back."

"So that's where I come in," I said.

"Yep. It wasn't hard to arrange for your membership and plane ticket. I've visited this time line before, so it wasn't a problem to call in a few favors and lay a trail to get you here. You're the only one I could trust with the truth."

"Thanks, I think. So where is it?"

"You're going to love this; it's on exhibit in the convention art show."

It was time for me to come out of the closet.

According to my watch it was 10 p.m. The art show had been closed for two hours. I, on the other hand had been in the maintenance closet for just over five hours.

I twisted one way, then another to work out the kinks in my leg and back muscles. Squeezing my five-ten frame into a small, smelly space for an extended period of time was not fun. For around the hundredth time since I had left Bucky, I found myself wondering what the hell I was doing. Why should I believe him? This whole thing sounded like something from a bad drive-in movie. Okay, he did look just like me, but they do say that everyone in the world has a double. He just happened to be mine.

The art show took up two large ballrooms, crisscrossed by pegboard and wire frame walls that formed a complicated maze winding hither and yon. I had wandered around the place for some time, trying to orient myself on what was where, and how best to get out once I had secured my prize.

I spotted the compass unit as soon as I walked in the main door; exactly where Bucky had told me it would be. A small metal tube, marked with gages and dials on the surface, lying with a number of other items in a very large treasure chest. That chest was wrapped by the tail of a large metal dragon sculpture.

There were too many people walking in and out, not to mention more than a couple of rent-a-cops prowling the area, so just grabbing it and running was not an option. So, instead, I hid out in the maintenance closet for five hours.

Outside of the room, I heard a mixture of laughter, conversations and that low ambient sound that crowds of humanity seem to make anywhere and anytime. I didn't see any sign of closed-circuit television and it was more than reasonable to guess that there weren't any high tech alarm systems or sensors waiting to be tripped, not on a temporary show like this one. I knew that there would be security of some kind. More than likely it would be the rent-a-cops probably checking the place every couple of hours. That was more than long enough for me to grab the unit and retire to my hiding place to wait for the show to open up tomorrow morning, and then I would just walk out with the regular visitors.

"I'd hold it right there, if I were you," said a muffled woman's voice from just behind me. I took a deep sigh and turned. I'd been dreading this moment ever since Bucky enlightened me as to who had busted my chops that morning.

After all, as far as I was concerned, she had been dead for two thirds of my life. I turned and looked at into the face that I could sort of see my twelve-year-old sister's features in.

"Evening, sis," I said.

"Good evening, little brother." She held a Styrofoam cup in her hands, and lifted it in salute to me. "I think we need to talk."

Bucky found me around noon the next day.

I had spent an hour wandering around the convention dealers' room; there were a hundred and fifty merchants set up if there were a dozen. They had everything that the sci-fi geek could dream of: fantasy jewelry, an endless supply of toys based on everything from comics to movies, computer games, has-been actors hawking their photos and even one or two dealers selling, of all things, books.

I was looking at collectable trading cards when I felt a hand on my shoulder.

"I thought we gave up baseball cards when we were fourteen," said Bucky.

"Please," I tried to put the right sort of irritation in my voice. "These are the ones that my girlfriend's son is nuts about. I score major points with her for keeping him happy, especially since he may be my future step-son."

Bucky chuckled, glancing nervously around the room. He was wearing a leather motorcycle jacket, along with wrap-around sun glasses. Not my idea of the best disguise, especially in late summer Atlanta, but who am I to criticize.

"Shall we," he said gesturing toward the room's entrance. Just outside the door, where two escalators brought a continuing flow of people up and down, there were several large banks of pay phones. Thankfully, no one was using any of them; but in this age of cell phones, how many times do you actually see anyone using a pay phone? I've always been an advocate of hiding things in plain sight; if you're careful, major secrets can change hands in the middle of a crowd.

"You got it, then?" he asked.

"Of course, I did. Let's just say it was easy and leave things at that," I said. Instead of going back to my hidey hole after I had retrieved the item in question, I had slipped out through the hotel employee's hallway; easy and simple. Complicated causes trouble.

I pulled out the compass unit, holding it up in my best Vanna White imitation. The look of relief on his face was major. He twisted his lip in the same way I did when I was contemplating a check from a satisfied client.

"I was seriously wondering if I would see that again," he said.

"Happy to oblige, 'brother'," I said. "Now, you haven't gone and misplaced the box, have you?"

Bucky shook his head and reached into his messenger bag to show me.

"May I?" I asked.

He shrugged and passed it over, as I handed him the compass unit. I trailed my fingers along part of the design, pressing down on an inlayed piece of ivory and on the corner of the box. Something moved and a drawer slid open.

"I'll be damned," Bucky said. I had a feeling that he had tried to open it but had failed and that was why he had been feigning indifference to the contents.

"I wouldn't move, gentlemen, and I would drop that box, if you please," said a tall figure in Star Wars storm troopers armor, standing a dozen steps away. Only, instead of a standard issue Imperial blaster, he held a .38 caliber police special.

Since I had no desire to add lead to my diet I did exactly what I was told. In the process I slid the drawer closed on the box and turned slowly toward our intruder, positioning myself so I blocked Bucky's view of him. In the process, I pushed the box back toward Bucky with my foot.

"You're a little short for a storm trooper, aren't you?" I asked

Then, in a move that I hope would have impressed my

martial arts sensei, I twisted to my right, launching a kick at the gun. The trooper pulled back before my blow could connect, but he didn't retaliate. Behind me there was a distinct whooshing sound, kind of a mini sonic boom.

"Crikey mate, that kick of yours was a little too close for my liking," said the storm trooper, as he reached to pull his helmet off.

"Reg, that was the whole idea," I said, looking back at the bank of phones where no one was standing now.

"So what am I going to do with you, little brother?" Elaine asked, speaking softly in spite of the background noise on the airport bound MARTA train.

"You could always pull a gun and pistol whip me," I said.

"There is that option. As I recall, I never did get even for you putting your iguana in my closet during that slumber party when I was in the fifth grade."

"Hey, a little brother's got to do what a little brother's got to do," I said.

It was still strange talking to her. Part of me remembered that irritating older sister who was mine alone to torment, anyone else stay the hell away from her, whose departure from my life on a rainy street ripped a hole in my soul that didn't heal for a lot of years. The little brother in me was very glad to have her back, even for a moment. Another part of me said who the hell is this woman?

"I still am amazed that you were able pull the whole thing off," she said.

As a matter of fact, I was, too, but I wasn't going to admit it. Right up until I heard the sound of air rushing into the space that Bucky had occupied, when he phased out to his own timeline, I had been convinced that the whole thing would end up as major failure. I was not eager to see my other self mad; I know how I am when I get mad, and it isn't a pretty sight.

"It was just a matter of letting him see what we wanted him to see and making him think what we wanted him to think—basic Stage Magic 101. You keep the audience looking at the right hand while it's the left hand that is getting into mischief. Of course, if he knew that you and I had talked, that might have skewed the whole thing," I said.

Reg had come onto the train with us, though he had taken

a seat several rows away, to give us the illusion of privacy. But I would bet my bottom dollar that he could hear everything we said and was ready to step in on her side, if for some reason she thought me departing from our little arrangement.

From my jacket I pulled a thin manila envelope. Inside were three foil wrapped packages, with names written across them, featuring a familiar figure in a red cape with an S on his chest. Elaine nodded, confirming that these were the items that my other self had "borrowed" from her.

"What's so special about these particular ones?"

"They come from a timeline where the creators of Superman, Jerry Siegel and Joe Shuster, did not get screwed by their publishers and had very long successful careers. You should see the other super heroes they created, amazing," she said, grinning. "Those cards are rare enough to begin with, there aren't that many timelines where they were actually produced; to have them signed by both Siegel and Shuster, well to say the least it quintuples their value. They are worth a fortune to my client, and that's why Bucky wanted them for his client," she said. "The madness of collectors; I have never understood it, but it has proved very profitable to me."

"What I didn't understand from the beginning was, why you didn't just grab Bucky and get them from him, without involving me."

"There was no way to know if he had opened the box, and if he had then he could have hidden them anywhere. Face it, downtown Atlanta is big and has more nooks and crannies than I care to contemplate especially when you are looking for things as small as trading cards."

I pushed the envelope toward her, but pulled it away before Elaine's fingers could touch it. Out of the corner of my eye, I saw Reg turn, and he was obviously ready to step in if things got out of hand.

"So, now, about my finder's fee," I said.

Elaine pursed her lips for a moment and then smiled. "I anticipated that, little brother. If you check your bank account, you will find a substantial payment has been deposited. Your regular daily fee tripled, plus a bonus for your time."

"That sounds fair. Can I trust you?"

"I'm hurt. After all, we're family," she said.

Just then the door between cars flew open and a couple of teenagers came in, two young men maybe sixteen. From their outfits, baggy pants, vinyl vests and do rags, they could easily have been the same ones who had been there when I rode in from the airport, or at least of the members of the same gang. They were arguing about the relative merits of a rap group named "The Deep Ones" and a Goth band called "Death's Big Brother," and got rather loud about the whole thing. Elaine looked at them with some distaste and then turned back to me.

"I think that concludes our business," I told Elaine and passed the envelope to her.

"It's been a pleasure," she said.

Reg came back to where we were standing; they both produced small silver tubes similar to what I had given Bucky, and made some quick adjustments. They didn't fade away; they were just simply not there. The whoosh of air rushing into the space the two of them had occupied was in no way as a loud as when Bucky had shifted time lines, but it was noticeable.

"Damn," said one of the gang bangers who came up next to me. "Two people just disappearing, there's something you don't see every day."

"Indeed you don't." I nodded and passed him another picture of Mr. Franklin to go with the one I had given him and his friend earlier when we made our arrangements. Cold cash does have a way of silencing any sort of awkward questions that might come up.

Once I was alone I pulled three foil wrapped packages out from under my left leg and smiled at the figure in the red cape on their front. If what Elaine had said was even half true in this time line, then these should fetch a nice price, more so than the ones I had switched them for when she had been distracted by the gang bangers. I knew some crazy collectors, too

But even if, in this timeline, these things weren't worth anything, I felt good about the whole matter. It had come down to whether I trusted my "sister" Elaine or my "brother" Bucky.

I learned to trust my gut a long time ago; that's how I've stayed alive all these years in this business. In this little matter my gut had told me not to trust either one, they'd both been playing me and I doubted that I had gotten the full story from either one of them. Instead, the safest path was to trust one person and one person only. Me.

Hey, it's a family tradition.

Who Stand and Wait

Bradley H. & Susan P Sinor
Space Grunts
Flying Pen Press

"Hi, Honey, I'm home!"

The words had barely left Command Master Sergeant Ricardo "Ricky" Molina's lips before he knew that something was wrong.

The small two-room compartment that had been his quarters since being assigned to McArthur Station two years earlier was dark and the air had a musty, stale tinge to it.

Ricky laid his hand, again, on the censor pad next to the door, the soft material of the scanner forming around his fingers. A dull blue light ran across his palm.

"Identification confirmed," said the computer. "Welcome home, Command Master Sergeant Molina. Shall I raise the lights to station normal?"

"Affirmative."

The light rose slowly, allowing Ricky's eyes time to adjust. The room was almost empty, except for the standard issue things that most assigned quarters had—chairs, a table, a fold-down computer terminal. Nothing that couldn't be found in most of the other quarters on the station.

"Tasha?" he said.

From the level of dust, it looked like the place had not been cleaned in weeks. This was not right. He was a slob, and admitted it, but Tasha was a fanatic for cleaning and would never allow it to get like this. Besides, where was everything; the teddy bear that Tasha had dubbed Mr. Tigger and who always sat on the bookcase near the door, her grandmother's jewelry box and the picture of the two of them taken outside the Excalibur Club.

"Tasha?" This time Ricky's voice was lower, and this time, as before, there was no answer.

He glanced at his belt com unit. The time display read 2230 hours. The unit was still showing shipboard time; it wouldn't synch up with station time until midnight.

"Computer, locate Natasha Molina."

"Working, Command Master Sergeant."

The few seconds of silence that followed seemed to run forever. Every possible scenario dashed through Ricky's mind, from Tasha working late to this being part of an elaborate surprise party that she had planned.

"Search completed," said the computer. "Do you require the results at this time, Command Master Sergeant?"

"Yes, damn it! Report!"

"Affirmative. There is no one named Natasha Molina currently assigned to this station."

"That's impossible. She's been here with me for over two years. I saw her just two weeks ago when The Lancelot left on patrol."

"Command Master Sergeant, if you can supply more information concerning this individual, I can expand the search parameters."

"To start with, she's my wife."

Tasha Molina stood at the entrance to docking bay number 12 where she could see the SS Lancelot on the main monitor.

Located at the far edge of Confederation space, Macarthur Station, known as Big Mac to the people stationed there, wasn't the newest or the biggest station in the service. However, since the beginning of hostilities with several breakaway human colonies and their Javialan allies in this sector, it had seen a five-fold increase in ship traffic, much of it military.

In spite of being a civilian employee, as well as a military dependent, Tasha still had to pass through several security checkpoints to get to the dock. She arrived just as the first wave of crewmen on leave disembarked. Many were familiar faces, some even friends who called out to her as they passed.

Only, her husband Ricky, more precisely Command Master Sergeant Ricardo Molina, wasn't among them.

She tried to call him again, but there was some sort of problem with the comm system, which didn't surprise her; around Big Mac malfunctioning equipment had long since become the norm. Oh well, she'd left him a message earlier, during the Lance's approach to the station.

Tasha had been a military wife, and a military brat before that, her father being career Mobile Infantry, tried not to worry, or at least not to admit it when she was worried.

Sometimes things happened to delay leave, so she wasn't too mad, though she might not let Ricky know that too quickly when she saw him.

"May I help you, ma'am?" The voice had come from behind her.

She turned to see Engineer's Mate George Carter, a tall lanky man in neatly pressed coveralls, standing near one of the airlocks.

"Oh, it's you, Tasha."

"Hi, George. I was just waiting for Ricky, but I didn't see him in the first shore leave party. He didn't get restricted to the ship for dumping the captain's palm tree out the air lock again, did he?" she asked.

"Palm tree? Airlock? I have no idea who the reprehensible thugs that were responsible for that stunt might be. After all, it was in gross violation of regulations, not to mention civil law, no matter what it did for the morale of the crew," he said in mock indignation.

"Yeah, right," said Tasha

Just then several small blasts of steam came from one of the conduits that crisscrossed the ceiling of the docking bay. Tasha barely noticed them.

The station was nearly a hundred years old and showed its age in many ways: the sounds of metal shifting and groaning, repair patches on top of repair patches, and a hundred other little things that had all become part of normal life on Big Mac.

"Don't worry, Ricky will show up as soon as he can," said George. "If he doesn't, you can always call me."

"Thanks, George. I'm sure your wife would love that," said Tasha.

Rick came out of the elevator and smiled as he looked down the corridor. It was identical to several dozen others on the station, but a welcome sight for him, because he knew that at the end of it and to the right were his quarters, home.

Before The Lance had docked, Rick had expected to be remaining on board to supervise the upgrades on the tachyon drive. There had been a few rough moments with that temperamental piece of machinery during the patrol, ones that needed to not be repeated in combat.

"Molina, get out of here," Chief Engineer Edwards told

him, his voice conveying the idea that there would be no argument allowed. "You've been working here as-well-as with your men for the last week, almost without sleep. So get lost for the next seventy two hours!"

Rick reluctantly admitted that Edwards was right, some uninterrupted rack time would be good for him, but from the growling in his stomach he also knew food came first.

The main mess hall had looked different, as though it had been redecorated or rearranged while he was gone. He couldn't precisely put his finger on just what had been done, but he knew something was different. Any thoughts about the décor of the place had been quickly forgotten when he caught the odor of steak and fried potatoes hanging in the air.

Rick hadn't gone more than a couple of paces through his front door when a small female figure exploded into his arms, kissing him very intensely. When suddenly being kissed, Rick realized, there was only one logical thing to do; kiss back and enjoy the moment.

The moment, and the kiss, ended abruptly with the girl pushing back from him.

"Where the hell have you been?" she demanded.

For the first time, the stranger became more than just a blurred image and a set of lips that were trying to occupy the same physical space as Rick's.

She was maybe five foot two or three, with shoulder length brown hair that framed her round face, and looked to be in her mid-twenties. Rick searched his memory, but could not place her.

"Wait a minute," he said, grinning. "I think the more important question is, who in blazes are you?"

The girl stared at him for a moment and stepped back, a sheepish look on her face. "Okay look, I'm sorry about that argument before you left. That was two weeks ago and I've had more than enough time to regret getting mad."

Rick looked around, seeing things that he didn't recognize in the room, mixed in with things that did belong to him. "What are you talking about? Who are you?"

"Ricky, you're scaring me," she said. "I'm Tasha. You know, your wife."

This was not a good thing, Rick thought. He scanned the room for some sign that this was part of an elaborate practical joke.

"Wife?" he said finally. "Wife? What wife? I'm not married, never have been and certainly don't have any plans to be. Let me guess. I got drunk at the Star and Comet and we had the bouncer marry us? Look lady, if that was the case I hope we had fun that night, because I don't remember any of it. How the hell did you get in my quarters, anyway?"

Tasha put her hands on her hips and glared. "I'm here because I live here—with you, the same as we have for the past two years. Look, let's drop the joke, it isn't funny. It's been hours since The Lance docked, why haven't you called?"

"I was hungry, and I—wait a minute. Nobody lives here with me," said Rick. Okay, he'd come close a couple of times, but there had never been anyone who, in the end, he wanted to spend his life with.

"You bastard," Tasha muttered and then hauled off and punched him. The sound of her fist impacting his face echoed off the walls.

She didn't start crying until she was in the hall and halfway to her best friend's, Christy's, 'partment.

"Tell me about Tasha," asked Dr. Miles Lander.

Ricky sat and stared at the photograph that hung to the left of Lander's desk. It showed a fog-shrouded city street with a single figure standing near a lamp.

"Where is that?" Ricky asked.

"It's Red Square in Russia on Earth. My wife took that picture about ten years ago. Have you ever been to Russia?" Lander wasn't military; he was a civilian psychiatrist, but his office still had a military feel to it.

Ricky leaned back in the chair facing Lander. He understood why he was here, orders from his commanding officer. After three days of trying to convince everyone that Tasha was real he had been told to "go see the shrink, now!"

"Doc, you've got my DD15 file, so you know that I grew up on the Daedelus colony, and the closest I've come to Earth was Advanced Infantry training at Lunar Seven. Besides, I thought you wanted to know about Tasha?" said Ricky.

Lander, a small man, with an engaging smile, picked up a stylus and made a few marks on a hand unit.

"Making notes on me?" asked Ricky.

"Actually, I'm working a crossword puzzle. Any suggestions for a five letter word that means bizarre? Or do you want to talk about Tasha?"

"Try weird, like this situation," Ricky said. "Okay, Doc, once more. Natasha Molina is my wife. On April 13th we will have been married five years. She's the assistant managing chef for the station mess; she was trained at the Cordon Bleu school in Paris."

If he closed his eyes, Ricky could still remember the party where they had met. Tasha was sitting on the floor in the corner, not talking to anyone, when Ricky had strolled over and asked if he could sit down.

"Only if you promise not to come out with any highly predictable pick-up lines."

"Okay," he said. *"Are you as bored with this party as I am?"*

"Predictable; you can do better than that," she'd said.

"Next year I'll be rotated Earth side. We've been talking about starting a family then," said Ricky.

Lander pursed his lips for a moment. "Sergeant, I've triple checked this. You've never been married," he said. "According to station records for the last five years, there's never been anyone by the name of Natasha Potemkin Molina assigned here, in any capacity, civilian or military."

"That's impossible," said Ricky, balling his fists around the arm rests of his chair.

"I did find twelve Natasha Potemkins in the last forty years in the European Union census records," Lander continued. "The only one that fit the information you gave me was living in Russia until six years ago. She was killed in a train wreck on the way to attend cooking school in Paris. When did you say the two of you met?"

"It was at a party on Lunar 7, five years ago when she came to visit her brother who was stationed there. We were married within three months," he said. Ricky slid his ring, his wedding band, off his finger, staring at the inscription, identical to the one in Tasha's ring.

"Ricky & Tasha, Forever."

Engineer's Mate George Carter filled his coffee mug and added four packets of sweetener and five small milk crystals. A few seconds later the liquid turned caramel colored and he took a sip.

"How can you drink it like that?" Tasha asked him as they

stood near the huge coffee machine at the far end of the mess hall. Someone had attached a hand-lettered cardboard sign to the machine that read "Holy Water."

"One swallow at a time, dear lady," he said, smiling. "Oh, by the way. I talked to Ricky. He looks the same, but he still maintains that he's not married, no matter what everyone else on the station says. I tried to pound some sense into him, but it didn't work. He also keeps saying that his name is Rick, that no one but his grandmother calls him Ricky."

"His grandmother died when he was three," said Tasha.

"Interesting. Ricky also mentioned that you broke into "his" quarters and came onto him like gang busters."

Tasha grinned for a moment, but the smile faded away. "I was just happy to see him. Although, thinking back now, there was something different in the way he kissed me," Tasha said.

"You're the expert in kissing Ricky, so I defer to you in that area. Has he been back home yet?"

"Not that I know of. I spent that night at my girlfriend Christy's place. When I went back, there was no sign of him. I haven't checked The Lance; he may be bunking on board," she said. "Where did you see him?"

"It was at the gym, coming out of the showers. When did he have that scar on his left arm removed? It looked strange not to see that crisscross thing there. Matt and I have always tried to talk him into covering it up with a tattoo, but he never would," said George.

"Because he knows I hate tattoos. Besides, he didn't get rid of it. He's proud of it; calls it his dueling scar, so it's still there," she said.

"No, actually, it isn't," said George as he took another sip of coffee.

Ricky, I wish you were married. That way I could stop being afraid I was going to call your current date by the wrong name and get you into even more trouble than you are capable of getting yourself into," laughed Gunnery Sergeant Matthew McQuay.

It was early afternoon, station time, and there were a lot of people in The Star and Comet, the station's main bar. The thing was, Ricky couldn't bring himself to go into the central mess hall, knowing that Tasha should be there and wasn't.

Ricky shook his head and motioned for the waitress to bring several more beers to their table. Matt McQuay, in the meantime, reached across the table and grabbed the half sandwich that lay in front of Ricky.

"Hey, that's my lunch!"

"Well, at least you've still got an appetite," laughed McQuay. "Besides, what are you doing eating a ham and cheese sandwich? After all, aren't you supposed to be married to a Cordon Bleu chef? Or was it the heir to the 52nd Anterean dynasty you married?"

It took all of Ricky's will to keep from coming out of the chair and throwing a punch at McQuay.

"Cut it out, Matt! I'd think you, of all people, would believe me. Tasha is real, not some Traumatic Stress Hallucination." Ricky leaned his elbows on the table, his head in his hands. "Matt, I miss her so much. When we've been out there in combat or waiting in some cold, wet fire base in the middle of the night for something to happen, sometimes the only thing that has kept me sane has been knowing that I'd be coming back to her." Ricky's words trailed off, but his friend nodded, not needing to hear the rest.

"Unless you've somehow managed to keep it a secret, and knowing you I can't see that happening, you've never been married," said McQuay.

Staring at McQuay, Ricky felt his heart sink even further than it had already. He laughed a dry, sad laugh. "You were madder than a wet hen that we didn't wait for you to get back before we got married," said Ricky "You said, how could I have a best man without you being there, since *you* are the best man?"

"That does sounds like something I would say," McQuay nodded. "But I still don't remember it."

At the far end of the room a retro Kaldian band began to play. It was a song that Tasha loved and would sing along with all the time. Ricky took another drink and wished with all his heart he could hear Tasha's voice right then.

Exactly when the thought occurred to him, Ricky didn't know. He just found himself reaching for his personal comm unit, looking at the screen, then putting it on the table. It was standard issue data and communications setup; McQuay had one just like it on his belt.

"Matt, you better look at this. Check the received list,"

Ricky said, not looking up from the table. He knew what he wanted Matt to find, he also was afraid of what his oldest friend might *not* find.

"What am I looking for? A call from your bookie?" asked McQuay.

"Just look."

Shifting screens with the edge of his fingernail, McQuay brought up the list of calls that Ricky had received over the last three days since just before The Lancelot had returned. He stared for a moment at one of them.

Ricky said nothing as he reached over, without taking the comm unit from his friend's hand, and touched the play button. The voice that emerged from the speaker tore at Ricky's heart.

"Hey, you handsome devil, you. It's me. I've missed you terribly and cannot wait for you to get your ass back here to me. I won't be able to meet you at the dock. I've got three cooks out this shift. But, babe, I *will* be waiting for you. I'm here for you. I'll always be here for you. I love you."

The comm unit screen indicated who, and where, the transmission had come from: Natasha Molina, Central Cafeteria McArthur Station.

"Matt, I'm not losing it."

"Are you going to deck me again?" Rick asked as he found himself facing Tasha. The two of them stood in the corridor outside the mess hall. Rick had just come from the direction of the station bar, "The Star and Comet." There was the odor of more than a couple of strong drinks about him.

"No, I just want to talk. I'm sorry about hitting you the other day," Tasha said slowly. "You're not my husband, but somehow you are him."

"If you think I look confused, then you're right. Even though I think this whole bucket is confused. They keep telling me that I'm married to you, but I know I'm not. I mean, you're a great-looking girl and all, and I sure wouldn't object to getting to know you better. If I was to get married, it might be to you, but I'm not interested in being tied to anyone for a while. Sorry," said Rick.

"I want to say I understand, but I don't, not really. Let's walk," said Tasha. She wasn't at all sure even what she was going to say. "Confusion seems to be the order of the day. I said that *you* aren't *my* husband. I do have one, though. His name is Ricardo Montoya Molina; he's been known as Ricky all his life. I don't know where he is or how you got here, but somehow you're here, he's not and I've got to find him."

Rick and Tasha had to move against the wall as three automated low gravity cargo carriers shot toward the loading docks. There had been more than one injury when people had not gotten out of the way of them fast enough.

"You're saying that I've got a doppelganger, that he's your husband, and that he's stationed here, on McArthur. It's like he and I got switched." As he spoke, Rick pushed his hair into place with the back of his hand in a gesture that mirrored one of Ricky's habits. Tasha had to look away for a moment when she saw it.

"This whole thing sounds like one of Matt's crazy theories," said Tasha.

"McQuay? Yeah you should have heard him in seventh grade claiming to have uncovered some centuries-long conspiracy over the secret formula for Coca Cola," said Rick.

Tasha stopped in front of the 360 degree holographic bulletin board displaying everything from commissary announcements, to current general station information, to the list of the latest vid epics set to play in the big auditorium on level six. At the edge of her awareness, Tasha heard an announcement about the confiscation of some exotic pets that had been smuggled onto the station.

"So, how did McQuay explain all this?" she asked.

"It was a bit far out, even for Matt, stuff about parallel worlds, and crossing timelines," said Rick. "It boiled down to the theory that there are a million, billion possible versions of reality, all based on every decision that everyone makes. If the conditions are right, you can step from one reality to another, sometimes without even knowing it," said Rick.

"If that's so, how do I find Ricky again?" she said softly.

"I don't have a clue. It all sounds like a lot of hokum to me. But, on the off chance that Matt is right, I'd think that the place to look would be somewhere that meant a lot to the two of you. Maybe "Ricky" will find his way there as well. That makes as much sense as anything else that's happened in the last few days," said Rick.

Then, without any preamble, she leaned close to Rick and kissed him on the cheek.

"Thank you," Tasha said, before she headed off down the

corridor. "Excuse me; I've got to go see if I can find my husband."

Ricky stepped through the bulkhead, stopping to dog it closed behind him without even a thought; in space there were some habits that became as normal as breathing. If the station were hit, avoiding explosive decompression definitely seemed like a good idea.

He'd left McQuay back at the restaurant muttering things about parallel worlds and dimensional barriers that, under weird circumstances, could be crossed.

All Ricky knew was that he needed to be alone to think and try to sort things out. And the only place that he wanted to be was The Cave.

Two months after Tasha and he had first arrived on Big Mac, she had overheard two maintenance techs talking about The Cave and whether it was real or not.

After three weeks of scanning old diagrams and station layouts, and tromping up and down corridors that no one had been in for decades, they found the place. Once, The Cave had been the headquarters of the construction crew that had built Big Mac, with banks and banks of monitors and sensors to oversee every step of the construction.

That no one had been there in years was obvious. Most of the sensors were long since burned out, though amazingly, after a link to the station power grid had been rigged, the monitor screens still worked. The Cave was on the edge of the station's gravity generator field, so that if you weren't careful, you would end up flying across the compartment rather than just taking a small step.

"You realize that someone besides us has to know about this place," Tasha had told him as they shared a picnic lunch to celebrate his birthday. The monitors were ablaze with starscapes, so that it was just the universe and the two of them alone in the dark.

Ricky spooned himself another bite of the chocolate mousse that was one of Tasha's specialties, and one of his favorites.

"Obviously some people have heard of it, but they usually classify it as just some old legend, like the great Ghost Fleet or the Magdalenian Serpent," said Ricky.

Tasha had grinned and reached over to where her shirt

lay. "Yeah, if someone shows up they might get the wrong idea about what was going on here."

"My dear lady, we are married, after all."

"Prove it," she said sliding her arms around him and pulling Ricky up against her.

As he dropped into the chair in front of the control panel, Ricky heard the old metal spring groan under his weight. The steady humming of the air vents was a comforting sound. He understood combat, one side fighting against another, all the stuff that McQuay had been spouting just made his head spin.

Ricky didn't know how long he had been in The Cave when he heard the sound of one of the bulkheads opening. He let out a sigh and closed his eyes. He began to massage the bridge of his nose, eyes closed, wishing that the last few days had been a bad dream and that he would wake up in bed with Tasha next to him.

It figured that *now* would be when someone else would find this place.

The footsteps grew closer and then stopped.

"Ricky?" said a familiar voice.

Even in the dim light cast by the monitors, the dark brown hair with the single blond streak running through it, hanging almost to her shoulders, was visible, framing a face that was filled with equal parts fear and astonishment.

"Tasha?"

The two were in each other's arms before Tasha's entire name had left Ricky's lips. Long moments later Ricky relaxed his hold on her long enough to look down at the eyes of the woman he loved.

"If I'm hallucinating, I don't want to know," he said.

"Trust me, I don't know what the rest of the universe has become, but I am not a hallucination and you better not be one either," Tasha said.

"The last three days have been insane. The doctor claimed that you were just a post-traumatic stress hallucination," said Ricky. "He claimed that you had died before we even met."

"I'm real. I'm real," she repeated, tears pouring. Tasha pushed back a few steps from Ricky, her eyes running up and down him, her face ablaze with doubt. Then she grabbed his shirt and pushed the left sleeve up. The crisscross scar was there.

"Authenticating me?" he asked.

"I don't know if I believe that junk about parallel worlds and reality stretched thin and walking between worlds. I just want to make sure I've got the right you," Tasha said. "But know this, mister, I would cross a million universes to find you."

"Sounds like you've been talking to Matt again," laughed Ricky.

"Nope, somebody who is a lot smarter than Matt ever was."

"Who would that be?"

"You, you handsome devil, you," Tasha grinned.

Before Ricky could say anything else the monitors behind them filled with static for a few seconds, then went totally black, plunging the rest of The Cave into darkness. It was a full ten seconds before the room filled with the flickering, far-too-weak emergency lighting.

"This isn't good," Ricky muttered. Beyond the monitors there were very few working controls. He scanned each of them in turn, and felt his stomach tighten as he saw the readouts.

"There's been an overload somewhere in this section. It's a potential hull breach. This looks like we're venting air and plasma and that it can go critical anytime between thirty seconds and ten minutes from now if it keeps escalating."

"Look, I don't know how we managed to get back together again, but I have no intention of losing you this quickly," Tasha said.

"Babes, me neither," said Ricky "We need to move."

Tasha ran ahead of Ricky, moving through the darkness without bothering to ask anything else. The next few minutes were a combination of darkness, pounding hearts and the sound of metal on metal as Big Mac cried out in pain.

With every step, with every hatch that they opened and closed behind them, Ricky expected to hear the sound of the emergency doors sealing off the affected area before the damage spread to other parts of the station. At least this was something he could understand and potentially do something about. If he and Tasha were going to die, at least they would die fighting to live.

"Damn it," said Ricky as he leaned against the final hatch. His face was streaked with sweat, his muscles twisted into hard knots as he fought to force the door open. He had tried to use the controls but they had sparked and arced and forced him to stop. "This damn thing won't move."

"I didn't find you again to have it end up this way," he muttered.

"Neither did I," said Tasha. She smashed her hand in frustration against the door controls. Burning pain coursed through her fingers, but whatever combination of wires she had jammed together proved enough to pull the door open.

"I don't know what's on the other side of this door. I hope it's our world, but whatever it is, you better be part of it with me." Tasha said, grabbing his hand.

"Sounds like a plan to me," said Ricky, pushing her through the door, his other hand on her shoulder. "Ladies first, Mrs. Molina."

"I'm not sure if I even like this ship anymore," said Ricky.

Tasha turned and stared at the dozen or so people who filled docking bay 37 and looked over at the side of The Lancelot.

The ship was being readied for a three week cruise near the demilitarized zone with the Juvial Empire. Most of the fighting with the rebel colonies had shifted far from Macarthur Station, but there were still people who liked to shoot at the confederation.

"You don't have to like her, as long as she works and brings everyone back safely. Besides, what's wrong with the Lance?" asked Tasha.

"Nothing, except she is keeping us apart, and that I don't like," laughed Ricky.

"Not a whole lot we can do about it," his wife said. "I'm going to miss you, mister."

"You definitely showed me that last night, not to mention a number of our neighbors," Ricky said, pulling his wife up against him.

"Hey, I can't help it if the comm system was on broadcast," she giggled.

The couple's lovemaking had gotten quite vocal the previous night, a fact they discovered when station security had shown up at their door due to a noise complaint.

"Maybe they learned something, or maybe they were just jealous," observed Tasha.

"Or just wanted to sleep."

A young man in a service coverall came down the gangway

toward them. Ricky didn't recognize him, but while The Lance was always short of crew, there were usually one or two new faces every patrol.

The man stopped a respectful distance from the couple, and then snapped a salute when they turned toward him.

"Command Master Sergeant," he said after his salute was returned. "The Captain sends his compliments and requests your presence on the bridge before launch."

"Please convey my compliments to the Captain. I will join him as soon as possible, and let my people know that we will be having a full inspection as soon as we are underway," Tasha snapped.

"Yes, ma'am," he said, heading back into the ship.

"You scared the hell out of him," said Ricky. "Not bad, not bad at all."

"Hey, I had a good teacher, and I hope you did too," she told him. "I just hope I remember everything."

"You don't have to know it, just make them think you do. This may not be the reality that we came from, but I think we'll get along just fine," said Ricky. "Of course, I may have a bit of trouble with that recipe for Chocolate Mousse when I try to run the mess hall."

The Memory of Desire
Susan P. Sinor

She closed the book, placed it on the table, and finally decided to walk through the door. She had restrained herself from throwing the volume across the room only because of her reverence for books. It wasn't very long, but it had taken her longer than usual to get through. The words inside the book, however, were enough to tear her heart out and leave her in a puddle on the floor. Almost.

Steeling herself, she followed through on her decision. Outside, the world seemed normal. People walked up and down the sidewalk on their way to their own destinations. She, however, had no destination. She felt at sea, awash in emotions unknown for a long time. Why had she picked up the book, that book? She didn't even know where it had come from. There had been others available, but the title intrigued her: *The Memory of Desire.*

She had never expected to find that it was about her. The names were different, but the experiences of the heroine, the loves and losses, mirrored her life. The memories it brought back to her were often painful, sometimes pleasant. A few were joyful. She clung to those. As upset as it had made her, she had finished the book.

She looked around, watching the people on their way. She had no place to be, but she started walking, anyway. Random turns took her to places she had never seen, although she had lived in that city for most of her life. She had always been too busy to search out new experiences. She had been too shy to search out new people.

Now that she had nothing else to do, she was doing nothing. Reading, watching television and listening to music filled out her days, but she had tired of the same old things. Perhaps reading that book had been the best thing for her, to break her out of her shell. She almost felt like chirping like a new chick. She *was* a new chick, freshly hatched.

Eventually she found herself in a dead-end alley, a cul-de-sac. Instead of the backs of buildings, there were houses. Walls in pastel colors with potted plants on top surrounded gardens. The walls all had gates that opened into the alley, and one of the gates stood open. Curious, she peeked through the opening.

The garden was lovely, paved with flat stones, with open areas for gardens of iris, tulips, marigolds and peonies. On a paved area near the house was a table with four chairs around it. At the table sat a man reading a newspaper. He looked up and saw her standing there.

"Come in," he said to her. Against her better judgment, she walked toward the table and sat in a chair.

"Would you like some iced tea?" he asked.

"Thank you," she replied, and he poured her a glass from the pitcher on the table.

He looked at her for a moment, then said, "Welcome to my home, Mary."

She was almost not surprised that he knew her name. Things seemed strange to her now. As she looked at him her past seemed to wash away, leaving room for something new, something different. Perhaps, something exciting. As if recovering a memory she never had experienced, she said, "Thank you, John." As they drank their tea, gazing at each other, it occurred to her that had she not read that book, among all the others, she would have not left the house, roamed the streets, found the one place she needed to be, and the one man she needed.

To Sleep, Perchance To Dream
Sue Sinor

Mike had been having the dreams, or nightmares, for weeks. The beginning varied, but the ending was always the same. Whatever else was happening, a phone would ring.

Mike was one of those people who could not ignore a ringing phone, even if it wasn't his. He wasn't really OCD; this was just a quirk. Not the only one he had, but the most annoying for his friends when he answered their phones, and inconvenient for him when he couldn't find the phone that was ringing. More than inconvenient, really. Sometimes terrifying.

These dreams always woke him up in a cold sweat. Sometimes he could remember them, sometimes not. What he did remember was answering the phone to silence. He'd repeat "Hello," but no one would answer. The times he remembered past that point were the worst. Always, after the silent call, would come vague terror, some indefinable squamous creature threatening him. He couldn't remember why he was afraid, but he'd wake up screaming. It was a good thing, he figured, that he was single. At least he didn't disturb anyone else. After those dreams he would get up, no matter what the time. He would watch TV, a comedy or talk show, or read a humorous book. He'd do whatever it took to stay awake.

After a while, he suffered from nervousness and lack of sleep. His co-workers and, worse, his boss, noticed.

"Mr. Conner, have you been staying out all night? Your work is suffering," his boss said to him one day.

"No, Mr. Bliss, it's just that I've been having nightmares," he explained.

"Well, stop it. If you can't handle your work load, I'll have to find someone who can."

That's all he needed, more stress.

"I'm sorry, sir. I'll do better, I promise." He didn't know how, though.

He started taking sleeping pills, hoping that they would prevent the nightmares. Those made him oversleep, and kept him groggy all morning. That took so much of a toll, that one day he arrived, late, to find a pink slip on his desk. He cleaned out his cubicle and went home.

With nothing to do, he decided to take another pill. Sleeping should help him get through the day. And if he didn't wake up? "I have nothing to live for," he thought.

For several days, he would wake up, take another sleeping pill and go back to sleep. He didn't eat much, and never went out. He couldn't make himself look for another job. What's the use; he wouldn't be able to keep it, anyway.

He got into a routine of sleeping, and sleeping some more, and then sleeping again. The pills had worked, keeping the nightmares away. "Maybe they've stopped entirely," he though, and decided to try sleeping without the help of the pills.

That day he stayed awake. He ate a good breakfast and went out to buy more food; his stores were running very low. He hadn't shopped in two weeks. He walked to the supermarket around the corner, carrying a large shopping bag, which he carried home filled to the top. He decided to fix a nice sandwich for lunch, and maybe a steak for dinner. He'd take a walk after dinner to tire himself out, and go to bed late for a restful sleep.

After dinner, he washed his dishes, put them away, and took a hot shower. He watched television for a while, and, at eleven o'clock, lay down in his bed.

It didn't take long for him to drop off. He had a pleasant dream about sailing on a lake, then woke up to get a drink of water. After he went back to sleep, things got darker. He dreamed he was back at work. His boss was yelling at him for coming in late and threatening to fire him. In the middle of the tirade, his phone rang. He picked it up and said, "Bliss Brothers, my name is Mike. How can I help you?" There was silence. "Hello? Hello? Is anyone there?" He was feeling panicky. He screamed again, "Is anyone there?"

"Hello, Mr. Conner? This is Advertisers Clearing House. I'm calling to inform you that you are the winner of ten million dollars in our contest. We'll come by your house this evening to present you with the check. You'll be famous, Mr. Conner. See you tonight."

Mike woke up and started screaming.

Bad Day
Susan P. Sinor

Janice was having a bad day. It was the day after Christmas, and Janice had been assigned to the return counter at the discount store where she worked. She figured she must have done something to piss off her boss, since her regular job was as a checker.

This was the worst job to have on this particular day and the several after it.

"Welcome to Save-A-Bunch, sir. How may I help you?" she said to her first customer.

"I want to return this toaster I got for Christmas. My sister-in-law gave it to me and it's not what I want," the man told her.

"Do you have the receipt? It's much easier if you do," she replied.

"She didn't send it with the gift, and I don't want her to know I returned it."

"Did she buy it at a Save-A-Bunch?"

"No idea."

"Was there a problem using it?"

"Haven't used it. It's not what I want, as I said."

Janice inspected it. "It's not a brand we sell at Save-A-Bunch. She had to have bought it at another store."

"Look here, lady. This store says it will accept returns from any store on the day after Christmas, which this is."

"I can offer an exchange. But, since we don't sell this brand, as I said, we can't offer a refund." The line behind the man was growing and she needed to get him taken care of quickly.

"I don't shop at this store. I don't like the merchandise you sell. It's cheap, like this toaster. If you won't give me a refund, I'll go to the top and complain. I'll get you fired for this!" The man took the toaster and stalked off.

Janice sighed. "May I help you, ma'am?"

The woman standing at the counter tossed a dress at Janice and said, "It doesn't fit me. I'd like to exchange it for another size."

Janice looked at the tag. It said XXL, which was the largest size the store sold. She was pretty sure XXL would be too small for this woman.

"Certainly, ma'am." She wrote a number on a slip of paper and handed it to her. "Here's the price of the dress. Just bring the replacement item back to me and I'll ring you up."

"Thanks," the woman said and walked away.

"May I help you, sir?" she said to the next person in line.

The day went more like her first customer than her second. By lunch she was frazzled and by the end of her shift at eight o'clock p.m. she had a raging headache and her back was killing her. As she clocked out, her boss went up to her and said, "I need you to do a double shift tomorrow on the return counter. I'll see you at seven in the morning."

Janice just looked at her and started to shake. She couldn't afford to lose this job, so she couldn't yell and scream, or even protest. She just nodded and her boss walked away.

DeWayne was having a bad day. As a minor angel, his duties lay in the protection area. He was a Guardian Angel, but his guarding had been lax lately.

He had let one of his charges, a little old lady, cross the street by herself, failing to provide a Boy Scout to help her.

His second infraction had happened when a little boy climbed his back-yard fence and went exploring. His mother had not found out until she called him in and couldn't find him. She had had to run two blocks to catch up with him.

Then a teenage girl had gotten into a fender-bender while texting. DeWayne was pretty sure that he had inserted the thought into her head awhile back that texting while driving was against the law, but he could have just thought he had.

The rest of day went in the same direction, until his supervisor, Leon, had reprimanded him. "You must pay better attention," Leon told DeWayne. "I want you to grant the next request one of your charges prays. No exceptions. I'll talk to you tomorrow about this." Leon wafted away to supervise someone else.

DeWayne had one more charge he hadn't checked up on. This one worked at a discount store. Janice, he thought her name was. He had never had any problem with her, so he seldom followed what she was doing. Today, though, he discovered her slumped on a stool in the employee's lounge, sighing. He went closer to see what was going on when he heard her say, "Oh Lord, kill me now."

He knew what he had to do.

Doors
Susan P. Sinor

"What's this?" I asked, holding out an object.

"Don't know. Where'd you get it?" she answered.

"My pocket. What do you think it is?" I passed it over.

"Looks like some kind of key. Strange, though. How'd it get in your pocket?"

"Don't know."

I had gotten home from work, frazzled and angry, and reached for my house key. This wasn't it. I had to knock to get in the house.

"But it's the only key I have. My house key has disappeared. It's a good thing you were home or I'd still be standing outside. This has not been a good day."

"Poor baby. Well, at least it's Friday. We'll get another one made tomorrow so you won't have to stand outside in this awful weather." She grinned because we had had lovely fall weather for a week, with more of the same in the forecast.

The house in question was old. Not just Art Deco or Art Nouveau old, but Baroque or Rococo old. Centuries old. We were living in Germany because of my job. It was just a temporary assignment, but we'd been there ten years already with no end in sight. We'd been renting the house all this time so it felt like home. A cousin of hers owned the house, which had been owned by members of her family for centuries.

After breakfast out the next morning, a high point of the week, we returned home with a shiny new house key. Or so I thought. I had put it in my pocket. I know I had. She had seen me put it in my pocket. I had felt it though the fabric after I had put it in my pocket. But it wasn't there.

Instead, I found the same key I'd pulled out the day before. Or another one like it. The first key was on the dresser at home.

Fortunately, she had her key. She always had whatever we needed. No mysterious key-things for her.

I went straight to the bedroom to see if the new house key had magically changed places with the other key-thing on the dresser. No key of any kind there. I searched my pocket again.

Then the other one. Then the back pockets. Nothing.

"I think the universe is trying to tell me something," I told her.

"What would the universe want to tell *you*?" she asked on her way to her reading chair with a thick book in hand. "I mean, after all, I don't think the universe really cares about the contents of our pockets."

I thought about that for a while. She may be right, but there has to be a reason I can't hold onto a house key, but can't get rid of a funny-looking key-thing.

I spent the next few days with the key-thing in my pocket instead of my house key. Knocking to get in my own home was getting old.

"SOMETHING MUST BE DONE," I proclaimed, finger pointing toward the ceiling.

She just looked at me. I wasn't known for my proclamations.

"I mean about this key-thing problem."

She stirred the pot of our dinner, and then put the spoon down and turned to me. "This must be happening for a reason. Have you looked for keyholes the key might fit? I think you're supposed to use it somewhere. Why else would it keep appearing in your pocket?"

She was probably right. She was always probably right. I should learn to trust her judgment.

"Okay," I said, and I went out looking for keyholes.

The obvious one was our front door. I knew it wouldn't fit that one, so I went on my way. I didn't think the neighbors would appreciate my checking out their door locks, so I looked for other likely places.

The stores around our neighborhood were starting to close, so I surreptitiously tried the key in each one, pretending to try to enter. Nothing. I looked at tree trunks to see if any of the bark formations resembled keyholes. I looked at the rocks placed in ornamental patterns around any landscaping I could find. Still nothing.

By that time it was starting to get dark, so I headed home. At the front door I automatically pulled a key from my pocket and put it into the lock. It fit. Still without thinking, I opened the door and started to step in.

Something was different. It looked like the inside of our house, but strange. The furnishings were ones that had been there when we moved in and hadn't replaced yet. I heard voices from another room; one sounded like her.

The other sounded like—me.

I took a step back and closed the door. I looked at the key. It was the key-thing, all right. And it fit my door. But the other side of the door wasn't—exactly—my house.

I knocked on the door and she opened it.

"I wondered when you'd be back. Did you find anything?"

I hesitated, but only for a moment. Did I want to tell her what I just saw? Maybe not yet.

"No. Didn't find anything. Might try again tomorrow, though." Then I went in and ate dinner.

The next day, after another excruciating day at work, I wandered around the other way from the house before I went home. I paused, trying to decide whether to use the key or knock. Well, nothing bad had happened the day before when I'd used the key; might as well do it again.

This time the furniture was more different. I mean, it wasn't ours and it wasn't what I'd seen the day before. I heard my voice again, but the female voice wasn't hers. A different wife? A girlfriend? As I stood there a dog walked into the room. It looked at me and started to growl. Then it stopped, with a puzzled look, and looked back at the room where the voices came from. The poor thing couldn't figure out why the man at the door smelled familiar, even though it could hear the person it thought I was talking in the other room.

After a moment I remembered the time a friend brought her dog over for us to keep for the weekend.

I closed the door and knocked again. She let me in.

"No luck. What's for dinner?"

I didn't look again 'till Saturday. We went out for our customary breakfast at the cafe down the street. I made a show of looking for keyholes on the way back and trying any I found. When we got home I made sure I was talking, distracting her from what I was going to do. I had the key-thing out and stuck it in the keyhole.

"Whoa, look at that!" I exclaimed. "It fit our door. I never thought to try it here."

I turned the key and opened the door. There was yet another set of furniture in the living room. I showed surprise, since I hadn't told her anything about what I'd found on the other side of our front door the two other times.

She pushed around me and stepped inside before she even registered what she saw.

"What the...?" She stopped short and stared at the old-fashioned sofa, chair and coffee table. "That's not our furniture." She looked around the rest of the room. The far end had the same style dining room suit as the living room did. The pictures on the walls were of hunting scenes and landscapes. It wasn't ours, but the furniture finally fit the time period our house was built.

She looked at me. "Where *are* we?"

"Don't know. The outside looks like our house, but the inside sure doesn't. Come back out."

She stepped back and I closed the door.

"Maybe you should open it this time." I moved aside so she could use her key.

"No," she said. "Let's try yours again. We don't have to go inside, though. We can just look."

So I did. It was yet another style of furnishings. These seemed older than Renaissance, Gothic, maybe?

And we tried again. Each time, the furniture and decor looked older and older, meaning from earlier time periods. If we kept trying, perhaps our bungalow would completely disappear.

We discussed the situation at length. Neither one of us was especially happy at work. We didn't have family anymore or friends that we cared about much. It was just us.

But what we didn't know was how the key worked. It fit our door, but would it fit the locks of the 'other' doors? Would the occupants see us or the open door? If we both went in and closed the door, would we still be able to get back to 'our' house? And what would happen if we went back so far that the house hadn't been built yet? That was a lot of questions.

We talked it over and decided to test the situation.

The next time we used the key we left a note for her cousin. It read: If you find this note, we have taken a chance on a fantastic adventure. Don't worry, we'll be fine. And don't look for us; we won't be anywhere you could find us. There's money in the envelope to cover any costs our disappearance might incur.

We'd packed anything we thought we'd need or couldn't part with into two backpacks, or rucksacks, as they were probably called. We didn't know what we'd encounter, but we knew whatever money they used would be so unlike what we had that we left almost all of it behind. If our experiment didn't work and we returned to the same place and time that we had left, well, all our belongings would be waiting for us.

We hoisted our luggage and left the house, locking the door with her key. For luck, or something, we walked all the way around the house before unlocking the door with my key-thing.

We paused a moment before opening the door to hug and kiss each other.

"Well, here we go," I said, taking her hand.

"At least we're together," she replied, squeezing mine.

And I opened the door.

Fairy Story
Susan Sinor

"Time for bed, my dears," I said, scooping up my treasures. "I'll tell you a story."

"About faeries?" said Amelia.

"About dragons?" said Tobias.

"About faeries AND dragons. And magic," I said, setting them down. "Scurry on." I followed them up the stairs and into their small room. Between their beds was a chair that the children called The Throne.

It was the storyteller's throne and I sat in it once they were properly clothed for bed and covered by blankets.

"Once upon a time," I started. "Faerie and dragon tales always start with 'Once upon a time'."

"We know!" cried the twins. "Go on!"

"Very well, then. Since you know the beginning, perhaps you know more. What comes next?"

Amelia thought for a moment, and then said, "There was a beautiful princess."

At the same time, her brother said, "There was a fearsome dragon."

I said, "Well, which one is it?"

"A beautiful princess captured by a fearsome dragon!" they said together.

"Very good!" I replied. "There was a beautiful faerie princess named Alexandria who had been captured by a fearsome dragon. Her father, King Alexander of Faerieland, was very distraught about the situation. He loved his daughter very much. What do you think he did?" I asked them.

"He asked all the princes in the kingdom to save her, of course. And promised her hand in marriage to whichever one did." Amelia had heard a lot of stories like that.

"But it was a small kingdom, and the only princes around were her brothers. Any other ideas?"

They shook their heads, so I continued. "So he asked any unmarried young person in the kingdom to save her. Any young man who rescued the princess would be made an official prince so that he could marry her. If, by some chance, it was a young woman who rescued her, she would be made an official princess and marry one of his sons. As you can imagine, every unmarried young person in the kingdom ran out immediately to save the princess. But there was a problem. What do you think it was?"

This time Tobias spoke up. "They didn't know where to find her."

"What a smart boy you are. No, they didn't. If the king hadn't been so upset about his daughter's plight, he might have found it amusing to watch his subjects running around, thither and yon, to find her."

"Didn't they know that dragons live in caves in the mountains?" Tobias asked.

"Very good question, dear. You would think so. Anyway..."

"How did the king know that a dragon stole Princess Alexandria?" asked Amelia. "Did the dragon send him a ransom note? Did the dragon grab her in front of people? If it did, why didn't the people follow it so they'd know where it went?"

"Those are all very good questions, too." I thought quickly. "As it happened, someone did see it, but the dragon flew off so quickly that he couldn't follow fast enough. But he did run immediately to the palace to tell the king. The king was so grateful to hear the news so quickly that he gave the man a gift."

"What kind of gift?" they asked in unison.

"The king gave the man a bowl made of gold, which would provide his family with whatever they needed for many years. Since the man was married, he could not marry the king's daughter as a reward for finding her."

"Did anyone find the princess?" Amelia looked close to crying.

"Of course someone did. In fact, a young man who was unknown in the kingdom showed up at the palace, informing the king that he would find Princess Alexandria and bring her back. Then he would marry her and take her to his kingdom."

"Didn't that make the king sad? The taking away part, I mean?" Amelia asked.

"Well, the finding part he liked, but, no, he didn't like the taking away part, although he knew that if she hadn't been stolen away, she would have married a prince from another kingdom and gone to live there, anyway. Okay?" I reached over and hugged Amelia to keep her from getting too excited.

"Okay," she said, settling down.

"Anyway, the young man, he was called Frederick, assured the king that he could find her, so the king gave the young man his blessing. Now, Frederick knew exactly where Princess Alexandria was. You see, Frederick had a secret. Frederick lived by himself in a very comfortable cave in a mountain not too far away. But he was lonely. He wanted someone to live there with him and keep him company and he wanted not just any someone, either. He wanted Princess Alexandria. He had another secret, too. He was a dragon. He could turn himself into a young man when he wanted to, but most of the time he was a dragon. And he had a third secret. He was the dragon who had abducted Princess Alexandria. He had, on occasion, walked the streets of the town in human form. The first time he saw Princess Alexandria, he fell in love with her. He didn't know who she was then. He saw her walking with several other young women, chattering and laughing. She was the most beautiful one of them all, and she had a regal air about her, which, of course, was because she was a princess. He decided right then to steal her away when he could and take her to his cave to be his wife."

By that time Tobias was settling in his bed, his eyes drooping. Amelia, however, was wide awake and excited about what would happen next.

"So then he got the princess and brought her back and they got married and went back to live in his cave and lived happily ever after," Amelia rattled off.

"Not quite," I said. "He couldn't tell the king all this because the king would be very angry and something bad would be bound to happen. No, he went back to his cave in dragon form and told the princess that he would be gone for a little while and that she should be good and stay where she was. She agreed, because the dragon had treated her very well. He had made her comfortable and had provided her with everything she needed. They would play word games and tell each other stories. She thought of her imprisonment as a sort of holiday from her duties as a princess. Then the dragon left, flying to the other side of the mountain where he changed into his human form. It was quite a trek, climbing around and up the side of the mountain where his cave was, but he didn't want to show up right away and he wanted to look tired; otherwise, the princess might be suspicious. So he took his time. He was dressed in armor and had a sword. Dragons can be wearing anything they want when they change to human form, you see, because they are magic. So he didn't need to keep human clothing around. Anyway, he made a big show of approaching the cave.

He called out to the dragon as he climbed, "Hey, dragon! I've come to slay you and rescue the princess. Come out to meet your doom."

Yes, that was a little cheesy, but that's the way they talked in those days. The princess came to the opening and called down, "The dragon has gone for a while, but I don't want to leave. I promised him I would stay until he returned."

"Your father, the king, is very worried about you and sent me to rescue you. My name is Frederick," he told her. "You must come back with me."

"Oh, my. I don't want Father to worry," she replied. "You go tell him that I don't want to come home yet. I'm having a very good time here with the dragon."

That made Frederick feel very good, but he was afraid to reveal to her that he was the dragon.

"But he won't believe me. He'll think I failed to rescue you and worry even more."

"Oh, pooh. I guess I'll have to come with you and tell him myself," she said. "Then I'll just have to come back quickly, so the dragon won't think I broke my promise. I'm very fond of the dragon."

This also made Frederick feel good. He was sure that she was falling in love with him. She quickly climbed out of the cave's doorway and down the mountain. When she got to the bottom, she looked around. "Can you show me which way to go to get home?" she asked Frederick.

"Of course," he replied, and started out the way he thought was right. He knew the way to go when he was flying, but walking there was another matter. They walked and walked, down valleys and across foothills, until they were both lost.

"Oh, dear, now I don't know how to get back to the dragon's cave, either. He'll get back and find me gone and he'll be very angry." Then she began to cry.

"Don't worry, princess," he said. "I'll get you home, I promise. But first I have to tell you a secret."

She looked at him, drying her eyes, and said, "A secret? I

love secrets."

"Promise me you won't get mad?" he implored.

"Why would I get mad if you help me get home?"

"You'll see," he said, and began to change to his dragon form.

"When Princess Alexandria saw this happen, she gasped and turned to run away.

"No! Princess, please stay. You know I won't hurt you," the dragon called.

She recognized his voice and stopped. "You? You are Frederick?"

"Rather, Frederick is who I am when I change to human form," he said. "I have loved you since the first time I saw you. The only way I could think of to get to know you was to steal you away for a while. I hope I haven't frightened you."

After Alexandria got over the shock of what she saw, she said, "Actually, I had begun to fall in love with the dragon, but now seeing you as a man, I must say that things have changed. You'll have to convince me to trust you."

"But I'm the same, er, man that I am as a dragon," he exclaimed.

"You deceived me! You kept that secret until now, when you had to reveal it."

"Please forgive me. And don't forget your father. He is very worried about you." Frederick had changed back to human form and was almost on his knees.

"Oh, yes, my father. He will be very angry with you. I'm sure he will deny your suit."

"I've already talked to him, and he promised me your hand if I should bring you back unharmed."

"I see. You've gone behind my back. What if I don't want to marry you?" the princess said.

"But your father has promised you to me," replied Frederick. "And why would you not want to marry me?"

"Because I would like some say in the matter. You have wooed me as a dragon; now woo me as a man." At that, she walked away and found her own way home.

"Her father was overjoyed when she returned, not only because she found her way home herself, but because he wouldn't have to honor his promise to the young man.

"The king gave a ball to celebrate his daughter's return, and things got back to normal at the palace."

"Wait!" Amelia cried. "Is that the end? Doesn't the princess marry the prin..., er, dragon? Isn't there a happy ending?"

"Of course the ending is happy," I answered. "But can't it be happy without the princess marrying the dragon?"

"I suppose," said Amelia, but she didn't look happy about it.

"Yes, it can. But in this case, that's not the way it ended." My little girl perked up.

"In fact, the princess became bored as life went on. She missed her time with the dragon, and was willing to accept the man to get the dragon back. But there wasn't anything she could do about the situation. She didn't know how to get hold of the dragon or the man, and she didn't know her way back to the cave."

Amelia looked sad again.

"But one day, several weeks later, the man, Frederick, came back to the palace and requested an audience with the king."

"To tell the king he wanted to marry Princess Alexandria," Amelia filled in.

"In a way. Frederick wanted the king to host a competition. Since the princess had gotten home on her own, he wanted King Alexander to invite princes from other kingdoms to come and participate in a contest to win the hand of the princess."

"And the king said yes, of course," said Amelia.

"Not at first. You see, the princess was still very young and her father wanted to keep her at home a few more years."

"But he promised her hand in marriage to anyone who could find her," she protested.

"Yes, but that was only to men in the kingdom, so she would have still lived there. This was different. Whoever won this competition would take her away from the kingdom to live."

"But the dragon lived in the kingdom, didn't he?"

"Yes, but the king didn't know that. He didn't know anything about Frederick. He hemmed and hawed and thought and pondered. He sent one of his advisors to find out whatever he could about Frederick." I paused.

"Well, what did he find out?" Amelia asked, impatiently.

"He found out...nothing. He couldn't say that Frederick didn't exist, because Frederick was there, but he couldn't find out who he was or where he lived or anything. The king refused Frederick's request for a long time. But Alexandria knew what was going on, and she really wanted to marry Frederick, so she wheedled and cajoled, and finally the king consented to invite the princes from the other kingdoms to come and compete for the princess's hand in marriage."

"Wasn't she scared that some other prince would win? Then she'd have to leave the kingdom."

"Not really. She knew that Frederick could use all his dragon strength and his human intelligence in the battle. What she didn't know was what the competition would be. Often contests were jousts or swordfights, or sometimes wrestling. She knew Frederick could win those. But what if it was something else? What if it was playing chess or dancing? She didn't know if Frederick knew how to do either of those. Finally, she asked her father."

"Your Majesty," she said, being very polite. "Might I ask what type of contest you will ask the princes to compete in?"

"I have thought about that, my dear," he answered. "I have decided to riddle them for your hand. It will be a difficult riddle, so the most intelligent will win."

"What will the riddle be?" she asked.

"I have not finished making it yet. You will hear when the rest do."

"That worried me a bit. I had never been very good with riddles, so I put my thinking cap on. Presently, I came up with one that seemed to work."

"When the king had called all the princes together, he explained that the contest was a riddle, and exclaimed:

> I met a man with no feet; he went upon his way.
> I met him again; this time he had no hands.
> Again I met him, ascending a mountain,
> Making his way with no road.
> The fourth time I met him,
> He had all that he had lacked before.

"Name the man and you may marry the princess."

Frederick started, knowing exactly what the king was saying. How could he confess to being the dragon the king was talking about?

"Your Majesty," he began. "I seem to recall hearing stories about a creature that could turn itself into a human. A dragon, I believe. Could this be the answer to the riddle?"

The other contestants scoffed at this answer. "We have

heard no stories about a dragon which could turn into a person," Prince Benedict of Swiftwater cried.

"None-the-less, I put forward this answer to the riddle. How say you, Your Majesty?"

"The answer was a relief to the king. Princess Alexandria had told him about what had happened when the dragon had abducted her. She convinced him that she would run away if anyone but Frederick won the contest. At least with the man/dragon she would still live in the kingdom and visit her family often.

"I say—that the prize goes to this young man, who answered correctly," the king proclaimed.

"There was much grumbling among the other contestants. Princess Alexandria was very beautiful. But they could do nothing. Frederick had won and that was all there was to it.

"So they got married and lived happily ever after," stated Amelia.

"That's right, sweetheart; they did. Now it's time for you to go to sleep. See, your brother is asleep already. Goodnight." I kissed them both and went back downstairs.

"How did the story go, Lexa? It seemed to take a long time," my husband asked.

As I was about to answer, Amelia appeared at the doorway. "Mama? Is Daddy really a dragon? And are you really a princess? And did all that really happen?"

Ricky and I looked at each other, wondering how to answer the question.

Then we said in unison, "What do you think, princess?"

It's a Miracle
Sue Sinor

Linda was desperate.

"Anything! I'll do anything to lose weight!" she cried, sinking down onto the overstuffed sofa and burying her face in her hands. This was the last straw. All she could stand. She was mad as hell and she wasn't going to take it anymore! But the question remained, what was she going to do about it? As she looked up again she noticed a magazine lying open on the coffee table.

It was showing another of those full-page diet program ads. She had tried a lot of them over the last few years, but they hadn't really helped. This one looked to be just like all the others, but she started to read it, anyway.

"Do people stare at you as you walk down the street? Do your friends call you 'thunder thighs' behind your back? Do you feel like you've been buying your clothes from Omar the Tentmaker?

"Well, NOW you can do something about it!! The IT'S A MIRACLE WEIGHT LOSS PROGRAM will melt those pounds and inches off. Results guaranteed! For more information call 1-800-555-LOSE.

Linda stared thoughtfully at the ad for several minutes, then began to flip through the rest of the magazine. She bought several magazines of this type, saying that she only read the fiction they printed. But each and every month, as regularly as clockwork, she started on whatever that issue's featured diet happened to be. Grapefruit diets, banana diets, seafood diets. Linda had tried them all, most of them more than once. But those diets were printed in the magazines. This one would cost money.

Linda stared at the ad again, and then flipped back to the cover. "Now, this is very odd," she said to herself. "This isn't one that I usually buy. When did I pick this one up? Oh, well, I guess it doesn't really matter. But this diet plan... I wonder if it really works. It does say that it's guaranteed, and none of the other ads I've seen have had 800 numbers. They're all 900 ones, an arm for the first minute and a leg for every minute thereafter. Thirty minutes minimum. Who has that many limbs?"

She picked up her cell phone which was lying on the couch next to her and dialed the number.

A pleasant, genderless voice answered on the fourth ring. "It's A Miracle Weight Loss Program. May I help you?"

"Yes. I read your ad in the, uh, *Star Inquirer* and I, well, I want more information," Linda said. She spoke in a rush, afraid she'd chicken out and end the call in the middle of a sentence.

"Of course," the pleasant voice said. "You want to know how *It's A Miracle* works. It's really very simple. Just take one of our patented miracle pills each day. Then you just 'Think away the pounds'."

"Think away the pounds?" Linda asked. Brother, this was beginning to remind her of one of those infomercials on late night TV.

"Oh, I know it sounds ridiculous, but it really works. I know; I used it and I lost 70 pounds in three months." The pleasant voice sounded excited. "I know it can work for you, too. Why don't you give it a try?"

"70 pounds in three months? I don't know. That seems awfully fast. I've always read that it's better to lose slowly. You can keep it off longer that way."

The pleasantly excited voice continued. "I know. I read that, too, but this really works. It's not one of those phony celebrity diet schemes. Although I could mention a few names you might recognize that are on our program.

"I've kept my weight off for two years now on our maintenance program. I just take one pill every month, and the pounds stay away. I call it my 'weight repellant pill'," the voice giggled.

"But what about the diet part? And exercise? What do I have to eat, and not eat?"

"Why, nothing any different than what you eat right now. You see, the pill does all the work. Just take one every morning and you can eat anything you want. You just think about losing the pounds, and you do."

The voice was very convincing. Linda didn't take long to ask "How much?"

"A trifle compared to what you'll get. We'll send you one month's supply of pills, a handy carrying case that fits in your purse, and a booklet with instructions on their use. And after you start taking them, you get the body you've always dreamed of.

"This first month's supply will cost you *only* $59.95, and each month thereafter will be *only* $39.95. If you are not delighted, just return the remaining pills to us and we will refund your money. But I'm sure you will be *very* satisfied! Now, all I need is your credit card number, name and address and your first step toward a perfect body will be underway." The voice sounded very sure of itself.

Linda fought uncertain excitement as she gave the information needed and ended the call. Soon, she was sure, she would be able to see the pounds melting away.

"Finally, I'll be able to show up Rachel Mason and everybody else at work!" Her pulse raced at the prospect. Now, if she could only wait the week needed to receive her first month's supply of the "It's A Miracle Weight Loss Program."

On Monday she arrived at work with a smile on her face, not at all as usual.

"Linda, you sure seem happy today. Did you have a nice weekend?" Rachel asked.

"Just fine, thank you," Linda replied. Rachel might act friendly to her, but she knew what Rachel was thinking: It couldn't have been a date; she's too fat for anyone to look at. They were all that way, friendly to your face, but making fun of you behind your back.

"Just you wait, Rachel Mason. I'll show you, and everyone else, too. And maybe I'll finally have a chance with David. When I'm thin and beautiful he won't even look at Rachel," Linda muttered to herself.

"Ms. McGee, time to get to work," her boss, Mr. Harrison, reminded her in no uncertain terms. She'd get him, too.

The next Saturday, Linda answered her doorbell to find a United Parcel Service man standing there, electronic thingy in hand. Resting in the crook of his arm was a small package with the words "It's A Miracle" in the upper left-hand side.

"Delivery for Linda McGee sign right here thank you have a nice day," he said in one sentence.

She stood there after he had left, just staring at the brown paper, her future in a box no bigger than her hand.

She carried it carefully to the couch, holding it tightly, as though it might suddenly disappear. Almost breathlessly, she picked up her scissors and cut the tape sealing the box. Inside she found a bottle with small pink tablets, an unobtrusive plastic case with a snap lid, and a booklet.

Hands quivering, she opened the brochure and read. "Be everything that you want to be with the *It's A Miracle Weight Loss Program.* Just follow these simple directions and you will begin losing unwanted pounds within days. Lose as much as you want with the patented 'Miracle' pill.

"Just one pill a day with breakfast does the trick. As you take the pill, think of the weight flowing away from you into something else, the trees in your front yard, your flowers, anything you desire. You'll be amazed how well it works. Guaranteed to work or your money back."

Linda didn't move a muscle as she read the booklet, cover to cover. She couldn't wait to start, but it said to take with breakfast and it was past lunchtime already.

"Maybe I'd better wait until tomorrow," she said. That was the sensible thing to do, though she stared at the little case of pills for a long time. "No, I'd better wait," she finally said, putting it on her kitchen table.

She usually slept late on Sundays, but the next morning Linda was awake at 7:00 a.m. The first image in her mind was of the small bottle of pills sitting on her kitchen table, then of herself in a bikini no bigger than a man's handkerchief.

"Time for breakfast," she thought. And time for a pill. Toast and coffee was what she usually had, but this morning she decided to have a full-blown breakfast: scrambled eggs, sausage, biscuits and gravy, orange juice and coffee. And the pill, the little pink pill. After all, the instructions said to eat all you want.

As she swallowed it, Linda found herself thinking, *Am I crazy? How can taking a pill and thinking make me lose weight?*

Then she sighed, "Oh well, I've paid for them, I might as well give them a try for a few days. You never know."

She started thinking about weight leaving her and settling on a potted philodendron in her front window. It had always been a little scrawny. She was no gardener, but she stubbornly refused to give up on that plant. Now, if she could transfer some extra pounds from herself to it...

After a half hour of just staring at the plant, she couldn't see any difference in it. So much for this idea, she thought. But the next day Linda tried again. By Tuesday she could see a definite change in the plant. The stalk had gotten thicker and the leaves were fatter. She thought about that philodendron all day, and when she got home that evening, it was bigger still.

"I can't believe it; it really worked. Maybe I'd better lay off the plant 'till I can repot it." She laughed. "I'll try the tree out front. The poor thing looks like a stick."

The next morning, when she took her pill, she concentrated on the maple tree. She was still eating larger breakfasts than normal, but she had noticed that her clothes were not quite as tight as usual.

After a few days of thinking about the tree, she could detect a noticeable difference in it. It was taller and had more leaves than before. The trunk was thicker, too.

Two weeks after starting on the program, she stood admiring herself in the mirror, wearing a dress that she hadn't been able to get into for quite a while. It was working. Linda's waist was thinner. The fact that she could tell that she even had a waist was something of a miracle, itself. Before, she had always described herself as having a "beach ball body."

Linda's legs weren't bad, even if she did say so herself, not that she would have ever shown them to anybody. She just didn't wear shorts, or swimsuits, either. It was a pity, because she loved to swim.

"The first thing I'll buy when I'm thin enough is a swimsuit. A French bikini," she promised herself. "And I'll wear it to the beach."

She had been getting curious stares at work, but no one could quite figure out what was different about her.

The neighbors were noticing things, too. Mrs. Evans from across the hall commented on how the tree out front was growing.

"Must be some new fertilizer the gardener is using." The neighborhood cats were getting larger, and the Doberman down the block that Linda was afraid of was getting absolutely fat. Pretty soon he'd barely be able to move, she fervently hoped.

Linda loved cats, but not only that, she hated dogs. She had tried to find an apartment she could afford that would accept pets, but they all demanded exorbitant deposits before they would consider allowing an animal in the place.

She was saving for that deposit, but until then, she made do with stuffed cats, cat figurines and other miscellaneous cat-related objects. At work she had a cat calendar over her desk. Some of her co-workers called her "Cat Woman," like that character from the Batman movies. Although she knew that they were just making fun of her, she was secretly pleased. She wouldn't have minded at all resembling Halle Berry. One of these days, she promised herself, she would. She'd look like all the movie stars she had ever envied.

All she had to do was take the pills and believe.

"Linda," Rachel whispered into her ear one morning at the office, "You've got to start concentrating on your work. Mr. Harrison has noticed you day-dreaming a lot, and I'm afraid he may fire you."

"You'd hate that, wouldn't you? Then you all wouldn't have anyone to laugh at anymore." Linda smirked coldly. "Well, you won't be able to laugh at me much longer."

"Linda, what are you talking about? Nobody laughs at you."

"Sure."

But Linda knew Rachel was right about one thing. She couldn't keep her mind on her work because she had to look for new targets for her pounds. She had already exhausted all the prospects in her apartment building.

"Linda, just look at Pookie. I don't know how she has gotten so fat. I don't feed her that much. Now she can hardly waddle across the floor," Mrs. Johnson had complained when she caught Linda in the hall that morning. She was very fond of her little Yorkie, but Linda hated the yappy little thing.

It occurred to her to try her power of thought out on the food in her refrigerator. Maybe that sirloin would get bigger and last for two meals instead of one. But, after trying for two days and getting nowhere, Linda decided that the trick only worked on living matter, like plants and animals... and people.

Could it really work in reverse on other people? She thought of Maryann, her best friend. Maryann had always been thin. In fact, she could eat anything and not gain weight at all. Linda was quite tired of hearing Maryann complain about her skinny arms and legs and her inability to gain even an ounce. Actually, Linda was resentful of what she considered to be Maryann's luck. She'd show her what it was like to be fat.

For the next few days, Linda thought of Maryann when she took her pill. She imagined skinny arms and legs filling out, ribs disappearing under a layer of fat, and just the hint of a double chin forming.

After three days of concentrating on Maryann, she decided to give her a call and find out if it worked.

"Maryann, it's Linda. How have you been? I haven't talked to you for ages. What's new?" Linda tried to conceal a smirk as she waited for Maryann to give her the news she was expecting.

"Linda! My God, you'll never believe it," Maryann cried. "You're just got to see me! Let's have lunch tomorrow. How about the deli on Third Street? I haven't eaten there in weeks. No, I won't tell you a thing. You'll just have to wait."

The next day Linda arrived at Noodleman's Deli before Maryann got there. She grabbed a table at the window so she could get an advance look at her friend.

In a couple of minutes she saw Maryann walking toward the deli. "She's not fat! What happened? Maybe I didn't take long enough. Maybe a few more days..."

"Maryann, you look great! What have you done to yourself?" Linda gushed as she got up to join her friend in the "order here" line.

"Nothing! I don't know, just suddenly, a few days ago, I started filling out. I haven't been eating more than usual. One horse a day is my limit!" They both laughed at the old joke.

"But, Linda, what's happened to you? You look like you've lost thirty pounds. Have you been sharing with me? I appreciate the thought."

Linda tried to keep a straight face at Maryann's accidental guess of the truth.

"Twenty-five, and you wouldn't believe it. Actually, it's just a new weight loss plan I found. It seems to be really working. I can get into the thin clothes I've saved for five years."

Finally, they were at the head of the line. "I'll just have a salad and iced tea, please," Linda told the counterman. She might as well pretend she was on a diet. She could always have a snack later.

After they sat down, Maryann asked, "What is this terrific diet plan you're on? If I keep gaining weight, I may have to go on it, myself."

"Oh, it's called... Lose-Mor. I found it in some magazine a month or so ago. I'm sure you won't need it; don't worry about it."

"Well, if I ever do, I'll know who to call," Maryann replied. "How much more do you want to lose?"

"I'm not sure," Linda replied. "But I think I'll know when I get there."

By that time they had finished their lunch and it was time to go back to work, but they made plans to meet for lunch once a week for a while.

Back at work, Linda started thinking. Maryann didn't seem upset; in fact, she seemed excited. Linda felt a twinge of conscience. Maryann was her closest friend. She never chided Linda about her weight, never told fat jokes. She was always just what a friend should be, and Linda had tried to be mean to her. She felt really guilty. She suddenly was glad that it had turned out all right for Maryann.

However, Rachel was an entirely different matter.

Linda was proud of how she looked. She had lost several inches in her waist and several around her hips. Fortunately, she hadn't lost any bust size. Until now, it had never been one of her prominent features. She had celebrated by buying some new clothes that showed off her new, improved figure. She wasn't at the end of her diet yet, but she was getting much closer. Just another twenty pounds, she thought, and she could begin the maintenance program and cut the pills back to one a month. Time, she decided, to get her revenge on Rachel.

They had been rivals, of a kind for as long as Linda had been working with Rachel. Several years earlier, Linda had gotten a promotion that Rachel had wanted. Ever since, Linda had suspected that Rachel was jealous of her. Linda had the better job, but she envied Rachel's success with the opposite sex.

"Rachel, are you still dating David Hughes in accounting?" Linda inquired at the coffee cart one morning.

"I sure am," she answered with a smile on her face. "In fact, I think he might be getting ready to propose," she added in an excited whisper. "Now, please don't say anything about it. I'd feel really silly if it didn't happen."

"If he does, what will you tell him?" Linda asked, conspiratorially.

"Yes, of course! Linda, I really love him, and besides, I'm ready to get married. I'm not getting any younger. Now, promise you won't tell?"

"I won't say a word."

"Thanks."

But the next morning, over breakfast and pill, Linda began to think furiously about Rachel. She'd had her eye on David Hughes for a long time, but knew she had no chance. Now, she considered him to be fair game. All she had to do was make sure that Rachel got fat. David would dump her, and Linda would be first in line.

Three days later, Linda could see that her efforts were bearing fruit. In fact, if she could manage it, she would make Rachel end up looking like a pear.

That morning, Rachel arrived at work looking miserable. She was wearing a shapeless dress with no waist, and she almost looked like she had been poured into it.

"What's wrong, Rachel? You don't look too good. Are you getting sick?" Linda asked, sympathetically.

"I don't know," Rachel wailed. "All of a sudden I seem to be putting on weight. I just keep getting bigger, and I'm hardly eating anything at all. I just don't understand. This is the only dress I could find that I could even get into."

"Oh, you poor thing. I think I may have a few things you can borrow for a while. I've had to buy some new clothes since I started losing so much weight."

"That's right. You've lost quite a bit, and you look wonderful. How did you do it?"

"I'll tell you all about it sometime, and don't worry. I'll bring you some clothes tomorrow."

"Thank you so much; you're an angel." Rachel hugged Linda and was about to say something else when Linda cut in.

"Time to get to work. We don't want Mr. Harrison after us, do we?"

The next day Linda brought Rachel a sack full of some of her least favorite and least attractive "fat" clothes. By that time, Rachel was grateful to have anything to wear.

Over the next week, Rachel seemed to blow up like a balloon. It was all Linda could do to disguise her satisfaction.

Early on Friday morning, Linda had just walked into the office when she heard her name called. It was Rachel. The other woman was sitting at her desk, dejectedly looking at a framed photograph.

"Oh, Linda, it looks like David will never propose now. I don't blame him. Look how fat I'm getting. I feel awful. David isn't acting any differently, yet. But he *seems* to be worrying about my health. I think he's just worried about my *size*." Rachel was starting to get the little-girl whiny voice that Linda had hated since the first day she had met her.

"Don't worry, dear. If he's going to be like that, he's probably not worth having in the first place. Now, you just go home this afternoon and try to have a nice weekend. There's some interesting TV shows on Saturday night. I'm sure you'll find something you'll like."

Linda walked away, thinking about shopping for a new dress to wear to work Monday; one that would knock David's socks off.

Two weeks later, after trying everything she could think of, Linda still hadn't gotten anywhere with David. He was still hung up on Rachel, in spite of her new body.

Linda had been paying more attention to David than to Rachel lately. She figured that he'd eventually get tired of the "new" Rachel. Until Monday morning.

Linda arrived at the office, ready for another week's work on David, when she got a look at Rachel. Something was wrong, but she wasn't quite sure what it was, so she walked over to Rachel's desk for a closer look.

She was thinner!

"Rachel, you look different. What have you been doing, exercising?"

"No, but I have been doing something. I got so desperate a couple of weeks ago that I did something I swore I'd never in my life do. But it seems to be working."

"What?"

"You know that David has never said a word about my weight. I guess he really loves me. But I can't take it anymore. The other day I just happened to glance at a magazine lying open on my table and this ad was showing, so I started reading it and, well, I sent off for a diet program. Now, I've never believed in them before, but this sounded so convincing. The funny thing is, I don't even remember buying the magazine."

Linda could feel her skin getting cold and her heart pounding. "What's the name of this program?"

"It's called "It's A Miracle Weight Loss Program", and you won't believe how it works."

Petal Attraction

Sue Sinor

Edna looked out her kitchen window, mentally listing the day's chores. First, she would work in her vegetable garden in the backyard of her two-story house. The house faced east, so the backyard would be in shade for a while. She worked there each morning, and when the shadow of the house moved over to the front, she worked in the front yard, in the flower garden. Edna didn't like being in the sun, but she did love to be outdoors in her gardens.

She was proud of the vegetables her garden produced, but the weeding, spraying and thinning were so boring and time consuming.

Working in the front garden was so much more enjoyable. That's where she grew her flowers: hyacinths, tulips, marigolds and roses.

Edna especially loved roses. Her father had planted a rose bush, just for her, in the front yard of this very house on her eighth birthday. It had been her favorite-ever birthday present. From that time on she had cared for it, eventually caring for all of her father's flowers after he died. She had wanted to care for them while her father was still alive, so he could see that she did a good job, but he wouldn't hear of it. In fact, he never thought she was a good caretaker of her own rosebush, although it always bloomed beautifully, with no problems from pests or diseases.

After her father's passing, she had married George and they had come to live in the family home. George had fancied himself quite a gardener. Without so much as a by-your-leave, he had taken over the flowers, relegating Edna to the backyard vegetable garden.

No matter that her vegetables had won more awards at the county fair than his flowers ever had, George still considered himself the gardener of the family. Mentally, she compared him to her father, lumping them both in the generic group: MEN.

Then, after thirty-five years of marriage, George had died, and Edna got her front garden back. A heart attack had left him sprawled across the delphiniums, where Edna had eventually found him. She had rushed him to the hospital and had stayed with him every day for hours, listening to him complain about the nurses, the food, his doctor, and the fact that he couldn't go home to tend to his flower garden, until he finally died of another heart attack.

All-in-all, Edna considered it to be an even trade, George for the flower garden.

Today as usual, after finishing her duty to the vegetables, she would sit in her front porch swing, eating lunch and reading a gardening book. Then she would get to work on her flowers. She loved tending the flowers; loved sitting under the big willow that shaded the house, just looking at her beautiful flowers.

With a start, Edna woke from her daydreaming and looked at the clock over her kitchen range. It was just now 8:00. She dried her last breakfast dish, put it away, and then tied a kerchief around her gray hair. It wouldn't do to muss it so soon after her visit to the hairdresser. Now, time to go out and weed.

She went to the gardening shed in the back yard, picked up her gloves, a trowel and the hoe, and proudly surveyed the plot before getting to work. There were a dozen neat rows, each one labeled in her precise handwriting: tomatoes, broccoli, squash, beans, cucumbers, lettuce and the rest.

Suddenly, she saw something that didn't belong.

"My heavens, what on earth could that be?" she said.

She put down her trowel and hoe, and looked more closely. Midway down the row of half-grown lettuce heads, neatly fitting in as if it were supposed to be there, was—something.

Something red.

Edna knelt down next to the lettuce row, staring at the intruder. It was a flower of some kind, but like none she'd ever seen before.

From the next yard came the screeching of two of the neighborhood cats as they clashed over something, which set off the dog in the yard beyond that. The sound faded from Edna's hearing as she studied the intruder.

This coloring was impossible. The outside of each petal faded from deep red at the base to pale pink at the tip and was a vivid blue on the inside. Each perfectly formed leaf was attached to the stem at exactly positioned points.

Whatever this was, it was simply the most incredibly, wonderfully, intensely beautiful flower she had ever seen.

Edna had to know what this flower could be. She ran to the house, almost tripping on the back porch steps. In the living room were gardening books: hers, her father's and even a few of George's.

She had always considered herself to be quite knowledgeable about plant life typical to this particular region of the country, but this species wasn't familiar to her at all.

Three hours later, Edna laid down the last of her books. There was nothing, not the slightest reference anywhere, to any kind of flower, or even a vegetable, remotely like this one.

A new species! Was it possible that she had found an entirely new species?

She hurried out to her shed, got spade and pot, and took them to where she had found the flower. It was still there, smiling up at her. Edna gazed down at The Flower, enraptured.

Protect it. Yes, Edna knew what she needed to do. She must protect it, save it from garden vandals: marauding rabbits, neighborhood cats, dogs out to bury their bones, moles. Carefully she set her spade, digging into the black earth. Cautiously she lifted the spade full of soil. Oh, so gently, she placed the precious plant in the pot, making sure that none of its roots was injured. She patted the soil down around the stem, watered it and took it into the house.

How proud she'd be at the next Garden Club meeting when she showed off her new discovery. How envious the other members would be.

Wouldn't they wish they'd elected her president instead of that Norma Baldridge? Norma, who couldn't grow a good iris or cabbage if her life depended on it. Well, she would show them. She had never felt that she had received from her fellow club-members the proper respect due a "true" gardener such as herself. They were just like her father and George.

Edna cleared off a small table and set it in front of the south window in her dining room. This would be an excellent place to put this lovely flower: in the dining room, where everyone who came to visit could see it. She watered it well and gave it a pinch of the best plant food she had.

For a fleeting moment, she wished George was still alive, just to see this gorgeous creation that had grown in "her" garden. Then he'd have to admit that she was just as good a gardener as he was. Not that he would have, of course. That wouldn't have been George.

Every once-in-a-while during the day she went to the little table and looked at her flower. It seemed to look back at her. She imagined it saying to her, "You are a wonderful gardener. You have rescued me from a miserable existence among the carrots and onions. I owe you my life, and I shall repay you."

Repayment? The proper respect from her garden club would be payment enough.

The next day was her club day, but she wouldn't take The Flower with her. It was too precious to be taken out. Instead, why not invite some of the women to tea on Friday? Yes, and just happen to leave the new flower where they could properly admire it. She wouldn't let on that she had anything special to show them, but when they got there, they'd see.

Edna sat up late that night, looking at the flower. It made her feel special; gave her confidence. She could have looked at it all night, but that wouldn't get her work done. She knew that she had to go to bed; she had a big day tomorrow.

The next day, Edna almost decided not to go to the garden club meeting; she'd rather just stay home with her flower. But then she thought about showing it off: the expressions on their faces when they realized just what she had. She did want her friends to see it. She was looking forward to her little tea party.

There would be three for tea. Two were friends, Thelma Hanson and Caroline Rogers; the third had to be Norma Baldridge. She especially wanted to see Norma's expression when she saw "The Flower".

The women arrived precisely at 4:00. They exchanged greetings, and Edna invited them into the dining room where the table was spread. She had prepared sandwiches, cinnamon cakes and a special blend of tea, but she fully expected her table not to be noticed because her Flower was in that room.

The women chattered as they entered the dining room. They exclaimed over the table, and then their attention was drawn toward the little table under the south window.

"What an interesting flower," Thelma said.

"Where did you find it?" Norma inquired.

"Oh, it's my own discovery," Edna admitted, proudly. "I don't think there's another one like it."

"Well, it's a very lovely flower, Edna. You should be proud

of it. Now, weren't you going to tell us about your granddaughter, Norma?" Caroline said, turning away from the flower and ignoring it.

They all gathered around the table, filling their plates and looking for chairs.

Edna was astounded. Where was their admiration, their awe? Where was her respect for having this glorious flower in her possession? She didn't understand their reaction, or lack of it, to her Flower. Well, they were obviously not the right people to have shown it to; it was apparent they didn't have the good taste to recognize a true work of nature's art.

Edna could barely conceal her contempt for them as they chattered away over their cake and tea. She hurried them off then with the excuse of a headache and went back to the dining room. The flower sat there, nodding in the late afternoon sunlight. It didn't seem upset at being ignored by the clubwomen. Indeed, the plant seemed oblivious to the whole episode.

"I'm sorry," Edna told it. "I should never have brought common people to see you first. I should have known they'd not appreciate you. I know; my cousin's son-in-law is a professor at the university. I'm sure he knows someone there who would be interested."

Edna called her cousin right away, only to be told that the son-in-law was out of the country on sabbatical and wouldn't be back for months. No, the cousin didn't know anyone at the university who might be interested in seeing her plant. Edna hung up the phone, disappointed. Maybe someone closer to home. No, she couldn't think of anyone important enough, influential enough, to show her prize to.

She went back to look at her flower, pulling in a comfortable armchair from the living room and placing it in front of the table. She couldn't get enough of the sight of the strange flower.

Hunger and a need for sleep were what finally drove her away for the night.

The next morning, Edna took her breakfast to the same chair. The flower seemed to have grown some overnight. She watered and fed it again. And then just looked.

She thought she should perhaps go out and work in her vegetable garden, as she did every day. Reluctantly, she went out the back door and approached the garden. It looked so bleak with nothing but vegetables in it.

She pulled a weed or two, set the hose to water it, and then gave up.

She just wasn't in the mood to stay there. She thought about the flower garden in the front yard. Wouldn't it be a good idea to vary her routine this morning and work there first? She walked around the side of the house and looked. It was the nicest flower garden in her neighborhood, but today it seemed washed-out, pale in comparison to The Flower. She didn't feel like working there, either.

"I hope I'm not getting sick," she thought to herself. "I just don't feel like being outside today."

She went back in, got herself a cup of tea, and resumed her place in the dining room. It was so restful, just looking at the flower. In fact, it was somewhat like a trance, like meditation.

"I'll just sit here for a few minutes, and then I'll do some housework," she thought.

A loud noise from outside woke her suddenly.

"Goodness, I had the strangest dream. Well, I'd better get something done around here." She looked at the clock and was astonished to find that it was one o'clock.

"Could I have slept three hours? It seemed like only a few minutes. I do feel better, though."

Edna puttered around her house for a while, then went back to sit in the chair. She felt drawn to the flower, as if looking at it was the most important thing in the world she could do.

During the next week Edna spent much of her time in that chair.

She would get up, eat breakfast, work half-heartedly in her gardens, do some housework, and spend the rest of the day in the armchair.

Looking at the flower, she seemed to see backwards, into her past, into her past lives, back to the beginning of time. At the same instant, she could see all the lives in her future. How very nice to suddenly become omniscient.

Over the next few days, she would rouse for food and sleep, but little else. At the beginning of the third week Edna began sleeping in the chair. She started bringing food from the kitchen and setting it on a table by her chair so that she wouldn't have to get up when she got hungry.

The flower seemed to be thriving under her care. It had grown and was forming buds. Soon there would be several flowers just like it on the same plant. A bigger pot was fast becoming necessary.

Soon, she had forgotten about everything else. The vegetables were ripening, then going to seed, while the flowers were being strangled out by weeds.

Edna's neighbors thought something might be wrong because she had never let her yard go like that. Even when she was gone, visiting her daughter, she would hire someone to take care or the gardens and yard.

They had no idea that she was inside, mesmerized by the strange flower she had found in her vegetable garden.

Her friends grew concerned about her when she missed the next garden club meeting, but when she didn't answer any phone calls, they decided that she must have gone to her daughter's and neglected to tell anyone.

"Mrs. Hanson, this is Margaret McAlester, Edna Conrad's daughter. I can't seem to get hold of Mother. I've tried for several days. I even called Mother's sister, my Aunt Gertrude, and her cousin, as well. Neither one of them had heard from her, either."

"Oh, dear. We all thought that she was probably visiting you," Thelma replied.

"I don't like this; I don't like this at all. Would you please go by her house and check for me? I'm getting really worried about her. Call me or tell her to call if she's all right. I'd really appreciate it," Margaret asked.

"Certainly, dear. I'd be glad to. I'm worried, too."

Thelma left right away to check on Edna. She found the yard overgrown and the house locked up tight. The mailbox was stuffed with mail, and weeks' worth of newspapers were on the front porch.

Thelma went back home and called Margaret immediately.

"I'm sorry, dear, but I think something's wrong. The yard is a mess. The papers and mail haven't been taken in for, it looks like weeks. I couldn't get in because the house is locked, and the shades are drawn, too. All except the one at the dining room window, and I'm too short to see in."

"Now I'm really worried. Thank you for checking for me. I'll fly in just as soon as I can. I have a key to the house; I'll be able to get in."

"Margaret, have you thought that there might be foul play involved? I think that you should have a policeman go with you. Why don't you come over here, first, and we'll call the police department," Thelma suggested.

The next afternoon Margaret, Thelma and a police officer arrived at Edna's house. They knocked on the door, and, when there was no response, unlocked the door with Margaret's key and entered.

They found Edna in the chair in the dining room. She appeared to be looking at the flower, which had grown considerably since it had first been dug up from the garden, but which was now beginning to wither. Edna seemed withered, too, and much older than the last time Thelma had seen her. She had obviously been dead for at least a week, yet she still sat in her favorite armchair.

After the medical examiner had been there, and Edna's body had been taken away, Margaret at last looked at what apparently had held her mother's attention for so long. She went to the table under the south window in the dining room and looked at the flower. What a curious looking flower, she thought. She had never seen one like it before. Margaret sat down without thinking in the chair so recently vacated by her mother. As she looked at it, the withering flower seemed to come back to life. Its petals became once again healthy and straight.

"What a beautiful flower," Margaret thought. "How perfect in every way. I can't leave it here; I must take it home with me and care for it."

The flower seemed to say to her, "Please take me with you. Don't leave me here to die. Take care of me and I will repay you."

About the Authors

Bradley H. Sinor has been writing for five/sixths of his life, and has written many short stories, most of them published in a variety of anthologies and three short story collections. His new collection – The Game's Afoot: A Sherlock Holmes Miscellany, published by Pro Se Productions – is now available on Amazon. He lives in Tulsa, OK, with his wife, (writer and copy-editor) Sue Sinor, and three cats. He can be contacted on his Facebook page as Brad Sinor.

Sue Sinor started writing at the urging of her husband, Brad. She has stories in several Yard Dog Press publications: "International House of Bubbas", "Flush Fiction" and, in collaboration with her husband, the chapbook "Playing With Secrets" and a story in "Houston, We Got Bubbas". They have collaborative stories in the anthology "Rotten Relations" and in "Grantville Gazette 4". She also has two stories in the charity anthology *Small Bites*. She is involved with community theatre in Tulsa, both on and off stage. Together, she and Brad are the caretakers and household staff for one older cat, Pewter, and two teenage cats, Mycroft Holmes and Ms. Watson. They live in Tulsa, OK. She can be contacted on her Facebook page.

About the Cover Artist

Melanie Fletcher is an expatriate Chicagoan who currently lives in North Dallas with her husband the Bodacious Brit™ and their five fabulous furbags JJ, Jessica, Jeremy, Jemma, and Jasmine (yes, they were following a theme, moving along now). When not herding cats, she turns into SF Writer Girl, and has the SFWA membership card to prove it. Her recent SF sales include "The Groom Wore Wings" (Debris and Detritus: The Lesser Greek Gods Running Amok, Story Spring Publishing). She also writes speculative fiction romance under the name Nicola M. Cameron, and her latest novel Degree of Resistance (Pacifica Rising 1) was released in February, 2017, from Belaurient Press.

Yard Dog Press Titles As Of This Print Date

A Bubba in Time Saves None, Edited by Selina Rosen
A Man, A Plan, (yet lacking) A Canal, Panama, Linda Donahue
Adventures of the Irish Ninja, Selina Rosen
The Alamo and Zombies, Jean Stuntz
All the Marbles, Dusty Rainbolt
Almost Human, Gary Moreau
Ancient Enemy, Lee Killouth
The Anthology From Hell: Humorous Tales From WAY Down Under, Edited by Julia S. Mandala
Ard Magister, Laura J. Underwood
Assassins Inc., Phillip Drayer Duncan
Bad City, Selina Rosen & Laura J. Underwood
Bad Lands, Selina Rosen & Laura J. Underwood
Black Rage, Selina Rosen
Blackrose Avenue, Mark Shepherd
The Boat Man, Selina Rosen
Bobby's Troll, John Lance
Bride of Tranquility, Tracy S. Morris
Bruce and Roxanne from Start to Finnish, Rie Sheridan Rose
The Bubba Chronicles, Selina Rosen
Bubba Fables, Sue P. Sinor
Bubbas Of the Apocalypse, Edited by Selina Rosen
The Burden of the Crown, Selina Rosen
Chains of Redemption, Selina Rosen
Checking On Culture, Lee Killough
Chronicles of the Last War, Laura J. Underwood
Dadgum Martians Invade the Lucky Nickel Saloon, Ken Rand
Dark and Stormy Nights, Bradley H. Sinor
Deja Doo, Edited by Selina Rosen
Dracula's Lawyer, Julia S. Mandala
Dragon's Tongue, Laura J. Underwood
The Essence of Stone, Beverly A. Hale
Fairy BrewHaHa at the Lucky Nickel Saloon, Ken Rand
The Fantastikon: Tales of Wonder, Robin Wayne Bailey
Fire & Ice, Selina Rosen
Flush Fiction, Volume I: Stories To Be Read In One Sitting, Edited by Selina Rosen
Flush Fiction, Volume II: Twenty Years of Letting it Go!, Edited by Selina Rosen
The Four Bubbas of the Apocalypse: Flatulence, Halitosis, Incest, and... Ned, Edited by Selina Rosen
The Four Redheads: Apocalypse Now!, Linda L. Donahue, Rhonda Eudaly, Julia S. Mandala, & Dusty Rainbolt
The Four Redheads of the Apocalypse, Linda L. Donahue, Rhonda Eudaly, Julia S. Mandala, & Dusty Rainbolt
The Four Redheads: The Wrath of Satan, Linda L. Donahue,

Rhonda Eudaly, Julia S. Mandala, & Dusty Rainbolt
The Garden In Bloom, Jeffrey Turner
The Geometries of Love: Poetry by Robin Wayne Bailey
The Golems Of Laramie County, Ken Rand
The Green Women, Laura J. Underwood
The Guardians, Lynn Abbey
Hammer Town, Selina Rosen
The Happiness Box, Beverly A. Hale
The Host Series: The Host, Fright Eater, Gang Approval, Selina
      Rosen
Houston, We've Got Bubbas!, Edited by Selina Rosen
How I Spent the Apocolypse, Selina Rosen
I Didn't Quite Make It To Oz, Edited by Selina Rosen
I Should Have Stayed In Oz, Edited by Selina Rosen
In the Shadows, Bradley H. Sinor
International House of Bubbas, Edited by Selina Rosen
It's the Great Bumpkin, Cletus Brown!, Katherine A. Turski
Judas Gene, Gary Moreau
The Killswitch Review, Steven-Elliot Altman & Diane DeKelb-
      Rittenhouse
The Leopard's Daughter, Lee Killough
The Lightning Horse, John Moore
The Logic of Departure, Mark W. Tiedemann
The Long, Cold Walk To Mars, Jeffrey Turner
Marking the Signs and Other Tales Of Mischief, Laura J.
      Underwood
Material Things, Selina Rosen
Medieval Misfits: Renaissance Rejects, Tracy S. Morris
Mirror Images, Susan Satterfield
Mirror, Mirror and Other Reflections, James K. Burk
More Stories That Won't Make Your Parents Hurl, Edited by
      Selina Rosen
Music for Four Hands, Louis Antonelli & Edward Morris
My Life with Geeks and Freaks, Claudia Christian
The Necronomicrap: A Guide To Your Horoooscope, Tim Frayser
*Of Two Minds: Location Shoot, It's a Miracle, and Other Strange
      Stories,* Bradley H & Sue P. Sinor
The Pinnacle, Gary Moreau
Playing With Secrets, Bradley H & Sue P. Sinor
Redheads In Love, Linda L. Donahue, Rhonda Eudaly, Julia S.
      Mandala, & Dusty Rainbolt
Reruns, Selina Rosen
Rock 'n' Roll Universe, Ken Rand
Shadows In Green, Richard Dansky
Stories That Won't Make Your Parents Hurl, Edited by Selina
      Rosen

Tales from Keltora, Laura J. Underwood
Tales Of the Lucky Nickel Saloon, Second Ave., *Laramie,*
Wyoming, U S of A, Ken Rand
Tarbox Station, Rhonda Eudaly
Texistani: Indo-Pak Food From A Texas Kitchen, Beverly A. Hale
That's All Folks, J. F. Gonzalez
Through Wyoming Eyes, Ken Rand
Turn Left to Tomorrow, Robin Wayne Bailey
The Twins, Selina Rosen
The Undead Ate My Head, Ethan Nahté
Wandering Lark, Laura J. Underwood
Weirdough, Inc., Selina Rosen & Sherri Dean
Wings of Morning, Katharine Eliska Kimbriel
Zombies In Oz and Other Undead Musings, Robin Wayne Bailey

Double Dog
(A YDP Imprint):

#1:
Of Stars & Shadows,
Mark W. Tiedemann
This Instance Of Me,
Jeffrey Turner

#2:
Gods and Other Children,
Bill D. Allen
Tranquility, Tracy Morris

#3:
Home Is the Hunter,
James K. Burk
Farstep Station,
Lazette Gifford

#4:
Sabre Dance,
Melanie Fletcher
The Lunari Mask,
Laura J. Underwood

#5:
House of Doors,
Julia Mandala
Jaguar Moon,
Linda A. Donahue

Just Cause
(A YDP Imprint):

The Bitter End
Selina Rosen

Death Under the Crescent Moon
Dusty Rainbolt

Getting It Real
Selina Rosen

The Ghost Writer
Selina Rosen

*It's Not Rocket Science: Spirituality
for the Working-Class Soul*
Selina Rosen

Meditations of a Hoarder
Melinda LaFevers

Not My Life
Selina Rosen

The Pit
Selina Rosen

Plots and Protagonists: A Reference Guide for Writers
Mel. White

Vanishing Fame
Selina Rosen

Fantasy Writers Asylum
(A YDP Imprint):
Blood Songs
Julia Mandala
Gateway to Corimar
Julia Mandala & Linda L Donahue
Tale of the Black Heart
Linda L. Donahue

Non-YDP titles we distribute:
Chains of Freedom
Chains of Destruction
Jabone's Sword
Queen of Denial
Recycled
Strange Robby
Sword Masters
Selina Rosen

Three Ways to Order:

1. Write us a letter telling us what you want, then send it along with your check or money order (made payable to Yard Dog Press) to: Yard Dog Press, 710 W. Redbud Lane, Alma, AR 72921-7247

2. Use selinarosen@cox.net or lynnstran@cox.net to contact us and place your order. Then send your check or money order to the address above. *This has the advantage of allowing you to check on the availability of short-stock items such as T-shirts and back-issues of Yard Dog Comics.*

3. Contact us as in #1 or #2 above and pay with a credit card or by debit from your checking account. Either give us the credit card information in your letter/Email/phone call, or go to our website and use our shopping carts. If you send us your information, please include your name as it appears on the card, your credit card number, the expiration date, and the 3 or 4-digit security code after your signature on the back (CVV). Please remember that we will include media rate (minimum $3.00) S/H for mailing in the lower 48 states.

Watch our website at
www.yarddogpress.com
for news of upcoming projects
and new titles!!

A Note to Our Readers

We at Yard Dog Press understand that many people buy used books because they simply can't afford new ones. That said, and understanding that not everyone is made of money, we'd like you to know something that you may not have realized. Writers only make money on new books that sell. At the big houses a writer's entire future can hinge on the number of books they sell. While this isn't the case at Yard Dog Press, the honest truth is that when you sell or trade your book or let many people read it, the writer and the publishing house aren't making any money.

As much as we'd all like to believe that we can exist on love and sweet potato pie, the truth is we all need money to buy the things essential to our daily lives. Writers and publishers are no different.

We realize that these "freebies" and cheap books often turn people on to new writers and books that they wouldn't otherwise read. However we hope that you will reconsider selling your copy, and that if you trade it or let your friends borrow it, you also pass on the information that if they really like the author's work they should consider buying one of their books at full price sometime so that the writer can afford to continue to write work that entertains you.

We appreciate all our readers and *depend* upon their support.

Thanks,
The Editorial Staff
Yard Dog Press

PS – Please note that "used" books without covers have, in most cases, been stolen. Neither the author nor the publisher has made any money on these books because they were supposed to be pulped for lack of sales.

Please do not purchase books without covers.